&
HARPER

FISHER AMELIE

To C.Z.P.
This is for you because you need
to know that you're worth
dedicating a book to and
because I think you've forgotten
who you are. Simply put, you're
incredible and I love you.

Acknowledgements

There's a few people I'd like to thank. First, my Plumes. You guys are my other halves. Nobody gets me the way you guys get me. You're all supremely talented and, to be honest, I'm not sure how the heck I got so lucky to call you peers. Also, book tours would be totally lame without you. J.Nunez, you are possibly one of the most sincere people I know. You jumped on my bandwagon and you lead, my friend. Thanks for the advice and the time you took in reading this little story. T.Watson, as fans go, you have to be the best of them all but you're more than a fan, you're a lovely friend and as sweet as the day is long. p.s. Say hi to your mama for me. Grandma, the fact that you sit at your table with me and listen to me drone on and on about my characters' lives as if they were real people makes me want to cry. You're more generous with me than anyone I know and I love you more than you could possibly comprehend. Thank you for putting up with me. JuJuBean, when you cry 'mama' in the mornings, you give me reason to live. And last but certainly not least, the Hubs. You're the inspiration for my Callums, Elliotts, and all future heroes. You are my very model...*of a modern major general?* No, scratch that. I'm trying too hard. Fact: I love you. So very much. Always have. Always will. p.s. Where do you want to eat? I don't know. Where do you want to eat? Repeat.

Chapter One
Where is My Mind?

Callum

I was sitting next to one of the most beautiful girls I'd ever seen in my entire life. She was so intriguing, I could actually feel the sweat dripping down the back of my neck at the effort it was taking to keep from staring at her. I hoped to God she couldn't tell...or smell.

If I were to guess, I'd have said she was about five foot, five inches, she had wicked long coppery hair and hazel eyes that looked more gold than green. Her eyes killed me. I believed I could peer into those eyes all day long, maybe on a blanket on the grass, in Central Park, that we could've *shared*.

Get it together, Callum, I thought. *You're probably*

making her nervous. You've too much shit on your plate, dude. I paused, mid thought, remembering where we were. *She* is *sitting in the same office you are, bro. Yeah, Callum, she is,* I debated with myself, with only a fleeting thought toward how mentally unstable people who talked to themselves were. *But the last thing this lovely probably wants is to mess around with someone with as much drama as you own.*

She tucked her chin into her chest and glanced my direction but when she caught me staring back, she quickly fixed her eyes onto the floor. *Then again....*

"Harper Bailey!" A social worker yelled out. Gold eyes stood up. *Harper Bailey. What an appropriate name.* She even *looked* like a Harper and that made me want to smile for some reason. Harper Bailey looked back at me and flashed a perfect row of white teeth making me melt a little into my seat.

Harper

Oh my God, I think I just melted a little bit into the floor. The guy I'd been sitting next to that entire time was bona fide swoon worthy. If I'd showed a picture of this guy to a hundred girls and asked their opinions, they'd all, without fail, would've said, 'swoon worthy'.

If I were to have guessed, he was probably six foot two or three. He had brown hair, piercing green eyes and a jaw line that screamed 'I might just let you kiss me here'. There's something about strong jaws that sing to me but his shoulders and back didn't look so shabby, either. Yet another feature he owned, I could say I wouldn't mind running my hands across.

I could feel his eyes on the back of my head, heating me up from the inside. I shivered involuntarily. Never had someone affected me like that and I was stupefied because I was Harper Bailey, self-professed bachelor and lover of singledom. 'Rely on no one because people inevitably fail you' Harper Bailey.

"Callum Tate!" A social worker called. I whipped my head around and watched him walk to their desk. Callum Tate. I liked the sound of that. It sounded sweet, like, 'Hi, my name is Callum Tate and I'm going to take care of you, Harper Bailey', which is exactly what I'd always openly confessed as stupid but also *always* secretly wanted. *Yikes, Harper. Crazy much?*

He looked over his shoulder at me. We stopped pretending and smiles ensued. He had a slightly crooked smile which somehow looked amazingly adorable on him.

"Miss Bailey?" I heard. *Oops.*

"Yes, Mrs. Carson?"

"If you can trouble yourself to pay attention to me, baby, I can give you some information. Now, when did you turn eighteen?"

"March seventeenth, ma'am."

"Alright, did you finish high school?"

"Yes, ma'am."

"Alright, why did Mrs. Drawing ask you to leave her home?"

"Isn't it obvious?" I said, dropping my arm over the back of the chair next to me. This was my attempt at feigning indifference. I don't think I was fooling anyone. Truth was, I was scared, no, terrified of being alone. "She won't be receiving benefits for being my foster mother any longer since I've turned eighteen. Her free lunch ticket expired, if you catch my drift."

"Harper, you're always so cheeky, maybe if you'd bite your tongue you wouldn't have been asked to leave."

"Oh, Mrs. Carson, that's why I love you. You make it seem as if it's my mouth that got me kicked out of all those homes when in truth, it was my fists." *And a little bit my mere existence.*

"There you go with that mouth, young lady. You're telling me, of all the fights you were in, not *one* of them was your fault?" Her eyebrow arched over one eye. That brow screamed 'bullshit'.

"I know it's hard to believe, Mrs. Carson, but when someone calls you a variation on the word orphan enough times, it does something to your heart and there's only so many occasions where a person is expected to endure it before they end up punching that someone in the face."

"Hmm," she said, "maybe you're right, baby." We both laughed loud enough to draw Callum's attention and that tickled my stomach slightly. *That's smart, Harper. Focus your attention on mister perfect and forget all about how pathetic your situation really is.*

"Okay, well," she sighed. "There are homes for those in your situation but this is New York City and they're full up, not an opening in the foreseeable future."

Of course. "That's fantastic news, Mrs. Carson. Well, that was invigorating, I think I'll leave now." I stood.

"Sit, Harper!" I sat. "Calm down now. I've got some other options for you." She frowned at the mess of papers in her hands. "Harper, the best we can do for you here is to put you on the waiting list for a few homes but until then, you'll just have to make do with the night to night facilities in the city."

I'd heard all sorts of stories about these places. If you didn't get there early enough, you missed your chance to stay and when Mrs. Carson said 'night to night' she meant you literally had to fight to stay there from one night to the next. I'd recently read about two homeless men who'd gotten into a fight vying for a chance at an open spot in line and one of them killed the other for it.

"Alright, put me on the list then and jot me down a few places I can stay until then."

"Already have a printed list." She said, handing me a piece of paper that had been Xeroxed so often it looked solid black. "Here ya' go. You call me in two weeks and I'll let you know the progress of your name on the permanent housing list."

"Thank you, Mrs. Carson."

"No problem, honey. I'll see you in two weeks."

I stood to leave and gathered the bag that housed every belonging I owned. So essentially, inside my small canvas messenger, were two pairs of jeans, a few button up fitted flannels, one striped dress, and a pair of flip flops. Also inside, was my signed copy of 'To Kill A Mockingbird' by Harper Lee, my namesake and hero, which I'd won at a county fair when my foster family at the time, traveled there to visit their own extended family. I wore my only other pair of jeans and a fitted t-shirt that read, 'Save The Drama For Your Mama'.

When I turned around, I saw Callum heading for the door and my stomach clenched in anticipation.

Callum

Oh dear Lord, we're leaving at the same time. If she hadn't stopped attempting to hide her smile, I would've been forced to reveal my plans to toss the stranger outside against the brick and kiss her face until the sun set.

She passed ahead of me and I caught a whiff of her shampoo, involuntarily sending my eyes into the back of my head. This chick was a walking version of the Pixie's "Where Is My Mind?". Sexy. As. Hell. Though, now that I

13

think about it, is hell *sexy*? I'm guessing not. I continued to watch. Her hips could have kept time with the damn beat.

"Here, let me get that for you," I said, throwing open the door. The sun cascaded down her copper hair and made her eyes feel transparent.

"Thank you," she shyly said but offered up a cute lopsided grin as if to say 'good boy'. *Thanks for the bone, buttercup.*

She took the wrought iron steps down to the sidewalk two at a time, which told me she was in a hurry and since it was nearly sunset, I was willing to bet that she and I were heading in the same direction. I scrambled at what to say while her feet scurried along the pavement.

Say something! "Where you headed?" *Clever.* She stopped and turned.

"Uh," she said, seeming embarrassed. She thought twice for a moment before stiffening her body and raising her chin. "I'm headed to..." Confusion set in. She glanced down at the same piece of paper I, as fate would have it, held in my own hand. "Hope House, on One Hundred and Second," she finished.

"What a coincidence," I teased with a slight grin.

"You too?" She asked, one eyebrow raised.

Cynical, a product of the system.

"Yup, what can I say? Looks like we share the same amount of luck."

"Which would be?" She asked.

"Nil, if you're going to Hope House."

She laughed at our dire situations which was pretty much all you could do.

"Want a ride?" I asked. She didn't answer me, obviously not willing to trust me, so I offered, "Listen, by

14

the time you walk there they'll be closed and definitely won't have any spaces open. If you ride *with me*, at least we have a chance of getting a spot for the night."

She sighed. "A valid point," she said, looking around for my car.

I'm embarrassed by this. "Uh, " I said, scratching the stubble on my chin with the backs of my fingers. "I don't actually own a car." I point to my vintage nineteen-fifty Indian motorcycle. "Come on. It's better than walking, right?" I stuck my hands out in offering.

She smiled slowly in appreciation, her mouth curling up at the sides and her eyes squinting into the sun. Her head bobbed slowly up and down on her neck. A silent yes. "I'd probably pick this over any car on this street." She stood back and admired it. "Solid black," she said. I nodded, intrigued. "Nice," she simply added.

"*You think so*? I plan on fixing her up when I get the time and, of course, the money. She's been good to me, though," I said, patting the handlebars. "She's pretty much all I have in this world." Harper looked at me as if in pity or maybe it was understanding. I really hoped it was understanding because if a girl that beautiful pitied me, I didn't think I could stand it. "Hop on," I said. She straddled the back of the leather seat and slid her duffel across her chest to sit behind her. "Uh, you might want to, uh," I said awkwardly, struggling with how to ask her to push her hair back so I could fit my helmet on her.

Instead, I set the helmet on the seat between her legs and brazenly ran my fingers through her hair. It flowed off her shoulders and settled onto her back. The scent of her shampoo bombarded me one more time and I swayed slightly at the assault but regained my stance. I grabbed the helmet off her lap and fit it onto her head. She giggled at the awkward familiarity of it.

"Sorry," I said. "But I wouldn't dream of putting you on the back of my bike without this."

"It's alright," she said, but paused. "*Why*? Are you an unsafe driver?"

"No, uh, my parents died in a car accident when I was four," I said matter-of-factly.

"Oh, I'm so sorry." She had the decency to look sincere. That was pretty refreshing, actually.

"It's alright," I sighed, shrugging my shoulders. "I barely remember them."

"I don't know *anything* about mine," she said, studying her feet, then realized what she was doing. "Harper Bailey," she said cheerfully, holding out her hand, revealing a dimpled grin.

I buckled the clasp around her delicate chin, resting my hands on the top of the helmet playfully. "My name is Callum Tate and I'm going to take care of you, Harper Bailey."

Her extended hand dropped into her lap. Her eyes went wide and her mouth dropped open. "Wh...*what* did you say?"

Shit. Was that was too forward? "I'm sorry," I said, shaking my head. "I'm Callum Tate. It's a pleasure to meet you, Harper Bailey." I grabbed her thin hand and a shot of warmth crept up my veins and shocked my heart into a frenzy.

The smile that had so quickly faded before came back with a vengeance. She squeezed my hand in greeting and whispered, "It's very nice to meet you, Callum."

I climbed on to the front part of the seat and started the engine. Harper settled her hands on the side of my ribs and I couldn't think of anything I wanted more than her arms wound tight against my chest. Suddenly, I couldn't get on the road fast enough.

Harper

I think Callum Tate can read minds. It's either that or there was something seriously *strange* going on between the two of us.

He started the motor and pulled the bike up on its wheels, lifting it off its stand and balanced our combined weight effortlessly.

He turned slightly to face me, exposing a flirtatious off-kilter grin, "You might want to hang on." My stomach flipped in circles as I tightened my hands around his chest and I could feel his heart beat furiously against my palm which only served to make mine race faster.

"You okay?" He asked over the purr of the motor. *More than okay.* "Yeah," I try to say as coolly as possible.

He revs the motor before placing his left hand over mine. "Hold on tight," he said as if I'd ever let go. As if I *could* ever let go.
Heat coursed through my arm and when he removes his hand, I felt a lacking I'd never known I could possess.

The wind whipped my hair behind me as I breathed in the warm summer air, letting it fill my lungs. With each breath he took, his chest expanded tightly against my stomach and hands and I can do nothing to stifle the tingling electricity that came with each one, sending my heart into violent trembles.

The Hope House is nothing like I thought it would be because it was worse, which is incredible as I expected awful. The building, though old and beautiful in architecture, was dark and extremely dirty, lines of sickly, equally filthy people huddled against the frame of the structure waiting and desperate to hear they have a place to rest their own heads in a cot for the night rather than the alternative and that was more than likely a cardboard box or a bench. I heard three gunshots go off as well as a woman's screams but the hundreds queued paid no heed, obviously accustomed to the harrowing sounds.

"Hold on," he said loudly before popping the curb and settling the bike near a lamp post.
He swung his leg over the seat and unbuckled the strap to my helmet before lifting it from my head. He grinned mischievously.

"My hair is stuck to my head at weird angles, isn't it?" I asked, a blush already descending upon my cheeks.

He studied me carefully before bursting out laughing. "Maybe," he teased. "Here," he said, smoothing out the unruly mess. The contact he makes with my skin gives me an involuntary shudder. "Are you cold?" He asked, raising one eyebrow.

"Uh, no, just...just got a glimpse at where we were and gotta' admit, I'm a bit un-enthused but beggars can't be choosers, right?"

"Poor Harper," he said with a slight frown. "You most certainly are not a beggar but I will admit we've not any choices," he playfully winked, sending me into yet another frenzy. "Come on." He placed his hands on my waist and lifted me off the seat.

"Good gosh, Callum!" I say, lifting my voice to the level of my now boiling blood pressure. His touch is intimidating, making me choke on the sharp inhalation its spark gives to me.

"What?"

I'm flustered. "I just wasn't expecting you to lift me is

all."

"I'm sorry," he apologizes. "I'm acting too familiar with you and I just can't explain why. I'm usually more polite than this. You just affect me differently than most."
Don't read too much into that, Harper.

"Alright," he says, wrapping a large, thick chain around his bike and the post beside it before attaching the largest lock I've ever seen made. "Shall we?" He gestured toward the rows of people.

We walked toward the end of the line and sat in uncomfortable silence, each probably wondering if we knew what we were doing.

Callum

 I don't know what I'm doing. I think I might have offended her by grabbing her waist without asking. I don't know why I did it either because the last thing I want is to offend this incredible girl.

"So, tell me, how were you orphaned?" I asked. Shock colors her face. Nice start there, goofball. Really sensitive. "I'm sor...," I start, but before I can even finish, she bursts out laughing.

"I've never actually had anyone ask me that so blatantly before yet it doesn't seem like such an unnatural question, seeming as we share the same plight."

"And what plight is that?" I ask.

"Oh, I don't know. The one where we meet in the lobby of social services after being kicked out of our foster homes for being afflicted with the 'eighteen disease'. Not to mention the part where we're standing in line together at The Hope House, a relief center that can't accommodate the demands being asked of it."

"God, you're plucky," I blurted out.

"You know it, but to answer your question..."

"What question?"

"The one where you asked me how I became an orphan?"

"'Kay."

She took a deep breath, readying herself to spew the prepared speech all us orphans kept at the tip of our tongues. "I'm not truly an orphan. My mother is alive and I'm hoping well somewhere out there but I've never met her. She left me at the hospital she gave birth to me at, slapped the name Harper on me, before peacin' it out and wishing me the best.

"I was adopted almost immediately into a young family who thought they could handle the demands of an infant. When they discovered that they couldn't handle one addicted to drugs, they passed me over. At three, I began the tireless process of being passed around once a year in the foster system. I assume my dad is some deadbeat crackhead, probably doesn't even know I'm alive. Anytime I pass a dude beggin' for change, if he could be my father's age, I slip him a buck or two in hopes he sees something in me he could recognize."

"Has it worked?"

"Nah, but my fingers are crossed," she teased.

"Wow, that is a sad, pathetic story," I prod.

"Tell me about it."

"My story's better than your story, though."

"That so?" Both her brows are raised in challenge.

"Yeah, double the pathetic, *quadruple* the sad."

"No kidding."

"As I said before, my parents died in a car wreck when I was four. I barely remember either of them. From what I can gather from my limited memories, though, they were loving. I think my father may have been an attorney because he was always on the phone and I remember the words brief, client, and evidence were at the top of his vocabulary.

"I remember my mother was sweet and kind and that we'd always bake cookies on Sunday after church. It's my only distinct memory of her. I would sit at a kitchen island on a stool and we'd mix all the ingredients, then she'd ask me questions about whatever difficulty my four year old life could conjure up while they baked and when the bell tolled, no pun intended, we'd grab hot cookies, dip them in our milk and life would be peachy.

"I don't remember the day they died. I suppose I may have blocked it out but I *was* in the car with them and the car seat they paid a freakin' fortune for may have saved my life but left me utterly alone."
Her breathing got deeper.

"My mom was an only child," I continued. "My dad had a half-brother who was only ten at the time of my parents passing. He was raised by his maternal grandparents. So, basically, there was no one to take care of me."

"Damn, Callum. That's tragic," she said, the teasing losing its potency.

Suddenly, our attempts at trying to make light of our misfortune lost their charm. I hung my head against my chest and breathed deeply, exhaling acceptance with each blow. I was no longer interested in acknowledging my lot in life. I was in line, begging to stay on a revolting cot, that'd had probably slept a thousand others before me. The worst part was I had no idea if I'd get to have even that.

Sensing my discomfort, Harper took initiative and wrapped her hand within mine, squeezing reassurance into my heart. I looked over at her and smiled as lightheartedly as possible. She squeezed harder. It's funny how this total stranger could relate to me better than anyone else I'd ever met. It was as if I'd known her my entire life.

"It's like I've known you my entire life," I stupidly admit.

But she doesn't rebuff me as I anticipate. No, instead, she says, "I think, in some ways, we have. Only you could know what I've been through; the humiliation, the judgments, the unwanted pity and none of it at your doing. We may not have known each other our whole lives but we've definitely lived them in parallel."

We waited in line for three hours, marking the time with idle chit chat that held no meaning whatsoever, but felt strangely vital to have at the time.

"Your favorite color?" I asked.

"Green," she said. "Yours?"

"Same."

"Liar."

"I'm not lying."

She eyed me disbelievingly, "Mmm-kay."

"I'm not! Seriously, it's always been green."

"Alright, I believe you, I guess."

"Favorite food?" I continued, changing the subject.

"You first," she says.

"Afraid of an unoriginal answer?" I teased. She raised both eyebrows. "Okay, my favorite food is Tex-Mex. Good, authentic Tex-Mex though and as you may not know, that does not exist in this city."

"Have you ever even been to Texas?" She mocked.

"Yes, I have, miss. When I was sixteen, I went there for a Latin competition for school. So there."

"A Latin competition!?" She scoffs.

"Don't make fun!"

She attempts to straighten her face, "I'm sorry. Really."

"Yeah, that burst of laughter your hiding is really convincing."

She sobered up, after some effort I'm unhappy to report. "I didn't even know they taught Latin anymore," she said. "I thought it was considered a dead language."

"It is *not* a dead language! Your language is based in it, Harper."

"I'm sorry. I can see that this subject is a sensitive one for you."

"Obviously, I'm insane. I'm defending myself as if I was Roman. Listen, I took the language in high school because I thought it would give me a good foundation vocabulary for my intended college major."

"Oh, I'm dying to know what major you've chosen that *Latin* could possibly create a good foundation for," she teased.

I feel the corners of my mouth twist up. "I'm going pre-med."

Her eyes bug wide, "Seriously?"

"I know it's a lofty goal, even for people who come from money but I'm determined and it's been a dream of mine since I was small, so..."

She's staring at me.

"It's not lofty Callum. It's brilliant that you have dreams. You should do it."

I was taken aback.

"I wasn't expecting that," I grinned. "I mean, my teachers were always supportive but I got conflicting messages growing up. My foster parents constantly told me I'd amount to nothing."

"But you didn't listen to them, did you?" She asked with a twinkle in her eyes.

"Stop looking at me like that."

23

She shook her head. "Like what?"

"Like I'm already a physician," I grinned.

"What kind of doctor do you want to be?" She asks, ignoring me.

"Uh...a pediatrician."

"How ya' going to do it?"

"Well, there's this thing, see, it's called a university. You apply..."

"Very funny. Seriously, how are you going to pull it off?"

Before I could answer though, a woman came out. Harper didn't know it, but we were about to get word that we were sleeping outside that night.

"I'm sorry," the woman callously announced, "but we're full tonight!" And with no other explanation, she shut the door behind her. The veteran homeless scrambled to the nearest restaurant dumpsters in hopes of finding new cardboard, resigned to their evening's fortune. Others stood gaping, unsure of what that exactly meant. I turned toward Harper, ready to speak but instead found myself studying her. She brought her hands to her mouth, her fingers trembled against her lips. She felt lost, I could tell, her tough outer facade was beginning to crack.

"Come with me," I said, quickly grabbing her hand, leading her through the dispersing crowd toward my motorcycle.

"Where are we going?" She whispered.

"Away from here."

Tears threatened the corner of her eyes and I caught one with my thumb before it slid down her cheek. I pushed her hair out of her eyes and strapped the helmet to her head without another word, before plopping her small frame toward the front seat of my bike, afraid she was too dazed to hold on to me. I got on and straddled the seat behind her, her lovely back against my chest, kicking on the motor and driving off the curb onto the street.

I leaned in closely to her ear, hoping she'd be able to hear me through her helmet, "You know everything's going to be okay, right?" She shook her head. "Trust me," I said. "I'll figure it out. Promise."
She slowly nodded her head, but I wasn't sure she really believed what I'd told her.

I stopped at a nearby gas station, narrowly avoiding a cab who cut me off but it didn't seem to faze her.

"Stay here, Harper. I'm going to call my friend Charlie, see if he'll let us crash on his couch." Her reply was a soft grin.
I held the receiver to the pay phone a few inches from my ear, nothing is grosser than a New York City pay phone. It rang three times before I got Charlie's voicemail. *Hey, Charlie here. Leave a message and I'll ring you back.*

"Charlie," I sighed, "I'm in need of a couch tonight, dude. Maybe you can call me back in the next five? I'm at 555-9876," I said, eyeing the number on the payphone. "I'll stick around for a bit. Also, I've picked up a stray. She's cool, you'll like her, just, *please*," I begged, "ring me back soon."

It was hit or miss with Charlie, he was a roadie for a mediocre band and he had mentioned a few weeks back that he'd be going to Japan with them soon. I just hoped he hadn't left just yet. The phone rang before I even got an opportunity to turn around.

I placed my hand on the receiver. *Please, God, let this be Charlie.* I picked it up.

25

"Hello?" I asked.

"Yo, Callum. It's Charlie."

"Oh ,thank God!" I exclaimed a little too loudly.

"Calm down, dude." He laughed. "Got your message. I've got some good news and some bad news. I'm not in the city tonight." *Damn.* "And I left my spare key at Cherry's and she's doing some waitressing job in the Hampton's this weekend for some extra cash so she's nowhere near you *but* if you *want*, you can crash at my studio tonight. There's a random shower in the back of the shared common space, if you remember, not ideal but all yours."

I breathed out an audible sigh. "Thank you so much, dude, seriously."

"No problem, man. I'll call Henry, let him know you're coming, he'll let you in, just mention my name."

"Thank you so much, Charlie. I can't thank you enough."

I hang up, invigorated.

I turn and slap my hands together. "Okay, Harper Bailey, you're comin' with me."

"I am?" She said, looking hopeful.

"Yeah, it's not going to be ideal," repeating Charlie's words, "but it's going to be better than staying the night outside in this heat."

We arrive at Charlie's studio around eight thirty in the evening. I ride my bike over the curb and onto the sidewalk, next to the entrance. Harper takes her helmet off and I get assaulted by her fragrant hair again and almost lose my balance.

"Where are you going to lock up your bike?"

"I'm not." I smile.

"Aren't you afraid it'll get stolen?"

"Nah, because I'm taking it inside."

"Can you do that?" She asked.

"Yeah, I've done it a million times, all the floors are concrete where we're going and I always promise Henry, the owner, to keep a mat beneath it to catch any oil." I point to the second story window above the door. "That's his apartment right there."

"Will he be cool about all this?" She asks, skepticism leaking from her tone.

"Yeah, I think so. Henry knows my situation. He never lets me stay more than one night, though. I suppose he's afraid I'll move in and that's against some sort of tenant code city thing. He's not licensed for that and a real stickler for the rules. The city has it out for the rockers, I guess." I winked, like a dumbass. I immediately regretted the cheese move.

I pressed the buzzer in awe of my total loss of cool. This girl seeped the 'smooth' outta' me.

"Henry," Henry announced in a static voice.

"Henry, it's Callum. Did Charlie call you?"

We hear another buzz for the door and I opened it. I clicked the buzzer again and hear the other end connect but Henry says nothing.

"Thanks, Henry."

"No problem, Callum. See you in the morning, dude."

"And that was Henry."

"How old is he?" Harper asked.

"I don't know, like thirty?"

"Cool."

"Alright, hold the door for me?" I ask.

She whips inside the covered alcove and holds the door as wide as it will go. I give my bike two hard shoves and it lurches over the step to the alcove and into the building foyer. I lead Harper to Charlie's studio in the very back.

"It's the last door on the right."

She jumped ahead of my bike and opened the door for me as I wheeled in the bike. Charlie's studio space is large and it should be, because it costs him a small fortune but apparently it paid for itself when he recorded for random bands when he wasn't on the road.

Harper let out a low whistle.

"Incredible," she said, turning around.

I set my bike up in an open corner of his instrument room and opened one of the only closet doors near the entrance. I pulled out a large rubber pad that Charlie kept inside for my motorcycle and tossed it underneath the motor.

I turned around and caught her watching me. It reminded me that I was alone, with an unbelievably beautiful girl, and that no one was around. I tucked my hands in my back pockets to keep from seizing this stranger and kissing her until she gasped for air.

"So," I said, rocking back on my heels. I grabbed my bag. "Listen, I've done this a couple of times. It gets old fast but the one thing I've learned is to take advantage of anything you can while you can because you may not have the opportunity to do it for awhile which means I recommend we shower, then take any dirty clothes we have to the laundromat close by."

"This isn't your first rodeo then?"

"Not by a long shot. I'll go first, ensuring you'll have privacy later."

I grabbed my towel, something noticeably missing from her "luggage", also something I plan on addressing later, and head for the shower with my soap and shampoo in hand.

The "shower" was a drain in the floor, a poorly pressured spout, and a thin plastic shower curtain in the corner of what at one time must have been a pre-war locker room. The water was lukewarm at best but better than I'd had for the past two days, which was sponge baths in subway restrooms. Even though the water temperature was crummy, I had never been in such a good mood and was positive it was from meeting Harper. There's nothing more thrilling than meeting someone new for the first time, especially if that someone new was freaking gorgeous as hell.

I stepped from the shower feeling better than I had in a very long time and toweled off. *Shit,* I thought as I looked down at myself, *I forgot my clothes.* I wrapped my towel around my lower half and trudged along the hall back to Charlie's studio, already turning beet red at what I was about to do.

As I near the studio though, I can hear loud music trembling through the air and one miss Harper Bailey singing at the top of her lungs. I edged toward the slightly ajar door and quietly pushed it open, hoping to grab my bag next to the wall nearest me and holding my breath that she'd be too distracted to notice me but when I catch a glimpse of her, I become engrossed.

Forgetting my towel and my bag, I leaned against the door jamb just watching her dancing around, singing Aerosmith's 'Dream On'. I couldn't believe how remarkably entertaining it was to see her shuffling over the floor like she was, her hair falling over her shoulders and in her face. I can tell it was probably the most free she had felt in quite awhile making her face flushed and excited and her body swaying to each beat. I wondered if the words meant anything in particular to her and suddenly didn't know if I was intruding. If this was some sort of therapeutic ritual for her, I'd feel like an ass if she knew I was watching. I leaned forward and grabbed my bag just as she turned and saw me standing there.

"Agh!" She squealed, turning down the music.

Her face a deep red. "How long have you been standing there?" She asked, her chest heaving from the effort of her song. Her eyes followed the lines of my body until they stop at the towel. "Why aren't you dressed?"

"Uh, I didn't mean to intrude," I said, the heat of a blush creeping up my neck. "I forgot my bag with my stuff and came back for it and, um, I accidentally saw you and..."

She looked like she was about to cry, her hands flew to her mouth and I reached for her, "I'm so sorry, Harper. I didn't think. I'm sorry."

But she burst out laughing, the tears streaming down her face her obvious attempt at holding it in and not from humiliation. I breathed a sigh of relief and my smile began to match hers. She sucked in air harshly and started laughing harder.

"Oh my Lord, Callum. This is so embarrassing!"

"You're embarrassed! Look at me! I'm in a towel, dripping water all over the effing floor."

She snorted, making her laugh even harder. My laughter harmonized with hers, tears streaming down both our faces now.

Harper sobered suddenly and we stared at each other for at least a minute. I made a cautious step toward her, my face inching toward hers. She laid a hand on my damp shoulder but instead of meeting my kiss, her eyes brightened and she turned her head in embarrassment.

"You have to get dressed, Callum."

"I'm so sorry, I forgot," I said, as I grabbed my bag and headed for the common room one more time. When I returned, dressed and slightly flustered, I found Harper playing an acoustic guitar in one of Charlie's recliners.

"Wow. You can play guitar too?" I asked.

"Nah, I just dabble."

"I noticed you didn't have a towel and although mine's a bit wet, I wouldn't care if you used it, if you want."

She set the guitar aside and stood, smoothing her wrinkled jeans down her legs and stood before me.

"Thanks," she whispered, grabbing her bag and throwing the towel over her shoulders.

She returned a few minutes later, her coppery hair wet and hanging at the middle of her back, already starting to dry in soft waves. Her eyes were brightened by the shower and her lips were plump and red. *What I wouldn't give to kiss those lips.*

Chapter Two
Dream On

Harper

"How long have you been on your own?" I asked Callum, as we walked to the laundromat three blocks down from his friend Charlie's studio.

"Probably three months or so."

"How did you manage to finish school?"

"Well, I'd shower in the locker room. I'm ashamed to say, I was forced to get the free luncheons and I'd take as much food as possible from there for dinner that night as well. I slept pretty much anywhere."

"Keep your grades up, doc?"

That made him smile. "Hell yes I did."

"Wow, Callum, that is simultaneously alarming *and* extraordinary."

"Nah, I did what I wanted most of the time. It wasn't as bad as I think I'm making it sound."

"You're an awful liar, Tate." I said, using his last name, sending a secret thrill up my arms from the familiarity of it.

"What about you?" He asked.

"Well, I didn't turn eighteen until after I graduated so my foster mom pretty much had no choice but to feed me my senior year."

"I meant your grades but I'm happy to hear you ate, even though it doesn't look like you do," he teased, inspecting my body and heating my cheeks to a bright red.

"I'm gonna' ignore that," I squeaked out. "My grades were decent enough, nothing lower than a B but I didn't really care all that much because my teachers hated me regardless."

That clearly intrigued him. "And why would they hate you?"

"I suppose you could say, I was a *troublemaker*."

"What kind of trouble could you possibly make, Harper Bailey?" He asked, with a raised brow.

"The kind that changes your opinion of someone, therefore, you'll never find out." I laughed out.

We arrived at the beat up laundromat. Its sign flickered neon green and buzzed throughout the electric summer air. Random insects crashed into the lights and spiraled to their deaths. Callum opened the door for me.

"Don't think for a second that I won't get you tell me what kind of hell you stirred up."

I eyed him carefully, a twist of a smile tickled the corner of my mouth.

He started to unload our clothes into a washer and I couldn't help but notice that he slid mine in with his. My stomach stirred with butterflies. *Seriously, Harper? It's not that he feels comfortable with you, he's*

33

just trying to save money. I scolded myself for thinking that this stranger was starting to think of me as a friend rather than the acquaintance we'd really end up being. He filled my palm with a few quarters and pointed to the wall machines selling detergent. As I walked away, I couldn't help but revel at the tingle his fingers gave me when he dropped the coins against my palm. I bring back the detergent and placed the leftover quarters back in his hand. His hand lingered on mine then and gave me a flirtatious smile.

"What are you doing?" I asked, fighting a giggle.

"I'm doing *our* laundry, miss." The way he emphasizes the word *our* heated my chest and the blaze met my cheeks, betraying me bitterly. He looked way too satisfied with that, so I turned and pretended to examine my surroundings but I could still feel his eyes on my body.

"How about we make a deal," he pipes up.

I paused for a moment, deciding whether or not I should even hear his terms, before answering with an obvious, "What kind of deal?"

"You ask me one question, however embarrassing you'd like it to be, and I'll answer honestly."

"And you?"

"I'll be informed of one trouble making incident for every answer."

"Deal."

"You acquiesced too easily."

"Maybe the reveal is worth it. I've got some ridiculous questions for you."

"Man, I think I'm starting to regret this game already."

He dropped the steel lid to the washer and slid over the top of the churning machine. I slid onto the lid beside him. We were utterly alone, no one even manned the service desk.

"So, Callum, have you ever bought a Creed album?"

"Damn. You're good and yes, unfortunately, in a fifteen year old haze, I apparently bought their first album but everyone bought that album, Harper!"

"Hey, no need to make excuses."

"Very funny, miss. Alright," he rubs his hands together in preparation. "Tell me one."

"Oh alright," I huff. "Alright, in ninth I photocopied my principal's cell phone number and passed it around to all my classmates."

"Oh Lord, Harper. Why?" He asked in disbelief. *Jeez, this is one of the tame things I did. I'm scared to reveal the naughtier ones.*

"Well, he suspended me for three days for something that wasn't my fault."

"Harper?"

"I mean, I am a troublemaker but it truly wasn't my fault that time." I sniffed.

"Well, what happened?"

"I was using the restroom and there were two girls in the handicap stall smoking cigarettes. I didn't think much of it because it was a common thing in my school but when my principal walked in, she saw me and just assumed it was all my fault. You know, reputation and all." I sighed out loud. "Anyway, I tried to explain that it was two girls in the handicap stall but she refused to check and dragged me to her office. When I sat down, she explained to me they had a no tolerance policy for smoking and didn't even give me a chance to speak in my own defense. She just waved her hand in my face and picked up her phone to ring my foster mother.

"That was the last straw for that camel, so to

speak, and I was placed in a new home the next week. I suppose it was easy for her to assume it was me but you don't do that to kids, ya' know? Always give them the benefit of the doubt. She had no idea the headache she caused me just for jumping to the wrong conclusion."

"Jeez, Harper, I'm sorry," he said, sympathy gracing his brows.

"Nah, I got her back."

"Obviously," he smiled. "Did they ever find out it was you?"

I winked. "Nope. Alright, your turn again."

"Shoot."

Just ask, Harper. "Who was your first kiss?" He blushed and attempted to fight a smile. It was the cutest thing I'd ever seen. *He* is the cutest thing I had ever seen.

"Um," he struggled, "her name was Keiko Nguyen." *I think I hate Keiko Nguyen.*

I cleared my throat, "Oh, that's cool. Was she, like, your girlfriend or whatever?" *Smooth.*

"No, it was eighth grade and we were all playing spin the bottle."

Whew! Alright, Keiko's cool now.

"But I purposely spun the bottle so it'd land on her. I liked her, I guess," he said, shuffling his feet back and forth, his heels bouncing against the machine in uncomfortable nervousness.

Nope, officially hate Keiko now. I inwardly sighed. *Harper, you're an idiot.*

He peered his head over his shoulder and smiled at me. I smiled back like an idiot.

"My turn," he said, waggling his brows.

I rolled my eyes, fighting to hide my giddiness at his slightly flirtatious behavior. *He's only charming, Harper.*

36

He probably does this to all the girls. Don't be a fool.

"I purposely set off the indoor sprinklers with a match and a crumpled ball of paper my sophomore year."

"Holy crap, Harper!"

"I know!" I said, burying my crimson face in my hands. "I was an idiot."

He shook his head. "Again, *why*, Harper?"

"Well, you see, I had this friend. His name was Chris." Callum narrows his eyes at me, in dare I say, *jealousy*? I continued trying to stifle the butterflies that gives me. "Chris couldn't use his legs and was bound to a wheelchair. Well, our stupid basketball coach got it in his head that Chris was gonna compete in a friendly scrap between the basketball team and a team everyone jokingly deems 'the incompetent misfits'.

"It's a scrimmage my school put together every year at the beginning of the year. They usually get the chess club or something to compete and they do this at a pep rally in front of the *entire* school. Chris didn't want to be treated any differently then he already was, which was totally lame because Chris was cool as shit, so when coach asked him to play, he agreed.

"So, fifteen minutes before the game was scheduled to start, while the bleachers were starting to fill up, I filed in behind the lemmings and caught Chris' eyes. He looked so distraught, I *had* to do something.

"I plunged my hands into my pockets and pulled out the detention slip I'd gotten that day in one hand and a lighter in the other. It was all I could think of."

When I finished, I noticed Callum stare at me with wide eyes.

"I know it was wrong...," but before I can finish Callum grabs me and hugs me tightly to him.

"You did that for him?" He whispered into my hair.

"Anybody would have," I said into his rock hard chest.

"But nobody else did, Harper."

"Yeah, technically but…"

"No, you're amazing."

"I am not!" I scoffed, pushing him off me, but he only pulls me tighter against him. "I'm a heathen according to everyone I know."

"No, you're not. You're all hard shell, bad ass on the outside but soft and sweet on the inside. You're a freakin' Tootsie Pop!"

I snort but can't think of an argument. *You cry during Charmin commercials, Harper Bailey. You're positively lame.*

I subtly breathe in the scent of his shirt and have to stop myself from burying my face into his neck. He pulled away and I felt a loss from it, wishing he'd just hold me a little bit longer. *It's been years since someone hugged you, Harper.* Callum cupped my cheek with his hand and rubbed his thumb against my jaw bone, smiling in my face like a massive goof. I laughed out loud. *Just looking at him makes me laugh.*

The washer stopped chugging and we both reluctantly turned to open the lid. Callum reached in and removed the wet clothes, setting them on the edge of the washer. I take pile after pile to the dryer and toss them in. We work in silence and unison as if we've done this hundreds of times before together, yet another reason I need to check myself. *Already getting attached.*

Callum

    I'm getting attached. She's too much for me and I find myself wishing she'd just leave before she breaks my heart. *You can't get attached. Attachment is death for someone like you, Callum.* It weighs more to me than it does for regular people. I glanced her direction as she lifted a pile of wet clothes into the dryer. She peeked over her shoulder at me and smiled before turning back and starting the machine. *Stay with me, Harper,* I find myself silently pleading.

I don't know what it is about this girl, but it feels like nothing to want to take her on as if I can afford to double my responsibility load and, you know, I think she may have felt the same way. *What is wrong with you, dude? You can barely feed and clothe yourself.* I'd been at it for a few months longer than her and it was painfully obvious, even if she hadn't already admitted to it. This was obviously her first night on her own.

I knew it was our pasts that united us. Though, I've met others with a similar bond, none had ever believed in me as implicitly as this naive girl. *Did you hear how she told you your dreams would become real?*

She'd obviously lived through a harsh childhood too but, somehow, remained as trusting as she did. It was refreshing. Refreshing and incredibly *dangerous* in a city like New York. I knew if didn't take care of her, she'd be eaten up and spit out, then shoved into a gutter and left for dead.

"Tell me a little about yourself," I said, desperate to hear her talk.

She pinched her eyebrows with a smirk. "What do you want to know?"

She reached me and I tossed her by the waist onto the machine at her back. *God, she weighs nothing.* She bit her bottom lip and turned her head, attempting to hide her blush. I really hoped that blush belonged to me. I turned and pushed myself onto the machine next to her.

"Who's your favorite band? And don't tell me it's MilliVanilli or something because I'll have to kill you right here," I teased.

She blushed, every inch of her face covered in a rosy hue.

"MilliVanilli? How *old are you*?" She joshed.

I smiled before clearing my throat. "Um, does 'Dream On' mean anything in particular to you?"

"Yeah," she said, quietly, looking introspective. "It reminds me how fleeting life can be and how those around you can steal you from yourself...if you let them. It reminds me to protect myself." I wanted to ask her who she needed protection from so I could beat them to a bloody pulp but she distracted me once more with her lovely mouth as it began to speak. "Anyway," she shrugged, "Enough about that." She laughed nervously. "Depressing. Um, Barcelona's my favorite band. Their lyrics are especially meaningful. They're especially sweet, to me anyway. I mean, their song 'Please Don't Go'? I've *always* been a sucker for violins." She meets my eyes. "Ever heard of them?"

I reach into my back pocket and pull out a flyer. "Oh who? Them?" I ask, nonchalantly, pointing at the name at the top of the flyer.

Harper snatches it from my hand.

"Where did you get this?" She questioned, her voice raising an octave in shock.

"Oh, they're just touring with my buddy's band."

She shook her head in disbelief and swallowed audibly.

"They'll be here in two weeks," I continued. "Why don't you come with me?"

"In two weeks?" She said. "Two weeks?" She repeated.

Commit to knowing me in two weeks, Harper. Don't make me beg.

"I think I would love that."

"You think?" I joked as I exhaled an inward sigh of

40

relief.

Chapter Three
Look What You've Done

Callum

"Tell me why you didn't apply for college," I asked her as we walked back to the studio at ten to midnight.

She narrowed her eyes at me. "How do you know I never applied?" She said.

"Well, I just assumed. You told me you weren't going to school."

"I did apply, to several schools, actually."

"And?" I asked, both eyebrows raised, but she didn't respond. "Don't leave me in suspense."

"I got into a few," she added cryptically, a smile tugging at the side of her mouth.

"I don't understand. Why aren't you going to

college then?"

"Honestly?"

"Honestly."

"I can't go."

"Why, Harper?"

"Because...," she sighed, her shoulders drooping in resignation, "because I wouldn't be able to do it. I don't think I *can* do it." She suddenly steeled herself, standing tall, pushing back her shoulders and raising her head. "It's too late now anyway. It's nearly June. There's no way I could even enroll."

"How would you even know that Harper? Unless you tried?"

She smiled and ducked her face in her chest, her chin shook back and forth.

"Where were you accepted?" I asked, moving on to the most important part.

"A bunch of state colleges." She cleared her throat. "NYU."

I playfully push her as if to say 'get out' but she doesn't expect it and almost toppled over. I reached for her clumsily, caught her by the waist, and brought her into my chest.

"I'm sorry," I murmured into her ear.

She stared up at me, so beautiful, lips full, eyes bright with excitement. Her sweet breath smelled of the strawberry lips gloss she had a habit, I noticed, of applying every half hour. She was so close I could smell her hair again and I forgot myself, openly inhaling her.

"What are you doing?" She asked, straightening herself from my grasp, cheeks flamed.

"Smelling you," I stupidly blurt, removing my grip from her small waist.

She bit her bottom lip to keep from laughing and

wrinkled her nose. "Wh-what for?" She stammered.

"Because you smell like oranges, pineapples and the ocean. It's the most unusual scent I've ever smelled and it's addictive," I confessed. Her face lost its playfulness. "I first smelled you in that lobby, Harper and I wanted to bury my face in your hair then, too." Harper's breathing sped up as she studied my face, looking for something but I'm not quite sure what. "Anyway, I'm sorry," I continued. "It won't happen again, I apologize."

I started walking, the embarrassment too much to shoulder and cowardly hide through my false determination to reach the studio. Harper slowly caught up with me and we walked side by side for the majority of the walk in silence.

"So," I uttered suddenly, nearing the door, trying to make light of what happened, "journalism and NYU, I've heard, are a fantastic combination."

Harper laughed out loud. "It does, one of the best actually."

"*So*?"

"So, what?" She shrugged her shoulders.

"So come with me tomorrow morning. I have to get some paperwork done and it will give you the opportunity to pick my advisor's brain."

She stopped me at the door, her soft hand on my forearm. I instinctively flex to prevent myself from covering her hand with the one resting on the door.

"Why would I do that, Callum?" She asked me earnestly.

"Why wouldn't you, Harper? What do you have to lose?"

"Absolutely nothing, I guess," she answered honestly.

I opened the metal door and let her in, walking ahead of her to the studio. Inside, it was slightly warm but not uncomfortable.

"Music?" I asked, walking over to the studio's soundboard.

"Mmm," she answered, breaking open the laundry bag and separating our clothes into two piles. The smell of the freshly laundered clothing filled the tiny space with a bursting fragrance.

"Thank you," she said quietly as I flipped through tracks.

I turned around to face her back. "For what, Harper?"

"For clean laundry, for taking me in, for seeming interested in what I do with my life," she said, her hands coming to rest on the table in front of her.

"I *am* interested in what you do with your life."

She curved her body around to face me. "Why?" She asked bluntly.

"I don't know," I answered honestly, shrugging. "You just feel important to me, for some reason."

She leaned her backside against the table, seemingly for support. "But you don't even know me, Callum." Her bottom lip trembled.

"You're a kindred spirit," I offered up, but I say this only to stop from revealing the whole truth. The partial was all I could give her without sounding insane. If I was being candid with her, she'd only find out that I felt something for her that could only be the equivalent of a gravitational pull towards the center of the earth. She was a magnet for me and I was powerless to resist. It was more than a mere attraction.

"I guess we do have eerily similar backgrounds," she agreed.

"Yeah, look at where we met."

"Exactly," she winked.

I picked up one of Charlie's acoustics and sat on the

swivel chair next to the soundboard. I absently began to play a song I wrote months ago. It had a melancholy melody and I'd never really played it for anyone. It wasn't my intention for Harper to hear it, it was just second nature to pick up Charlie's guitars and start playing with paying no mind to who's around. I wasn't used to anyone else hearing me play except for Charlie and his band.

"Callum, that is beautiful," she exclaimed.
I stopped playing, a heat creeping into my face and up my neck.

"I-I didn't realize I was even playing," I said, attempting to shake the humiliation from my face.

"Don't stop," she begged quietly, sending my blood to an ultimate boil. She moved to sit in one of the other swivel chairs next to me.

I coughed into a fist. "Um, okay. Any requests?"

"Well, since you're actually familiar with *Barcelona*. Could you play *Please Don't Go*? If you know it, that is?"
I smiled. I did know it and immediately start singing it to her, strumming the strings softly. The melody is simple but beautiful. It incited waves of intensity to roll off Harper and they hit me like a hydrogen bomb. My fingers almost stilled from the shock of it. *She's ridiculous extraordinary*, I admitted to myself. She closed her eyes and grinned at the lyrics.

While most people act awkward and uncomfortable when others sing to them, Harper surprised me by letting it be what music was, natural and beautiful. She moved her eyes with mine and it seemed to be the most unfeigned, unpracticed thing in the world. She even sung harmony with me for the chorus and I was completely taken by her by the end of the song.

She leaned in closely with glinted eyes. "Play another," she whispered.

And I did. Four more, actually and Harper Bailey made me feel like a freakin' rock star instead of the nobody I really was. She wrinkled her nose adorably and sang along, scrunched her eyes closed and bit her lip to prevent herself from beaming a bright smile at her obviously favorite parts, and raised her hands, dancing and twirling around during songs with an accelerated beat, her hair fanning around her.

When my fingers could take no more, I set the guitar down and slumped into my chair. Realizing I was tired, Harper turned on a few tunes through the soundboard.

"Come on," she said, grabbing me by my hands. A shot of pleasure that *she* reached for *me* sent me reeling with an unreasonable need to bring her close. "Dance with me?" She asked, giving me the out I would have paid a million dollars for at that moment.

We threw our arms out and shook our heads as we screamed the lyrics of three songs at the other, yet exhaustion never took me. Harper gave me energy enough to last for weeks. Despite the unusually dark room, I felt like I could decipher the smallest lines of her face. That's how attuned to her I'd become in those few hours and I studied every expression, memorizing what notes made her happiest.

What are the odds? I thought, as *Barcelona's* 'Please Don't Go' suddenly played softly, magnifying our loud breaths caused by the effort of dancing around. I held out my hand to her, my face sobering quickly. She hesitated for only a second before sliding her hand into mine. I brought her body close and my breath sped up even more but not from the earlier exertion, no, this was from proximity.

Harper laid her head on my shoulder as we

swayed back and forth to the resonating piano, the long, low strokes of the violins, and the soft, meaningful words. We sang the lyrics to each other, letting the impact of their words sink into our hearts.

And when the last note rung through our ears, and the music stopped altogether, a deafening silence filled the room. We stilled, neither of us wanting to remove one another from our embrace. *It's not you she wants, Callum,* I chided myself for believing for even a moment that it was *me* she wanted. Me, a complete stranger. *We've been neglected all our lives. Hugs are a rare commodity,* I reminded myself.

"You're warm," she said gently, breaking my train of thought.

Not able to stop myself, I inhaled her hair again.

"Uh, *Callum*?" She giggled.

"Yes," I said, a grin hitting my reddening cheeks. I purposely kept her cheek to my neck to avoid her stare. *You're the king of humiliation.*

"Are you-Are you smelling me again?"

"No," I said, before breaking out into laughter.

I felt her chest shake in amusement before I hear the chuckling. She tried to pull away and I hugged her tighter but instead of pushing harder against my chest to break free, she held tighter and my stomach dropped to my feet.

I have perfect timing because I decided to yawn embarrassingly loudly.

"Tired?" She teased into my chest.

"I might be," I conceded. I cleared my throat. "Uh, Charlie keeps egg crate foam in here," I said, pointing to a closet she couldn't see. *Doofus.* She said nothing to that so I broke away from our hug, still avoiding eye contact. I reached into the closet and start pulling out clean sheets and the egg crate. "Sometimes Charlie stays so late he doesn't feel like cabbing it home so..." I trailed off.

I unrolled the foam and it came spilling out in one large square, taking up most of the little studio booth. The studio is large but compartmentalized, leaving a series of medium to small rooms. The soundboard booth was the smallest besides the voice recording booth but it was the only one with an air conditioner to keep the expensive equipment cool. "So," I continued, "he keeps all this junk here. I secretly think he keeps it here to help me more than to help himself. I called him on it," I rambled, setting out the clean, folded sheets, "but he insists that he's a selfish jerk who thinks only of himself and that I should watch my mouth because he has a reputation to uphold."

"But why would he make sure the sheets are clean if it was only for him?" She stated.

"Exactly."

"I think I like this Charlie," she teases.

"He's kind and I think he's going to love you," I said, without thinking, assuming she and I would know each other long enough for her to even get to know Charlie. *She did commit to the concert in two weeks, Callum. Guess she'll meet Charlie after all.* Then a heavy stone of realization settled in my stomach. *What if she meets Charlie and he takes to her?*

Charlie had a knack for getting girls. I can't tell you how many times I'd liked a girl and he'd gotten her instead. It's not like he steals them or anything, he probably doesn't even know I was interested in them, but girls just flock to the guy. *Oh God, what if Harper likes Charlie? What if they hit it off and start dating? I'll have to endure them together or fight Charlie.* Either leaves a bitter taste in my mouth.

"So," she interrupted my rambling thoughts, forcing me to take note that I'd been standing over the egg crate just staring down at it like an idiot.

"Sorry," I said, shaking my head. "You can have the pallet and I can sleep in the chair."

"Absolutely not," she vehemently disagreed. "If you hadn't helped me when you did, I would be sleeping on a sidewalk somewhere." I didn't have the heart to tell her that's, more than likely, where we'd both be sleeping the next night. "So, it's only fitting that I sleep in the chair. Besides, you're much taller than me. You take the pallet. I'll be more than comfortable in the chair."

"Well," I said seriously, "if you made me sleep on that pallet, I wouldn't get a wink of sleep knowing you were in that chair. Then, finally, when my body couldn't take it anymore, succumbing to sleep too late, I'd sleep through my alarm. I'd wake up late, miss my appointment with my advisor, and lose my scholarship.

"Then, I'd be forced to take a job waiting tables while going to a community college and as we both know, no one finishes community college. So after dropping out and enduring six years of working in the food industry, they'll offer me a management position and I'll be forced to take it to support the eight kids I had with the girl I met at ju-co in my theater electives class but left me to pursue her 'acting career'. I'll be bitter and grow a beer gut..."

"Okay! Okay!" She giggled. "I'll take the pallet but *only* if you take the pallet with me."
My throat instantly dried and the smirk that graced my stupid face fell.

"Wa-*with* you?"

"Yes," she said turning her back toward me and taking a t-shirt and some shorts from her piles of clothing and heading for the door. She stopped at the edge. "You sleep with your feet at this end and I'll sleep with my feet at that end."

Harper winked at me before leaving to change.

"Oh," I said to no one, the blood returning to my face but disappointment following soon behind. *You're still sleeping right next to her, genius.*

I used the time she was gone to ready myself for bed. I usually slept in my boxers because I didn't make it a habit to sleep with women, hardy har, har, but wasn't sure what to do because I didn't have anything else. I scrambled through my belongings and found a pair of old Adidas track pants. I removed my t-shirt and threw on the pants.

Harper

I can't believe I suggested we sleep on the pallet together. I know *why* I did it. I genuinely couldn't let him sleep in that gosh awful chair but if I was being honest with myself, it wasn't the *only* reason why I did it. *You can't lie to yourself, Harper.* And I couldn't. *Alright, fine.* I did it because I wanted to know what it was like to lie next to a warm body, to feel close to someone sincere because sincerity is one of those rare human qualities that feels a bit like discovering a lost treasure. It is a rare commodity but once found, is absolutely priceless. That was Callum, pretty much in a nutshell. And I, to be perfectly frank, could count the people I'd found to be genuine on my right hand.

I came to the door and knocked before stepping in, so as not to disturb him getting ready.

"Come in," I heard.

But there wasn't enough preparation in the world to ready me for what I saw when I opened that door.

Callum, standing above the pallet, the lights out but the faint glow from the hallway glistening across his perfect chest and highlighting the eight pack that painted his stomach. I gulped audibly. I stood there, staring like an imbecile.

"Uh, Harper?"

I shook my head. "Um, yeah?" A blush crept up my neck and plastered my face in crimson.

"You okay?"

"Uh, huh. Why do you ask?" I said, biting my bottom lip to keep from a nervous laugh and staring at everything in the room *but* Callum, a feat in and of itself.

"Because you're just standing there. Listen, if you don't want to sleep with me on the pallet, I understand."

"No, it's okay." I answered as breezily as I could. I set all my stuff on the table with our clean laundry and headed for the soundboard to turn on some low tunes. "Do you mind?" I asked.

"Not at all," he said. "I can't sleep without it."

I look at him, surprised. "Neither can I." It's how I used to drown out the nightly yelling my last three foster parents used to embark on every evening after getting drunk or when they were getting in a fight or when I just wanted to drown out my situation.

I turned and walked over to the pallet. He watched me settle in before laying on top of the blanket I was underneath, his feet at my head, pulling another quilt at his side over his own body. Basically, we were as far apart as two people sleeping next to one another could get. After a few moments, he turned out the lights and it became pitch black and *that's* the moment I chose to start laughing uncontrollably which, in turn, caused him to follow suit.

"What's so funny?" He asked me.

"Everything, Callum. It's all so incredibly surreal and this is incredibly awkward but I'm going to ask anyway."

"Okay, shoot," he said, still laughing.

"Can I sleep up there with you? Right next to you, that is? And before you turn me down..." I started but he interrupted me.

"Come here," he said.

I climb up to his side of the pallet and get underneath my blanket again, the very thin blanket that still separated our skin.

"I've never slept with anyone before," I stupidly say. This makes him laugh and suddenly I'm extraordinarily grateful that it was dark because I'm sure my face lit up like a Christmas tree.

"Neither have I."

"I meant that I've never literally gone to sleep with someone." I paused. "Actually, I've never *slept* with anyone before, either," I admitted, staring up at an invisible ceiling.

I heard him turn toward me. "Neither have I," he admitted.

"Seriously?"

"Really," he said, "and this is incredibly embarrassing to admit to anyone, especially a hottie, but I figure, what the hell, I'm lying next to you shirtless and that's about as intimate as one can get with a stranger, I think. Or, you know what I mean.

"Anyway, I've never done anything because I just feel like it's the one part of myself that I still have control over. I have nothing to give anyone, really. It's the one gift I can give that has any kind of value. It makes me feel worthy."

I couldn't believe what I'd just heard. I mean, I struggled a little after the hottie part, of course, because

Callum had this school boy effect on me and all. *He thinks I'm pretty*, I stupidly and giddily admitted to myself. I stayed quiet for a moment just absorbing what he'd said before answering. "I think that is just about the sexiest thing I think has ever come out of a man's mouth," I blurted.

"Are you sure?" He asked. "Because you've never seen me spit to hit a mark."

"See, now you just killed it."

Callum snorted. "I think you're the only person on this planet that seems to agree with me on that particular subject," he joked.

"Not at all, dork. I can think of a million girl's names right here and now that would be right there with you."

"But not you?" He boldly asked.

"Callum Tate! I'm riding the v-train with you, aren't I? Got the ticket and everything. Gotta' admit, it's the slowest and most boring train ride ever but, sheesh, I know the destination will be worth it. Give me a little credit, will ya'?"

"Alright, alright," he laughed. "I'm sorry. It's just, we're sort of a unique pair, the two of us."

"I know," I said. "You just gained a heck of a lot of respect from me. You know that?"

"Same here, Harper Bailey. You're an enigma."

"In more ways than one," I said.

"So, do you want to do it?" He asked.

"Callum!" I screamed, laughing. My face turned another shade of red. Like I said, thank God for the dark.

He laughed. "I'm joking! I'm joking!" He said, laying flat, tucking his hands behind his head.

I turned to face him and felt his breath move my hair. Callum surprised me by reaching out and tucking it behind my ear but doesn't return the hand behind his head like it was before. Instead, he laid his left hand on my own and we drift off to sleep, each lulled by the warmth of a sincere body.

The next morning, I woke groggily to quiet and pitch black but Callum's hand wasn't on my own. I instinctively reached out but it continued on to the end of the pallet. *He's gone.* I sat up, wondering why Callum would have left for his advisor meeting without me. Deciding to stand, I stretched and lifted myself up to search for the light switch, fumbling along the wall for the raised plastic rectangle. In my haste to find the switch, I forgot to feel around at my feet and ran into something hard, falling to my knees.

"Crap!" I said, my hand going to my right knee. My fingers come back warm and wet. *Bleeding, great.* I hobbled toward the door but before I could reach it, it opened, revealing a casually dressed Callum. I take note that t-shirts and jeans should be his clothing of choice, regardless the occasion. *I'd marry that t-shirt and jeans,* I thought to myself. *Wait a minute. Where did that come from?* He strode in and flipped on the light. I squinted my eyes at the sudden brightness.

"Sorry, I didn't wake you, did I?" He asked, then noticed me bleeding. "Oh, crap!" He set down the cups of coffee and bag he was carrying on the table with our clothing and knelt at my level. "You okay? Here." He grabbed his bath towel and pressed it lightly against the small laceration.

"It's really not that bad," I offered, slightly embarrassed but growing fascinated by the masculine hand still at my knee. Callum surprises me by taking my hand but before I can read too much into it, he replaces

54

his hand with mine.

"Keep pressure on it," he said, before standing and spinning toward, what I assumed, was our cooling breakfast.

He reached for the bag and pulled out two bagels and cream cheese.

"I hope you like bagels," he smirked.

"I like them. You did good, Callum."

"How do you take your coffee?" He asked.

I don't have the heart to tell him that I don't actually drink coffee. I'm a tea kinda' girl but at the risk of ruining a lovely breakfast I say, "sugar and cream, please." I can drink it, I just don't like it all that much.

We sit in companionable silence sipping our coffee, well, he was sipping, I was gulping to get rid of it, and eating our bagels.

"Your hair looks fabulous, by the way," he teases.

A deep flush creeps up my neck and settles smack dab on my heated cheeks. I quickly stand and cross the room to the glass above the soundboard, smoothing out my crazy locks, attempting to tame them into a somewhat normal style.

"I didn't say I didn't like, Harper. Sit down," he laughed. I sit but smooth my hands down the part and twisted the length around my hand. "Seriously Harper, it's sexy as hell. Stop messing."

I blush yet again. I didn't know what it was with this boy. He said flirtatious things with such confidence I questioned whether or not it affected him as his words implied.

"So, I thought we could head to the university in a few minutes. My appointment's at nine fifteen," he said, shifting uncomfortably in his chair. *Oh God, he's going to bow out.* "Did you...Did you still want to come with me?"

55

"Uh, only if you want me to," I answered, suddenly interested in how well the cut on my knee was scabbing up. He didn't answer right away so I glanced up.

Callum furrowed his eyebrows. "Why wouldn't I want you to come? I invited you, didn't I?"

"Yeah, it's just, sometimes people change their minds," I answered, shrugging my shoulders.

"Well, not this person. So, get dressed already. You're gonna' make me late," he playfully snapped.
I hopped up and grabbed my belongings. I decided it was probably a good idea to shower again as the summer heat would dry my hair quickly and I could tame the dried creases from the night before.

When I was dressed, my wet hair combed out, I decided to put a little bit of what was left over from my makeup stash. It wasn't much and had dwindled considerably but it was all I had to work with so I ended up improvising a lot. Like, I didn't have eye liner so I took an old wine cork from my old foster parent's house, wasn't hard as they peppered their flooring like confetti. I would take a lighter and burn the ends. I'd use the burnt charcoal to line my eyes and it worked perfectly, giving them a nice, smoky effect. Also, I had this reddish liquid eye shadow, which looked hideous on the eyes but worked nicely as blush. I topped it all off with mascara and some lip gloss.

I study myself in the mirror. *Not bad, Bailey. You may impress him after all.* I shook my head as if to clear the stupid idea. I hauled butt down the hall to an awaiting Callum, complete with both our bags, packed and ready. I didn't even want to think about the fact that he had to touch my underwear, how embarrassing. I met him and he immediately took my hand, leading me down the hall.

"What about your motorcycle?" I asked.

He looked at me and smiled. "You look amazing, by the way." I blushed, again. *See! Oh hush, Harper!* "I'm leaving my bike here because, well, unfortunately I have no idea where we'll be staying tonight and would rather leave it locked up here. We can take the subway."

Sure enough, the five minute walk in the sun to the tunnels dried my hair into its natural waves and by the time we crossed the turn styles it was full and met my elbows again. We squeezed through the crowd and stood side by side awaiting the subway, pushing through the doors quickly as it pulled into the station. Callum and I were forced to sit in between two men so I squeezed as closely to him as possible to avoid touching the guy next to me. I noticed that he kept eyeing me strangely so I snuggled even closer to Callum. Callum swept the hair from the right side of my face and grinned.

"You okay?"

"Mmm, hmm. So, what is this meeting all about, anyway?" I said, trying to distract us both.

"My advisor has some stuff for me to go over and sign. It should only take a few minutes."

"Cool," I said, but I was having a hard time concentrating because the creepy guy next to me pushed his thigh into mine. I looked up at him and shook my head but he just smiled. I turned my attention back to Callum. "Why do you want me to go with you so badly?"

"Because, I think the reason you, and I quote, *'can't* go to college', is because you're intimidated and unsure what to do. I just want you to talk with Sylvia and maybe, just maybe, she can enlighten you and I'm hoping you'll change your mind."

Creepy guy decided that his right hand should be resting on his thigh where his pinkie just happened to find its way to my leg. He started making lazy circles with it across my jeans.

"Stop it," I ordered him, slightly over confident since I had enormous Callum sitting next to me.

"Stop what?" Callum asked, confused.

"Oh nothing. Hey, can we stand? I don't feel like sitting anymore."

"Uh, sure," he said, standing up and taking my hand. No sooner had I stood than two women holding groceries took our seats. There was really no place else to stand because the car was crowded and we're forced to hold the ceiling hand rails next to Creepy. The car shifts back and forth, causing the occupant behind me to accidentally fall into me. My nose pressed firmly against Callum's chest and I got a hefty dose of fresh laundry.

"Sorry," the patron offered.

"No biggie," I said, non-chalantly checking my bag for missing items and finding everything in its place. I looked into Callum's eyes and see that they're twinkling with mischief. "What?"

"Oh nothing. I just like this."

"What?"

"Standing close to you like this."

"Oh," I brilliantly said, no doubt turning bright red. *This is, like, a new record for me. Pathetic*, I laughed at myself. "I can't say that I am *that* adverse to it. Your shirt smells amazing."

Callum's eyes squint, revealing a wicked grin. The inside of his left arm rubs against my cheek and sends a spark through my skin, heating up my stomach. My own arm felt too heavy to hold up anymore. He leaned his body closer to mine and the crowd around us turned invisible, leaving us alone with our cumbersome breaths, our chests heaving heavily with anticipation and a promise of things to come. He brushed the hair on my left shoulder back before sinking his face against the crook of my neck and breathing in deeply.

"Have I told you how amazing I find the way you smell? You make me dazed. I feel punch drunk around you."

The breath I didn't know I was holding rushed out all at once. I sucked in an even deeper breath when he kissed the little bit of collarbone exposed by my t-shirt so lightly I could barely feel it. It was a chaste kiss but felt so intimate my eyes rolled to the back of my head. I closed my lids to prevent myself from passing out right there and when I opened them, Callum's face was but a few inches from mine. I could feel his warm breath against my cheek, his lips a provocative invitation. I could only stare as his radiant green eyes searched my face.

"Harper," he whispered but before he can finish we're both slammed into the direction we're travelling as the car comes to a screeching halt.

We can only stand, gaping at the other at the lost moment but something escaped his eyes, making me feel uncomfortable. I thought I read regret in them but what kind, I wasn't sure. Regret he couldn't continue? Regret that he stepped over a line?

"Sorry," he said, "that got out of hand. I shouldn't have done that."

"It's alright," I offered, hoping the supreme disappointment I was truly feeling wasn't coming through.

The doors to the car slid open and people started spilling out. Callum took my hand and guided me out to avoid getting trampled. We walked in silence until we reached the doors to NYU's administration building. Callum grabbed the handle to the large wooden doors but stopped before walking in.

"Come here," he said, dragging me to the side.

"But you'll be late," I said, trying to avoid eye contact so the tears welling up wouldn't spill over and embarrass the hell out of me.

That's the kind of humiliation I just didn't want to have to endure. I'd endured all kinds my entire life but this one I at least had control over. I'd be damned if I shed a tear over a boy who owed me nothing because that was beyond pathetic and I was tired of being pathetic. In fact, it was me who owed him and I realized that just because he wasn't interested in me the way I was interested in him, it wasn't his fault.

Callum stared up at the large clock on the building's forefront, noticing the time, and rushed through the doors, dragging me along with him, his previous speech forgotten. We turned a corner and approached a set of double doors. He pressed his hand to the knob but sighed before turning. A young student with insane green spiked hair and a studded collar manned a sort of desk at the front of the room.

"May I help you?" She asked cheerily, wearing a massive smile, negating every assumption I instantly made of her.

"Yes," Callum said. "I have an appointment with Sylvia Lengrand at nine-fifteen."

"Of course, if you'll take a seat," she said, gesturing to a line of simple upholstered chairs. "I'll see if she's ready for you."

The girl stood, revealing a cute little pixie figure. She was wearing a short black skirt, fishnets, and combat boots that met her shins. She had a black camisole under a shredded t-shirt and piercings in every part of her body imaginable but she was obviously a sweet girl. She was just another walking example of why you should never judge a book by its cover. I can't stand 'cover judgers'.

60

She returned with a petite brunette with brown eyes.

"You must be Callum," she said with a bright smile, shaking his hand before turning to the girl. "Thank you, Bridget."

"No probs, Syl," she answered. "Can I offer you two anything to drink?" She asked us before sitting down.

"I'm okay," I said.

"Me too," Callum offered.

"Okay, if you need anything, just ask," she said before taking her seat again.

"And who's this?" Sylvia Lengrand asked.

"Oh, I'm sorry, that's so rude of me. Sylvia, meet Harper Bailey," he said, bringing his hand to my lower back. Heat pooled into the skin where his hand rested and I wished I could glue it there, permanently. I took her hand and smiled. "Harper was accepted here and I'm trying to convince her to attend."

"Oh, that's wonderful! I'm glad you came, then. I'm just the person to talk you into it," she winked, pulling my hand toward her. "Alright, this way, love birds," she said, walking toward the back.

"Love birds?" We said in unison.

She stopped and gawked at us. "I'm so sorry. Did I assume incorrectly? You just seem so comfortable with the other. I apologize. I'm always making a fool of myself with you young folks."

"Oh, it's okay. I was just curious as to what gave us away," Callum said, poking me in the ribs with his elbow. *Oh good gracious, I think I'm in like with Callum Tate.* Sylvia smiled and opened her office door.

"Take a seat," she said.

We sat side by side and Callum playfully dragged my chair closer to his, with me in it, as if I weighed nothing, his muscles bunched as he pulled and I had to fight myself to prevent a bite to his forearm. *Get a hold of yourself, Harper.*

"Alright, let me just gather a few files," she said, diving into a file cabinet, her back toward us.

I stare at Callum and he sticks his tongue out at me which makes me burst out laughing. Sylvia turned around. "What?" She asked.

"Oh, I was just teasing her," Callum admitted, but his cheeks pink, revealing an even more adorable him, as if that's possible.

Sylvia returned to her files only to pull out a stack and sits at her desk. She stares at the stack while music pumps through a speaker above. I bit my bottom lip and sarcastically bumped my head to the cheesy ballad. Callum grinned and slid an air guitar he supposedly kept strapped to his back into his hands. Totally immersed in our pretend jam, we finally emerged when Sylvia yelled Callum's name.

"Sorry," we said in unison.

"That's okay, you were obviously in your own little world but as adorable as the two of you are, I need Mister Tate to sign a few forms for me." She slid the papers over to him. "I've marked all the spots you need to sign for me, Callum." She handed him a pen and turned her body towards me. Callum smirked at me and dove in. "Now," Sylvia said, turning slightly towards me, "did you have any questions about NYU, Harper?"

"Uh, not really. Callum dragged me here against my will. He's actually holding me hostage."

"I am not!" He exclaimed before realizing I was joking and rolled his eyes.

Sylvia smiled. "Listen, Harper. Obviously you have reservations about attending school here but that's why I'm here. I can smooth out all your worries, all you have to do is talk."

I sighed in resignation.

"Okay, just remember, you asked for it."

"Go on," she said. I noticed Callum's pen stilled as he feigned interest in the top paragraph of the paper he just signed the *bottom* of.

"I'm an orphan. My parents abandoned me to a system that failed me. I've been kicked from my foster home. I have no money, no job, no home, no hope. College is a pipe dream. Just because I got in does not mean I have the capability of attending. I can barely survive, Sylvia. I'm not college material."

I let the words spill from my mouth in a blur. Both Callum and Sylvia paused, barely breathing.

"That's ridiculous," Sylvia said suddenly.

"Excuse me?" I said, offended.

She grabbed my hand. "I'm not saying your life isn't tough. I can only imagine what you're going through but you can do anything you want to, Harper. Stop letting your past effect your future. You're in charge. Now, listen to me. I want you to fill out this half-sheet," she said pulling out a piece of paper from a side drawer. "It's everything I need to look you up in our system and find ways to get you attending classes, whether that's with tuition, books, food, or shelter. I can find it. Are you willing to do that?"

I hesitantly looked at the sheet of paper, twirling it in a circle on her desk when Callum slid his pen over to me. I looked up at him and his encouraging eyes plead with mine. I simply nodded and took the pen.

Chapter Four
Dream On

Callum

Harper and I left my appointment with Sylvia with yet another set for the both of us the day after the concert.

"First things first," I said to a stunning Harper. Her eyes were bright with hope and shone with speckled bits of glittery gold.

"What's that?" She asked.

"We figure out how we're going to survive the night."

"Tell me what to do, Callum. I feel like I'm taking advantage of you."

"Hush, Harper. Now, listen." I looked around for the time. The clock on the building's face read eleven thirty in the morning. "Crap, it's too late to get work at the docks." An idea crept in and I snapped my fingers. "Okay, I got it. I know a guy in the Village who owns a restaurant. He lets me bus tables for cash *under* the table but you have to get there early. Up for hauling butt for a few blocks?"

"Anything," she said, stopping my heart. *A fighter.* I smiled at her and grabbed her hand. We started weaving our way through people on their way to lunch. I can only hope that we'll make my guy's place before it's too late and he turned us away.

Martin's cool. His place always has people lined up around the door for lunch rushes and he can never seem to keep his bussers. I'm banking on the fact that he'll be just as desperate for help as we're in a desperate way for cash.

By the time we reach his restaurant, people are already lined up, a good sign. Harper makes her way to the front door but I stop her short.

"No, through the back," I whispered in her ear. We rounded the exterior of the building and entered through the back. Martin's Italian and loud and amazing.

"Martin," I said, interrupting his yelling at a few cowering cooks.

He turns toward me, surprised. "Callum," he said. Only, it sounds like Cowlum. "Where have you been, my boy? I've been in need of help for weeks!"

"I'm sorry, Martin. I've been barely staying afloat recently. I haven't been on this side of town."

"Hmm," he said, eyeing me carefully. "Is okay! You are here now!" He started to walk away but he stops, noticing Harper standing next to me and obviously taken with her.

"Martin, this is Harper. Harper, Martin," I said, introducing them to one another.

He offered his hand and Harper took it. Martin kissed the back of her hand, making me roll my eyes. "A pleasure," he said.

"The feeling's mutual," Harper said, charming him down to his leather clad feet.

He could only stare at her. She's a natural magnet.

"Uh," I interrupted, "Harper and I are looking to see if you're looking for any help."

"Of course! Always!" He said, breaking his stare from Harper.

"Martin, what are you talking about? You've turned me down several times for getting here too late."

"But you've never brought me such a charming creature before."

Harper winked at me but I can only sarcastically roll my eyes while Martin starts to walk off.

"Okay, we'll need to get you an apron," I said to Harper but Martin stops short.

"Uh no, Harper can host this afternoon. *You* can bus tables."

Too tired to argue with him, I nodded in agreement.

"Introduce her to the other girls up front then come back and Rodrigo will give you your apron."

"Okay," I said and began to lead Harper toward the front of the restaurant.

Harper looks up at me. "I'd rather bus tables with you," she whispered, pulling me short halfway toward the podium. Her hand rested on my forearm, sending a concentrated heat to my shoulders and it fell into my chest. "I mean, I'll be okay up there and everything but I just wanted you to know that I'd rather be with you today."

I looked down at her face and grinned. "Duh, Harper. I want you with me today, too. If Rodrigo could

speak English, I'd make him take your place."
We both laughed.

"I mean, seriously, it's okay, I just, well, sort of wanted you to know that I can't wait until this is over with so we could hang out a little more," she admitted, red cheeks and all.

"The time will fly by," I said, "like this." I snapped.

And *snap*.

Harper and I worked eight hour shifts, earning two hundred dollars apiece. We took our cash and headed out into the evening. We were both exhausted, though.

"Okay, should we even bother heading to The Hope House?"

"I think we should try, Harper. If it's one thing I've learned on the streets it's that money is precious. We shouldn't waste it, if we don't have to."

"Agreed. Let's go."

It was the weekend, and fortunately for us, the weekends were The Hope House's least busy times of the week what with people partying and staying with friends and all. Harper and I stood in line close to the stone interior after I convinced her that her bra was the safest place to place our money. That was a strange argument but one I will never forget. She even turned her back toward me to place it. I have never wanted to laugh so hard in my life.

"I have the most incredible sense of deja' vu," she teased after fifteen minutes of silence.

"Huh, what do you know! So do I!" I winked. "Wait, except, I don't remember doing this before." I push the side of my knee into the back of hers and she stumbled forward but I caught her before she lost her balance completely. This has an unexpected effect and the moment from the subway we had yet to talk about resurfaced in both our eyes and breaths, our bodies close yet again.

Time seemed to stand still for a moment, a song blared but died away as a car passed, a man and woman scream at one another but we barely registered it. I can only stare at her, breathe her eyes in. Our faces inch closer and closer, barely half an inch separates our mouths but neither of us takes it any further. The ultimate teasing. The ultimate flirtation.

"What are we doing, Callum?" She asked, her breath warm against my lips.

"I don't know," I whispered, desperate to close my eyes and marry her mouth to mine.

We're so close, I can feel her eyelashes on my cheeks, get drunk off her hair. Just another half inch and we'd be kissing. One. Half. Inch. "God, you smell good." I admitted, swallowing loudly.

"So do you," she panted, her bottom lip jutted out the slightest bit, narrowing the half inch gap.

My hands trembled on her waist. Her hands gripped my shoulders hard. She pulled away slightly and I almost cried out for her to close the distance again but before I can do it, Harper runs both her hands along my jaw line, silencing me with the skill of her touch.

"You have stubble already," she stated quietly, bringing her mouth close to mine once more, making my stomach tighten in response, in happiness.

"I know. An Irish curse, I think."

"I didn't know you were Irish," she whispered, slowly closing her eyes and opening them equally as languidly, just as inebriated with the moment as I was.

"I'm magically delicious," I mock delivered.
We both laugh, her bottom lip brushes mine and it sobered us quickly.

Yet, we still didn't commit, the anticipation growing, butterflies taking residence in both our stomachs. She closed her eyes completely and I follow her silent instruction. I took a deep breath through my nose, letting the buzz swirl through my head.

"Callum!" I heard, breaking our perfect, flawless moment.
Our eyes shot open, regret can be read all over her face and I know mine screams one word, 'why?'

"Callum!" We heard again, louder. I tore myself from her, studying the direction I heard the voice coming from. "Callum! Over here!" I look to my left and recognize Cherry.

"*Cherry*? What are you doing here?"

"Oh, just bustin' my hump trying to find you. Charlie insisted I give you this," she said, handing me a key to his flat.

"I think I love you, Cherry," I said, lifting her six foot frame up and twirling her around.

She gave me a goofy face and peeled herself from my hold. "Okay, sweets. I did my part. I got work to do. Tell Charlie he owes me for leaving the Hamptons early for you." She winked.

"I'll tell him. Thank you so much for this," I said.

"No problem, honey. Anything for you." She pinched my cheek and winked one more time. "Who's this, baby?" She asked, gesturing toward Harper.

"Cherry, this is Harper. Harper, Cherry."

Harper holds her hand out. "Nice to meet you, Cherry."

"Oh, baby, one thing you gotta' learn about me is I don't shake hands." Harper pulled back, offended. "I hug," she finally offered, pulling Harper in fast. "And any friend of Callum's, here," she said, eyeing me dubiously over Harper's shoulder, " is a friend of mine, baby. Anything you need, you let me know, 'kay?"

"Thank you," Harper said.

"Alright, got places to be, people to see. I'll see you 'round, C." She smiled then leaned in and whisper teased, "Who is this girl who's stolen my Callum Tate?" She pulled back and waved at Harper. "Take it easy, Harper. Nice to meet you, honey," she said, heading toward the busy cross street, already signaling for a taxi. "By the way," she yelled, I'll put yours and Harper's name on the list at The Bowery. We go on at eleven." We watched her get in the cab and it sped off.

"Let's go," I said to Harper.

"To Charlie's, I assume?"

"Of course. We've got ourselves a bath tub and a washer and dryer, again. We hit the jackpot, baby," I said, borrowing a word from Cherry's vernacular.

Charlie's flat is in the Village, which is unfortunate that we hadn't stuck around Martin's restaurant as it would have spared us the subway fare to The Hope House but then again, I would have missed the kissing dance outside its exterior and I would have paid a million fares to experience that again. It's an amazing flat but up seven flights and no elevator. By the time we reached the top, we were both slightly winded.

"I don't know how he does this every day," I admitted, resting on the wall outside the top of the stairs.

"No kidding. Good gracious, at least he gets his cardio in."

I opened his door and welcomed Harper in. She stepped through into his cozy loft and glanced around.

"It's small and he pays a fortune for it but just look at it."

Inside the five hundred square foot apartment is a small living and kitchen area, a bathroom complete with tub and a platform library loft that houses the bedroom. The entire thing, save for the bathroom, is open with fifteen foot high ceilings and dark stained shelves as far as the eye can see, accept the kitchen wall, even the stairs leading to the library loft have built in shelves. And they're all *full* of books. Charlie was the most prolific reader I'd ever met in my life.

"This is amazing," Jules said.

"Truly," I said. We both looked in awe upon our cozy surroundings. "So," I continued, clapping my hands together, "shall we?"

We threw both our bags onto the floor behind his mid-century upholstered sofa, which ran parallel to the long kitchen island. It was an ingenious use of the small space, making it feel much larger than it actually was. I took her to the window in the kitchen next to his small dining set. Through it, was a balcony with wood decking and a virtual ceramic pot garden with ivy growing up the brick facade. Cherry did all of this for Charlie. No, not for Charlie, *for* Charlie. The girl was head over heels in love with him but he was too busy being blind as a bat to see it. Not wanting to interfere, I never said anything, but the blockhead was taking forever to notice. *Maybe Harper might have an idea as to how we can awaken him to the idea? Wait, dude. The last thing you want is a gorgeous, charming Harper talking to Charlie. He'll steal her.* I shook my head to clear it. *You're an idiot. She's not even yours. She can't be stolen if she isn't yours,* I argued with myself.

"This is beautiful," she whispered, her hair dragging across her face as she leaned further out the window to admire the balcony's garden.

"Yeah, Charlie writes all of his songs out here." I turned toward Harper. "Lots of inspiration."

She grinned.

"Laundry?" She asked.

I can't help but chuckle. "What is it with us and clean clothing?"

"We're hygienic, I guess?"

"Yeah, again, you never know when we'll get the chance to clean them again. I'm what you call, 'opportunistic'."

"I can relate." She sighed. "Trust me, I can relate."

"How about this," I offered. "We shower and all that jazz, get ready for Cherry's show, take our stuff and do a load, then head to The Bowery."

"Deal. I'll go first so I can dry my hair."

"You're hilarious."

"Never lived with a girl before?"

"Actually, no," I said thoughtfully, just now realizing the truth of that.

"Alright, go."

"Thank you, Callum."

"Of course. Think nothing of it."

"No, *thank you*."

I nodded as she traipses off to the bathroom.

Once I heard the shower running, I sat on Charlie's sofa and picked up the book he was reading before he left, face down to save his page. I started reading the first paragraph. The main character, Elliott, professed his life and his love for this girl named Jules. Pretty good, but not my flavor, if you catch my drift. I prefer non-fiction. When I heard Charlie's blow dryer start, I smiled, thankful that the doofus had long enough hair that he could supply Harper with what she needed to tend to her own silky strands.

Twenty minutes later, the door opened. Still sitting, I glanced up, full intending to return to my page but was struck dumb. The book slid from my grip, spilling to the floor. I had to remind myself that she was standing there, expecting me to speak but was literally driven mute.

Harper stood under the door frame, her feet were clad in black combat boots but she pulled them off well with a horizontal stripe black and white floor length cotton dress that painted every curve of her body. Modest. Modest yet sexy as hell. Her lengthy locks flowed to her waist and curved at the ends.

But the show stopper were the eyes. Those incredible eyes I could spot from a mile away, sharp and almost a translucent gold.

"Good God, Harper. I can't go out with you looking like that," I blurted.

She set both hands on her hips, "And why the heck not?"

"Because I'll be in jail before Cherry can even go on. I'll have to fight off every bloke who tries to talk to you. No, you have to change. You're going to get me in trouble," I said, sincere as I've ever been.

It was true. I couldn't step out of Charlie's flat with her looking like that, not if I didn't feel like leaving her side wearing a pair of handcuffs. Also, now, I'd never admit to this out loud, but I wanted to slide my hands down every curve she owned, every striped covered curve.

Harper laughed. "Oh, I get it. Ha, ha, Callum. You think you're so funny. Now, you better tell me that I look nice or we're going to have issues because this is all I have and it matters to me to look good, for you...I mean,

I don't want to embarrass you," she covered up.

I wonder if handcuffs come in my size. Surely, they're one size fits all. "Harper, you look incredible."

A slow smile crept across her mouth and she nodded in acknowledgement. "Thank you. Now, you're turn."

The Bowery was the busiest I'd ever seen it. Chris was working the door and we were on the list so we were able to bypass the seemingly mile long line.

"Chris, what's up, man?"

"Callum Tate! Long time no see. What've *you* been up to?"

"Oh, you know, a little of this, a little of that."

Chris eyed Harper up and down. "I can see that."

I furrowed my brows and tried to overcome the screaming voice inside my head telling me to kick this acquaintance in the chest. Instead, I said through gritted teeth, "Chris, this is Harper. Harper, Chris." *The freaking introductions lately.*

They shook hands and I had to quell the urge to snatch her hand from his grasp. *Get a hold of yourself, Tate. Jeez, man.*

"A pleasure," Harper said with a charming smile.

Chris held his arm out after crossing our names off the list, gesturing us inside. I grabbed Harper by the arm and pulled her close to my body. This served many purposes. It sent a clear message to Chris, it kept her safe because The Bowery was packed, and, well, it just brought her close to my body. I loved being near her. *Careful, Callum.*

"What time is it?" She yelled in my ear.

"Ten fifteen. Cherry doesn't goes on for another

forty-five minutes," I yelled back, digging the proximity the band currently playing was forcing us to take.

"'Kay. Hey," she yelled, leaning in closely, "this band blows. Let's find some place to talk while we wait." Just what I wanted to be, alone with Harper Bailey.

But that was not going to happen because the second we stepped onto the rooftop I lead her to, although the music was dulled and the breeze was wonderful, Cherry, her band mates and a few of our friends were already there, as if in waiting. *You can't turn around and drag Harper with you, Callum.* When they saw us coming, they whooped and hollered, thoroughly embarrassing me.

"Ladies and gentlemen," Cherry started, rising and bowing at her engrossed crowd, "if I may have your attention, please! Introducing, for your entertainment, a one mister Callum Tate and his lovely assistant, Harper!" The dramatic group all rose to their feet and clapped at our approach.

"I'm sorry about this," I whispered at Harper but she only laughed. "Thank you! Thank you!" I make a slight bow myself.

"Speech! Speech!" Freddy yelled.

"Freddy. *Pink* hair? Seriously?" I teased.

"What kind of speech was that?" He joked.

"Harper, pink-hair-dude is Freddy." Freddy waved. "This is Tie-Dye Tom, as you can tell from his tie-dye t-shirt." Tom stuck his hand out.

"Tie-Dye, eh?" Harper asked.

"Yes, milady. I own seventy-seven of them."

"Congrats?"

"Thank you."

75

"And you know Cherry," I say. Cherry hugs her hello. "And this is SO." I point out our most Gentleman's Quarterly member.

"A pleasure," Harper said. "SO, is it?"

"It's not my real name," he corrected smoothly.

"That's right, SO's real name is Henry or something stupid like that," Cherry chimed in.

"What does SO stand for, then?" Harper asked, ignoring Cherry.

"Smooth Operator," we all said in unison, then laughed out loud.

SO takes Harper's hand and kisses the knuckles. "Did I mention we are a dramatic bunch?" I asked. I point to each remaining member of the group as I mention their name. "Kelly, Cross, Marty, Aaron, Nat, Jared and Josiah, but we call them 'the twins' because, well, they're twins, and last, but not least, Sam, short for Samantha."

Everyone smiles and nods, finally taking note of Harper, mesmerized by the sheer beauty of her. Samantha patted the seat next to her and Harper took the offered seat. I found an empty place next to Cherry and watched Harper talk to Sam.

"You're smitten," I heard to my left.

"I'm not," I tell Cherry.

"You're smitten, dude. It's obvious."

"No, I'm not!"

"Callum, you wear your emotions all over your face. Plus, Harper's sitting directly next to Sam, whom, by the way, I would have bet money on that you were in love with just two days ago, and you barely took note of her. You're smitten with that girl."

"I can't help it," I blurt out. Cherry laughed. "I really can't, Cherry. I'm going out of my mind. I'm mad at you, by the way."

"What? *Why*?" She demanded.

"We had this moment earlier. The one *you* interrupted. Ring a bell?"

"Oops," she laughed. "Sorry."

I forgave her with a reluctant smile.

"Oh my God, Cherry. I have never met anyone like her in my entire life."

"What exactly *did* I interrupt?"

"It's embarrassing but it was this strange flirtation. We were close enough to kiss but we never closed the gap." I gripped the sides of my hair with my fists. "Gah! She is like no one I've ever known. She drives me batty."

"And Sam?"

I shook my head. "Sam who? She's a poor man's Harper Bailey."

"Damn, boy. Never thought I'd see the day you got over Sam."

"Sam's Charlie's, anyway." I said without thinking. I cringed when I realized what I'd said then peered over my shoulder at Cherry. "I'm sorry."

"For what?" She pretended.

"I know you're in love with Charlie."

"I'm not," she said, her eyes wide.

"Cherry, come on. You and I are the king and queen of unrequited love."

She shoved her shoulder into mine. "Am I as transparent as you?" She teased.

"Shut up," I laughed then smiled stupidly. "Probably not." I watched Harper's mouth. "I want to kiss her so badly, Cherry." I turned back to Cherry, leaning my head on the railing.

"What ya' tellin' *me* this for? Tell her," she said, bringing my attention back to Harper, who was now staring and smiling at me.

I stood and walked over to Harper, grabbing her hand, barely acknowledging Sam. "Come with me."

"Where are we going?" She asked.

"We go on in fifteen, Callum! Don't stray too far!" Freddy yelled.

"We'll be there," I yelled back, keeping my eyes on Harper.

I looked across the rooftop deck and found a dark corner with our names written all over it but Harper surprised me by bringing up the furthest topic from my mind.

"Callum, when Charlie comes back from touring. Where are we going to stay?"

What surprised me the most in that question wasn't the fact that she was concerned about what was going to happen but what's going to happen to *us*.

"Don't worry, Harper. I'll take care of us." And I meant it. I'd figure out a way. "We're going to be fine. I have two weeks to figure something out. We can save our money and cross that bridge when we come to it. Now, for tonight, stop worrying?"

"Alright," she grinned.

I tucked a stray hair behind her ear and hugged her tightly.

"Callum Tate," we heard over the scratchy speakers. "You're needed near the stage."

I sighed loudly. "I'm gonna' kill Cherry. Come on," I said, dragging Harper back down the stairs and into the main hall.

We dug our way through the crowd and stood close to the edge of the stage. Cherry poked her head from between the curtains and winked at us. So many beautiful sounds surrounded us and I grabbed Harper's hand as I listened to them; glass bottles clanked like bells against others, happy people laughing all around us, the pumping of awesome tunes coming from up above, Cherry's band tuning their instruments.

"So, who's in the band?" Harper yelled in my ear.

"Oh, Cherry's on keyboards, Nat's on drums, Freddy's lead singer and lead guitar, Sam's on bass, and Tie-Dye Tom is rhythm guitar."

"Oh, very cool," she smiled. She looked around her a bit before leaning into me. "Uhh, at the risk of sounding rude, I've observed that they're all older than you," she added.

"Yeah!" I laughed. "They're probably mid to late twenties, the lot of them. I seem to relate to them better than kids our age. Maybe because at this age, they know what it's like to be the only one responsible for yourself."

"I can see that," she said. "Older's cool. Except for Sam, though, right?"

"Yeah, Sam's our age."

"Mmm, yes." She cleared her throat. "I know."

"What?" I furrowed my brows at her.

"Oh, nothing. It's just...I think Sam may like you."

"*What!* What gave you that idea?"

"Well, when we were talking earlier she sort of gave me the impression that I wasn't to touch you."

"You've got to be kidding me. That is really weird."
"Why? You're kind of a catch," she teased.

That made my chest swell. "No, it's just that Charlie and Sam are sort of dating."

"Are they exclusive?"
"No, I don't think so."
"Well, that explains it then."

I was embarrassingly sort of flattered by that but peeved at the same time because she *was* dating Charlie and although they probably *weren't* exclusive, why would Sam all of a sudden take an interest in me? Unless, she's one of those 'I want what I can't have' sort of girls which are the worst kind of girls. Nothing is less attractive than that quality.

"I wouldn't go out with Sam for anything in the world," I honestly said.

"Why?"

Well, besides the fact that she's dating Charlie, she's not you. "Because, I just never would." Harper eyed me strangely but turned back to the stage.

The curtain began to peel open, revealing a marvelous Cherry and band.

"Cherry pie!" I yelled out inciting a little dance from Cherry at her keyboard.

"She's wonderful," Harper said, laughing at Cherry's antics.

"I know."

"Hi, we're The Ivories," Freddy said.

Their first song was my favorite because it did wild things to the chest and stomach, filling both up with anticipation, and making the heart beat violently. It didn't help that Harper held my hand the entire song. I'm not complaining. I loved sensation.

The crowd swayed and bent like wheat in the wind. The Ivories were the reason the crowd was what it was. I watched Harper's eyes widen with every song they played. They were truly talented but this was something I am newly reminded of living the songs anew through Harper. She was so incredibly charming dancing and laughing. At one point, Cherry reached out and waved at her. You should have seen Harper's reaction. She was so adorable.

When The Ivories set was over, I pulled Harper towards the back wall to cool off.

"Can I get you something to drink, my dear?" I asked.

"Uh, a water would be wonderful," she said, smiling from ear to ear.

"Okay, don't move or I'll never be able to find you again," I only half-teased.

The line to the bar was ten people deep but Quinn was tending bar that night which was awesome. Quinn was another member of our group of friends. I lifted my hand signaling two. He threw two waters over the crowd without me asking and I silently thanked him over the awaiting heads.

I waded through the crowd, inhaling a woman's overkill perfume, stepping on a guy's foot, which almost got me killed, but finally got close enough to spot a fidgety Harper. I walked faster because the look on her face screamed, 'help me'. I lifted my head higher to get a better look at her situation and noticed a tall idiot had practically boxed her in, chatting her up.

"That's amazing, Brandon. You're their number one salesman, are you?" I heard her say.
I slowed my approach and listened in.

"Yeah," blockhead said, "I work on commission. I make at least thirty thousand a month and that's if things are going slowly."

"I don't think I've ever been so impressed in my life." I almost lost the water I had just taken a swig from. "Tell me, what sort of car do you get around in?"

"I drive a panty dropper, Jenny." *Okay, that's it. Wait, Jenny?* "I drive an Audi Coupe. Paid cash for it just last week. Cherry red."

"That's incredible. I have a friend named Cherry. So,

81

tell me, Brandon, what kind of gas mileage do you get?"

"Well, *what*?" Blockhead was surprised.

"Gas mileage, Brandon. Keep up, man. What kind of gas mileage do you get?"

"I'm too rich to care, baby." He cheesily recovered.

Oh my gosh, I'm going to tear this sucker in half. But just as I neared the two of them, Harper winked at me over the guy's shoulder signaling for me to sit back and enjoy the rest of the show. I stayed close, anyhow.

"Well, in that case, you probably wouldn't mind driving me out of town this weekend?"

"Depends, is your place out of town?"

Lame.

"As a matter of fact," Harper said, "I need a ride to pick up my kids. They're mine this weekend. We were planning on a trip to the zoo. Do you like elephants, Brandon?"

"Kids?" He asked, stepping back slightly. "But..b...but, but you look too young to have children," he stuttered like a blubbering fool.

"Oh, do I? Well, if I was being honest, I started quite young."

"That's nice. Listen, I see my friend calling me over to him. It was nice to meet you, Jenny?"

"Yes, Jenny. Oh, but wait, Brandon. You didn't ask for my number."

"Oh, well, I don't," he spit out.

"That's okay, Brandon," I chimed in. "She's with me, anyway."

Brandon looked so incredibly relieved, I almost laughed.

"Good luck to you, bro," he said and bolted.

Harper and I leaned against the back wall, holding in our guts.

"So, Jenny, what are these kids of yours named?"

"Oh well, there's Bosephus. He's my youngest. Just two months old."

"That is hideous, Harper."

"I know, but it's his grandpa's name."

"Oh, well, then it's understandable." I smiled at her. "You're a goofball."

Harper and I laughed ridiculously hard when we noticed Brandon talking animatedly and pointing our direction.

"I think you may be a genius, Harper Bailey."

"You know it."

I turned my body her direction, my left shoulder leaning against the brick wall. She followed suit and leaned on her right, facing me. I brushed her hair behind her shoulders and blew at her neck, trying to cool her off. She closed her eyes, enjoying the makeshift breeze, her lips parted slightly. She inadvertently succeeded at driving me insane. I instantly stopped and drank her face in. Her eyes popped open.

"And here we are again, Callum. We really must stop playing these games."

I swallowed hard. "What could you possibly mean, Harper?"

"Oh, just that you and I are walking a razor thin line and I'm trying to find out if it's sharp enough to actually hurt us."

"Anything can hurt you, Harper. Even things you're supposed to be able to count on can hurt you."

"These things you speak of, do they include how we're supposed to rely on mothers and fathers never to die or leave us alone?"

"Exactly, but that's life, Harper. Nothing is guaranteed."

"You're right."

"But I *can* promise you that I would never intentionally hurt you and, although a promise is not a guarantee, it *is* still a promise and you can ask anyone I know, I'm good on my word."

"I don't know why but I believe you."

"Harper, I..."

But Sam interrupted us.

"Hey, you guys!" Sam said emphatically, a little too emphatically. *Great.*

"Hey Sam," I said, never taking my eyes off the glorious Harper. Sam forcibly distracted me from Harper, grabbing my arm and twisting it around her own waist. "Uh, what are you doing, Sam?" I asked, unwinding myself from the death grip she held on the hand she placed at her hip.

"What am I doing? You are a silly goose. I'm saying hello to my friend." She narrowed her eyes at me. "*Oh*, I see. Am I interrupting?"

"No, it's okay, Sam," Harper said politely.
I beg to differ.

Sam turned towards me. "A few of us are heading over to Cherry's afterwards. I would love it if you could come, Callum."

"And?" I asked, looking pointedly at her.

"And, *what*?" She played dumbly.

I snorted sarcastically. "It doesn't matter," I said, refusing to buy into her game. "Harper and I have had a crazy day. Unless, wait a moment." I turned toward Harper. "Would you want to go, Harper?" She shook her head no, fighting a smile. "Yeah, we're probably going to go crash at Charlie's soon. You remember Charlie, don't you, Sam?"

All the color drained from her face. "Of course I remember Charlie. What kind of question is that?"

"Oh, nothing, Sam. I just wanted to make sure you still did, is all. Tell the gang I'll catch up with them later, will ya'?"

I captured Harper's hand in mine and lead her toward the exit. We burst out into the hot summer night, relieved to be away from the sweltering bodies inside.

"All I want to do is crash out," I confessed.

"No kidding. First, shower, then, bed. I'm exhausted," she said.

I smiled down at her. "I'm happy you came with me."

"They were surprisingly awesome," she admitted.

Chapter Five
Holdin' On To Black Metal

Harper

Callum and I readied for bed in very little time as we were both drained but also because, I suspect, we were eager to talk. This was one thing I loved about Callum. He was actually interested in things I had to say, something I'd never experienced before and made me feel extraordinarily special.

"You take Charlie's bed. I've made a pallet on his couch."

"Okay," I conceded without argument. It would've been useless.

I've learned that he loves to argue, which I believed falls just short of his love for *winning* an argument. I climbed the bookcase stairs into the elevated loft. It was open to the living room just below and I could see Callum clearly.

"What are our plans for tomorrow?" I asked him, burrowing my legs beneath the soft sheets.

"Oh, I was thinking the docks. The pay is better and we only have to work for half the hours we would have to for the restaurant for the same pay. It's slightly harder work. Think you're up to it?"

"I am."

"Harper?" He asked.

"Yes?"

"Where did you grow up at?"

"Well," I said, laying on my back, settling in for a long explanation. I tucked my hands behind my head. "It depends on my age at the time. I really don't remember any of my foster parents before the age of three or four. I do have memories that fall back father than that, though it's not so much a visual memory as it is a memory of how I felt."

"Oh, yeah? Like what?" He asked, laying back as I did. The lights from the city cascaded through the window next to his body, creating deep shadows over his muscles, making my fists clench beneath my head.

"Oh, I distinctly remember feeling hollow."

"Hollow," he repeated thoughtfully.

"Yeah. I didn't realize until much later in my life that the hollowness was basically a complete lack of feeling loved."

"God, Harper."

"What?" I said, sitting up.

Callum sat up just as abruptly. "I know *exactly* what you mean. My void existed until I'd say, sixteen or so and became friends with Charlie and Cherry. That's when I realized what I'd been missing."

We just stared at one another but not in pity the way so many people would look at us. No, this was a look of understanding and empathy. Callum half-grinned. I fought the urge to jump off and hug him until he turned blue. The moment passed and we both laid back down.

"So, the first foster parents I can distinctly remember were Mr. and Mrs. Campari. They actually *made* me call them that. I was four and already realized they weren't in it for the long haul.

"Mr. and Mrs. Campari lived in Brooklyn, Dyker Heights to be exact, a pleasant neighborhood with manicured lawns and middle income families.

"I don't remember them being cruel, just detached. I suppose they knew they couldn't keep me and decided it be best not to form an attachment. I don't blame them in the slightest."

"When did you leave the Campari's?" Callum asked quietly.

"I think I was six?" I stated, trying to fight through the memories. "I remember something about Mr. Campari having some sort of heart surgery. Anyway, that's when I was moved to another household. I endured four new foster families until the age of ten. They were normal, nothing particularly strange about them. They just couldn't handle my acting out. At eleven, I moved in with the Strauss'." I paused, to gather myself and catch a single tear falling down my cheek. I caught the hitch in my throat. "They were my favorite. They were kind and gave me, I think, my philosophy on life as well as the morals I carry and live by. I was lucky to have them.

"I was with them until the age of fourteen. They're responsible for my most treasured possession."

"That book you keep wrapped in a cloth?"

I laughed. "Yeah, that."

"What book is it?"

I stood and descended the bookcase stairs, hopping down each step with a lightheartedness I hadn't felt in years. I was going to show Callum Tate my favorite thing in the entire world. I'd never shown anyone for fear they'd try to take it from me. It'd been hidden in my possession for so many years, it felt liberating to finally feel comfortable enough to show someone.

I grabbed my bag and dug my hand through my meager belongings. When my hand hit the carefully wrapped book, I gently pulled it from the bottom and walked over to the coffee table next to Callum's makeshift bed. I knelt to sit on my ankles and placed the wrapped book on top of the table. I nodded my head at the lamp above Callum's head and he turned it on.

I unwrapped the book carefully, exposing its cover.

"*To Kill A Mockingbird*," he said with reverence, "by Harper Lee."

I flipped the hard cover open and revealed Harper Lee's signature.

"Signed!"

"I know!" I said giddily.

"How did you get this?" He asked, bringing his face reverently toward the signature.

"I won it. If you can believe that."

"But *how*?"

"The Strauss' took me with them on a summer vacation to visit family they had in North Carolina. It was the best and only trip of my life," I said, looking back on the memories. "Anyway, there was some sort of beach carnival going on. Apparently, they'd been planning it for weeks because they had this jar full of buttons sit on the

89

front counter at their local grocery store. You would pay twenty dollars to enter a guess at how many buttons filled the jar.

"Well, I didn't even know the prize but I, now don't freak out on me," I laughed, "but I am a freak when it comes to guessing these things. I've never lost."

"Never?"

"Not once. Of course, the other prizes were always lame. Although, I did win a bike once when I guessed how many cherries were inside a canning jar when I was nine but that was taken from me."

"What? Why?"

"My foster parents thought I stole it. I mean, I was a bit of a thief back then but when I tried explaining to them that they could verify my story, they refused to check on it. I think they just wanted to give the bike to their niece who lived in Jersey."

"That's pretty shitty."

"Yeah. Anyway, so I entered with some leftover birthday money from the Strauss' not even aware of the prize. A couple of days later, I had forgotten about it, actually. We went to the beach carnival and rode a few rides but an hour into our visit, that's when it happened.

"I can remember everything about that moment like it was yesterday. I was wearing a white linen sundress that was a hand me down but still so beautiful. I had my hair up in a pony tail and was carrying a pink cloud of cotton candy on a paper cone. My flip-flops smacked against my feet as we walked the sandy beach.

"I didn't think I could be happier until we all heard a buzz over the carnival P.A. system."

"What did they say?" Callum asked. He'd sat up for the story and was on the edge of his seat.

"They said, and I quote, 'Harper Bailey of New York

City, you are the winner of our button contest. You have one hour to claim your prize.'

"I was so ecstatic, I dropped my cotton candy on the ground and Philip Strauss, who was just a year younger, followed me closely until we reached the carnival gazebo. People were milling about waiting to see the girl who won and the prize she was gonna' get.

"I walked right up the steps to the gazebo and yelled, 'I'm Harper Bailey!' I don't think they were expecting someone so young. You should have seen the look on the man's face." I said, laughing a little. "He asked if I could provide some sort of identification. I whipped out my New York State I.D. so fast, his head spun. "Then he revealed my prize.

"I'm gonna' be honest with you, Callum. It was the furthest thing from my mind but it was the most wonderful thing I could have possibly gotten. My favorite book of all time *and* the author was my namesake. I was in the local paper and everything. It was such a strange coincidence."

"That's wild, Harper."

I sighed. "I know."

We sat in silence as I re-wrapped the book and placed it back in my messenger bag.

"Why did you leave them?" He asked, breaking the sleepy quiet.

I took a seat on the edge of Callum's couch and my chin sunk into my chest. "I didn't. They left me.

"Harper, I'm sorry. I shouldn't have asked."

"No," I said, looking back over my shoulder at him. "It's okay. I don't mind talking about it."

"What happened?" He asked, sidling closer to me and laying his hand on my shoulder.

I placed my hand over his. "Dad, I mean, Henry

Strauss, got a job offer in Chicago. I wished so badly that they'd adopt me but as we neared their moving day and I was prepared for yet another transition, the offer never came. I was silly, really, hoping they'd make me a part of their family. It was then I realized that I was really, truly on my own, that no one was going to love me the way I wanted to be."

"Harper. You don't really think that, do you?"

"I don't know," I threw out quickly. "Anyway, that's when I went off the deep end, getting into hella' trouble and getting a new family every six months. The all time record was one month. I'm sort of proud of that one.

"The foster families got worse as I got older. Either my reputation preceded me or, you know, they just didn't like taking the older ones, which was pretty common."

"I know," Callum said.

I shrugged my shoulders, scooting against the back of the couch and getting comfortable beside Callum. I lay my head on his shoulder and he reached his arm around mine. We sunk into one another.

"The last few foster families were just atrocious," I admitted to the room. "I'd just turned sixteen and gotten thrown out of a bad family for breaking into the school."

"Why?"

"It's a long story. Basically, I had this friend named Lauren who unfortunately got pregnant. She was kicked out and sent to one of those magnet schools for 'troubled teens'. Anyway, she had a few things in her locker along with some money. They wouldn't let her enter the school to retrieve it. They'd said they would retrieve her belongings for her and forward them on but she was desperate for the cash inside and was afraid the shady janitors would pocket it and claim there was nothing else inside.

"We came up with this plan to leave a classroom window open nearest her locker during school and then we'd come back later and get into her locker."

"I don't get it. Why didn't she just give you the combination to her locker and you do it during school hours?" He asked.

"Because if anyone and I mean *anyone* saw me get into her locker, even with Lauren's permission, I'd have gone to jail and I couldn't have *another* arrest on my record."

"I guess I can understand that."

"Well, I left a window in the wood shop classroom open and we returned that night but Lauren was too big to fit through, so I agreed to go in without her. I was in an out in less than five minutes with all her stuff. I thought it the perfect pseudo-crime." I paused.

"But?" He asked, eyebrows raised.

"*But*, turns out, a few kids, who hated me, saw us while playing basketball on school grounds and turned my name in."

"What jerks, dude."

"No kidding."

"So, then what happened?" He prodded.

"I told the school but to them it didn't matter why I did it. They expelled me anyway. I was just thankful they didn't press charges."

"That's when you were forced to change families?"

"Yeah, that was the straw that broke that camel's back, I think. If I had known what kind of family I would have been moved to, I never would have broken into the school."

"What kind of people were the new family?"

"It wasn't the family so much as it was the other foster

93

kid I had to share the house with. The first day there, I had a pretty pleasant conversation with the parents about their expectations and all that crap. You know the drill. We were just sitting at their kitchen table, talking, when I heard the door open and this hulking guy around my age fills the door way.

"'Harper,' the old lady says. 'This is John Bell. He's the other foster child here.' I stood up and shook the guy's hand. He sat down with us and seemed pleasant enough through conversation. We all ate dinner together and then watched a little television. All nice and neat and pretty, right?

"Anyway, the next day, John introduced me to the kids at my new school and others in the neighborhood. I was really starting to believe he would be cool and that this family could be one I could stick it out with, at least for a little while.

"I couldn't have been more wrong," I said solemnly.

"What happened?"

"Well, that night, while I was sleeping, I heard the wood creak below someone's feet just outside my door. I sat up, turned on the lamp and looked at the time. It was just after two in the morning. I called out but heard nothing else. I just assumed it was John going to the restroom so I fell back to sleep.

"The next night, at the same time, the same thing happened but this time I stayed quiet and kept the light off. That's when I panicked a little." I grabbed Callum's hand and held it tightly at the memory. "My bedroom door opened a crack and I sat up quickly but no one came in. It was an old house and I figured it just fell open. I scolded myself for being so paranoid. I chocked it up as an overreaction to a new home.

"Two weeks later, I became pretty comfortable again,

not experiencing anything weird at night again. John and I had also become pretty good friends but one school night, I woke up to him sitting beside me on the bed." Callum squeezed my hand. "I asked him if he was okay and if he needed anything but he just sat and stared at me. I sat up and scooted as closely to the headboard as possible but John lunged himself at me. I opened my mouth to scream but his big, meaty hand stifled it. 'Don't speak', he told me. I shook my head in agreement, hoping I was misreading what was going on. He kept his hand over my mouth though and I knew I should most definitely be concerned. 'Harper,' he said, 'I want you to sleep with me.' I shook my head hard but he just clamped his hand tighter across my mouth. 'Not to have sex with me but to sleep next to me,' he said. He laid his body next to mine and drug me into him. I'd never felt so frightened in my life. John was so much larger than me, I couldn't fight him. He cruelly dug his nails into my arms to keep me in my place. He whispered in my ear that if I left or told anyone what he was doing that he would kill me. I just nodded and endured the night next to his sweaty, awful body. I eventually fell asleep and woke to no one there. I didn't know if I'd dreamed it or not but when I stood up and noticed his nail marks in my arm, I knew.

"That morning, I showered, trying to wash him off of me, then dressed. The foster family I was staying with made it very clear I couldn't be late for breakfast. So, I nervously trudged down the stairs and entered the dining room. Everyone was sat there, including John. The foster mother scolded me for being late and I apologized. John sat directly across from me and smiled. He said, 'Good morning, Harper. How'd you sleep?' I almost spit up the orange juice I'd nervously downed. I told him I'd slept terribly. He said that he thought that a shame. I couldn't bear to look at him the rest of the morning. I avoided him at school but at the end of the day, he forced me to walk with him home."

"My God, Harper. Please tell me you got out of that house."

"I tried, Callum," I said, a single tear falling down my cheek. "I tried so very hard. I went to my social worker but I stupidly didn't tell them what John was doing to me and they told me there was no need to change my home, that I needed to adapt.

"It was all about power and possession for John. He would force me to do strange things like sleep on the floor while he slept in my bed, or tie his shoes for him, or clean his laundry. Once, he made me go to a dance with him but forced me to sit in a corner. He told me if I moved that he'd kill me. He always threatened death.

"Finally, after a few weeks, it dawned on me that I'd forgotten who I was. I'd forgotten that I was friggin' Harper Bailey and that I didn't take shit from anyone.

"I knew I couldn't get out of that foster home without some sort of proof of his craziness so I figured out the perfect way to get him. John couldn't stand being out of control so I started locking my door at night. At first, he ignored it, deciding to take my decision out on me later but I endured it all and kept on locking my door. He'd knock softly and ask me nicely to open up but I refused. He'd threaten me the next morning but I'd ignore him, patiently waiting for him to lose control. Finally, after the sixth night, John couldn't take it anymore and began to beat at the door violently, waking our foster parents. They wanted to know what he was doing and John, not being a very bright guy, told them I'd taken a cd from his room without asking. I told them that

I did nothing of the sort and that the cd he was referring to was actually in his stereo as we spoke. They confirmed it was true and I was given my out."

"Harper, that is awful."

"I know," I said laughing, trying to avoid the sob threatening to leak from my throat.
Callum, sensing how tense I was, hugged me closer.

"Where did you go after that, Harper?" He asked.

"An alcoholic's but, to be honest, it felt like a reprieve. They were winos, their floor was littered with corks. I lived in a literal sea of corks but I didn't mind it so much. They were cool as long as you left them alone and whatever trouble you got into didn't directly affect them.

"I stayed there for at least a year, but social services paid a surprise visit to them and they hadn't cleaned up yet. So..." I shrugged as if that was explanation enough.

"And you were forced out?"

"Yup."

"Then where'd you go?"

"To the last foster home I'd ever have to endure again," I said.

"Was it as awful?"

"Depends on your definition of awful," I offered. "Was it as bad as John Bell? No. As laid back as the winos? Nope. It was somewhere in between. They weren't physically abusive or anything but they would scream at one another every night over money and I was sort of endured because I provided a steady stream of the very cash from the state they'd yell about."

"And when you turned eighteen?"

"See you later, alligator."

Callum

97

I had it pretty bad growing up but Harper seems to have endured every awful situation a person could conjure up, short of rape and even that I think she narrowly escaped. I wanted only to wrap her in my arms and tell her that everything would be okay but that would have been a lie. I didn't know if everything was going to be okay. I did know, however, that whatever we *did* go through that we were going to sustain it together, that I was quite certain of.

"And then you met me," I said.

"And then I met you," she said, smiling softly.

"And all was right with the world," I joked.

"Exactly," she said seriously.

"I was only joking Harper," I said, sitting up a little to get a better view of her face.

"Of-of course," she giggled, fidgeting next to me. "I know that."

I studied her closely before turning off the lamp next to me. The moonlight fell across her gold strands, looking for all the world like copper threads. I half expected them to sing in clinking charms every time her head moved. I hugged her closely to me, hoping to squeeze the bad memories from her life. I'd absorb them from her, if I could. Just take them and endure the obvious ache they caused her.

"When my folks died," I confessed, "I remembered feeling sadness, an overwhelming sadness, but I was too young to realize what it meant. I have memories of visiting a cold, unwelcoming room where they would force me to draw pictures of how I supposedly felt. They'd ask me if I remembered my mom and dad, and even then I thought they were stupid for asking such an obvious question.

"I wondered why I left my home, wondered when

my mom and dad would come and pick me up. I would often tell my foster mother that I was ready to call my parents to have them pick me up but she would just smile and settle me on her hip, never really giving me the answer I was looking for."

Harper thread her fingers with mine, burrowing her shoulder deeper into mine.

"When I was slightly older and had almost completely forgotten about my parents," I continued, "I began school and quickly noticed that my life was very different from my classmates. Many of them would talk about their families and I just couldn't help but fear that I didn't share their fates.

"I went home my first day of first grade and asked my foster mom if she was mine. She gave me a round-a-bout answer and that's the day I knew I was different. That was the day I knew I belonged to no one and steeled myself for a difficult life. I don't know how I knew, but at six, I had already figured it out.

"I was a pretty good kid, school became my life because I had nothing else. I made it my life's goal to be worth something to myself as I was the only one interested enough to care. I, too, was thrown from family to family for one reason or another. I tumbled about New York City never really forming friendships for fear they'd just disappoint me further than I already was. I was afraid that a loss like that would be the bitter pill that would kill the little spirit I had left.

"I trusted no one, until the age of fourteen, when a boy introduced himself to me as Alan Moss. He was cool and non-judgemental. I started hanging with him a lot.

"By the time we were fifteen, Alan and I had become best friends. I didn't allow myself to get very close to the guy, like I said, I never allowed that void to be filled until

Charlie and Cherry but, I admit, Alan was a really good friend and I was as loyal to him as I possibly could be.

"By our sophomore year though, Alan became distant. We hadn't talked for weeks but out of the blue he called me and invites me to this party, letting me know that Keiko was going to be there. This was after our kiss in eighth grade, of course, but I still liked the hell out of her. So, I told him I'd be there. I met up with him that night but the party was not what I thought it was. People laid about like idiots, laughing at the most ridiculous things and I knew they were high as kites.

"Alan came bounding up to me, acting so different. He teased me incessantly until I agreed to try the small purple pill he held out to me in a tiny plastic bag." I sighed audibly. "I stupidly swallowed the pill.

"After that, Alan and I got high every weekend for two months. We both became addicted but I believe Alan was even more so than I. The first week we decided to ditch class to get high, I knew I needed to stop and I did. Cold turkey. And it wasn't as hard as I thought it would be but Alan...Alan couldn't do it. He started ignoring me once again, ditching class, then school altogether.

"Several weeks later, I got a frantic call from him. He'd been to his dealer's house to get more stuff but ran out of money and the guy was essentially holding him hostage for the rest of his money. Alan begged me to bring him some cash. I agreed but on the condition that he agreed to seek help, immediately.

"When I showed up, they'd already beat the living hell out of the guy. I refused to hand the dealer the cash personally and made Alan come get it from me. When he returned from paying his dealer off, I practically had to drag him home. Alan refused to go in and I knew that if I didn't stay with him that the guy was going to kill himself.

I brought him to my foster parents and snuck him into my room, stupidly thinking he hadn't taken any drugs at the dealer's house, that he needed the money so desperately to pay off old debts.

"But I was wrong. I'd fallen asleep after babysitting him for a few hours. I woke up early, around five or so, to a sleeping Alan, or at least I thought he was sleeping.

"Oh, God. No," Harper said, brining her hand to mouth.

"I tried to shake him awake but he wouldn't," I choked out. "I beat the hell out of his chest, begging him to wake but he wouldn't. My foster parents came into my room and tried to revive him but there was no use. He'd been dead for hours.

"My foster parents refused to believe I wasn't using as well and kicked me out. I ended up at my last foster home that week."

Harper unfolded her legs and faced me, sitting on her ankles. I face her as well, on the verge of losing my cool from the memory of my friend's dead, lifeless face. She cupped her hands around my face and kissed each of my cheekbones, then each brow, brushing the hair back from my face and threading strands through her fingers, holding it in fists above my ears. I pull her closely to me, hugging her tightly. It was what we both needed in that moment.

I don't believe two people have ever led lonelier lives than the lives Harper and I had led.

"I think I've been waiting my entire life for you, Harper Bailey."

"I think I have, too," she whispered.

I don't remember falling asleep but I do remember feeling the best I'd ever felt in my entire life.

Chapter Six
The Knife

Callum

For the next two weeks, Harper and I worked our fingers to the bone day and night, saving every penny we earned, knowing Charlie would be returning and we'd eventually have to figure it out for ourselves. Oh yeah, it sort of also distracts me from having to deal with the growing attraction I was feeling for her.

No matter what I did, I could *not* stop myself from falling for Harper Bailey.

Every day, like a vision, she struck me like a starting gun with a sweet smile and a generous nature. She always made me a toasted bagel with cream cheese in the morning. A few days into our friendship, I discovered she didn't even like coffee, the little liar, so I bought her a box of tea, instead. You'd think I'd given her a diamond when she saw the damn box. She was so elated, she'd begun to cry.

She was the hardest working person I'd ever met. She was frugal yet generous. She was an enigma and funny to boot.

"Good morning, Harper Bailey," I said toward the ceiling, still lounging on the couch despite the fact that the sun has almost risen completely, meaning we'd lost any chance for work at the docks. But that was okay because we had worked at The Bowery the night before for enough cash tips that we should be alright to skip one morning.

Harper and I had several jobs. At three thirty in the morning, we usually headed for the docks, earning about a hundred dollars a piece there. We'd leave there at six thirty and catch the train back to Charlie's where we would sleep until ten thirty or so, then head to whatever restaurant would take us. We usually pocketed an additional two hundred there and headed home once more where we'd sleep from around four in the afternoon until seven, only to work The Bowery until three in the morning, where we help clean up then head straight for the docks. In all, we earn around five hundred dollars a day and caught around seven hours of sleep. It was rough but we planned on getting an apartment together which was going to be difficult as hell for me knowing how I was starting to feel about her but it was the only way.

"Good morning, Callum Tate," I heard her say. "We missed work this morning," she said around a yawn.

I sighed. "I know. It's alright, last night I think we

earned three hundred altogether. We can afford to miss one morning."

"I hope you're right," she said. "Because Charlie comes home today and we haven't looked at a single apartment yet." She stood on the bed and looked down at me. "We better skip work altogether today and clean this place up, then search for our own place."

I leaned up on my elbows. I felt a definite crease in my hair and was slightly embarrassed knowing it was more than likely laying at strange angles. I attempted to run my hand through it but judging by Harper's amused expression, I'd only made things worse.

"Okay," I said, "let's clean up, wash all the sheets and blankets and then count our loot before the apartment hunt."

It only took us a few hours to finish everything up, leaving the apartment cleaner than how we'd found it. While the last load of sheets were drying, I popped around the corner and bought a paper to circle a few options close to campus before trudging back up to Charlie's apartment to get an idea of what we'd saved.

When I walked in the door, I noticed Harper on the phone.

"Um, yes. Sure, sure. No, no, that's okay. No, really, it's alright." She giggled politely. "Yup, alright. Bye."

"Who was that?" I asked, shutting the door behind me.

"Oh, that was social services." She cleared her throat. "I had my name put on a list, the day we met, for permanent housing."

I felt supreme disappointment for a moment.

"Oh," I said. "Well, what did they say?"

"No openings in the foreseeable future but I

really only called to remove my name from the queue. You know, since *we'll* be living together."

Relief washed over me.

"Oh," I said as coolly as possible. "Shall we?" I asked, pointing at the paper in my hands.

"Sure."

"Wait," I said. "Maybe we should figure out what our budget will be before we start looking."

"Right, that only makes sense."

We dumped our cash onto the floor and separated the bills by likeness. We had a few hundreds and twenties but the lower denominations dominated. I knew Charlie kept cash straps around his house because his bands usually paid in cash so I got up and rummaged through a few drawers before finding what I needed. In the end, we had five thousand seven hundred thirty-six dollars in bills and seventeen dollars in coins.

"I don't think I've ever seen this much money in my entire life," I said.

"Well, we worked our freaking butts off for it," Harper said. "What does it mean, though? We can't rely on this kind of money when school starts, can we?"

"No, I don't think we can. I'd say the most we could rely on would be..." I said, as I did a mental calculation in my head... "probably fifty a day, before taxes."

"What? Why so little? What is that, like, fifteen hundred a month?"

"Yup," I said, "and if I were to guess, our monthly apartment budget shouldn't be more than seven or eight hundred. Fifty a day is just a guess, Harper. it's so little because we'll each be taking twelve hours of classes or, in my case, fifteen. We aren't going to have time to work the way we have this summer."

Harper stared at the floor, thinking. "We aren't

going to be able to do it."

"Why would you say that? We'll figure it out. I promise. Listen, we have a week before school starts, right?"

"Yeah, if I was even able to get in."

"Harper, you were already accepted."

"I *know* that. I'm just not going to get my hopes up that Sylvia may have found the funding needed.

"Okay, so we've got five grand in our pocket. We earn another thousand this week bringing the grand total to six thousand. We're in school ten months." I tallied up an estimate, on a hand held calculator. "Leaving us an additional six hundred a month in added income. We can do this. We just need a little creativity."

"Yeah, you're right. We *can* do this! Gee, you're like a regular motivational speaker, Callum. I think I'm going to start calling you Tony from now on. Certain medical school is your true calling?" She teased.

"Ha, ha."

"Just stay away from me in the mornings. Note to self, keep megaphone away from cheerleader Callum."

"That's it!" I said, tackling her onto the couch, tickling her until tears spilled from the corners of her eyes.

"Please stop," she begged. "*Please*!"

She giggled uncontrollably. I released her but only long enough to allow her to think I was letting up. She sat up and took a deep breath but before I could tackle her again, a look flashed into her eyes. A look that told me she wouldn't mind if I placed my hands on her body again. She sucked her bottom lip under her top teeth, her breathing was labored, her cheeks flushed. Did I ever want to place my hands on her figure. I sat up on my knees and walked them toward her. She instinctively sat on her heels and I placed my hands on either side of her legs, crouching over her.

"Harper, are we ever going to talk about that day outside The Hope House?"

"Don't forget the subway," she challenged.

I fought the smile tugging at the corners of my mouth. "Or the subway?"

She breathed a sharp intake of breath when there was a hard knock on the door.

I sat back onto my heels as well. "Seriously. Everyone I know is still asleep. Who in the world could it be?" I asked the ceiling.

I climbed off the sofa and walked to the door, forgetting I didn't have a shirt on. I swung open the door and there sat Sam, her eyes grazing every inch of my chest and stomach. I tried to cover myself up which only made her laugh out loud.

"What are *you* doing here?"

"I came to open up Charlie's house. Clean it up a bit before he came home tonight."

"That's bull, Sam," I said, calling her out. "You knew we were here while he was away."

"Alright, fine, but...Wait, *we*?"

"Yes. We, as in Harper and I."

"Did Charlie know you let some stranger stay in his apartment?" She practically yelled, knowing full well Harper was within hearing range.

"Um, yes, he did, not that it's any of your business."

"Shit, Callum. I'm his freaking girlfriend!"

"No, you're not and you know it. Charlie was never exclusive with you. You said so yourself." She tried to open her mouth but I interrupted her, "What's the real reason you're here, Sam?"

She made a motion to come inside but I placed

my hand on the door jamb, blocking her way.

"Fine," she said, rolling her eyes. "Are you coming to the show Saturday night?"

"You knew I would be."

"Are you bringing *her*?"

"Who?" I played dumb.

"Harley."

"Harper!" Harper corrected from the living room. I wanted so badly to howl in laughter.

Sam crossed her arms and slowly tapped her foot. "Well?"

"Yes, I'm bringing *Harper*. I want her to meet Charlie."

Her face brightened with realization.

"Yeah, I want Charlie to meet Carper, too," she said, barely stifling her glee.

"Harper."

"Yes, I'm sure Charlie will find her as delightful as you do," she challenged, voicing the very fear I was so terrified of.

"Alright, well if that's all, then I'll see you tomorrow night," I said, closing the door.

It clicked shut. I faced the door, shaking my head. *What in the world did I ever seen in that girl?* I wondered if I should mention it to Charlie or just see how things played out.

"As I said," Harper chimed in, clearing her throat. "She likes you."

I scratched my head. "Yeah, maybe you're right," I said more to myself than to Harper. "I don't get it. I've chased her for years, practically drooling at her feet and now, all of a sudden, she acts like she wants me? So frustrating." I didn't think I'd ever been less attracted to a girl once I knew she possessed that quality and I found myself almost feeling sorry for Charlie rather than my usual jealous.

I look up at Harper but she averted her gaze.

"Um, yeah," she said at the wall. "Well, shall we, um, look through the listings?"

The paper held several affordable options in Washington Heights but we agreed that Manhattan was not a requirement and by the looks of the prices, neither was a two bedroom. We searched around the city and visited a few options near campus but found nothing really worth anything. Our last stop was in Queens, an Astoria one bedroom.

I rang the buzzer to gain entry to the building.

"Yes?"

"Uh," I said, "we're here to view the one bedroom."

There was a distinct buzz and an audible click before I opened the door for Harper. She squeezed past me, her front brushing mine, her hair floating beneath my nose. Warmth flushed over me. We both smiled at one another before footsteps interrupted us.

"Hi, I'm Kenny. I'll be showing you the apartment," the stranger said, before holding out his hand.

I shook it firmly. "Pleasure, Kenny. I'm Callum and this is Harper," I said, gesturing to her at my side. I loved to see her there, at my side.

"You two look awfully young to be interested in an apartment," he said, eyeing us skeptically.

For some reason, Harper took massive offense to this for some reason. "Yeah, seeing as neither of us have parents and all, we don't really have a choice now do we?"

"Oh, I'm so sorry. I shouldn't have..," Kenny

stuttered.

"It's okay," I interrupted the man, before shooting Harper a 'what's wrong with you?' look.

"What? He was the busy body who started making assumptions."

"*Harper*," I admonished under my breath.

"Uh, right this way," Kenny said pointing to the elevator.

It was a long ride up to the top floor, the enclosed space felt stifling thanks to Harper's defensiveness.

"It's, uh, right here," he said quietly, pointing to thirteen-oh-seven, the last door on our left. He removed keys from his pocket and opened the door. "I'll leave you two to look around. I'll be on the first floor if you have any questions." He closed the door behind him and we just stood there looking at each other, listening as he stepped onto the elevator.

I broke the silence. "Even if we wanted this apartment, I doubt he'd rent it to us."

"Uh! Why?" She asked, looking confused.

"Maybe because you were rude to him, Harper?"

"*What?*"

"Harper, he may have overstepped his boundaries a bit but he meant no harm by it."

She sighed audibly, opened her mouth, but snapped it shut instead, releasing a hard breath through her nose. She walked off toward the bedroom, examined the plaster ceilings and walls. I followed her as she inspected the size, before she moved on to the bathroom.

"It's nice," she said to me, failing to meet my eyes.

"I agree," I said in a hushed tone.

She stopped, examined the white hexagon tile beneath her feet. She ran her toe over the black grout. "Do you really think I botched our chances?"

"I don't know, Harper," I sighed loudly, running both hands through my hair and leaning against the marble countertop of the bathroom sink.

She sat on the toilet seat, burying her face in her hands. After awhile, I notice salty tears dripping from the sides of her hands. *Oh, God. You were too harsh, Callum.* I hastily grabbed some toilet tissue from the roll next to her and handed her a few squares, moving to sit on the edge of the pedestal tub beside her.

"I'm such an idiot and I'm sorry. *Please* stop crying. I don't know why I was so short with you." I paused for a second. "Well, it was probably because Sam came over today and anyway, please forgive me."

She sniffed loudly and wiped at her nose. "No, I'm sorry. I'm just in a horrible mood. I'll apologize to the guy."

"Why? Have I upset you?"

"No! No. I mean, of course not. You've been nothing but kind to me. It's just, well..."

But before she could continue, Kenny opened the front door.

"Hello!" He called out.

I squeezed my eyes shut. "We're in here!" I yelled, wishing we could have had just five more minutes. It felt like the world didn't want us to talk about anything of substance.

Harper quickly wiped her tears away in front of the mirror, attempting to erase all signs that she was upset. I could tell it was something she was practiced at because when we met Kenny in the ancient wood floored bedroom there was no trace that she had been crying less than two minutes before.

"Kenny?" She asked, humility seeping from her pores.

"Yeah," Kenny said, trying hard to be light hearted but

failing miserably.

"I'm really sorry about downstairs. I'm having a crap day and I took it out on you."

"Oh, that's cool," he said but I could tell it made him feel a lot better because his face brightened a bit. "So, are you guys interested?"

"What's the rent?" Harper asked, a slight grin tugging at her lips.

"Um, this unit is nine seventy-five. We've had difficulty letting it."

I could barely contain the excitement in my voice. "What do you say, Harper? It is the best one we've seen all day and we don't have much time before school starts."

She took a deep, cleansing breath and her eyes sparkled a bit before she answered, "I think it's amazing. We'll take it."

An hour worth of paperwork later, Harper and I were ready to sign the dotted line.

"I'll just need the first and last month's rent and a five hundred dollar deposit," Kenny says.
Harper reached for her bag to pull out our cash but Kenny stopped her.

"Not yet. I'll need to see if you're approved first but as soon as we get the thumbs up, you can swing by and we'll take care of it then. Do you guys have a number I can reach you at?"

"Do we?" Harper asked.

"Uh, sure. I'll give you Cherry's cell." I grabbed a sheet of paper and jotted the number down. "Just let her know who you are and why you're calling and she'll take the message."

"Alright, I'll let you know in a few hours," Kenny said.

Harper

Before Callum and I boarded the packed train back to Charlie's to put all the sheets back on his bed and put up a few things, Callum found a nearby pay phone and rung Cherry to let her know to expect a call from Kenny.

"So, where should we go after Charlie's?" I asked as I plopped next to Callum on the subway.

"I'm not sure, sweet. I haven't gotten a chance to think it through yet."

I could tell he was sort of sweating it. He kept rubbing the palm of his hand against the back of his neck, running his long fingers through his hair, and scrubbing his face.

"Dude, if you're getting cold feet about moving in with me, remember that you don't have to do it. I understand if I scared you with that crap I pulled back there. I don't blame you if you want out."

"What? Shut up, goof. I'm stressed about Sam."

My stomach plummeted toward my feet. "Oh, I understand."

When he revealed that he liked her back at Charlie's, I wanted to burst into idiotic tears which was so unlike me. As I was fighting the urge, the burn subsided a bit because I realized that Callum had softened me like a stick of butter left in the sun. It scared the shit out of me, actually. The last thing I wanted was to feel weak in a vulnerable situation and here I'd gone and let him do it without my knowledge. I wanted to clobber him and kiss him all at once. The fact that he liked Sam was like a punch to my gut.

"Really? Well then what do you think I should do about it?" He asked me.

"I think you should, well, listen to what your heart

says."

His brows furrowed. "That's vague and not at all helpful," he teased with his glorious, slightly crooked smile. "It doesn't matter anyway because I don't think Charlie cares for her that much," he stated.

So, he for sure likes her, then. Why would he say that otherwise? Is he worried that Charlie will be offended if he asks Sam out? God, I am such a dweeb. He was never interested in me. He's just a master flirt.

I promised myself that I'd stop liking him, move on. I turned my head toward him and actually watched him think about her. I wanted to kick my laughable ass all the way back to social services. I wondered if he thought about her hair the way I wanted him to think about mine. I wondered if he fantasized about the way she smelled or memorized her lips. Just the thought of him wanting her the way I wanted him made me nauseous. I was so pissed at myself for thinking that he was starting to become mine.

I opened my mouth to let him know that I was the one who was going to bail on our deal because I'd started to fall in love with him and I just couldn't deal when a man tripped over my bag and sprawled face first into the floor of the train.

"Shit! Are you okay?" I asked him, standing up. Callum stood and helped the guy to his feet but he just walked to the end of the car without so much as an acknowledgement.

"Weird," I said.

"Yeah," Callum said, sitting back down.

The walk to Charlie's was quiet and uncomfortable. Callum was preoccupied with, I'm sure, thoughts of Sam but he surprised me when he said, "Our appointment with Sylvia is on Monday."

"I know. What made you say that?"

"Just wanted to remind you is all, can't have you bailing on me," he teased down at me through a gleaming smile.

"Wouldn't miss it for the world," I said. *Are you flirting with him? Ugh! You are such an idiot.*

He grabbed my hand and practically dragged me to Charlie's floor. I could feel his muscles bunch and strain through the back of his t-shirt, sending me spiraling down an imaginary tunnel. *Good God, Harper! Get a hold of yourself.*

When we reached the door, an unexpected sight greeted us. Sam and an unbelievably gorgeous man I could only assume was Charlie were sitting and talking on the couch.

"Charlie!" Callum said.

Charlie stood. "In the flesh!" He said, dramatically extending his arms from his sides. Charlie had the thickest English accent I'd ever heard and was tall, probably six foot three. He was blonde with clear blue eyes and longish hair that stuck out at strange angles. It would most likely look ridiculous on anyone else but it seemed to fit Charlie to a T. "And who is this lovely?" He asked, walking toward me, his stride long and confident.

"Charlie," Callum said, still holding my hand tightly, looking down at me with what seemed like pride. "This is Harper. This is the girl I was telling you about." He squeezed my hand a bit harder.

"Harper," Charlie said warmly, a smile reaching the corners of his eyes. "It is an absolute pleasure to meet you." He took my free hand and lifted it to his lips, kissing the knuckles softly. I'd be lying if I told you it didn't feel nice or that I wasn't completely charmed by him in that moment and just as suddenly I finally got to see what

115

Callum had been talking about.

"You, too," I lamely said back.

Charlie righted himself and winked at me before turning to Callum and hugged him with heavy slaps to the back. He lifted his friend off the ground and shook him around.

"Good God, Callum. It is so good to see you."

"What do you think of Harper, Charlie?" Sam piped in, seemingly from out of nowhere.

It's a miracle! She does know my name.

Charlie laughed slightly, the smile meeting both his eyes. "She is breathtaking, Callum. How in the world did you find her?" He asked.

"We met at social services of all places but I'd like to think it was fate," Callum said, tucking me into his side. Blossoming warmth seeped into my body and I felt the blush reach even the tips of my ears as it swept across my face.

"That's sort of cool," Sam said, pathetically wrapping Charlie's arm around her shoulders. "Did your parents die too, Harper?"

"Samantha!" Charlie said.

"I'm sorry. Did I say something offensive?" Sam asked him, feigning innocence. *God, she's good.*

"Sam, apologize," Callum said, his body tensing beside mine.

"No, it's okay," I tell him, squeezing him around his waist. "No, Sam. Actually, I have no idea who my dad was but my mom was young and addicted to drugs when she gave me away at the hospital."

Sam seemed appropriately horrified for a moment but her expression cooled as she wrinkled her nose in mock sympathy.

"So, uh, Harper and I have to leave," Callum said abruptly, surprising everyone in the room, including me.

"We have some paperwork to attend to and need to catch up with Cherry. I can't thank you enough, Charlie for letting us crash here. How can I ever repay you?"

"Just have Harper here save me a dance on Saturday and we'll call it even," Charlie flirted. Despite what Callum said, I can tell that Charlie is just being polite, albeit a bit cheeky, and really meant no harm but Callum's grip on my hip tightened slightly, sending a secret thrill up my side.

In that moment, I glanced Sam's way and she had Callum's attention with her brow raised with an invisible 'I'll have you yet, Callum' hanging in the air. Callum hugged Charlie once more and we left them alone inside as the door clicked behind us.

"It feels weird leaving there," I said.

"I know. It was our first home together," he said absently, not realizing what that meant to me to hear him say.

Callum and I found the nearest pay phone and rung Cherry to see if Kenny gave us the apartment or not.

"Cherry bomb! What's up, baby doll. Hey, any word from Kenny?" Callum's eyes widened and he nodded at me. I am so excited, I can barely keep myself from jumping up and down, screaming. "Okay. Alright, cool. Thanks, Cherry berry. Love you! Bye!"

Callum hung up the phone. "We got it!" He yelled, picking me up and swinging me around. His arms crushed around my torso and I selfishly wished he would squeeze me harder. His hands were the most amazing things I'd ever felt in my entire life and I found myself threading my hands in his hair and kissing his neck in glee. He slowly set me down, sliding my body down his. We both shifted uncomfortably, staring at one another, slightly embarrassed.

"What did she say?" I asked, trying to move our attention towards something slightly less awkward.

"She Kenny needs the first and last month's rent in a cashier's check. She mentioned it'd probably be smart for us to open a bank account."

"Alright then. Well, where should we go?"

"Cherry banks right around the corner. That's as good a place as any, I think."

"Alright, lead the way, Mister Tate."

Callum and I flew around the corner and entered the bank, breathless and oh so high off where our hard work was taking us. We signed our names onto the list to see a banker and sat on a non-descript sofa side by side. There was several people there and I was forced to wedge myself close to him, his warm, hard body felt so good next to mine. Callum grabbed a pen off a nearby desk and we played tic-tac-toe on the back of a deposit slip while we waited. It ended in a draw every single time.

"Cat's game," Callum says. "How many is that?"

"Eleven draws."

"Why do you think they call it a cat's game?" He asked me, leaning his head against the back of his chair and rolling the deposit slips into a tube.

I leaned my head as well but tilted my face towards him a little. He met my eyes and smiled.

"It's called a 'cat's game' because no matter how many times a cat chases his tail, he can never truly latch on. He does it anyway because it's still fun to chase," I explained.

"Seriously? How do you know that?"

"I don't know if that's true but it's what I heard once."

"Cool."

"Harper Bailey and Callum Tate!" The banker called out with a little bit of deja vu'.

We stood and walked arm in arm toward their desk.

"Hi, I'm Asa." He gestured towards the chairs and we sat. "What can I do for you guys today?"

"We'd like to open a checking account," Callum said.

"We also need a cashier's check before we leave," I chimed in.

"Alright, that shouldn't be a problem. I'll just need two pieces of identification and a minimum of one hundred dollars opening deposit."

We both nodded our heads.

Fifteen minutes later, Asa is wrapping up everything he needed. "I'll just get these copied for you. If you'll just get your deposit ready for me. Here's the opening deposit slip. Just fill it out and I'll be back shortly." He stood and entered a room in the back.

While Callum filled out our deposit slip, I reached for my bag and pulled it up into my lap. I opened the top flap and reached toward the bottom for our cash but it wasn't there. *Must be in the front zipper*, I thought to myself. I unzipped the front pocket and felt around inside. Nothing. My adrenaline started pumping furiously through my veins. I stood up and tossed the insides of my bag all over the seat of my chair.

"What are you doing?" Callum asked, confused but I can't really hear him.

I rummaged through my belongings, knocking things off the sides of the chair, desperately searching for the bands of cash but there was nothing. At this point, Callum stands up realizing what's going on and frantically started searching with me. I found my bag on the floor, unzipped all the pockets, tearing my hands through every inch of every compartment. Callum took the bag from me and turned it upside down, shaking it out, like he could force the money to fall out. My hands begun to tremble and I fell to my knees on the harsh, grey carpet. My

119

entire body shook with disbelief. I brought both hands to my mouth to stifle the sob I was getting ready to let escape but Callum startled me before I could.

"No," he said quietly. "No, it can't be. Not after how hard we worked. Please, there's no way this could be happening."

"What do we do?" I asked, shell shocked.

Callum turned towards me, as if seeing me for the first time since our discovery. He shrugged his shoulders in defeat and joined me by falling to his own knees, barely able to keep himself upright. He hung his head and I couldn't help but feel like the whole thing was my fault. I was so ashamed that I couldn't even look at his beautiful face. *He's going to hate you forever for this*, I though. *I would. Why didn't you zip it into the bottom compartment?* I asked myself.

"I'm so sorry, Callum," I barely choked out.

Abruptly, Callum stood and crossed over to me. Instinctively, I held my hands over my head, readying myself for the blow but it never came. Instead, Callum grabbed me by the shoulders and brought me to my feet. He pulled me into the tightest hug and I lost control of myself, sobbing into his shoulder.

"I'm so sorry, Callum," I cried.

"Shh," he said, stroking my back. "Did you really think I was going to hit you?" He asked.
I nodded in response unable to speak.

"Jesus, what kind of life did you have before me?" But it was a rhetorical question and when I opened my mouth to speak, he just shook his head and hugged me tighter.

"So sorry," I mumbled out, still shaking with sadness.

"It's not your fault, Harper. It's not your fault," he whispered. "It must have been the dude on the subway."

I nodded my agreement, sniffing loudly against his chest.

Asa chooses that moment to walk into his tornado blasted office, interrupting our full blown meltdown.

"What *happened*?" He asked.

"We, uh, lost over five thousand in cash. It was stolen actually."

"Oh my God. I'm so sorry. Here," Asa said to Callum, helping him place me in Callum's chair. "Shall I call the police?" He asked.

"Please," Callum said, before bending down and gathering all my belongings into a neat pile.

I bent down next to him and helped him fold my laundry and place my stuff back into my messenger bag. The salt from my tears must have clouded my eyesight and I was having trouble controlling my trembling hands because I kept losing my grip on my toothbrush. Callum grabbed it from me and placed it in the front zipper. He closed the top flap of the bag and placed it by my chair. When he stood, he brought me up with him one more time and hugged me closely. He kissed the top of my head but instead of comforting me, it sent me reeling down a spiral of guilt and the tears flowed nonstop until the police arrived.

The police took our statements but both Callum and I knew, we were never going to see that money again. We left the bank a few hours later in utter disbelief. Callum clasped his hand tightly into mine and silently guided me toward The Hope House to wait out the night in hopes we'd get a cot. How long we stood, I don't know but I remembered suddenly being yanked from the line with a single curse from Callum. He dragged me to Central Park and sat me on a bench next to him. He dragged me closely to him, tucking me into his side much like when he introduced me to Charlie that same night. How quickly life can change. In an instant, you can lose your mother, your father, your life, your youth, your innocence, and your pride. Losing your money and possibly the best friend you've ever had seemed like too much, even for me.

"You're going to leave me now, huh?" I asked him.

Callum looked at me, stunned. "What? No. Never, Harper."

"Why not?" I said, staring blankly at him. "I just lost thousands of dollars. I lost any chance of housing for yourself and possibly just made going to school impossible for you as well as myself. Why even bother?"

"Listen to me closely," Callum gritted through clenched teeth, grabbing me by the shoulders, bringing his face closely to mine. "That money was stolen. You were no more responsible for it than I was. Stop blaming yourself, Harper Bailey! Shit happens! You know that just as well as I do but it's *because* it happens to us so often that he have to fight just a little bit harder.

"One day, you and I are gonna' wake up and be alright. Maybe not today, maybe not tomorrow but one day. One day. I promise you."

He brought his chest to mine and I buried my face in his neck, sobbing at the generosity of his words.

"Thank you," I whispered into his ear.

He buried his hands into my hair and kissed my neck. "No, thank *you*, Harper."

"For what?" I asked, tears staining the shoulder of his t-shirt.

"For giving me a reason to *want* to fight again."

Chapter Seven
Tide is High

Callum

"So, this is where we're staying the night, I guess?" Harper asked me.

I sighed. "Yes. I'm sorry but The Hope House ran out of cots."

"I figured."

Harper snuggled closely to me on the bench, a massive yawn escaped from her delicious mouth.

"Here, lay down," I ordered her. "We have no blankets, so you'll just have to settle for me," I teased, making her blush the most attractive shade of pink on her soft skin.

She gave in to me and I laid down, my front to hers. We tangled our legs together and I wrapped my arms around her little torso. She sighed, content, and for a moment I didn't feel like the care-taking failure I really was. Laying this close to her sent an oddly warm shiver through my entire body. My feet tingled and that same thread of shocking greatness traveled up my blood stream, affecting even the roots of my hair. I shivered involuntarily and Harper mistook it for my being cold, clutching me tighter, making my heart race and a crimson heat to pool in my stomach. She burrowed her face in my neck and, unable to stop myself, I inhaled the scent of her hair.

As I watched the shadows on her face from the lamp post, I couldn't remember a time I'd ever seen anyone lovelier than Harper Bailey. She was everything I could ever want in a girl and a new fever gathered in my chest when I realized what it meant. I was falling in love with Harper Bailey. The scales were tipping fast and furious in that direction and I was slightly alarmed at how comfortable I was at the rapid descent. Falling for Harper felt like the most natural thing in the world and, God help me, I liked it. Damn the consequences.

Just as she started to drift to sleep, Harper's eyes shot wide, making me grin. "What are we going to do now, Callum?"

"Don't worry about that now. We'll figure it out tomorrow. Just sleep," I told her, wrapping her tightly against me.

She nodded and closed her eyes. After a few minutes, her breaths steadied with sleep and I felt free to spend most of the night wondering just what in the hell we were going to do. Somewhere between the fantasy of winning the lottery and desperately considering knocking over the proverbial liquor store, I fell to sleep.

"Get up!" I heard someone yelling. I realized that someone was poking me with something hard in the back. I turned around and recognized the end of a police officer's flashlight. "Did you hear me? Wake up!" The officer said.

I stumbled up and helped a sleepy Harper sit up as well.

The officer shone the bulk of his light at our faces but as we shaded our eyes from the blinding brightness, he dragged the beam toward our chests.

"What are you guys doing?" He asked. "Have too much to drink tonight?"

"No, sir," a scratchy voiced Harper answered.

"No, we just didn't have a place to sleep," I offered.

The officer narrowed his eyes at us. "Why not?"

"We're homeless," I said and it felt so weird admitting it out loud.

"Run away?" He asked.

"No sir," I said. "We have no home to run from."

"Why didn't you stay at one of the city's night facilities?"

"We tried," Harper said, "but they ran out of cots."

"Have your I.D.'s?" He asked bluntly.

Harper and I pulled ours out and handed them over to him. He spoke into his sleeve radio and asked the operator to check us out. When he was satisfied we weren't wanted criminals, he handed us back our I.D.'s.

"You guys can't sleep out here," he said, bringing us to our feet and escorting us from the park.

"But we have nowhere to go," Harper said.

"That's not my problem, kid. Should have thought about that before you ran away from mom and dad. Maybe their rules aren't so bad now that you're sleeping outside on a bench, are they?"

Harper began to open her mouth but I just shook my head. "Come on."

We walked away from the park, towards the city and leaned against the nearest building. We both yawned loudly and laughed at the other.

"Bless my soul! I am so tired," Harper said.

I yawned again when she did. "Careful, or we'll be

trading these all night," I said.

"Where should we go?" She asked.

I shrugged my shoulders. I walked to a nearby store and although it was closed, pressed my face against the glass and read the time on the register. "Cherry will be home at five a.m. She'd probably let us crash on her floor."

"What time is it?"

"Four."

"Should we start walking toward her place?" Harper asked.

"Why not."

We arrived at Cherry's apartment, at four fifteen and sat outside her door. We must have fallen asleep because I woke to Cherry kicking my toe. Harper stayed asleep on my shoulder.

"Dude, what's up?" She asked, her eyes full of concern.

"We got kicked out of Central Park," I whispered, careful not to wake Harper.

"When?"

"Around four," I said, unsure.

Cherry leaned her face towards mine. "Were you both sleeping there? What happened to your apartment?"

I shook my head. "We had five g's stolen on the subway. Lost all our money."

Cherry placed her hand on the top of her head and exhales loudly, like she can't believe our luck and it accidentally wakes Harper. "Crap," she said, but I'm not sure if she meant that about waking Harper or about the money, probably a little of both. "You two just can't catch a break, can you?"

Harper funnily agreed, completely unaware of our topic but immediately laid her head back onto my shoulder and fell back to sleep.

"Come on," Cherry said, opening the door. "You can take the carpet underneath my coffee table. I don't have anything softer, I'm sorry."

Cherry lived in a little studio and her fold out sofa is her bed. She had a small kitchen that doubled as her laundry and a small bathroom with a stand-up shower. It was cheap but she somehow made it look like the Taj Mahal because she was crafty like that. I balanced Harper's head against the wall and stood before picking her up and carrying her into Cherry's.

"Lay your girl down here," she said, removing the coffee table and sliding the rug nearer to the kitchen. I started to lay her down but Cherry stopped me. "Wait, let me get an old sleeping bag in my closet." She left and returned with a maroon sleeping bag, unzipping the sides as she walked. She laid it flat over the carpet and I laid Harper on top. I immediately crashed on top. "Tired?" Cherry asked the room but got no answer.

She snorted and I could hear her toss two of her sofa pillows at us. A light quilt cascaded on top of us.

"I love you, Cherry bomb."

"I love you too, Callum. Good night, baby."

Cherry turned out the lights and I was asleep before the light bulb cooled.

Later that morning, while Cherry still slept, Harper and I folded her blanket and rolled up her sleeping bag. We both took showers and because I had taken a hundred out of our stash to keep in my wallet, Thank God, I went to get breakfast for all of us while Harper dried her hair.

As I stood in line, trying to figure out if they had real cream for Harper's tea or not, I heard a tiny voice creep into my ear.

"What are you doing here?"

I turned around to see Sam standing directly behind me. *Oh, dear God.*

"Oh, yeah," I absently remarked. "You live in Cherry's building. I must have forgotten."

She snorted. "Yeah, right. You've been in love with me for two years, Callum Tate. You knew I lived here."

I was taken aback by her truthfulness. In fact, I had remembered that she lived in that building. I just thought she'd be at Charlie's and didn't think more beyond that.

"So, you knew," I said, staring directly ahead. The person in front of me moved up and I followed suit as did Sam.

"Of course I knew. Everyone knew, including Charlie." That stung a little bit to hear.

"Why aren't you at Charlie's?" I asked, evading.

"He and I...Well, we've decided to see other people."

I laughed loudly but stopped and clear my throat. "I'm sorry to hear that."

"I feel it's for the best. I like to keep my options open."

"Is that what they call being dumped now? Keeping your options open?"

"Charlie didn't dump me, Callum," she scoffed. "I dumped him. He was too old for me anyway. I've got a taste for something younger now."

I almost choked on my own spit when I heard that. "*Okay.*"

"Next," I heard. *Saved.*

"Hi, I need three bagels, toasted. Uh, cream cheese. You know," I said to more to myself, "she likes strawberries. Let me have some strawberry jam as well. Let's do two coffees and a tea."

"Is that it?"

"Yup," I said.

I paid my total and picked up a few things of cream and sugar at the side stand. I started to walk off but forgot that Harper wouldn't eat the strawberries without a little bit of sugar and threw an extra few packets in my bag. I walked outside and remembered that Harper liked lemon with her tea and debated whether or not it was worth having to brave seeing Sam again. It was worth it. I walked back in and grabbed a plastic ramekin full of lemons. I tried to get away before Sam was done but got no such luck. She only just caught my arm when I tried to burrow my way out the large glass door again.

"I think I'll walk with you, maybe visit Cherry."

"You're going to see Cherry in a few hours. Why bother?"

"Callum, what is wrong with you?" She asked, keeping step with me.

"Nothing. I'm just not sure what's wrong with you, to be perfectly honest."

"Nothing's wrong with me. I'm perfect."

"And oh so humble," I snorted.

"It was a joke, bonehead. Seriously, I think I want to explore your feelings for me. Aren't you even the littlest bit curious as to how that might go?"

I stopped dead in my tracks and looked at her point blank. It took a few seconds for my mouth to catch up to my thoughts.

"No," I said succinctly.

"What?" She asked, her chin dropped to her chest.

"No, I can honestly say I am not in the least bit curious." I noticed and stared at the stop light ahead of me. The light turned green just as the truth of that hit me. "Huh. That's funny."

"What is exactly supposed to be funny here, Callum?"

"I don't want you anymore, Sam."

"Uh! What? That can't be, Callum. You don't stop loving someone just out of nowhere like that."

"I think what I felt for you was more lust than love, Sam. How can you truly love someone who harbors no real interest in you? I may have been pathetic but I knew I was worth more than the way you treated me. Besides, it wasn't meant to be. Trust me, it just wasn't meant to be."

I started walking towards Cherry's but she pulled my sleeve hard and I almost lost control of the bag I was carrying.

"Callum Tate, I'm giving you a chance. I think we both know you'd be missing out if you didn't take it."

"Ah, and there's that winning charm. You may still be a sort of sweet girl, Sam, but you really have no idea what humility is nor do you know what really matters in life."

Sam rolled her eyes. "Oh come off it, Callum!" I didn't acquiesce and that made her visibly angry. She tucked her hands at her side and leaned her head back. "And I suppose this Harper chick, she knows what's important in life? I already know how humble she must be seeing as her simple looks have probably already instilled that little life lesson."

I dropped the bag I was carrying and instinctively got closer to her face, my blood boiling underneath my skin. "If you ever talk badly about Harper again, Sam. You and I will never speak again." I picked the bag back up and started to walk off quickly but stopped and threw over my shoulder, "You and I both know that her *simple* looks are a little more *complex* than you're implying. In fact," I said, turning and walking back to Sam, to drive the point home, "I'd go so far as to say she's the most complex girl I've ever come across and that includes even the most

130

illustrious version of you, Sam." I stared her down and it took her quite awhile to remember to blink. "See you tonight."

When I walked in to Cherry's, Cherry and Harper were cuddled up next to one another laughing like they'd known each other their entire lives.

"What are you guys talking about?" I asked, already laughing.

"Oh, Cherry was just telling me about the time you were at one of her shows and were dancing with a girl with bright orange hair, lost control of yourself, then fell through the bathroom doors."

"Oh God! *Cherry*! You *told* her that?"

"Yeah, but I forgot the part where you..." I had already dropped breakfast on the nearby coffee table and was on top of Cherry, my hand covering her mouth, before the rest could come out.

"Don't even think about it, Cherry Bomb!" Both the girls were laughing so hysterically at me that I couldn't stifle the grin threatening the corners of my mouth. "Seriously, Cherry, if you tell her the rest, I'll never talk to you again!" She nodded but the laughing tears in her eyes told me otherwise.
I slowly unwound my hand from her mouth and she jumped up, running to the other side of the room.

"And then," Cherry said, betraying me, but she stopped talking just in time to escape my chase. She finished her story as I chased her in circles, as if I wasn't humiliated enough. "He couldn't stop the momentum and..."

"Don't do it, Cher, I beg of you!"

"He tripped face first into the urinal on the wall!"

I gave up the chase and fell to the ground, my back on the floor, and covered my face in utter embarrassment. "You did it. You told her."

"And the worst part is someone had their camera out and caught it all on film," Cherry finished, sucking in a labored breath.

Harper was laughing so hard, she couldn't breathe.

"Why is my life so hard?" I asked the ceiling.

"Oh my God, Callum. That is the best and worst story I've ever heard!" Harper said, falling to her back on the sofa in amusement. She sighed loudly, like she'd just caught her breath.

"I'm going to die of embarrassment," I said.

Cherry started to rummage through the bags, chuckling to herself. Harper stood up and laid down next to me. She wound her arm with mine and I let my hands slide off my beet red face to the floor. I turned my head to stare at her.

"You can't die of embarrassment, trust me."

"Can I die of humiliation?"

"No," she said, taking in my flushed face. "Well, maybe," she teased.

I elbowed her, then stood up before taking her hands and bringing her to her feet. Her body came dangerously close to mine as she stood and I had to shake my head to regain composure. All I wanted to do was attack her face and neck with my lips.

I walked over to the bag. "I'm going to kill you, Cherry."

"Yeah, yeah," she said, plopping herself on the sofa and taking a long swig from her coffee. "Ah, the nectar of the gods."

"You know," I said, removing my own coffee from the carton and setting in next to Cherry, "Harper doesn't drink coffee."

"*What*?" Cherry asked. "Get out of my house."

I laughed. By this time, Harper had started going through the bag.

"You got me strawberry jam? Oh! And extra sugar! I think I'm in love with you, Callum!"

Customarily, a statement like this would be passed over as exaggerated but an uncomfortable silence filled the room and Cherry took it as some sort of hint. Harper just stood with her back turned toward me, pretending to fiddle with the lid to her tea.

"I'm gonna' hop in the shower," Cherry said, winking at me and making me blush.

As Cherry, left the room, the silence grew so thick I could almost reach out and grip it in my hands.

"Harper," I said, clearing my throat. "I, uh, wanted to..."

A loud knock came at the door. *Damn it!*

"I'll get it," Harper said, setting down her tea but I realized who it might be and jumped up quickly.

"No, um, let me get it," I said, practically cutting her off.

When I swung open the door, Sam stood there again and Harper came to stand behind me.

"Oh, hi, Sam," she said, leaving the door way. I turned to see her attending to that darn lid.

"What's up, Sam?"

"Oh, nothing," she lied. "I just needed to talk to Cherry about tonight is all."

I narrowed my eyes at her and clenched my teeth but opened the door anyway. It wasn't my home to kick her out of and she was in the band with Cherry. I walked to the coffee table and picked up the bag. I watched Harper through the corner of my eye as Sam came in and closed the door behind her. Sam swung her arms as she sauntered toward the sofa and plopped down on top.

"It's so freaking hot outside," she said, removing her short jacket, revealing only a tank top underneath.

I rolled my eyes but Harper didn't catch it. She was too busy watching Sam. Before long, Harper's gaze flitted back to me, then back to Sam one more time. I sat in Cherry's arm chair, hoping Harper would make eye contact so I could tell her to squeeze in next to me but she wasn't paying attention and sat on the opposite side of the sofa from Sam. Another awkward silence filled the room. Cherry came out from the bathroom dressed but her hair wrapped in a towel.

"What's up, Sam?"

"Nothing really. I wanted to go over the set list."

"Oh, yeah. Cool. Let me grab my bag. I think I left it on the washer," Cherry said before leaving the room for the small kitchen.

Sam turns toward Harper without missing a beat, revealing the true reason she came. "So, Cherry tells me that you and Callum are getting an apartment together?" Harper turned the palest shade of white and gulped audibly. She looked at me, tears welling in her eyes.

"Yes, we are," I told Sam but looking intently at Harper. "We had a slight hiccup. It's not a big deal but we will eventually get an apartment together."

"Isn't that a little weird? I mean you guys barely know one another. Are you, like, *that* kind of girl?" Sam asked Harper with more acid than I felt necessary.
She wasn't even pretending to be nice and she was implying that Harper was not classy or something. I couldn't stand for that.

"No, Sam!" I said. "We'll have two separate rooms. We'll be proper roommates." I sat back in my chair, feeling satisfied that I defended Harper's honor.

Harper

Any doubt I had that Callum may have liked me,

completely vanished the instant he insisted to Sam that we were strictly roommates. I felt like such a complete fool. He liked Sam. And who wouldn't? Sam was gorgeous.

She was tall, well taller than me, with bright beautiful blonde straight hair that tapered down her back. She had light blue eyes and a body that could rival Brooklyn Decker's. Who, by the way, I finally realized she looked exactly like. I believe I was close to the exact opposite of Sam. Bigger hips, bigger eyes, bigger lips, bigger hair. Everything about me was bigger than her except for my height, *of course*. I had coppery hair and gold eyes which I'd always thought were sort of my best features until, that is, I met Sam, now I wasn't so sure.

Yeah, she was prettier than I was, maybe, but that didn't bother me. It never really bothered me to meet girls prettier than I was. I was jealous of Sam for a completely different reason. She had Callum's attention. I thought, at first, that he was getting annoyed at her but then I realized that he was probably annoyed *with* her. She belonged to Charlie and she was untouchable. That would be enough to drive anyone insane.

"Harper?" I heard but Cherry said it in such a way that it made me think she'd been trying to get my attention for awhile.

"What? I'm sorry. Did you need me?"

"I was asking if you wanted to borrow any clothes for the concert tonight."

"That's really nice of you to offer but you're like six foot tall, Cherry. I doubt anything would fit."

At that, Cherry only laughed. "Come on, girl. Just check out my closet. I think I may have a few mini's in there that would fit you. Any of them would look chic with a pair of combats," Cherry said, winking at me.

She picked me up by my arm and dragged me to a closet set deep within the wall. She opened the doors and an unbelievably amount of clothing practically burst out.

"Oh. My. Gosh." I said, in shock. "How do you even close the doors?"

Cherry laughed out loud just as Sam came to stand beside her.

"It is ridiculous, Cherry," Sam laughed.

"You say ridiculous, I say magnificent," she chimed in. "Alright, so let's see."

She dug around in her closet and pulled out ten or fifteen different miniskirts that looked more like tube tops to me and threw them at my feet. I bent to pick them up, examining each one as I checked them over. I held up a dark silver sequin one and thought it was the cutest thing I'd ever seen.

"I think that would look amazing with your hair," she said. "Here, I have this awesome fitted grey Led Zeppelin v-neck that would look great with this. It's too small for me so I'm certain it'd fit you like a glove." She turned toward her closet and I stood up. Just then, I noticed Callum casually leaning against the wall, his arms crossed across his chest.

"What?" I asked him, trying very hard not to let him effect me.

"Are...are, are you going to try those on?" He asked, gulping down hard.

Hmm.

Chapter Eight
6 Underground

Callum

    Cherry and Sam had left hours ago to ready for the show, leaving Harper and I to get ready on our own. When they left, Harper had been exceedingly quiet, barely speaking a word to me and I couldn't put my finger on what was wrong. I was lounging on the sofa, watching television, when she came out of the bathroom wearing the outfit Cherry let her borrow. My eyes literally bugged from my head. I stood, my palms beginning to sweat. I was forced to lock my knees to keep from falling forward.

    "Harper, you look *amazing*."

    "Thank you," she said and walked toward her bag, stuffing all its contents inside.

I watched the muscles in her exposed legs flex with every movement as the t-shirt clung to her flat stomach, making my head swim.

"You can leave that here, Harper. Cherry will let us come back for it."

"Oh, okay," she said, leaning against the sofa arm and crossing her legs at the ankles. I gulped down how sexy I thought that was.

"Uh, are you ready?"

"Yup," she said, shortly, refusing to look at me as she stood.

I started walking toward the door and heard her follow. "Are you excited to see Barcelona?"

"Of course," she answered.

She was so short with me.

"Is, I mean, did I do something wrong, Harper?" I asked as we descended the narrow stairs.

"Um, no, of course not," she said too softly.

"Well, you aren't acting yourself. What's up?"

"Seriously, nothing."

I didn't say anything back. There was nothing *to* say. She was obviously ticked off. I decided I'd just have to let it come out on its own.

We rode the subway there in complete silence and she barely looked at me the entire time. I put my hand around her shoulder to let her know that I didn't care if she was mad at me or not, I wanted to be near her and to my surprise, she didn't shove me off. Instead, she laid her head on my shoulder like she couldn't get close enough yet still refused to look at me.

"I thought we'd get off here," I said a few blocks from the concert.

"What for?"

"Charlie said I could park my motorcycle where all the

bands buses are. I need to pick it up."

"Alright," she conceded easily.

The concert was held in Central Park and was more like a summer festival. There was a main stage and several side stages, where The Ivories were supposed to be playing. We rode right up the path behind the main stage and were stopped at the fenced in gate.

"Whoa!" A security guard said. "What are you doing?"

"Sorry," I said, flashing my backstage pass. "I'm here with Charlie James."

The guy didn't say a word, opening the make-shift gate and letting us through. I slowly brought my bike toward the rear where Charlie said he'd be. I spotted Cherry first and stopped by their trailer. When I got off my bike, I helped Harper slide off the seat so her skirt wouldn't show anything. I got a small smile for that and breathed a slight sigh of relief. She stood beside me, letting me unbuckle her helmet for her and I could feel the eyes of the band and Charlie watching us. I got the helmet off and hung it on my handle bar but when I turned around, I saw Harper shaking out her hair. The scent assaulted me, a fragrant punch to the chest, and my fingers itched to run through every single strand, to feel its silk. I caught myself and turned toward my friends and was taken completely back. The girls were talking amongst themselves, laughing and joking...but the guys. The guys were apparently struck as dumb as I had been when they caught a glimpse of Harper. Instinctively, I reached for Harper but she had already headed for Cherry, doing a little turn to show how her outfit looked on her.

I strode over to the guys and punched Josiah in the shoulder.

"What the hell, dude?" He asked, rubbing his arm.

"Can you all pick your jaws off the floor?" I asked, a little bit peeved. "Charlie? *Charlie*?" I snapped my fingers in his face to grab his attention.

"What? Yes?" He asked and the others laughed.

"Can you, maybe, not stare at Harper?"

He shook his head to clear it. "Oh, of course. I'm sorry, Callum. She's extraordinary."

"I know," I said, sighing at the typical direction our conversations usually went. That's when I realized that Harper was one girl Charlie couldn't have. "Listen, Charlie. I know you and Sam are over or whatever but I'd appreciate it if you could not go after Harper. She's....She's..."

"Yours?" He asked, a twinkle in his eye.

The others had walked off at this point to visit with Harper, leaving us alone. "She's not mine. No."

"But you want her to be," Charlie said, stating it more as a fact than posing it as a question. He leaned against The Ivories' sleek black trailer they bought for the previous summer's tour.

"More than anything," I admitted out loud.

"Stop wasting time then or I can't be responsible for my actions," he teased.

This held me slightly on edge. "Please, I can't joke about this with you. You have no idea how much Harper's beginning to mean to me."

"I apologize, Callum," he said sincerely, throwing his arm over my shoulder in a peace offering. "I was only joshing. Honestly, I'll stay away." A small smile curved around his lips. "It'll be hard but I'll stay away."

"Charlie!"

"What? Callum, calm down. I'm teasing you!"

I eyed Harper, my jaw clenching, making the muscles in them flex. I opened my fists, then closed them, over and over. I wanted her more than anything in this entire world.

Charlie's hand came flitting over my face to break the trance.

"My God, Callum," he whispered.

"What?" I asked, turning his direction.

"You're in love with her."

"What? No, that's impossible. I've only known her two weeks," I said, watching her intently again laughing at something Tie-Dye Tom said. *They're standing awfully close.*

"That may be but you're either most definitely in love with that creature there in that fetching skirt or there's something between you and Tom you haven't yet discussed with me." I rolled my eyes but laughed. "I can't say I blame you. I've never seen you like this, Callum, not even with Sam."

My head snapped his direction again.

"You knew?"

"Everyone knew."

"Then why would you go out with her?"

"I didn't realize until much later. It's why I broke up with her last night. I thought you may still be in love with her and I didn't want to stand between that. I was only mildly interested myself." *Funny,* he *broke up with* her.

"But I'm not."

"I can see that now," he said, laughing a bit.

"I'm sorry I made you feel you had to do that."

"I'm not. I was ready to move on."

I stood there next to Charlie watching Harper and Cherry gossip closely.

"She's in love with you, by the way," I said.

"Samantha? No, she's not. She's only in love with herself."

"Not Sam, Charlie. *Cherry*."

This took Charlie by surprise.

"*What?* You're mad! She's my best friend!" He exclaimed in disbelief.

"She is and I can honestly say, I'll consider you the biggest idiot if you don't realize soon that she's perfect for you."

"I can't, Callum," he said, sighing loudly in exasperation. "She's the only person in my life, besides you, I can count on. If I fall in love with her, I could *never* lose her and that's scares me more than anything."

"So you've thought about it then?"

"Of course I have. I just never knew she felt the same way." Charlie swallowed and stared hard at the ground. "I don't think I've ever met anyone more beautiful then Evelyn. She's the kindest, most lovely girl."

"I agree. Well, almost," I said, nodding my head toward Harper, making Charlie laugh and shake his head. "Wait a minute! *Evelyn*?"

"That's Cherry's real name. It was her grandmother's. I think I'm the only one she's told."

"Wow. I've never thought to ask if Cherry was her real name or not."

"Nah, I called her that when we first met seven years ago. She was super tall, porcelain skinned, crazy deep red hair. When she stood next to me, she was only a few inches shorter than I and I was so intimidated by her. That was what made me think she looked exactly like a cherry bomb. Beautiful to look at but there was something alarming there as well, like a fire was nearing the end of her wick. Her eyes make me feel like if she exploded anywhere near me, I couldn't help but be a very willing casualty.

"Haven't you ever wondered why I've never tried it out with her?"

"Not really," I said honestly. "I just figured you weren't into red heads."

"No," he said emphatically. "She *is* the reason I don't date red heads."

"Damn, Charlie. You got it bad."
He laughed wholeheartedly and slapped me on the shoulder.

"What a pair we are, eh?" He asked.

"Listen," I said, seriously. "I promised her I wouldn't say a word about the way she felt and that makes me feel like the most horrible friend right now but after you confessed to that phenomenal crush, I don't feel as guilty as I probably should. Just, figure it out, will ya'?"

"I'll try," he said, readjusting against the trailer.

"You know, Harper's here for Barcelona. Particularly *Please, Don't Go*. Think you could...?"

"Already on it," he said, standing upright and smoothly walking away from our group.

When Charlie left, Harper walked toward me. I held my breath and with every inch she closed the distance between us, my body began to tremble more and more.

"Hey," she said.

"Hey." I swallowed hard.

"Should we, ya' know, head toward The Ivories' stage?"
I nodded my answer.

It was crowded so I grabbed Harper's hand so I wouldn't lose her. We weaved our way through sweaty bodies and watched The Ivories but I had a hard time concentrating on their set because I still possessed

Harper's hand and I finally realized she possessed my heart.

When The Ivories left the stage, Harper and I left to camp in front of the main stage to see Barcelona. The rest of the band told us they'd meet us after they broke down their equipment and placed it in their trailer. We sat on the grass, side by side, a silence building between the two of us and it was becoming shockingly awkward.

"Dude, Harper. Tell me what's up."

"Uh, noth..."

"Don't say nothing, Harper. I may have only known you a few weeks but we've practically lived a lifetime in those few weeks. I know you. You're upset."

She sighed loudly and brought her knees to her chest, resting her cheek on her knee, facing me. "I'm embarrassed to say," she admitted.

"Just tell me what's wrong."

"I'm jealous," she said bluntly, making me choke on my own spit.

"Wh-what?"

"I'm jealous of Sam. I don't like her for no other reason than that she obviously wants you. There, I said it."

Her face turned a bright red in the artificial light of the stage lights. I opened my mouth to confess everything but was interrupted by the roar of the crowd. Everyone stood abruptly, surrounding us as we stayed on the grass, staring at one another. I wanted to reveal all. I just needed everyone to quiet down enough that she could hear me.

"Hi, we're Barcelona," we heard over the thunder of the crowd. "Our first song is dedicated to Harper Bailey from Callum Tate," he said right before the first resonating piano note of *Please, Don't Go* began to play.

144

Tears began to fill Harper's eyes. I stood and offered her my hand and to my utter relief she took it. I enveloped her in my arms and brought her close, squeezing her tightly against my chest. I brought her hand in mine to my chest and splayed my free hand across the broad of her back.

I bent slightly toward her ear. "You don't have to be jealous of Sam, Harper. It's not her I want."

My hand rose slowly with her breath. We bent to the rhythm of our song, her face buried in my neck and my cheek resting on the side of her head. What I needed in my life was right there, in my arms. I closed my eyes and drunk in the most perfect moment of my life.

The song was over all too soon and we reluctantly pulled away from the other, realizing this meant there could be no more pretending.

"I think I'm fa..." I started to say but was cut short by the howling of my friends.

They teased us incessantly, embarrassing us both but I just held tightly to her hand to let her know we'd be talking, extensively, much later.

I enjoyed the rest of the music with everyone and was so freaking proud that they included Harper like she was one of us now. Well, everyone except for Sam but I was hoping that with time she would come around. I knew I was nothing more than a forbidden novelty to her. By the time it all came to a halt, we were all sweaty and full of smiles. All of us walked back to The Ivories' trailer where my bike and the gang's van was.

The alcohol was poured freely that night. It seemed everyone around us were drunk including some of our group but we lived in New York City for crying out loud. No need to worry because there was always a taxi available.

We sat on the concrete around the trailer, getting to know a few of the bands around us. Charlie had a keg on rollers that he spilled from the back of the trailer as a surprise. A million hands lifted in cheer and the after party had begun.

"God, what time is it?" A drowsy Harper asked.

I peeled my pocket watch from my jean's pocket and checked. "Twelve fifteen."

"It feels like four," she said laughing, laying her head on my shoulder.

"That's because the past few days were exhausting pieces of crap that no person, no, people, should endure."

I felt more than heard her chuckle in response.

"I need to talk to you, Callum," she said suddenly.

"And I need to talk to you. Badly," I said, looking at the top of her beautiful head.

Just then, Sam came up.

"Can I speak with you?" She asked.

"No," I said and I meant it.

"Please, it's...I just want to apologize. Please?"

I sighed. "Fine. Harper, excuse me."

She lifted her head and bit her bottom lip. I could tell she didn't want me to go.

I kissed her neck and whispered in her ear, "It's not her I want."

She nodded and I stood, following Sam to a dark space near the other side of the trailer. She wanted me to follow her farther away but I felt sick leaving Harper where I couldn't see her so I froze there, crossing my arms and waiting. Sam seemed to understand and came back up to me.

"I just wanted to apologize for earlier this morning," she began. "I overstepped some boundaries. I knew how much you wanted her and it scared me. I always thought you'd be there, waiting, and it just freaked me out that you weren't there when I wanted you."

"That's the lamest apology in the history of apologies, Sam."

"What? *Why*?"

"Sam, are you really this dense?" She had the decency to act embarrassed. "You just admitted to using me. Listen, I know you strung me along and before Harper I was just pathetic enough to endure it because I thought I loved you but since meeting her I realized something about myself. I'm worth more than what you think of me. I shed some crazy when I met her, took off my blurred visioned glasses and saw what you really are...not meant for me."

"Callum!" Sam yelled, showing a bit of crazy herself. She reached for me in desperation but I was distracted by yelling on the other side of the trailer. I ran into a crowd gathered in a circle around Harper and Charlie.

"I told you! She wants nothing to do with you!" Charlie said to a rather large man in jeans and a stained t-shirt. Harper clung to Charlie, her body visibly shaking.

"And I told *you*! That girl is coming home with me. She's mine," the man said with slurred speech.

"You've had a lot to drink, John. Let's just leave," a sensible friend of the drunk said, pulling him away from the circled crowd.

I finally reached the circle and broke through, wrapping Harper in my arms and trying to drag her away but the guy became enraged.

"Stay away from her!" John, the drunk, said.

"It's John Bell," Harper barely whispered, her lips quivering, her body shivering in fear.

I searched her face. *John Bell, John Bell. Why does that*

name sound so familiar? That's when I realized, John Bell was the sick psychotic who tortured her at her foster home.

"Oh my God," I said, sucking in a breath. I scooped her up by her knees and carried her to my bike. "Charlie don't let that man follow us," I said and he nodded.

By then, the rest of the group caught on to what was happening and circled around John Bell to prevent him from coming after us. I set a shaking Harper on the ground, started the bike then began to pull the helmet onto her head but a roar of anger came from within the circle that contained John.

Before I could even turn around, Harper yelled for me to watch out. I tossed Harper and I away from the direction she screamed and saw John barreling toward us, a crow bar in his hand. I could see Charlie, Aaron, Nat, Jared and Josiah running after him. He edged toward Harper, a crazed look in his eyes but three police officers caught on to the commotion and started running toward us. John saw this and not wanting to get caught, picked up my bike and hopped on, gunning it into the crowd around us.

Harper and I stood, staring in shock as John drunkenly tried to weave through the people but he wasn't fast enough and the cops almost reached him. We watched. My eyes wide in disbelief, Harper's hand covering her mouth, tears streaming down her face. John turned around to check his progress and saw that there was no way out. I expected him to slow down but instead he gunned it more and we were forced to watch him hit a woman, driving over her after she'd fallen before losing control and crashing my bike to the ground.

Panicked, we all run to the woman, laying still on the ground. One of the police officers grabs John, turning his unconscious body onto his stomach, cuffing him while he calls for an ambulance standing by. The woman was still, too still and Harper screamed when she realized the woman was dead. I bent, immediately beginning CPR. *Count thirty quick compressions, breathe twice, repeat.* Time seemed to flow so slowly. The woman was unresponsive but I refused to give up. It was *my* bike that killed her. The paramedics arrived and began where I left off. We all stood, dazed, praying she came back to life but we all knew that would never happen. The paramedics stood and called it as it was. Harper turned from me and vomited all over the pavement. I held her body up to keep her from falling. Cherry, Charlie, the band, the rest of our group, even Sam surrounded the two of us, keeping us both standing upright. I couldn't believe how quickly the night had turned.

"He killed her!" Harper screamed at the ground, doubling over. "That woman is dead because of me!"

"No! No you don't, Harper! Stop! Just stop it!" I screamed at her, hugging her closely. Hands came from everywhere it seemed, comforting, warm hands were placed on our shoulders, backs and heads, telling us we weren't alone.

"Oh God!" Harper wailed. "That poor woman!"

A police officer came up to our group and we noticed that they'd already begun to tape off the scene. We were asked to step aside to give statements as they brought John to an ambulance and it drove away, sirens screaming toward the hospital.

Harper and I sat on the concrete, watching as they took pictures, pulled my bike into a police trailer, and when they were finally ready for our statements, it was almost two in the morning.

149

While I recounted everything that had happened, I saw two firemen hose the woman's blood off the wide concrete driveway and couldn't believe she was dead. While Harper gave her statement, I stood next to her, her hand in mine and watched the scene around us. Charlie came and stood quietly next to us as did Cherry.

My stomach was queasy and I felt like vomiting every five seconds. And just when I thought things couldn't get any worse, Charlie and I noticed a man about Charlie's age running up to the scene, screaming the name Erica over and over. Two policemen intercepted him and the man fell to his knees when he saw them hosing off the concrete.

"No!" He kept screaming over and over, his hands tucked into his body, he face red at the effort of his screaming.

I prayed that Harper couldn't see him but when her body seized, I knew my hope was for nothing. She looked at me and tears began to stream down her cheeks. I shook my head at her, a silent 'don't'.

The cops told us that Harper needed to come to the station to give a written statement. Charlie and Cherry agreed to meet us there while everyone else agreed to go to Charlie's and wait. It was in this unfortunate moment that I realized that these people were my family. They truly loved me and wanted to be there for me, to support me.

Harper and I climbed into the back of a police car and silently watched the harrowing scene around us. There's something the lights on emergency vehicles do that make an already anxiety filled moment that much worse. As we drove to the station, the radio buzzed with static and updates on calls.

We walked up the steps to the station, Cherry and

Charlie quiet citadels behind us. The station was busy despite the late hour. Phones ringing, loud booted feet stomping the linoleum floor. We sat in benches, waiting to be taken to another room. The double doors to the station opened in a rush, the wind swirling our hair as they brought a cuffed man in.

A cuffed John Bell.

He recognized us immediately.

"I told you I'd find you one day!" He screamed at Harper, struggling to get away from the officers' grips. Instinctively, I hovered my body over hers. "You think to run from *me*?! I'm gonna' to get out of here and when I do, I'm coming after you! Just wait, Harper! Just. Wait!" One of the officers yelled for him to shut up as the other violently tugged him into a nearby hall through a door labeled 'Processing'. "I'm coming for you, Harper!" His voice echoed down the hall. "You're mine! Never forget that!"

Cherry and I covered Harper as her body began to wrack with sobs. An officer from earlier that night named Torres signaled for me to bring Harper into a nearby office. I sat her down and pulled up a chair myself.

"I'm sorry, son, but you have your own statement to write," Officer Torres said. He grabbed an official looking blank document and sat it in front of Harper with a pen. Another female officer sat in a desk opposite her as Officer Torres lead me out and into an adjacent office.

"I'll be right next door, Harper. I'm not leaving you," I said, as she reached for my hand. She nodded.

When both statements were written, we were asked to stay in touch since we didn't have a contact number in case they needed Harper or even my testimony at the trial, if it went that far.

"What will he be charged with?" Harper asked the detective who took the statements.

"We're not sure. Most likely vehicular manslaughter but considering the circumstances around the death," He said, making Harper wince, "he may get second or third degree murder. We'll let you know. Like I said, stay in touch."

"Can he make bail?" I asked, worried about Harper more than anything.

"He can. Unless the judge decides he's a flight risk." Harper began to shake beside me.

"It's okay, Harper," I said, rubbing the goosebumps that formed on her arms.

"He's going to find me," she said to no one.

"No, he won't," I said, we're not listed anywhere. We don't live *anywhere*," I humorlessly laughed. "Please, stop worrying."

"And the judge may consider his threat to you," the detective chimed in. "There is a chance he won't be given bail. Also, depending on the charge, his bail will be set fairly high. You'll just have to wait and see but you can't worry about things that haven't even happened yet. Go home, or wherever it is you go and get some rest. Call us tomorrow afternoon. We should have some answers by then."

"Thank you," I said, leading Harper toward the double doors of the station.

Cherry and Charlie stood on either side of us again but Cherry held Harper's other arm as we descended the steps. Charlie hailed a taxi van and we all climbed in.

Charlie's apartment was bursting at the seams when we walked in. A few had fallen asleep but most had stayed awake, the worry that lined the room was tangible.

"What'd they say?" Aaron asked, folding his arms.

"They took our statements," I answered him while setting Harper on a bit of couch that wasn't taken up by sleeping friends. "They aren't sure what charges will be given but they said we can call up their tomorrow to get a few more concrete answers."

"And who was that guy?" Nat asked. "Do you know him, Harper?"

"Yes," she said. "I used to live with him three foster homes ago. I thought he had been my friend until his insaneness started making an appearance. He's a psychopath." Harper looked up at me. "If only I had told someone about all that he'd done, that woman could be alive right now."

Everyone started to protest but I cut them short. "No, Harper. I told you, you can't blame yourself. You can't be responsible for his actions. Stop blaming yourself. Seriously."

"I can't help it," she said quietly. "I keep seeing her dead eyes staring up at me."

Those who were awake rushed over to her and soothed her with words and hands. I could visibly tell that her heart had lightened at their proximity. It was like they were absorbing her pain through touch. I loved them for this. They loved her for me. They loved her because she was amazing.

Chapter Nine
For The Longest Time

Callum

Harper and I didn't sleep a wink that night but finally succumbed around five o'clock in the afternoon the following Sunday, which worked out nicely as we had an eight o'clock appointment with my advisor, Sylvia, Monday morning. Both of us woke at five in the morning, silently getting ready in Charlie's apartment. Everyone had left sometime after we'd fallen asleep. When I woke, I found a note from Charlie saying he was going to sleep at the studio so we could get some rest. He was so generous to me. Also, we hadn't thought about it before but were awfully grateful that Cherry had our bags brought from her flat to Charlie's.

"Are you ready?" I asked Harper.

"Yes," was her simple answer.

We locked the door behind us and rode the subway toward campus.

A minute into our ride, Harper asked me, "What about your bike?"

"Who cares about the bike, Harper. I'm just glad he didn't hurt you."

"I promise I'll make it up to you," she whispered.

"Absolutely not. You have nothing to make up for, Harper. You owe me nothing. Shit happens, babe."

She smiled slightly. "You're incredible, Callum."

"I'm really not. If I was, I never would have left you alone in the first place."

"I'm not an invalid," the old, sassy Harper said.

"Oh, got your tongue back, have you?" She smiled wider. "We'll figure it out. We always do."

"I can't believe the past few weeks," she said, shaking her head.

"I know. You, kicked from your home, us, working all those weeks just to have our money stolen." Harper shook her head. "That's not your fault either! Then, that psycho comes after you and kills that innocent girl."

"That poor woman," Harper said, shaking her head.

"Her name was Erica," I said.

"I know, the detective told me."

"Her husband," I said, shuddering. "I don't know what I'd do if...I mean, I just don't know what I'd do." Harper grabbed my hand and squeezed hard.

At our stop, we got off the train and headed into the bright morning sun to Sylvia's office. The same punk chick from two weeks before stood up and waved energetically, like we were old friends and she hadn't seen us in a while. Harper waved back politely and she gestured for both of us to sit as she did the time before.

"Can I get you a water or anything?" She asked.

"I'll take a bottle," Harper said, surprising me.

The girl's eyes lit up and she bounded down the hall toward a kitchenette. When she came back she handed Harper a cold bottle of water and a napkin.

"Sylvia's ready for you now," she said, smiling sweetly.

Sylvia's office looked so much different to me now. It was like the past couple of weeks drained a little bit of color out of the way I looked at life. So much had happened and there was no way I thought I could ever get back that little piece of my innocence.

"Callum! Harper!" Sylvia beamed, completely unaware of the events that had transpired since we'd last left her office.

"Sylvia," we both said. Sylvia came around her desk and hugged us both tightly.

"It looked like you both needed hugs," she teased.

We smiled at her thoughtfulness.

"Okay," she said. "Good news! Harper, I've pulled a few strings. You've officially gotten a full ride here." Harper and I perked up at that bit of news. "Don't ask me how I did it," she joked. "A magician never reveals her tricks." Harper and I hugged fiercely and tears appeared in Harper's eyes once more.

"I didn't want to believe it," Harper confessed. "I knew if I got my hopes up that I'd just end up disappointed. Thank you, Sylvia. You have no idea what this means to me." She sucked in a breath to gain some composure. "Thank you so much."

Sylvia grabbed a few tissues from behind her and handed them to Harper. "Please, it was my absolute pleasure. Plus, it's my job to help out students Harper and you are officially a student here. Now, you're going to have to make an appointment with a counselor to figure out what classes you need to take. I found a grant to help pay for your books and supplies. You should be good to go, doll."

Harper looked at me through grateful tears and nodded repeatedly as if in disbelief. 'Thank you' she mouthed.

"Stop," I said, "you're making me feel all gushy inside. I don't do well with emotion."
She laughed and grabbed my hand. We just stared at one another deeply.

"Okay, love birds," she said making Harper and I smile wider. "I'll need Harper to fill out some paperwork. The same, ironically, you filled out last time, Callum."
She removed a stack of papers from her desk and slid them across the desk toward Harper and handing her a pen. Harper eagerly filled them out, making my heart swell with pride for her.

I leaned back in my chair, a small weight lifted from my chest. *Now all we need is a place to live*, I thought. I sat up. I had an idea.

"Sylvia," I began, "is there any way to get a grant to live on?"

Sylvia smiled kindly. "Well, it's too late to apply for housing, Callum. I'm sorry. Why? Do you not have a place to live?"

"No, well, we ran into a bit of bad luck," I said and noticed Harper's pen stop moving for a moment. "It's not a big deal but we basically have nowhere to live."

"Callum, I'm really sorry to hear that," she said sincerely, "but I have nothing to offer you. Housing applications were due at the beginning of summer. It takes several weeks to process them and are only done annually." Harper handed Sylvia her paperwork and she took it, turning her chair and standing before walking over to her filing cabinet. "Unless, you were married," she joked. "Then I could put in an emergency application but..." Sylvia said, turning around with the largest smile on her face, "but you aren't, so."

Sylvia bent to pick up a paperclip she dropped and I peered hard into Harper's eyes, my mouth dropped open. This was it. This was our out. Her eyes opened wide and she started to shake her head but I wouldn't hear of it.

"But we are," I blurted out.
Sylvia stood but stopped in her tracks, seemingly shocked.

"Excuse me?"

I cleared my throat to gain confidence. "I said, we are. Harper and I are marrying next Saturday."

"What?" Her hand flew to her chest. "I'm so sorry! Where are my manners! Congratulations! I had no idea. Well! That changes things a bit," she laughed, sitting back down only to stand right back up. "I have to get a few app's from my cabinet. Hold on."

With her back to us, Harper pinched my shoulder. She threw her hands up in question. 'What are you doing?' She mouthed.

I pressed the air, telling her to hold on but she kept staring at me, shocked. I held my finger up. 'Please,' I silently begged just as Sylvia turned back around.

"Alright," she said. "We'll start the paperwork now. I'll just need the marriage certificate as soon as it's finalized. The sooner, the better. Time is of the essence what with classes starting soon. Let's see." She grabbed her bottom lip between her thumb and forefinger, thinking. "I think I have everything I need for the application already in your files. Yup, just the certificate will suffice." She smiled at us. "Congratulations, you two."

Harper and I filled out the new application then stood to leave, Sylvia wrapped us each in a hug again and we left her office as coolly as possible. Harper waved to punk chick once and we swiftly walked as fast as possible without arising suspicion toward the exit. Harper busted through the large wooden doors, out into the sun.

"What. Was. That.?" She asked.

"Harper, listen. I know it sounds crazy."

"Crazy? I can't marry you! I...I...Why did you tell her that?"

"Harper!" I yelled, edging us toward a few benches near some trees. We were drawing people's attention. Quietly I continued, "Listen, our college is paid for. That's awesome, right? But how are we supposed to attend? We have no money. No prospects. No real jobs. No parents to rely on. We are utterly alone, Harper. It's just you and me. We've got the crap end of the stick our entire lives. Just...think about it."

She shook her head back in forth at the grass below us, her arms folded across her chest. "This is just too crazy, Callum."

"What other choice do we have? Huh? Tell me. How are we going to survive?"

"I don't know," she said honestly, "but this is not the answer."

"I know we haven't figured out all the particulars but this is the *only* way, Harper. You have to see that." She opened her mouth to answer but I cut her off. "No, don't answer. Just promise me you'll think about it?" She closed her eyes and seriously thought for a moment. I began to panic that she would say no.

"Fine," she said. "I promise to *think* about it."

"Thank you," I said, breathing a sigh of relief.

Harper and I worked at the restaurant for lunch, earning three hundred dollars altogether. It was a start. We had the choice of working The Bowery or heading toward The Hope House. We were sick of mooching off our friends so we opted for The Hope House. We sat outside the welcoming doors, not surprisingly the first ones there and settled on the sidewalk, leaning against the stone facade.

"How is this going to work?" She asked.

"Well, we sit here and around five o-clock when the line starts to swell to impossible numbers, we pray that no one tries to knock us from our choice spot."

"Very funny," she said. "I mean the marriage thing."

"I'm not asking for a real marriage, Harper," I said. Her eyes fell to her lap. "I propose an agreement."

"Alright." She brought her eyes to mine. "What are the terms?"

"We stay married until the end of the school year, then annul."

"You can't annul a marriage after a year, can you?"

"Okay, we divorce then but it's not a real divorce, Harper because we wouldn't actually be married. I mean technically we'd be *married* but we wouldn't *practice*," I said, clearing my throat at how uncomfortable the conversation had turned, "practice all the *things* married couples, you know, practice."

"Got it out there, buddy?" She teased.

"Shut up," I laughed, a red blush creeping up my neck and attacking my face. "God, this is embarrassing. Listen, I just want you to know that I wouldn't try to take advantage of you. There would be an understanding between the two of us. We'd live together as roommates, just like before."

"And if we, I don't know, wanted to start dating other people?" She asked, averting her eyes.

Would she want that?

"Um, I don't think that's a good idea, Harper. It's only for a year. Besides, I think we'll both be distracted with school," I offered, hoping she didn't see my obvious attempt at making her stay single when I was around. I couldn't stand the thought of another person liking her the way I did.

"That's not an unreasonable request," she said, shyly smiling back at me.

Oh my God. I think Harper is actually considering marrying me. My heart swelled in my chest and I felt an unbelievable amount of happiness roll over my entire body. Realization donned on me. I felt hot all of a sudden, unsure if I was fake-marrying her for the wrong reasons. Who was I kidding? I wanted to fake-marry Harper for the wrong reasons. *Nothing alarming about that, old chap.*

"Okay, let's just get through this night," Harper said, interrupting the alarming thoughts I cheerfully pretended didn't exist.

"Alright, here, save my seat," I said, standing up.

"Where are you going?" She asked.

I pulled the detective's card from my back pocket and flashed it her way. "Just going to check."

She nodded but I could tell by her tensed body language she was frightened.

"It'll be alright, I promise."

I walked to the payphone just across the street, still within view of Harper and stuck my quarters in before dialing the number on the card.

161

"Detective Mason," he answered.

"Hi, Detective Mason, it's Callum Tate. We just wanted to check on the status of John Bell's case. Have they decided on the charges?"

He breathed hard into the phone. *Not a good sign.* "Yeah, the D.A. decided vehicular manslaughter fit best. Sorry, Callum, I know you were looking for more serious charges considering the circumstances. Erica's family's pretty upset too."

"What about his threatening Harper?"

"Well, since he didn't actually do anything to her, there's nothing much we can do there."

"He threatened her life! And what about all the things Harper told you about when they lived together in the foster home?"

"Again, if she had filed charges then, we'd probably be able to get something on him now but we just can't, Callum."

"So, essentially he has to do something heinous to her in order for you to get involved?" I asked in disbelief.

He sighed loudly again. "No, but he technically didn't do anything directly to Harper. I'm sorry but my hands are tied. This does *not* mean that you shouldn't take his verbal threats seriously. Just be careful.

"Also, listen, he posted bail early this morning."
All the breath seemed to suck from my chest at those words.

"Alright, thanks Detective. Uh, I'll let Harper know."

"Keep her safe, son," he said.

"I promise," was all I could think to say and hung up.

I returned the card to my back pocket and stuck both hands in the front pockets of my jeans, dreading the walk back to Harper. She read my face from across the street and stood, wrapping her arms around her torso,

162

shifting her weight from foot to foot. Tears began to cascade down her beautiful skin.

"No," she simply said. "No, no, no, no, *no!*" She then screamed, bending to sit on her ankles and hugging her knees.

I ran to her, scooping her up into my arms and gathering her to my chest.

"Shh," I said, running the palm of my hand over her hair. "He can't find us, Harper. He can't do anything. He'll *never* be able to find you because I have a plan. You're going to fall off the face of this earth. He will *not* be able to find you."

"H...how?"

"We'll change your last name...to *Tate*."

She withdrew herself slightly and stared into my eyes, gulping hard.

"I'm considering it," she said, then buried her face in my chest once more.

We sat like we had before, but this time she pulled herself practically on top of me for comfort, not that I'd have complained. Her warm body overtook all my senses. All I could hear was Harper, all I could smell was Harper, all I could feel was Harper, all I could see was Harper, all I could *taste*...was Harper. I would do anything for her. I would *die* for her.

I'd only known her a few weeks.

But I was in love with Harper Bailey.

You're in deep, Callum, I thought to myself because I had just asked the love of my life to marry me but did it for all the wrong reasons.

Harper

I had no idea what I was doing. I practically agreed to marry a stranger. Except he wasn't a stranger, was he? He was Callum. Sweet, adorable, amazing Callum. Agreeing to marry him for appearance's sake only felt wrong, though, knowing how I really felt about him. I was falling in love with Callum and marrying him for the wrong reasons made me feel ill to my stomach, knowing I'd only end up breaking my heart in the end.

I knew I would do it, though. As pathetic as that seemed, I know I would. If Callum Tate ever asks you to marry him, you do it whether he loves you or not because he would treat you better than anyone else. I knew how stupid I was being but I literally could not help myself. Never had I ever lead my life with my heart. Why I was doing it now, I didn't know but I couldn't help but wonder if it was because I really did love Callum. It was a self-destructive decision. I had no real sense of self-preservation. *To hell with it.* I'll probably leave the imitation marriage with my heart scattered in pieces at my feet but at least I'll get to know what it feels like to belong to someone, *really* belong to someone, with papers to prove it and everything.

Since we're both using the other to survive is it really using? Yes. It was. I couldn't lie to myself but somehow it didn't *feel* like using. I knew Callum and I would figure it out *together* whether we went ahead with the sham marriage or not. That made me feel a little better about considering his fictitious proposal.

"We can't tell anyone it's fake," I blurted out to him.

"I completely agree. We couldn't let anyone know, not even Charlie or Cherry. It's just not smart if we don't take this all very seriously."

"I know."

"And, uh, I'm not sure how you feel about this but we can't get married in a church. This is not a promise we're making to God, only to the state."

I laughed. "Callum, I know that. Trust me, you've made that very clear. This is not a real marriage," I said, my stomach hurting knowing the pain I was purposely inflicting on myself. What a glutton for punishment.

All the color surprisingly drained from his face. "I'm sorry, I know."

"So, when would we do it?" I asked.

"We would have to apply for a license. It takes several days to process. Then get married on Saturday."

"And we're sure John would never be able to find me?"

"There's no guarantee, Harper. I mean, I'm just betting he's too stupid to check to see if you were married. We can ask about making the records private."

"Okay, and we're just doing this for a year? Just enough to save a few bucks and get our own place?"

"Right, then we get an annulment or divorce, whichever. I just don't see any other way to live while we go to school since we lost our money and I can't sell my bike now."

"You were thinking of selling your bike?" I asked, knowing I never would have ever let him do that.

"Yeah, we didn't have anything else to sell."

"Yes, we did," I said. "My book."

"Absolutely not, Harper. No way! I would never let you do that!"

"It's better to sell the book. It's all we have now, no thanks to me."

"Will you stop blaming yourself? And, no! I'm putting my foot down. No! That book stays in your possession come heck or high water. No, this is our only option."

I sighed loudly. "I think you're right," I said. "We're pretty desperate." I laugh without humor.

Minutes pass in companionable silence.

"Harper?" Callum asked quietly.

"Hmm?" I said, studying Callum's Converse, my head on his chest, his arm around my shoulder.

"Does this mean you'll marry me?" He asked, peeking down at my face.

I felt an embarrassing crimson heat flush spread across my cheeks.

"I think it does," I whispered.

We were both silent for a very long time, our chests heavy with labored breathing. This was it. We were actually going to do it. I couldn't believe myself. This felt like the best and worst decision I'd ever made.

"What do we have to lose?" He asked.

Everything.

"Okay, so we're not acting anymore," he said, thinking. "Well go to a pawn shop, buy a few rings, apply for a license, tell our friends."

I gulped audibly. "When?"

"Today, right now. Why? You got somethin' better to do?"

"No," I nervously chuckled. "Won't we lose our place in line?" I stupidly asked.

Callum eyed me. "Do you want to do this, Harper?"

"Yes," I said with conviction and stood. "Let's go. I think I saw a pawn shop three blocks down."

"I know the one," he said. "We'll try to be back before the doors close and just hope for the best."

"It is The Hope House," I lamely joked, making Callum contort a funny face at its dorkiness.

I laughed.

The pawn shop was old. You could tell the same owner

166

was in possession since the fifties and he still ran the counter.

"How can I help you?" A kindly looking older man asked.

Callum grabbed my hand and smiled down at me. "We'd like a few rings please."

The older man's face brightened as he stood. "No kidding! Well isn't that fantastic. Here. Here," he said gently but excitedly, rounding the corner behind his counter. "The rings are here. Anything in particular you'd like?" He asked.

"I've never thought about it," I said.
This surprised Callum and he shoved his shoulder into mine.

"Well, let's see what we have here," he said.
Callum and I bent over the glass display case and studied the array of rings before us.

"You pick mine," he said.

"Really?" I asked.

"Really, go ahead."
I perused the bands for men and picked a simple white gold band with straight edges and no embellishment whatsoever. It seemed so Callum to me, simple, classic, beautiful.

"This one," I said and pointed to the ring in the case.

The man brought the ring out and set it on top of the glass with a clink. Callum picked it up and examined it before turning to me. His eyes melted me to the floor where I stood, twinkling with happiness.

"It's the one I hoped you'd select," he said, swallowing hard.
I took a deep breath and laid my hand on his forearm.

"And for the bride?" The man asked, shocking us.

"You pick mine," I said, following Callum's lead.

"You don't want to choose your own?" He asked me warily.

"No, I want to see what you'd choose for me as well." Callum bent over the display case, considering all his choices carefully. He sat up and his shoulders sagged a bit.

"I don't like any of these for you," he said sadly.

"It's okay just pick the best one, then."

"No," he said with conviction, making my stomach dip suddenly. "It's not here."

The old man held up a finger and went to the back. He was gone for a good five minutes before finally emerging with a wooden case, setting it on top of the cabinet and opening the lid.

Inside were a crumpled pile of rings. I watched Callum's eyes shoot wide and his hand made a beeline for a ring, buried beneath a few others. I didn't even know how he saw it. I held my breath as he wrestled it from the heap and brought it up to the light above us. I gasped when he brought it down for me to inspect, burning tears threatening the corners of my eyes. It was everything I didn't know I wanted and was shocked into silence at the beauty of it.

The stone was round and framed within many small diamonds. It was art deco inspired, filigree following up the band itself and many more diamonds filled the band as well.

"That is the prettiest ring in this store," the man said, his eyes crinkled with a smile. "My wife found that at an estate sale before she passed away, God bless her." I smiled and my breath sped up as Callum slipped it onto my finger. It fit perfectly.

"Like it was made for you," the old man said happily.

Callum held my hand, sending warm sparks up my arm and into my chest, making my heart beat unnaturally.

"How much do we owe you?" Callum asked without looking from me.

"One hundred and fifty," he said.

Callum and I both turned to the man, stupefied.

"Only one-fifty?" Callum asked.

"Yes, for the gentleman's band," he said.

"But we'll take both," Callum said, gesturing to my ring.

"And I'll *give* you both but my wife would roll over in her grave if she saw me sell a ring that was only meant to be given. Trust me, it is my absolute pleasure."

"I wouldn't feel right," I said. "That's too generous."

"Something tells me generosity isn't a gift you two see very often," he said, not unkindly. "Please, I consider it more a gift to my wife. So, you see? It's mostly selfish."

Callum and I both smiled at the man, in awe of the his consideration for his wife even after she'd left this earth.

"Thank you," we both said, a bit breathless.

"There's a catch," he said, a mischievous glint in his eye.

"What's that?" Callum asked, chuckling.

"Just send me a pic of your family in ten years. Give an old man something to look forward to."

Suddenly I felt very guilty, my stomach fell and I wanted to pull the ring off my finger and flee the store. Callum, sensing my discomfort, grabbed my hand.

"We promise," he said, with suspicious confidence.

Callum

We paid the man, thanked him profusely again and headed straight for the Office of the New York City Clerk. The line to apply for the license was of ridiculous proportions as they handled all living documents, including birth and death certificates. We had been there close to an hour already but Harper and I were grateful just to be able to get out of the sun.

"Dude, this line is worse than The Hope House," I joked, feeling lighter in the chest than I had in a very long time.

She laughed.

They were pumping old hits through the sound system above our heads and Billy Joel's *For The Longest Time* started to play. Harper started to bob her head a little bit and I noticed several other people started tapping their feet or quietly swaying back and forth. I don't know what came over me but I took Harper's bag from her shoulder and set it at our feet. She just stared at me curiously but I refused to give it away, only smiling from ear to ear. I set my own bag down and wrapped an arm around her waist, twisting her into the middle of the hall, making several women around us ooh and awe. I sung the words quietly into her ear, trying not to worry at just how applicable the lyrics were to how I really felt for her. (Look them up, seriously.) And we danced, slowly, achingly slowly.

Her soft skin melted at my touch, malleable beneath my fingers it was so silky, smooth and cool like glass. At a lull in the lyrics, I pressed my nose into her hair and inhaled loudly, causing a breath to hitch in her throat. She drove me crazy, she was so sexy. We swayed around the little hallway, holding on tightly, her hand cupping beautifully in mine.

As the song came to an all too short end, we looked up to see that a few other couples had joined us, creating an impromptu Prom in the middle of a city government office. I dipped her unexpectedly, my hand sweeping around the back of her neck and resting at her throat. I wanted so badly to kiss her. People started clapping and whistling when I brought her back up and Harper and I stood back in line.

"That was...so fun," Harper said, her cheeks pink.

"What can I say? I'm a fun guy."

She laughed and bit her bottom lip, sending me into a frenzy. *Just do it, Callum. Take her lips with yours. Right now.* I ordered myself but became sane at the last second.

I bent to grab Harper's bag just as she did and we met on the floor, our faces close and breathing hard. We came up slowly, pulled into one another's stares. A woman next to us broke our trance.

"Getting married, are you?" She asked.

"Uh, yes," Harper said. "What gave us away?"

"The dancing for one and the way you two look at each other."

Harper and I got slightly uncomfortable when she said that. I don't know how we had gone so far with all the flirtations and near kisses without ever really discussing them. For God's sake, we were standing in a line that handed out marriage licenses! How had we never talked about our true feelings?

We reached the top of the line and waited our turn. My hands began to tremble so I threw them into my front pockets.

"Next!" We heard from a Hispanic woman behind a glass wall.

My feet felt heavy and I drug them to the counter.

"How can I help you?" She asked politely.

"Yes, we'd like to apply for a marriage license," I said with a shaky voice, like she could see what a fraud I was.

"Alright, I need both of your driver's licenses. Fill this out," she said, sliding a single sheet of paper our direction. "It's thirty-five dollars."

Harper began to fill out our information as I pulled my wallet out to pay. The sections she had no idea what to put she left blank and I filled them out after handing over our cash. I got a kick out of the fact that she was memorizing all the information she didn't already know.

"You're middle name is Philip?"

The lady processing our application looked at us strangely, like 'she didn't know that already'? I couldn't help but let the little part of my conscience that didn't think this was a good idea come out screaming but it was brief and I stamped it back into its box. When I was done, I checked over our application and saw that Harper's middle name was Lily. *Beautiful, like her*, I thought.

In less than fifteen minutes, we had a paper license that needed three days to be considered good in our hand, an appointment with a judge Saturday afternoon at three p.m., and a conscience full of tsk's.

"So what now?" Harper asked, folding the license and placing it in the front pocket of her bag.

I took out my pocket watch and glanced at the time. Five fifteen.

"We're a little late but we could try The Hope House. What do you say?"

"Yes, let's at least try. We can tell the gang tomorrow of our plans?"

"I was thinking the same," I agreed.

The line for The Hope House hadn't yet grown the way we thought it might and that was a slight relief. We'd have a chance, at least. When they were shuffling people inside, Harper held on tightly to my arm thinking we'd be left out as usual but when we reached the doors we were just guided in with the rest. Harper's mouth fell open wide and I couldn't help but feel surprised myself. Well, surprise and relief. Relief until we realized that the boys and girls slept in two separate spaces.

"I'd rather sleep in the street than leave you," she said, not realizing, I think, the honesty in what she'd said and giving me hope.

"Harper, it's just one night. We'll be fine," I tried to soothe her but I wasn't so sure myself. I'd gotten used to sleeping near Harper if not directly with her and my chest ached with just the possibility of her absence.

"Alright," she said, sighing as a volunteer there tried to move us along to clear the area.

"Remember," I said as she walked the other direction. "I'm right over here. I'll see you in the morning. Sleep tight."

Harper broke free from the volunteer's light hold on her arm and ran to me, wrapping her arms around my neck.

"Thank you...for everything," she whispered in my ear. "I don't know what I'd do without you. You're my family, Callum." She broke away to join the volunteer, giving me one last look over her shoulder.

I could only stand there, my hand grappled at my chest. I could feel my heart beating furiously against my rib cage. *Just marry her Saturday and you'll figure it all out later*, I told myself.

Chapter Ten
Joy of Man's Desiring

Callum

The next morning, Harper saw me and jumped into my arms.

"I missed you," she said, making me smile.

"I missed you, too. How'd you sleep?" I asked.

"Terribly," she teased and rolled her eyes.

We worked the entire morning at the docks, then the restaurant in the afternoon. In between jobs, Harper and I showered at Cherry's and let her know we'd like to have a little get together that night. She asked us what it was all about but we told her she'd have to wait just like everyone else. Cherry said we could use Charlie's, encouraging us both to come there after the restaurant to help her because she thought, and I quote,

'Announcements always go better with dinner'. We didn't know where she got the impression that it was an 'announcement' but Harper told me girls are freakishly intuitive and I left it at that.

We obeyed Cherry and showed up at Charlie's around three-thirty. Charlie and Cherry were both there and Harper and I both noticed how *friendly* they'd become of late.

"So what's this all about then?" Charlie asked in his impossibly English accent.

"You'll see," I said, holding plates in my hand, following Harper around like a little lost puppy as she placed them neatly on place mats around Charlie's table.

The gang started trickling in around five-thirty and Cherry passed around glasses of wine around as everyone chatted. They were all gracious enough not to mention John for which, I think, we were both grateful.

Then it was time to eat, a few of us sat around the table and up at the bar, the rest on random cushions on the floor near the table and on the couch. Harper and I chose to stand.

"We have an announcement," I said, extremely nervous. Harper placed a hand on my back, offering her support. "Harper and I are marrying."

We were bombarded with absolute silence, a few forks and knives fell on plates in clangs as all turned to stare our direction.

"Now," I continued, "I know this seems rushed but I've never been more sure of anything in my life and it was only a matter of time anyway. We thought it was stupid to wait."

Again, nothing.

Sam broke the quiet. "Oh my God, she's pregnant," she said with disgust.

"No!" I said emphatically. "Harper is *not* pregnant."
Harper snorted.

"But you've only known her for a few weeks!" Sam
said, whining out the last word.

I looked around, locking eyes with Charlie as he
processed the information I'd just laid on them. Then he
came full circle and stood.

"Congratulations, Callum," he said, slapping me on the
back and hugging me fiercely. He grabbed Harper's little
frame and hugged her just as tightly before pulling away.
He placed a hand on each of our shoulders and looked us
both in the eye. "This is wonderful news!"

And the dam broke. A sea of sincere congratulations
came gushing over us,

Cherry hugged me tightly and whispered in my
ear. "A very good choice, Callum."

I felt slightly guilty for the lies I was spewing but when I
really thought about it, it didn't feel like a lie. I truly
wanted to marry Harper despite how crazy it seemed.

Unexpectedly, Sam stood in a rage.

"This is ridiculous, Callum! You cannot marry someone
you just met! This is just stupid!" Sam yelled.

Harper shrunk into my side slightly, fisting her hands in
my shirt, sending a slew of butterflies swarming around
my insides. I gritted my teeth at Sam.

"You're too young!" She continued, the
waterworks at full force. "This isn't you! She did
something to you! Why are you doing this?"

"Enough!" We heard Charlie say behind us. "Sam, can I
talk to you in the hall please?"

Sam's face softened but not entirely as she followed
Charlie out the door.

A few minutes passed by and the awkwardness Sam
had caused, seemed to have left with her. I was stunned

at how everyone supported us. No one seemed to feel the same way Sam did. I was flabbergasted, to be honest. I expected more of an upset than this. I expected to spend a few hours convincing but instead Cherry popped a bottle of champagne and started to pouring it into glasses.

Charlie entered the apartment once more with a tear soaked shirt and I felt badly for Sam for a moment but knew she would get over it eventually. Getting over things quickly was her specialty actually. Sam huffed over to the side table by the sofa and grabbed her purse and jacket.

"Sam," I said, grabbing her arm. "Don't leave. Everything will be okay, you'll see."

"No it won't!" She threw harshly at me. "You're making a huge mistake. I don't know why you're doing this but I can promise you, you'll regret it." Then she walked to the door and slammed it shut behind her.

I didn't want to think about her any longer so I pushed my way through my friends toward my solitary stress reliever named Harper. She was talking and laughing with Charlie and Cherry and I stopped to watch her a bit. She was breathtaking to me. She'd decided to wear her striped dress again but went barefoot, her hair soft and wavy down her back, cascaded slightly off her shoulders. Her eyes struck me breathless, they were sparkling so under the lights of Charlie's apartment. She caught me staring and smiled, extending her hand to me. I swiftly walked her direction and took it in mine.

"So when is the big day?" Cherry asked.

"Saturday," I said, tucking Harper deeper into my side, she leaned slightly back to get a good view of my face and smiled.

"Saturday!" Cherry said, making everyone around her

jump. "How are we going to throw a wedding in less than a week?!"

"Oh, we're just going to the courthouse. It's not a big deal," Harper said warmly.

"Not a big deal! Just a minute, let me get the other girls over here." She turned. "Kelly! Marty!" They were laughing while they came over to stand beside us.

"What's up?" Kelly asked.

"Did you know that Harper and Callum are marrying this Saturday?"

"What? Why?" Marty asked.

"Because we just want to get it done and over with before school starts," I said. Not a total lie.

"Done and over with?" Cherry asked, disgust evident on her face. "Wait a minute! Did you even get her a ring, baby?"

"Of course I did!"

Cherry grabbed Harper's left hand and brought it toward her face. All three girls gasped loudly, cooing over how beautiful they found it.

"Well, at least you did that right," Cherry teased. "Fine. We got our work cut out for us ladies." And with that, she stepped between Mary and Kelly, linking arms and lead them to the kitchen.

"What in the world are they doing?" Harper asked before noticing Cherry stamp her foot near the end of the kitchen.

"Uh, I believe that foot tap is for you, Harper," Charlie said, laughing.

Harper sighed but couldn't hide her smile. I stared as Harper retreated to the lion's den. She peered over her shoulder, waiting for me to intervene but I raised my hands and shook my head. She stuck her tongue at me but joined the girls in a giant laugh.

"Quite a big step from a few days ago," Charlie said matter-of-factly.

"I know it seems like we're rushing and in all honesty we are a bit."

"A bit?" Charlie nearly yelled but his mile wide smile let me know he was only half-joking. "You're not a stupid man, Callum. If you feel this is right for you than I trust you. We *all* trust you."

His complete trust in me gave my stomach a sharp pain. I felt like we were duping them all and we were but it didn't feel as dishonest as it really was. That scared me. I knew I should feel worse about it than I was but it felt natural to marry Harper, too natural.

"It's decided!" Cherry comes out. "Van agreed to barricade the The Bowery's roof top Saturday night for free. We have a place to celebrate!" Everyone stood and cheered, much to my dismay. I was worried that Harper would feel badly about it but she looked happy from where I stood. I was grateful to Cherry for being so thoughtful.

Harper

I could not believe how amazing these three girls were being to me. It was a lovely testament to how much they loved Callum.

"Okay, you," Cherry said pointing to Marty. "Call Van and ask him to shut off the rooftop for this coming Saturday. Tell him it's for Callum and Harper."

"On it," Marty said cheerfully, skipping to Charlie's wall phone.

Spritely Kelly jumped up and down giddily. "Oh, please, Cherry. Give me a task!"

"Alright, call Benny at the theater and ask him if they still have those pretty string lights from the boat scene in *Roman Holiday* last year. You know, the one with large bulbs?"

"Yup, I remember. Got it."

"Okay, let's see," Cherry said, pinching her bottom lip between her fingers. She snapped. "The dress! Do you have a dress?"

"No, but I don't need one," I said, feeling slightly embarrassed and very guilty.

All three girls turned to me, mouths agape.

"No!" Cherry said, turning to Kelly. "You're about Harper's size. Still have that white silk slip dress from *The Great Gatsby*?"

"I do!" She gasped. "Oh, that would be so perfect! What size shoe do you wear?"

"Uh, a seven."

"Oh, phooey!" She said. "Oh well. We'll work something out. I'll search Costumes. They won't even know." She winked at me.

I couldn't believe my ears. These women were throwing my fake wedding together in practically no time at all. If I wasn't so amazed, I'd be ashamed.

"You really don't have to do all this," I protested.

Cherry furrowed her eyebrows. "Oh, hush, Harper!" She admonished before slapping me on the rear, making me yelp. "Okay! No veils. Let's see. Oh! Do you guys remember that feather butterfly fascinator I wore for The Ivories' photo shoot three years ago?"

"Oh that's *perfect*!" Marty exclaimed, hanging up the phone. "The Bowery is all ours for the night, by the way."

"So are the lights," Kelly said dramatically, moving to lean against the counter, tossing her cell aside and theatrically placing her arms on either side of her in a very melodramatic pose.

"Are you an actress?" I asked Kelly.

"Of course, honey. It's the only thing that can

explain my odd behavior."

I laughed into the back of my hand. She was so right and very cute.

"Alright," Cherry said, her eyes bright, rubbing her hands together conspiratorially. "Cross's girlfriend, Linda, works at that bakery on Ninth. She'll whip something up for us. She's fantastic by the way," Cherry said, turning to me. "Is there any flavor you'd prefer?"

"I don't care but I know that Callum's favorite is lemon."

All the girls smiled slowly at me. I'd surprised myself with that one, blushing a crimson red.

"Okay, we'll have to scrounge up a suit for Callum but that shouldn't be too difficult. Can we think of anything else?" Cherry asked us.

"Flowers?" I said without thinking. I slapped my hand over my mouth, making the girls burst out laughing.

"Tie-Dye Tom has that one," Marty said absently.

"Seriously?" I asked.

"Yeah, he works in the flower market mornings. That's his day job. He's really talented, too. I told him so once and he told me he'd kill me if I ever said anything like that out loud again. Oops." Kelly giggled and we all followed suit.

"Alright, good work girls. We've got a dress, cake, reception venue, pretty lights," Cherry said, winking at Kelly, "flowers. Marty, who's that photographer ex of yours again?"

"Oh, Eric?"

"Think you could...?"

"Oh, he's so there. We're still friends." I could also tell she wished it was still more.

"The Bowery will provide the tunes," she jested, elbowing me softly. "Do you have a song, Harper?"

I was caught off guard to realize that we did. "*Please Don't Go* by Barcelona."

"Oh yeah," all three girls sighed before bursting into laughter again.

"I'll tell Van," Marty said. "Gah! I almost forgot! Van said, as a wedding gift, he'd provide, and I quote, 'a few morsels and some bubbly'."

"I almost forgot!" Kelly chimed in suddenly. "We'll get Tom to play his acoustic for the processional." I almost cried at everyone's generosity. I wanted to bolt from the room and tell Callum we couldn't take advantage of them like that but knew it was what we had to do in order to live and for John never to be able to find me. I didn't have a choice and my heartfelt oddly light and heavy all at the same time. What a riddle.

"What time is the ceremony?" Cherry asked

"Three p.m. We're the only marriage he has that day," I said.

"We'll get the judge to meet us at The Bowery then."

"I doubt he'll do that," I said. "Why? Do you know someone who knows someone?"

They all laughed.

"No," Cherry said, "but never underestimate the power of a red head." She winked devilishly and I couldn't help but laugh.

"I'd love to see you pull it off," I teased.

"What's his name?" She asked.

"Judge Ryder."

"Just let me handle it," she said and somehow I believed she'd do it.

"We're done," Cherry said, slapping her hands together in a swiping motion. "See? Harmless."

"You just planned my wedding in less than an hour," I stated, flabbergasted. "And it didn't cost a dime!"

"I know!" Marty said, hugging herself. "It pays to know creatives, Harper. We may not be able to do your taxes but we can throw one *heck* of a wedding."

I smiled, knowing this was probably going to be one of the best days of my sad, lonely life.

Thursday rolled around and Cherry told me she got the judge to meet us at The Bowery and that Robert, yeah, *Robert*, and his wife Karol would be attending. I should have known that she'd be able to pull it off.

Friday came a little too quickly for my taste. Callum and I stayed our nights at The Hope House, working mornings and lunches earning roughly three hundred a day. Since Monday we'd saved fifteen hundred and that made us both feel a little bit more secure.

Friday night, Cherry insisted we have a girl's sleepover at her house and watch wedding themed films. Callum would stay at Charlie's. The whole thing was shockingly too much like a real wedding to me and I often found myself tamping down guilty feelings.

Not surprisingly, Sam wouldn't be able to attend the slumber party or the wedding as she was 'visiting family' in Idaho over the weekend and couldn't possibly reschedule. That was like music to my ears. I didn't really want someone who believed we were making a mistake there. Even if we were, it was our mistake to make. Period.

Cherry made popcorn and she, Kelly, Marty and I dressed in pajamas and watched *The Princess Bride, The Wedding Singer, My Big Fat Greek Wedding*, (Cherry suggested Father Of The Bride but I turned that down for obvious reasons) and at my insistence *Corpse Bride.* They all scoffed at the last choice but none could disagree Callum was marrying the perfect bride, which made me squirm a little in my seat. We gave each other manicures and pedicures, talking and giggling all night. The other girls painted their nails wild colors to match their equally wild outfits but I wanted a natural look and only painted a pale, pale pink to mine.

The late morning sun woke me after a good six hours of sleep, from what I could tell which surprised me as I thought I wouldn't be able to sleep at all. It seemed I was the last to wake up. I could hear their soft giggling from Cherry's closet/dining area.

"She's perfect for him," Marty whispered.

"I know. It seems impulsive but I know my Callum. He's made a most perfect choice," Cherry chimed in.

"I love her already," Kelly said. "I'm so happy Callum found her. He was so lonely for so long." Cherry and Marty mumbled in agreement. "It seemed no matter what we did to make him feel a part of our little family he never really committed to us the way we wanted. Harper has changed his confidence. I thought Callum was amazing before but now there's not a thing in this world I can imagine that could possibly stop that boy from being extraordinary now that he's with her."

They were quiet for a moment and I figured that was as good a time as any to let them know I was awake so I made an exaggerated noise before standing and stretching.

"She's up!" Cherry said and all three girls sprinted toward me like it was an annual shoe sale at Loehmann's. She turned me toward her bathroom and shoved me gently. "Get in the shower. We only have four hours to get ready." I obeyed. Cherry meant business.

The shower was lovely but not super warm. I noticed the other girls had already showered and done their hair.

Each was perfectly styled and fit them beautifully. I stepped out, wrapping a towel around myself. I leaned over the sink to brush my teeth, water dripping down my legs and back and I realized I'd have to kiss Callum today. I started to panic and dropped my brush in the sink. I picked it back up and brought it back to my mouth with shaking hands. I brushed longer than my shower had taken. *Silly girl.* Before I could even finish, though, Cherry came bursting through the door, taking me by surprise. I squealed like a little girl.

"How long are you going to brush your teeth, girl? They're clean alright! It's not like it's the first time you've ever kissed! Jeez!"

"You were *listening*?" *And it is the first time I'll be kissing him!* Suddenly I was more nervous about the kiss then I was about the actual getting hitched. Figure that out.

"Of course! Didn't I mention we have precious little time? Come on!" She dragged me to her little vanity area in her dining room and sat me in the velvet cushioned stool.

I looked at myself in the mirror and started to freak out a little. My hair was still wet, not a stitch of makeup, and I was completely naked underneath my towel. I was about as little prepared to get married as humanly possible. I began to wring my hands.

"No worries," Marty said, squeezing my shoulder. "Now! Blow dryer! Stat!"

Cherry, Marty and Kelly went into a mission like mode, buzzing around me like someone had just kicked their hive. Marty didn't say a word while drying my hair and it seemed like it took forever but when I glanced at the clock only fifteen minutes had passed. It was going to be a long day.

Kelly took over where Marty left off, a bright gold curling iron in her hand. She began to fashion spiral curls that tapered to the middle of my back.

"I learned this from our hair girl at the theater. It took a lot of practice," she said, laying a warm curl against my skin. "You're hair looks like copper, Harper."

"That's what Callum always says."

"Does he now?" She teased, wagging her brows up and down.

I blushed profusely. I knew there were going to be sex jokes this day but I didn't think they were going to start that early. I figured they'd come right about the time the champagne started flowing.

"Stop, Kelly," I laughed. "Don't you dare!"

Cherry pulled a chair up to my side, grabbing my hands in hers, seriousness was written all over her face.

"Now, Harper. When a man and woman get married..." she started and I pulled my hands free, covering my face. All three of us started to bust up.

"Callum's never done it with anyone before," Marty said, matter-of-factly flipping through a magazine.

"Marty!" We all yelled.

"What? He hasn't. It's written all over him." She looked at me pointedly. "He hasn't, has he?"

I cleared my throat, turning another dangerous shade of red. *I'm going to look like a lobster in the photos*, I thought. "I'm not at liberty to say," I said cryptically or maybe not so cryptically.

"I knew it!" Marty laughed throwing her head back. "What about *you*?" She asked.

Cherry could tell how uncomfortable I was becoming. "Marty," she admonished. "We're vexing Harper."

"No, it's okay. I'm not *experienced* either." Once I said so, all of the girls' faces turned expressionless.

"What?" I asked, feeling shy all of a sudden. I sunk slightly into my shoulders.

"That's nothing to be ashamed of," Cherry said.

"I'm not," I said and she winked.

When Kelly was done with my hair, I stood closely to the mirror. "I don't think my hair has ever looked this beautiful," I said honestly. "Thank you, Kelly." I hugged her fiercely, a tear beginning to slip.

"Stop, you're going to make me cry," she said, already crying. "Turn around, I need to spray it." I obeyed and she sprayed them in place but not too much because I told her my hair held curl well and I didn't want to look like plastic.

Kelly also did my make-up, a trick of her trade she told me. She sat me in the stool, facing her and took out a large bag, splaying out its insides on the table. I gulped at the quantity she owned.

"Calm down, Harper. It's not all going on you," she teased. She picked a few colors out and got to work. "I think I'll do gold for the eyes. What do you think girls?"

"Oh, definitely," Marty agreed. "Just like her eyes. Make it smoky looking." Kelly nodded her agreement.

"She doesn't really need much for the cheeks," Cherry said. "Her skin is perfect. Ugh. So jealous." I smirked at her.

"Do a natural glossy lip," Marty said, "or it'll clash with the eyes."

Once Kelly was done, all three girls stood, eyeing me carefully. "The fascinator," she said. Cherry left and came back with the most beautiful netted head piece with feathered butterflies on the band. It made me gasp it was so beautiful. Cherry and Marty pinned it to my head, folding the slanted net over my face. I tried to turn and look but Cherry stopped me.

"Not yet," she said. "Let's complete the look first. Stand up for me, baby." She whipped out a very light blue silky piece of underwear. It looked like a piece of scrap. She bent and held it open for me to slide my feet into. I laughed out loud.

"You're going to put my underwear on me?" I asked.

"Yes, unless you want to do it but you'll have to remove your towel and I can't have you move yet or you'll see yourself. Expose yourself or have me slip them on. Your choice."

"Fine," I sighed as she slipped them up my legs.

"Lotion," Marty said, handing a big bottle to Cherry. They both lathered their hands and started applying it to my legs.

"I can't believe I'm not embarrassed by this," I said, laughing.

"Meh, we're girls. Who cares," Marty said, finishing up my right leg.

Kelly left to the closet and pulled out a garment bag hanging on the door.

"The dress," she said dramatically, smiling from ear to ear.

"We'll have to tape her first," Marty said.

"Tape?" I screeched.

"Yes, you can't wear a bra with this dress. It's backless," she said like I was goofy in the head. I'd tried the dress on once and it fit perfectly but didn't even think about undergarments. I blushed slightly as I applied the nude colored tape to my breasts awkwardly under my towel.

Then they slipped the velvety soft silk garment over my extended arms and it cascaded over my figure and toppled to the floor. The only thing Kelly could find in my size in Costumes that wouldn't clash with my dress were a pair of white Dupioni silk ballet slippers with a satin ribbon that laced up my calf. They were comfortable and elegant and so unbelievably beautiful.

When the look was complete, the girls stood back a bit and admired their handiwork. All three started tear up, smiling at one another. Cherry did a little jump.

"Turn around, Harper," she said.

I turned slowly, a little afraid of what I'd see but was stunned to see that I actually looked beautiful. I couldn't believe how well they had thrown me together like this. The dress was white silk, a nineteen-twenties inspired floor length slip dress with a slight train. The sleeves gathered at the shoulders and twisted like pieces of rope that criss-crossed in the back. It was form fitting and hugged my hips and chest perfectly. I lifted my dress slightly to expose the lace that ribboned up my calves.

"You're stunning, Harper," Cherry said, a hiccup in throat.

All the girls came to stand beside me and we admired my slippers, gown, head piece, hair and makeup.

"Let's see," Marty said. "We have something old in the gown, something new in the underwear." We all laughed. "We have something borrowed in the shoes. What's her something blue?" She asked.

"The underwear!" Cherry laughed making us all giggle yet again. "It's working double-time. I thought of everything."

We stood still for a few minutes before a knock at the door startled us.

"That better not be Callum," Kelly teased.

Cherry skipped to the door, giddy no doubt at her workmanship. She peeked through the peephole. "It's Tom!" She squealed and threw open the door.

189

Tom had anticipated we'd all be right there because no matter where you stood in the studio you could see the door so he had posed like 007. His right hand at the top of the door jamb, his left at his chin, a hilarious smolder on his face. As goofy as he was, he looked incredibly debonair in a black suit and thin tie.

Cherry whistled and Kelly, grabbed my hand like she had just really noticed him for the first time and needed assistance standing. *Hmm.*

"Tom!" I said. "You look like a million bucks, man!" He winked but when he noticed me he stopped and clutched at his chest.

"Callum is one incredibly lucky man, Harper. You look like a cross between a Shakespearean fairy and a character from The Great Gatsby. You're stunning," he said, but I noticed he briefly drunk Kelly in. He quickly brought his right hand behind his back and stepped my direction. He stood a few feet in front of me, before presenting a bouquet of light pink ranunculus with a simple white Dupioni silk band around the stems. I gasped.

"Oh, Tom!" I said and hugged him fiercely. I caught a hitch in my throat. "I do not know how I could ever repay you for this! For any of this," I said to everyone around me.

"Just be good to Callum," Tom said. "That's all we could ever want."

I nodded, smiling.

Tom straightened. "I had several assignments. The flowers, the processional, and I am also here to escort you lovely ladies in my kickin' Sixty-Five Imperial because that's the kind of guy I am I guess. I bring hot ace women to weddings apparently."

Callum must have thought about that. I really thought we

were going to have to ride the subway to The Bowery. It was laughable now that I really thought about it.

I took Tom's hand and we started walking toward the door but Cherry stopped us.

"Wait!" she said. "Perfume!" She ran to her vanity and picked up a bottle of perfume. "Stand back Tom, unless you want to smell like a fabulous woman all night." He quickly hedged toward the door. Cherry spritzed my body twice then placed a dab on my wrists and behind my ears. "You're good to go."

"What is that?" I asked, breathing in its heavenly scent.

"It reminded me of you," she said. "It's got bluebells, persimmon, lily of the valley and eglantine. It's very elegant. Do you like it?"

"I love it," I said, almost drunk on its unbelievably yummy bouquet.

All five of us piled into Tom's most awesome Imperial and rode in laughter and fun to The Bowery. We were half an hour early but I preferred it that way.

"I can't believe you're not wearing Tie-Dye, Tom," I said.

"Oh, but I am," he said, yanking down the collar of his dress shirt to reveal a yellow tie-dye t-shirt, making us all lose it in the laughter department. It was going to be quite a happy day.

It was weird to walk into my place of work in a wedding dress but I just laughed at how I couldn't believe any of the stuff that had been happening to me lately had been happening. We walked up the steps to the rooftop. Cherry shielded my eyes as she wanted it all to be a surprise and led me to the ancient greenhouse. The glass was so old you couldn't see out and I was told to stay put while they readied everything outside. There was a little broken corner of glass on the door and it allowed me to see who was coming. I didn't expect anyone but was pleasantly surprised when I saw a few of our co-workers from The Bowery as well as the restaurant, including Martin and Rodrigo. I saw Van scrambling around a little bit and wondered what in the world he could be so flustered about. I saw our entire group of friends pass by. I saw a few people I had no idea who they were but figured they knew Cherry or Charlie or any of the others. I saw a few of the bands who would open for The Ivories often. There were a lot of people. I just had no idea they would have showed so last minute. Finally, I saw Judge Ryder in his robe and a lovely older woman I could only assume was his wife, Karol.

My heart jumped in my throat a little when I could hear Tom playing a soft melody on his acoustic as people arrived.

"Oh no!" I said out loud to no one, bringing my hand to my face. "Who's going to walk me down the aisle?"

"I am," Charlie stage whispered through my peep hole before laughing, startling me. He opened the door and shut it behind him quickly. He shook his head as he took me in. "My God, Harper. You are a vision."

"Thank you," I smiled.

"You don't mind?" I asked.

"It would be an absolute honor," he crooned in his charming English accent.

"Thanks, Charlie," I said hugging him.

"Your Callum is a nervous wreck," he said, his eyes crinkling in laughter.

"What?" I said, holding him at a distance to see his face.

"He is. He's beside himself. Pacing back and forth downstairs. I've just left him. I made him take a shot of whiskey to calm his nerves. I don't think it worked. He's too geared up."

Oh no! He's having second thoughts! Charlie noticed my beginning panic and put a stop to it.

"Not you too!" He laughed. "Stop worrying, miss. This is meant to be." He said it with such conviction I almost fainted. *Were we?* I was starting to believe we were.

Tom started to play *Jesu Joy of Man's Desiring* softly on his guitar and I could hear the crowd settle down. I began to hyperventilate a little but Charlie just grabbed my hand firmly and squeezed, wrapping it around his left arm.

"Enjoy this, Harper," he told me and I felt my heart rate calm to a normal level at his words.

Someone knocked lightly on the door and that was our cue. The door opened and I grabbed my bouquet as we began to walk out. Cherry was there and kissed my cheek before fixing my slight train then walking up the sides to sit up front next to the other girls. Charlie and I walked to the middle of the rooftop and turned right to head down the makeshift aisle.

And it hit me all at once.

Fifty white garden chairs flanked the middle of the aisle. Along the row of chairs at the center were incredible swooping garlands of peonies, ranunculus, miniature roses, and antique roses. The garland was fastened to the top corners of the chairs with exquisite bands of feathered butterflies. Scattered on the dark stonework, were thousands of antique rose petals. Balls of white pomanders seemed to float at different heights around the outside of the chairs, held up by iron stakes.

Charlie gently lead me down the aisle, the fragrance of the flowers assaulting me with euphoria. I couldn't help but smile as my eyes followed to the judge, standing beneath a simple chuppah. Hundreds of thin branches were tied to four large wooden posts. Woven within the thin branches were bunched, beautiful light pink flower bouquets. The canopy was a thin draping satin tied at the four corners, a foot beneath the tops of the posts. It dipped slightly in the middle almost reaching the judge's head and swayed lightly in the wind. It looked sweet and intimate, like a scene from *A Midsummer Night's Dream.* Tom had outdone himself. One of the girls must have gone to Chinatown and bought every white paper umbrella they had because each woman there held one to shield themselves from the sun. It was a feast for the eyes. A picture of elegance. A delicate piece of art.

Every chair was filled and many had to stand to the side. I was surprised to know that I knew most of these people. They were people who touched my life every day. I had no idea Callum and I were so loved.

I quickly moved my gaze to drink in Callum, standing strong and sure by the judge. He wore black, a suit similar to Tom's, vintage nineteen-sixties, a thin black tie. He looked astonishingly handsome. I tried to tell myself that he wasn't really mine but, for the moment, I just wanted to pretend.

When he saw me, his eyes widened, sending a private charge through my entire body. I locked eyes with him and he became the only one on that entire rooftop and I knew, despite the fact it was probably the dumbest thing I'd ever do, that I would be making a promise to a God I didn't think really existed until that moment. It was a private arrangement between Him and I.

Callum

Watching Harper come down the aisle left me gasping for air. She was *devastating*. I never imagined a woman could look as beautiful as she did in that moment. I had to stop myself from wanting to tear down the aisle and grab her just to be that much closer to her that much sooner. I wanted to beg her to be mine in the most real sense. I wanted her as my wife. No more pretending, no more deception. I wanted honesty and she was it.

I knew I would be promising my God to love and honor her regardless of what she wanted. I vowed to make her fall in love with me like I loved her or die trying. It was extreme. I knew it but I didn't care. I knew what I wanted and I wanted her.

Charlie brought Harper to me, unwrapped her arm from his and gave me her hand. I felt an instant calming relief when her warm hand fit inside mine. I gathered her hand and wrapped it around my own arm before turning us towards the judge. I never took my eyes from her nor did she take hers from mine. We stood at each other's mercy but we refused to turn away. We simply couldn't.

The judge began to speak and though I listened, nothing quite absorbed until he spoke my name and asked me to repeat after him.

With my eyes still on hers, I vowed myself to Harper. "I, Callum Philip Tate, take you, Harper Lily Bailey, to be my wife, to have and to hold from this day forward, for better or for worse, for richer, for poorer, in sickness and in health, to love and cherish, from this day forward until death do us part." *I promise this in God's name.* Then, I placed Harper's gifted ring on her slender finger. Harper sucked in a sharp breath, overcome and swayed slightly. I held her tightly to me and waited for her to repeat the words.

Harper

"I, Harper Lily Bailey, take you, Callum Philip Tate, to be my husband, to have and to hold from this day forward, for better or for worse, for richer, for poorer, in sickness and in health, to love and to cherish, from this day forward until death do us part." *I promise this in God's name.* Then, I placed Callum's ring on his strong hand.

Callum

My heartfelt lighter than it ever had. In the back of my mind, I knew my parents, her parents, should have been there but such was life and we don't always get what we want, do we? *But then again, sometimes we do.*

Judge Ryder had us turn to face him but we were still so unable to keep from staring at the other.

"By the powers vested in me, by the State of New York, I now pronounce you husband and wife. You make kiss your bride, Callum" he said happily with red puffy cheeks.

This was it. My lips had just pledged an oath to her and to my God and it needed sealing.

My first kiss with Harper and it was as husband and wife. I exhaled the breath I'd been holding and faced a stunning Harper. Her face was full of emotion, her cheeks flushed, her lips moist, her eyes bright. Both our chests were heaving with labored breaths. I had anticipated this more than anything since I'd met her. Her lips beckoned mine.

I slowly ran my fingers through her curls, sliding them off her bare shoulders and watched as the clean spirals bounced before resting on her back. I brushed her bangs back before cupping my hands on either side of her face, holding her jaw and moved achingly slowly toward her beautiful mouth. I watched her glinting eyes until the last possible second, wanting to drink in every single thing she was feeling.

Her breath was sweet and warm and I could feel her panting slightly as I moved closer and closer. This was real, no longer a flirtation. Today we would be closing the gap.

I captured her mouth severely at first and my knees almost buckled beneath me. I closed my eyes in drunken ecstasy, softening immediately, savoring every taste, every sweet flavor she possessed. I sunk into her body, running my hand to the back of her neck, sliding it slowly down her back, gripping her waist and bringing her tightly into me. She had to have felt my desperation for her but I didn't care. She silently answered a plea of desperation of her own when her hands squeezed tighter around my shoulders and I moaned lightly at the pleasure of it.

Her body leaned back and I hovered over her, holding her body close to mine with the same hand at her waist. Her hands fisted into my collar in a mad attempt to bring me as close as possible. A slight slip of her tongue met mine and I visibly shivered in happiness.

We were forced to break the kiss when the judge cleared his throat, reminding us we weren't alone. We both stood, dazed and consumed by the other. I was snapped back to reality by furious clapping and shouting. I smiled at Harper and she smiled back, her eyes brilliant in the setting sun.

"Ladies and gentlemen! I present to you, Mr. and Mrs. Callum Tate!" The judge roared over the crowd only making them shout louder.

Harper and I ran down the middle aisle as our guests threw handfuls of dried lavender over our heads, the scent was incredible and I knew I'd never forget all the overwhelming sensations that presented themselves to me that day.

Chapter Eleven
When We First Met

Harper

We ran into the little glass greenhouse as our guests continued to roar.

"We did it," he said, exasperated, leaning against the door and laughing.

"I know!" I squealed.

He grabbed me to him and hugged me mercilessly, kissing my neck and swinging me around in a circle. He placed me back onto the ground and we stood there, staring, daring the other to do *it* again. I almost did but a knock came at the door and we were greeted by Charlie and Cherry.

We exchanged hugs and laughed, Cherry and I wiping tears from our eyes.

"Good job," Charlie said to both of us. "I'm very proud of you."

"That kiss!" Cherry said, fanning herself, making us both blush. "Come on," she said, grabbing our hands and leading us to the 'reception area'.

Off to the vast side of the rooftop, eight rectangular tables formed a giant 'L' around a makeshift dance floor. Soft music pumped through the speakers and we joined the rest of our guests with appropriate 'thank you for coming's'.

Judge Ryder came up to us to sign our license and the photographer caught the moment on film making me feel so conflicted inside I felt sick. We thanked him, encouraged him to stay but he said he and Karol needed to get home.

The tables were breathtaking, earthy arrangements that matched my bouquet and the flowers used in the ceremony lined the centers, leaving no gaps between. Large pillar candles were lit inside antique lanterns nestled within the generous arrangements. The tables were set with the plain white china I knew belonged to The Bowery when they used to serve dinners fifty years ago. It was all so dazzling it made me dizzy. Champagne flutes sparkled in the candlelight, begging for their drink.

Callum squeezed my hand in disbelief and we silently made it our mission to find Tom.
He was hovering near Kelly and not so subtly watching her. When he saw us coming, he straightened up and bounded our way.

"What do you think?" He asked non-chalantly.

I hugged him tightly around his neck, kissing his cheek. I was openly crying and told him out right how I felt. "I am speechless Tom. This is magazine worthy. I just cannot tell you what this means to me. You have given us the greatest gift in your generosity. Thank you so much." I sucked in a breath at the emotion.

He pulled me from him to look at my face. "Thank you, Harper but I did have help. All the ladies at the market chipped their time in for free when they heard about what I was going to do for the both of you. The flowers were free, darlin'. Courtesy of the market."

"I'll be sure to come down and thank them," I said.

"Oh, those old bats love it," he teased. "Look what happens when they have creative freedom. They're very talented!"

"As are you," I winked.

He was gracious enough to accept with a nod and we were turned around by more guests. Martin and Rodrigo!

"Harper, you are sight! Aphrodite herself would cast you down in jealousy," Martin said, hugging me tightly, then Callum. "Congratulations."

"Thank you, Martin," Callum said.

We heard the buzz of a microphone somewhere and Charlie's complaining that no one could hear him.

"May I have your attention?" He said into the microphone. "I'm sure you're all as hungry as I am but I've been told by that lovely red head over there," he said, pointing at Cherry. She blushed and shook her head, "that I need to 'suck it up' because Callum and Harper's first dance as a married couple must, and I quote, be while the sun completely sets."

Everyone laughed and clapped as Callum drug me to the dance floor and swung me in a tight circle as Barcelona's *Please Don't go* began to play. He held me firmly and slowly guided me around the stone dance floor, my hand in the palm of his as he held it securely to his chest, my other hand around his neck. I leaned my face into the side of his neck as he sang softly into my ear the wonderfully delicious lyrics.

Suddenly, the strung lights Kelly had arranged for burst on over the dance floor. It was incredible and left us awestruck as we heard the ooh's of the guests around us.

Callum stopped and whispered in my ear, "I've never seen a woman look as beautiful as you do right now, Harper Tate." My breath caught in my chest, striking me mute. "Shall we give them a little show?" He teased, a glint in his eye. I gulped, expecting him to kiss me but was disappointed only for a moment when he didn't because my heart rate picked up as he lead me around the dance floor dramatically, like a professional dancer, making me forget all about my missed kiss.

"Kelly made me take lessons with her last year for a role she was trying to get. She didn't, by the way," he offered my dumbstruck expression as he effortlessly guided me around the stone.

At the last note, he dipped me dramatically and kissed my neck. The guests howled in elation. He picked me up and I felt dizzy, gripping tightly onto his forearms.

"Thank you, Mrs. Tate," he winked and led me to our seats.

Cherry led us straight to a sweetly decorated table with the most gorgeous little cake I'd ever seen. It was fairly small, but enough to feed about fifty, two tiers, simple butter cream frosting but you can tell Cross's girlfriend arranged to have Tom envelop it in flowers. Flowers seemed to be the theme for the evening. We cut into our cake hand in hand, completing yet another tradition, and fed each other lemon cake respectfully.

Callum was taken back that I remembered his favorite was lemon and rubbed my hand in his with a wink of appreciation.

The food, the champagne, the flowers, the dress, the guests. Everything was more perfect than I could have ever imagined. I felt so undeserving of it all knowing Callum never planned on continuing on. I felt sick at the thought.

"Hey," he said, noticing my face. "Are you okay?"

"Yes. It's just, I feel very guilty for pretending." *For many reasons.*

"Are you?"

"Am I what?"

"Pretending," he said, glaring hard.

"Of..of...of course I am," I lied.

"I'm not," he said with conviction.

"You're *not*?" I asked, hopeful for the first time in weeks. My heart beat in my throat.

"Not tonight, I'm not." *Not tonight? What does that mean?*

"No, I..." He started to say, leaning into me, making me breathless again. I felt butterflies wrestle in my stomach.

"Excuse me," we heard a voice from behind us, "but may I have this dance?" It was Cherry. Callum stood and took her hand, squeezing my shoulder.

As Cherry and Callum danced, I studied the way he carried himself around her. It was the same way he carried himself around all girls. All girls except *this* girl. I felt a twinge more hope knowing he was way more intimate with me than he was with anyone I'd ever seen him with. He wasn't a shameless flirt. He was genuine and wonderful and...my husband.

The food was plentiful, the champagne flowing, the

night lasted for hours. At two a.m., we could still feel the bass bumping around us but Callum and I both felt tired and ready to leave. We'd planned on using some of our money from the week to rent a hotel room but Charlie surprised us with a room at The Chatwal as a wedding gift.

We thanked everyone profusely, hugging each of our friends five or six times a piece. I lingered a bit at Charlie and Cherry and we were on our way, escorted yet again by the humble and talented Tie-Dye Tom.

The Chatwal was unlike any place I had ever been. We stood in its opulent lobby, waiting for the elevator and felt more pampered than we ever had and we hadn't even made the room yet.

Callum

Harper and I stood at the elevator, our key in hand. Charlie assured me everything was taken care of, our bags were already in our room, he had checked us in. All we had to do was enter the door. We entered the elevator in an amazing mood, riding all the way up to our floor in flirtatious smiles and teasing pokes. We stepped into our hall, passing an older couple. The woman gasped and briefly held her hand to her mouth.

"Congratulations!" She exclaimed passing us by, arm in arm with her husband. "You have a very beautiful bride, groom."

"I know," I said, "and thank you."

We reached our room and I unlocked our door. Harper tried to step forward but I swung her back, scooping her up in my arms and carrying her across the threshold. The door clicked behind the us. The windows were open, bathing the room in moonlight.

"We've gone this far," I teased. "Might as well finish this thing." As soon as I said it, I turned beet red,

203

setting Harper on the ground again.

I covered my face trying to hide my humiliation but her laughter brought me back out into the open and I peeked between my fingers.

"Please," Harper said, grabbing my hands and pulling them down, "I knew what you meant." I smirked and shrugged my shoulders. "It was funny, though," she said and I couldn't help but laugh with her.

"So," I said, suddenly realizing we were alone in a very posh hotel room with absolutely nothing to do.

"So," she copied.

"So," I said again.

"Okay, let's just get it out in the open."

"Get what out in the open?" I asked.

"You know." She hesitated.

"What?" I questioned, raising one brow. "Get what out in the open, Harper?"

She turned beet red.

"I'm beat," she said, chickening out. "I'll think I'll take a bath. I haven't had one of those since I was a little girl." This made my heart sink a little for her. She deserved daily bubble baths in giant porcelain claw tubs. I yanked her hand back as soon as she started to walk off. She crashed into my chest, breathing hard.

"Yes?" She said timidly.

"I meant what I said tonight when I said you were the most beautiful woman I'd ever seen," I said, studying her face.

She looked at the ground for an answer before bringing her eyes back up to mine. "I know," she simply said, pushing herself closer to me.

Suddenly the room felt smaller, too intimate, too dark.

"I can't believe you can kiss like that," I murmured before I lost my nerve, remembering the passion we had in our first kiss earlier that afternoon.

She swallowed hard. "I can't believe *we* kiss like that."

"We are very good at it," I whispered in her ear, bringing her cheek to mine.

"You're beard is coming in," she whispered back, making me smile.

"It *is* late. Sometimes that happens," I chuckled. She openly smelled my neck, making me laugh yet again.

"Are you smelling me, Harper Tate?" She laughed. I dug my nose through her hair and inhaled.

"Are you smelling me, Callum Tate?"

"Yes I am, Mrs. Tate." She brought her face from mine and looked at me.

"Do you like that I'm Mrs. Tate?"

"I do," I confessed but she moved further away, turning from me, confusing and wounding me.

She leaned over the dresser mirror and undid her hair piece laying it gently on top of the dresser.

"I'll run your bath," I said, walking to the bathroom to hide my bruised ego. I sat at the edge of the tub and turned on the water. On the countertop near the sink, sat a basket with a note that read, 'To Mr. and Mrs. Tate'. I peeled the ribbon off the top and opened its lid. Inside, were candles, bubble bath, chocolate covered strawberries, a bottle of champagne and two glasses.

"Harper come here," I said. When she stood next to me, I showed her the basket. She picked up the card.

"'To Mr. and Mrs. Tate'," she repeated then turned the card over. "'From Cherry, Kelly and Marty.'" Harper leaned against the counter top, facing me. "I love them," she said simply. "They are extraordinary kind to me."

"I think they love you too, Harper," I said

unexpectedly sad.

She walked over to the bath and felt the water.

"Perfect," she murmured under her breath. She poured the bubble bath the girls had given us into the water and let the bubbles get ridiculously huge. She turned back my way. I picked up a chocolate covered strawberry and took a bite. "Turn around," she said.

"What?"

"Turn around. I'm getting in."

"But *I'm* in here."

"You won't look. I trust you," she said, already slipping off the straps of her gown. I turned rapidly, finishing my strawberry. Did I hear tape?

"Is that...*tape*?"

"Don't ask," she laughed. "Okay, I'm in".

I turned back around slowly and gawked at her, hidden beneath a sea of foam, she flirted with me by winking. I couldn't see a damn thing but it didn't matter because I had never wanted to take a bath more in my life than I did in that moment and I didn't even like baths. I had to get out of there.

"I'll, uh, go put ice in the bucket to chill the champagne," I said, grabbing the ice bucket as I left the bathroom.

I heard her giggle and shook my head at her cheekiness. Our entire marriage was going to be nothing but a painful flirtation, I could already tell. I filled the bucket with ice then sat in the little room with the ice maker for a second to cool off. It wasn't working so I grabbed a few cubes and dragged them across the back of my neck. I'd been gone for awhile and decided to head back, hoping that I'd be able to just slip in and she wouldn't notice but when I reached the door I realized, in my haste, I'd forgotten my key. *DANG IT!*

I didn't want to but I had to knock. "Harper, I forgot my key!"

After a moment, a soaking wet, barely robed Harper answered the door, letting me in. I wanted to stick my head inside the stupid bucket at the sight of her. She thought nothing of it and returned to her bath. I followed her and stuck the champagne in the bucket, turning around just in time to miss what I didn't really *want* to miss.

"You can turn back around now," she said absently.

She was resting her head against the back of the tub, her hair clipped up so it wouldn't get wet, her long slender neck exposed. For a split moment, I considered vampirism. I would have ravished that neck that very second if I knew she had made the same commitment to me that I did to her at that afternoon. I needed to get out of there.

"Callum?" She said, running a sponge over her arms and upper chest.

"Ye-yes?" I sat on the edge of the counter to give the impression I was breezy. I doubt it was working. That was evident in her smirk.

"When will we get our marriage certificate back?"

"In a couple of days, why?"

"Hmm," was all she said.

"Why?"

"Oh, I was just thinking. Maybe you and I could use those days to shop for simple furniture for our new apartment? After working lunches? I know school starts in two weeks. That doesn't leave us a lot of time. I know we'll get our apartment but we'll have nothing inside it just as school starts? That's too much. We should try to at least get a few larger pieces." She lifted her silky knee from the water, making me reel. "Like a sofa, television, and bed."

The word bed was more than I could handle.

"Um, yeah. That's a great idea, Harper. Let's start tomorrow. We'll go to that Sunday swap meet they hold over by Charlie's. They shut down the entire street for the entire day."

"What a good idea!" She exclaimed, shifting the water a bit.

I ran. From that room, from that robe, from that enticing water and from her. I threw myself onto the bed, groaning into my pillow. She was going to kill me. Making my commitment to God made me feel like she was mine to do *things* with but she hadn't made the same commitment and now I was stuck in a marriage with a woman I loved, one that I was so incredibly attracted to, one that I wanted to touch all over including her mind and couldn't. I was a glutton for punishment and wanted nothing more than to gorge myself on that creature soaking in our wedding night tub.

When Harper got out, I left the room for her to dress, barely looking at her. I showered in the huge glossy black marble walk in shower. I let the steam roll around me and the heat work out my frustration. I had no idea what I was going to do. I was beginning to panic. I loved her so much I could barely see straight. I wanted her so much I could barely breathe straight. I needed her so much I could barely think straight. I hopped from the shower onto the warm tile floor and toweled myself dry, dressing in my long pajama pants, foregoing the t-shirt as it was too hot and turning off the light before I entered the room.

It was quiet and dark. Harper was hidden beneath the covers steadily breathing and I realized she may have already fallen asleep, causing an inexplicable ache in my chest. I slid into the silky sheets under the down comforter and laid my head on the soft goose feather pillow, staring at the ceiling. I threw my arm over my eyes suddenly unsure of what I'd done.

"Callum?" Harper whispered, startling me. I removed my arm from my eyes and looked at her. She shifted and rolled over on her side, propping herself up on her elbow. I followed her lead, doing the same.

"Yes?" I asked her beautifully moonlit face. She didn't say another word, just slid over to my side of the bed and wrapped her arms around my bare chest, fitting her head underneath my chin. I didn't want to think about how well her body fit next to mine but I couldn't help it.

After an hour of just holding one another, Harper spoke. "I'm glad I married you," she said before drifting off into a deep slumber.

"I'm glad I married you too, Harper," I whispered into her hair, "because I'm in love with you." But she didn't hear, gone into a dream.

Two Years Later

Please, for
reference's sake,
watch Hello Goodbye's
'When We First
Met' video.

Chapter Twelve
Sunburn

Callum

"Dude, your hair is getting ridiculously long," Harper teased, running her hands through it, sending a shiver of warmth down my spine and my eyes rolling to the back of my head.

"Think I should cut it?" I asked drunk on her touch, lounging next to her on the sofa, otherwise known as 'Callum's bed'.

The microwave beeped and Harper jumped up, tripping over the step into our kitchen as it was so dark. The smell of popcorn wafted its way into our little living room. She came back with it in a giant bowl along with two bottled waters.

"I wanted soda," I said, furrowing my brows.

She sighed but shoved her shoulder into mine as she sat. "I know that but you've already had four today. I'm vetoing a fifth."

"Fine," I sang not wanting to admit how much I still loved that she looked after me.

"And no way," she said.

"No way, what?"

"No." She cleared her throat, staring into the bowl. "I don't think you should cut it."

For two years, Harper and I had been playing the ultimate game of cat and mouse. Now, I know what you're thinking. 'I thought they were only going to marry for a year, then annul, divorce, whatever.' Well, truthfully, we liked being 'fake married' or as I like to secretly call it, 'faking that my marriage isn't real'. Also, unfortunately John Bell was only sentenced to a year in prison and had been released six months prior. Though, he'd yet to find us, I wasn't going to leave her defenseless while we were in school, so we decided that we'd stay married until the end of the school year. That was partly by design. I wasn't ready to leave her yet. I didn't want to.

We didn't need any more grants starting our sophomore year and had become completely independent. We belonged to no one. We owed no one. We were each other's family. This was it for me. There were things that had been happening lately that made me think this was also it for her.

"Your hair is getting long as well, Harper," I stated, unsure how to tell her that I loved it as long as it'd become.

"Do you like it?" She asked me, turning away from the screen.

"As a matter a fact, I love it," I said honestly. It

reached her elbows now in long, loose coppery waves, like when we'd first met. She'd cut it after we'd married just under her shoulders.

"Thank you. How's Krantz treating you this semester?" She asked.

"Like crap as always," I admitted, making her laugh.

"I told you not to take him for Bio-Chem. Everyone and their dog knows not to take Krantz, even journalism majors," she winked.

"Yeah, well I told you, I didn't have a choice. The only other option was when you were already off and I didn't want to have a conflicting schedule."

"Yeah, yeah. I think you just like torturing yourself." *You have no idea.*

A scary part of the film came flashing across the screen, making Harper scream and jump in my lap. She grasped my shoulders and pulled herself into me closely making my heart leap to my throat.

"Sorry," she whispered, scurrying off me quickly, a blush creeping across her gorgeous neck. I'd wished the scene had lasted longer just so she could have stayed in my arms.

"It's alright," I said, readjusting on the sofa.

Harper had decorated our apartment in a lot of different pieces. She dragged me to the Sunday swap meet near Charlie's practically every weekend that first year. We'd buy little pieces together and place them in our house, making it a home. She described our home's style as eclectic. I can remember every piece we bought together and why. For instance, the sofa we sat on was 'a tufted purple velvet Chesterfield'. I had no idea what that meant but I just nodded and agreed to its purchase as it was the first thing she'd found that made her squeal in excitement.

And the wingback in the corner? It was a piece of crap when she found it at the thrift store but she promised me it would look good once we recovered it in a funky pattern and, of course, she was correct. I refused to go to the cloth store to pick out the fabric and told her she had carte blanche. She came back with a mustard yellow print. I didn't have the heart to tell her I hated it but when she made me stay up until one in the morning recovering it with her, it'd grown on me and it ended up being my favorite piece we'd ever bought because of the conversation we'd had while covering it.

That's what I loved about the furniture in our apartment. I could care less what it looked like. Harper could have had the worst taste in the world and I would have loved it regardless. She doesn't, by the way. It was the fact that she was in every piece, in every corner, on every shelf. She was everywhere, reminding me how much in love with her I was.

In the two years we'd been married, I'd only kissed her once and that was on our wedding day. She tortured me with hugs which I gladly took. I'd kissed her neck more times than I could possibly count but it was starting to wear on me. I was too invested to confess all now. I was frightened to admit to her how much I loved her, afraid she'd bail, not wanting to torture me under my own roof. And I couldn't just be friends with Harper. It was all or nothing and nothing scared the ever living crap out of me. So I took all her friendship and pretended it was enough.

"Did you pay the insurance, Callum?"
"Yes, honey bunches of oats," I laid on thickly.
"Shut up," she laughed.

214

I stood up quickly.

"Where are my slippers and pipe?" I demanded, "And roast beef *again* for dinner? Woman! You are dangerously close to a spanking!"

"Take that sexist crap and shove it," she laughed harder, doubling over.

She surprised me by tripping me and I fell hard onto the hard wood floor. I was laughing too hard to get angry. She was laughing as she crawled toward me and lay down beside me. We both stared at the ceiling, our laughs dying out slowly until our breaths were the only thing audible beside the film.

She turned on her side, her head resting on the inside of my folded arm.

"I have a lot of fun with you," she said.

"Me too. I'm wonderful."

She slapped me playfully and I tickled her until she could barely breathe.

The next day was Friday and we were both off school that day but had to work at the campus library which proved useful for both of us as there was a lot of down time and we always needed to study. It also helped that when we got off, most of our work was already done and we could spend a lot of time with another.

"Get the mail, Harper," I said, juggling my back pack and keys, stepping off our elevator.

"'Kay."

Harper opened our little box with her key and removed four or five envelopes, shifting each one behind the other as she read off what each one was.

"Bill, bill, junk." She stopped on the fourth one. "Hmm," she said, eyeing the envelope. "It's a letter, for you."

"*What*?" I asked. "What's the return address say?"

"It says, 'I'm busy, leave me alone'."

"Ha ha. Seriously, who's it from?"

Her eyes bugged wide. "An Ames *Tate* in Seattle."

"No," I said, dropping my bag on the floor. "This is my dad's half-brother, Harper."

She smiled and squeezed my shoulder, handing over the letter. She tucked the remaining letters into her own bag and we headed toward the subway to get to work.

As we sat, our bodies leaning into one another, I opened the letter. Excited butterflies filled my stomach and I unfolded its short contents

"Read it to me," I said, handing it over.

She took it and began, clearing her throat.

Callum,

This feels so strange to finally be able to write you. I've been searching five years, since I graduated school actually. It was incredibly difficult but I finally found your records with the state and followed the homes you'd lived in. This address was the last listed in your name and I'm hoping it's the correct one.

You probably know nothing about me but my name is Ames Tate and my brother was your father. I remember little of him but from what I do, he was a good man and so was your mother. If it means anything to you at all, they loved you more than they loved themselves. They would have and did do anything and everything to keep you happy, healthy, and safe. Even one as young as I, was able to recognize this in them. They were in love with you as were us all. You were a bright, charming boy and their love for you reflected in the way you played and loved as well.

I'm writing because I wanted you to know that you do have family who still loves you, despite the fact that we've never met. You're my only family as well and I hoped that we could meet one day. I'm still single, though I'm working on that, and living in Seattle. I've attached a note with my address and e-mail. If you ever feel like dropping a line, please do.

Sincerely,
Ames Tate

Harper looked in my eyes, tears spilling from her own. "Oh my God, Callum. You have family."

I squeezed her hand in mine, accidentally crumpling the letter. "I already knew that."

She kissed my cheek and wiped away a stray tear. "Are you going to write him back?"

"Of course, I'll e-mail him as soon as we get to work."

"I can't believe this. It's so exciting, don't you think?"

"It is, kind of. I'm a little nervous, though."

"What for?"

"Well, I don't remember him at all but I remember my dad a little and I'm nervous to see how much they look alike. I just don't want to rehash buried feelings."

Harper nodded and wrapped her slender arm around my broad shoulders. She could barely fit it across and it made me laugh. I leaned back slightly and brought my own arm around her frame, hugging her close, kissing the top of her head.

"I love you, Harper."

"I love you, too, Callum."

We were always telling each other that but I'm not sure it meant quite the same thing coming from her as it did when I said it. When I said it, baggage was attached. When I said it, I was really telling her that I was *in* love with her, that I wanted to cover her body with mine at every possible second, that, in my heart, she really was my wife, and that I had been aching to make love to her. No, not have sex with her. I wanted to make love to her, intertwine my fingers and my body with hers, drink her in and inhale every inch of her, memorize her skin.

"How long have you been married?" A woman next to me asked.

"Two years," I said, still holding tightly to Harper. She raised her chin and smiled.

"Ah, the honeymoon phase," the woman teased. "I have a feeling you two will always live in the honeymoon phase. You have 'meant to be' written all over you."

"Thank you," Harper said, smiling at me and laughing. Laughing because we held a secret. A secret that only she really wanted to keep.

Work was work. I got all my studying done, which was ultra nice, wrote Ames and befriended him online, read a little, helped about five thousand people find books and teased Harper. We got home around ten and we both plopped onto the sofa.

"It's Friday, babe," she said, poking me with her bare foot in the ribs.

"Don't! That tickles," I said, laughing and grabbing my side. "I know, should we see if The Ivories are playing tonight?"

"That's a really good idea. I'm tired of staying in and I haven't seen Cherry in a week."

"I think Charlie will be there as well," I stated absently.

"Good, maybe he can jump off his 'dumb stool' and get with the program already."

"I know! It's been two years already. Make a move!" She laughed. So did I, but it wasn't out of humor. It was out of stupidity at my own statement. I was a massive hypocrite.

Harper put on a short skirt, not too short, I made sure of that. Yeah, I'm a Neanderthal but a sane Neanderthal and that's all I cared about. She wore her boots and a tight vintage tee. She let her hair down and it flowed to the middle of her back. As she put on her make-up, I walked by her open door to the kitchen and did a double take as she was slightly bent over. I couldn't help myself. I came to stand behind her and watched, running my hands through her copper strands. She closed her eyes lazily and swallowed hard.

"Stop," she said breathlessly. "You're making me sleepy."

I didn't listen, just kept right on threading my fingers. She slowly tried to apply lip gloss but I could tell her arms felt heavy and a deep, exciting blast of warmth shot through my legs and pooled in my stomach knowing I had that kind of effect on her. Her eyes drooped closed as she stood, then leaned back into me.

"Keep doing that and I'll end up spending what's supposed to be a fun night out in that bed instead," she said, making me close my own eyes at the unintentional double meaning. *I wish.*

I started to run my hands over her shoulders but wasn't able to stop them from running along her ribs and down to her hips, squeezing the bone. She let out a little gasp, her eyes still closed, the back of head resting on my shoulder, her mouth slightly open. I stared at her mouth and wished I could kiss her again the way I'd kissed her on our wedding day. *Run*, I told myself.

"Alright," I barely spit out and left the room, practically sprinting to the bathroom.

Once inside, I ran the cold water in the sink and splashed my face and neck. I stood and looked at myself in the mirror. *How long are you going to be able to do this?* I flushed the toilet to make it seem like I was in there for a reason rather than trying to gain some semblance of composure. I heard a knock at the front door, then Harper making her way to the living room, then opening it.

"Callum! Charlie's here!"

"Tell him I'll be right out!" I yelled through the door. I turned off the water, grabbed one of Harper's ridiculous guest towels and wiped my face dry. A few drops landed on my t-shirt but it was dark and I hoped she wouldn't notice. Charlie and Harper were laughing when I entered the living room.

"Alrighty," I said, trying to ignore the woman standing next to my best friend, my wife. "Let's go."

The Ivories were amazing that night. At least, I think they were amazing. I couldn't really concentrate because Harper was leaning against the bar top, facing the stage, talking to SO. They were just chatting. That didn't bother me. What I cared about, was the punk on the opposite side of her that couldn't keep his eyes to himself. Of course, Harper hadn't noticed, too engrossed in whatever she was talking to SO about.

I stood in a dark side of the room, watching her, like a freak. A cold shiver ran up my spine with no idea why. An ominous feeling crept through my veins. *Get a hold of yourself, Tate.* I clenched my hands in fists and released, over and over and over, pretending to watch the stage but every five seconds my eyes gravitated back toward her. She absently placed the back heel of her right leg on the footrest behind her, making her left leg's muscle tense under her shifting weight and the hem of her skirt rise a tiny bit. I wanted to fall on my knees in front of her and worship those legs.

The punk's eyes shifted to her thigh and I had to physically restrain myself from running over there and punching him in the face. Then he did the unspeakable. He turned toward her and tapped her shoulder. SO didn't notice and I wanted to yell at him to intervene. She turned toward him with a sweet smile on her face. 'Yes?' She mouthed. He said something to her and she laughed, sending a jealous, coursing storm through my veins. He shifted closer to her and I made a move to break it up but she moved back from his invitation and into SO. I breathed a sigh of relief knowing SO would now intervene but a young blonde across the room had caught his attention and he was entranced.

Harper shook her head back and forth with the same smile still plastered across her face. She raised her left hand and showed him her ring. 'Married'. She mouthed again. *Ugh! Good girl*! I felt my heart start to slow a little bit but pick right back up to ridiculous speed when the guy shoved her hand away and tried to push himself into her by her hip.

I'd had enough. I started shoving people as I made my way across the room to the bar. A few people shoved back but I didn't care. They could follow me if they wanted to do something about it. SO had left the counter to talk to that girl, not noticing Harper's predicament. By the time I reached her, Harper was frantically pawing at the guy to get him off of her.

"Stop!" I heard her yell.

Finally, I was within reach so I grabbed the guy and

shoved him back.

"Didn't you hear my wife?" I asked him. "She told you to stop."

Harper was wiping tears from her cheeks when she sidled up closely to me. I wrapped an arm around her waist.

"Sorry, dude," the guy said, throwing his hands in the air. He was drunk and could barely stand. He immediately noticed another girl he fancied and made his way over to her.

"What an idiot," she said laughing, trying to make light of the situation.

"He was drunk," I offered. "That was the only thing that prevented me from shoving him to the ground." I thought twice and remembered how scared her face looked. I began to charge him again.

"Don't," Harper said, flustered and pushing me back a little. "It's not worth it. Come dance with me."

All anger dissipated at the look on her face. "Alright," I said, cupping her cheeks and bending to kiss her forehead. We made it to the middle of the floor where the crowd watched Freddy sing one of their most popular songs. They were jumping and singing along, sweaty and red faced but happy. Harper and I sang along, jumping with the crowd. The floor was tight and Harper and I often bumped into one another. Her body was warm and soft and made me want to pick her up and wrap her legs around my hips in a searing kiss. I shook my head at the thought and found her staring at me, a mischievous twinkle in her eye, like she read every thought I'd just had. My face blushed furiously.

"What?" I screamed, still jumping.

"Oh, nothing!" She said and turned her attention back to Freddy.

I continued to watch her.

Something caught her attention in the corner. She furrowed her brows but she seemed to get over it quickly, turning her thoughts inward before snapping her head back to the corner. Her body seized before it begun to shake, making me stop.

"Harper?" I yelled in her ear. "What's wrong, love?"

"Go!" She said, turning toward me, pushing me, terror in her eyes. "Go! To the door! *Go!*"

I picked her body up and ran for the door, not caring who I hit.

Once outside, I got my earlier wish but under very different circumstances as she climbed my body, sobbing hysterically, wrapping her legs around me.

"Take me home," she begged, her hands curled around my collar.

I tried to peel her off of me but she would have none of it, so I started walking with her wrapped around me. I didn't care what people thought of us as they stared, bewildered.

"What happened, Harper?"

"John," she whispered in my ear.

I stopped briefly before picking up my pace, practically running. *No! There's no way he could have found us! It had to be a coincidence*, I thought.

"How?" She cried into my neck. "How did he find me?"

"I don't know," I told her honestly. "I have no idea. Maybe it was a coincidence."

"Nothing he does is a coincidence," she whispered, afraid that if she spoke any higher, it'd make it more true.

We were pretty far away from the club now and her body had calmed down a bit so I set her back on the sidewalk. I looked around us, trying to decipher whether he was near or not. People littered the darkly lit sidewalks, talking, laughing, flirting but I could see no sign of John. The coast was clear so I decided we could hide in a nearby alley. Now, you're asking yourself, is it really safe to hide in a dark alley at one in the morning in New York City? Yes, it is, if John Bell was the one chasing you. Those were chances you'd be willing to take.

Thankfully, we wouldn't share the alley with anyone else so I quietly hid us behind a dumpster just in case John had followed. I pressed her body against the brick building behind her, sheltering her body with mine, ready to ask what he was wearing but I stopped when we heard someone shuffling softly through the alley. An eerie quiet cascaded around us, only the soft padding of feet was barely audible. I put my finger to my lips, signaling for her to be quiet. She nodded but I could feel her body tremble beneath mine.

"Harper," John sang. Tears began to spill down her cheeks. I slowly shook my head from side to side. "I know you're around here somewhere. I can practically *smell* you," he continued menacingly. "It's taken me six months to find you, Harper and I've waited two years." He paused, breathing hard. "You owe me," he gritted harshly. "Just come out so I can look at that beautiful face of yours. I promise I won't punish you too hard for going off with that asshole."

He was inching the wall opposite the dumpster. He knew we were there. It was the only place to hide in the entire alley. 'Run' I mouthed to her followed by 'Police', remembering the mounted policemen outside the club and hoping she did as well. She shook her head, knowing I was staying to keep him from following her. I had no time to think of that. I gritted my teeth before pushing the dumpster his direction. She hesitated but I yelled for her to run and she miraculously obeyed me.

John immediately started chase as I threw my

224

body into his and we went crashing into the brick. He was bigger than I was, had at least twenty pounds on me and was roughly four inches taller, too. I was at a size disadvantage but for some reason my strength was holding him, my desire to protect Harper stronger than his want to harm her. I just hoped it would stay him long enough for Harper to get help.

John wrapped his fingers around my throat and it wasn't long before I could feel blood vessels in my eyes begin to burst. He was choking the life out of me and I knew I had to remove my body from his if I wanted to stay conscious. I let off a bit and he shoved me with a shoulder, hard into the chest, pushing me until my back and head slammed into the brick wall on the other side. I scrambled to push back but was weak from the lack of oxygen.

He wound his arm back, going in for a punch but I dodged it at the last second, making his hand hit the hard brick behind me. He wailed in pain and the rage built tenfold in his eyes. I could read the absolute evil this man possessed. It radiated off of him. I wanted nothing more than to get away, to avoid the taint. He grabbed my shirt at the shoulders with both hands, coiled his head back and brought it full force to mine, butting me and making me feel weak in the knees.

I surprised him by not passing out, making him chuckle. "What's your name?" He asked.

I shook my spinning head and the added dizziness made me want to vomit. "I'll never tell," I said, swallowing. I wondered what was taking Harper so long. I was beginning to worry.

He smiled, reached into the back pocket of my jeans and removed my wallet before I could fully force myself on him to prevent it. I staggered toward him, dazed from the head butt and was too slow, forced to watch as he yanked my license from my wallet, taking away the only piece of protection we both had. Our anonymity. I fell to my knees, resting a shoulder against the wall, panting heavily, trying to keep the nausea down.

"Callum Tate," he purred. "I was so patient and now I'm one step closer to finding her."

He was wrong. The address on that license was also hers but I wouldn't be the one correcting him. The thought that he now knew our last name made me want to vomit for an entirely different reason. I shifted a knee up to have something to push on as I stood. I was beginning to gain control of myself again.

Once I was fully up, no longer needing to lean against the wall, I said, "John, you will never find her. Never."

"But I already have. I promised her I'd come for her. She's such a stupid girl. She never believes me." He sighed as if exasperated. "She makes it so difficult for herself."

"How?" Was all I could manage.

He knew I meant 'how did you find us'. "The Ivories trailer. I knew they were friends of yours. I went to every single concert, waiting, biding my time. It took several months but it paid off. Tonight."

The trailer.

"Well, I've got to go," he said, tossing my wallet and license to the concrete. "I'll be seeing you around. Trust me, you'll be seeing a lot of me around. Tell Harper I look forward to seeing her again. Tell her," he said, smiling wickedly, "I'll enjoy every single minute."

Then he ran. And I chased, tried my damnedest, but he was too fast and I was too hazy to keep up. I could hear people shouting behind me and turned just in time to see

Harper with policemen in tow heading toward the alley.

"Over here!" I shouted. Harper turned direction toward me and the officers followed.

"Oh my God, Callum! You're bleeding!" She shouted as she reached me, running her hands over my bloody face. Her hand went to her mouth in a gasp. "Your eyes! What happened?" She asked, tears streaming down her face. I removed my t-shirt to hold over the bleeding wound.

"He got away," I said stoically and in disbelief.

I had promised myself that if I ever saw that guy again it would be the last. I felt weak and pathetic. Next time, *I'd be prepared*. Harper and I gave statements over everything that happened. They took pictures of my head for evidence. I hadn't glanced in a mirror since the attack and when I caught a glimpse of what he'd done in the photograph, I almost laughed. I looked like a hopped up serial killer. Blood ran down my face and my eyes were bloodshot, literally. Two red orbs stared back at me, letting me know just how serious John Bell really was.

"He...knows where we live," I stated to the officer quietly, not wanting to alarm Harper any more than she already was.

"Do you have any other place to stay while we look for him?"

"We do but I believe we'll be okay tonight. He knows we'd be waiting for him. He'll be waiting for our guard to be down."

The officer agreed.

Harper and I took a taxi home. It was three already and we both felt pretty beat up. I couldn't help but feel incredible anxiety as I slid my key into our door. I turned the knob, throwing the door open fully before stepping over the threshold. I placed my hand on the jamb preventing Harper from going in and listened. Not a sound. We both entered and I closed and locked the door behind us.

"Stay here," I ordered before examining every room for evidence he was there or had been there.

I came back out to a nervous, fidgety Harper.

"Do you think he'll find us?"

"I'm sure of it," I said, trying not to allude as to why.

"How...how did he find me?"

"The Ivories Trailer," I told her honestly.

Her jaw quivered a bit before she smashed her teeth together to still it. "Okay," she simply said, walking towards me with purpose and dragging me by the hand to our tiled bathroom.

She signaled for me sit on the toilet so she could tend to my wounds at eye level. My heart rate had steadied at that point and I was actually becoming very tired.

"Let's just sleep," I said.

"No, I won't have you bloody my nice white sheets," she said.

"You want me to sleep with you tonight?" I asked.

"Of course," she said. "I couldn't sleep any other way." I agreed. I would be too worried about her all alone to get any kind of rest whatsoever.

She ran the water in the sink, letting it warm, before grabbing a wash cloth from the cabinet. She let the water absorb into the cloth before twisting out the excess with shaking hands. She gently removed most of the blood before giving up and letting me know there was too much and I'd have to just wash my face. While I did, she grabbed her little emergency kit full of supplies I used to tease her incessantly we'd never need. Never again.

I sat back down and she pushed her fingers

through my hair to pull it away from my wound. I winced as it tugged a little at the tear and she moved her fingers slower, more softly. She blew into my hair to dry some of the moisture that had built at my hairline, where the wound was. I closed my eyes at how sexy I found that. Her lips were red and swollen from worry from biting at them for hours. It was quiet, so quiet it was deafening. I could hear every single thought ramble through my mind. *Kiss her*, I kept ordering myself. *Kiss her and tell her that you love her. Let her know what you would do for her.* She applied Neosporin to prevent infection and bandaged the wound.

"Sleep," she said, dragging me by my hand again to her bedroom.

I said nothing. I was already bare chested from having to remove my shirt to stop the bleeding earlier. I threw off my boots but left my jeans on as I tumbled into her bed. It was soft and smelled unbelievable. It smelled like Harper and awoke my senses. Abruptly, I was much more alert than I had been in our warm bathroom, not so quick to doze off but still very sleepy. Harper left to change into one of my boxers and t-shirts, like she always did, and it always sent my heart into a frenzy at the sight of her.

I pulled the covers over my back and laid on my stomach, tucking the pillow beneath my head and staring at Harper's door, waiting for her. When she came in, my stomach clenched. She was unbelievably beautiful to me. She was made for me. Never could I have imagined a woman could look as good as this one did in my clothes.

She crawled into bed, throwing the blanket over her shoulders and snuggled closely. I tossed an arm and a leg over her, making her nestle even closer.

"I love you, Callum."

"I love you, too, Harper."

Sleep came quickly for both of us. I couldn't remember feeling more relaxed in my life than I did lying next to Harper. Her, cradled in my arms, a welcome respite from the tedious anxiety John Bell had caused us that evening.

Chapter Thirteen
Good Ol' Fashioned Nightmare

Callum

The next morning, I woke to an empty bed and panicked.

"Harper?!" I yelled, scrambling out of bed in a stiff pair of jeans.

"I'm here!" She called out to me from our kitchen. I sighed in relief, heading for the bathroom to relieve myself. I hated sleeping in jeans. The next morning you always wake pissed a little that you forgot to take them off or, in my case, that you couldn't just sleep in your boxers next to your wife.

I flushed and washed my hands, inspecting my wounds in the mirror. A good night's rest helped tremendously. I wasn't as sore as I was the night before but my eyes still looked disgusting.

"Why didn't you wake me?" I asked Harper, rounding the corner into the kitchen before kissing the top of her head.

She was at the gas stove, flipping pancakes.

"You looked so pathetic there with your bandaged head. I wanted to make sure that you got as much sleep as possible."

I sat and poured a cup of coffee for myself. She always made me coffee even though she never drank the stuff. Another reason I loved her so much, so thoughtful.

"What are we going to do?" She asked me.

"For now? We're going to wait. We're going to be extraordinarily careful. We're going to stick to crowds and I'll walk you to all your classes. We're going to be alert and you will never go anywhere alone."

"No where?"

"I don't even want to be separated by a room."

"Not even a room?" She teased.

"Okay, maybe a few rooms you can be alone in," I said, laughing, making her laugh with me.

That's how we lived day after day, after day, after day. For three weeks Harper and I lived a very tiresome existence. We spent an unbelievable amount of time with one another, sleeping together, eating together, traveled together. We went to school together. I walked her from class to class and, to be frank, we were growing weary of the worry John Bell was causing us.

The Friday of our third week, we got into a particularly rancid argument, our nerves frayed. Harper and I never name called, never. We never really shouted either but this day, there was a lot of shouting back and forth.

"If I went out with them but promised to stay with

them at all times, would you let me go *then*?" Harper asked.

"No! Not one of those women could handle John's girth. I'm six-two, a hundred eighty pounds, Harper! And I'm in damn good shape! Even I can't handle him completely! He's a *monster*!" I yelled from my position on the couch. I was drumming my thumbs nervously on my thighs.

"I know that! You don't have to remind me, Callum!" Harper yelled back from behind her door.

She was trying to get ready to have a girl's night with Cherry, Kelly, Sam, and Marty and I wasn't going to let her. I was going to tie her to the radiator if I had to. I felt it was too dangerous. I saw what John's intentions were with her and he knew where we lived. Harper didn't know that but I thought maybe it was time she did, especially if she kept insisting that she was going out 'whether I liked it or not'.

I sighed loudly, hoping she heard. "Harper, why can't you just stay in until they catch him?"
She opened the door, stepping out in some dress that made my eyes want to roll into the back of my head. I almost keeled over at the pleasure of looking at her.

"No," she said succinctly. "I can't live my life, looking over my shoulder every five seconds and I'm going stir crazy sitting in this house all the time." She sat beside me, the skirt of her dress, tightening around her thighs, reminding me how shapely they were. All the more reason she should stay. "Listen, I love you but I need to get out of here. I need a break."

I sighed. "I know, Harper, but you can't go alone. Listen, I'll compromise with you. How about I come with you..."

"No," she interrupted. "I'll be fine."

"It's either that or you don't go. I don't care if I have to block the door myself. You are not going alone. Don't you even remember that night, Harper?"

She thought for a moment, sinking further into the couch cushion. "Fine," she conceded, "but you're invisible, alright? I don't want the girls to even know you're there. I'm breaking all the rules by allowing you to attend a girl's night. It's, like, sacrilegious or something."

I couldn't keep back my snort. "You'll never know I'm there."

They knew I was there. It enraged Harper but when they saw me sulking in a corner, they dragged me to their table. Eventually, Harper joined in on the fun, even apologizing to me later when she'd relaxed a little bit.

The other girls had gotten up to dance, leaving Harper and I alone. She slid across the leather booth to sit next to me.

"Hi," she said.

"Hello, love." Her hand was pressed into the seat of the booth and I placed my own on top of it. I leaned into her ear. "Dance with me, Harper."

She shook her head, glancing at the crowded dance floor. "No," she said, hurting my feelings and wounding my pride. I started to pull my hand away but she gripped it and brought her mouth to my ear. "I would much rather sit here with you, smell your yummy smell, drink in your handsome face, hear your lovely words."

"Wow, Harper. That was," I cleared my throat at the surprising turn of our conversation, "sexy."

"I know," she teased. "Fighting you brings out a feisty side, I think."

Note to self, fight with Harper more often.

We sat in silence for a few minutes.

"Do you ever think about our kiss?" I asked boldly, surprising myself. I didn't know where I got the confidence.

I'd said it before I'd lost my nerve and from the look on her face, I immediately regretted it but then she surprised me.

"All the time," she said, astounding me.

"Me too."

We were quiet for an awfully long time and I had no idea what to do. I knew if we took the conversation any further that things would be revealed or not revealed and I was too frightened to find out what either would be but it was hanging out there, practically begging to come out to play.

"I'd like to try it again," I said, possibly ruining the past two years worth of work I'd done.

The blood in my neck seeped into my face and I found myself hoping she hadn't heard me. I turned toward her and saw that she had. I felt sick in that moment, an instantaneous headache began to pound my brain but all ceased immediately when she grabbed the vest I wore over my t-shirt and slid the wool cap off my head. She let go of my vest and ran her hands through my hair, twisting her fingers through to the end right above my shoulders.

I couldn't believe this was going to happen to me. We both leaned into one another but I stopped abruptly, wondering something.

"Have you been drinking, Harper?" I asked her, curious why she'd become so forward all of a sudden.

She didn't have a chance to answer because my cell phone began to vibrate on the table. I went to push end, to ignore the call but it was our Super. I noticed it was late so I picked it up.

"Hello! Smith?" I screamed into the phone. I couldn't hear. It sounded like sirens blaring on both ends. Hold on!" I grabbed Harper's hand, refusing to leave her alone and led her to the patio outside the bar. "Smith?" I asked again.

"Yes! Callum! Is Harper with you?!"

"Yes! Why?"

"Well that's a blessing, I guess."

"Smith! What's going on?"

"I hate to tell you this, son, but the building's burning!"

"What?!" I yelled, gripping harder on to Harper's hand. She inched towards me, panic sobering her quickly.

"It looks like it started in your apartment!" He yelled into the phone. "You're needed here, Callum."

"We'll be right there!" I yelled back, ending the phone call.

I tugged Harper's hand toward the club. She'd heard everything and was in shock. I found the girls on the dance floor.

"Cherry!" I yelled, pulling at her sleeve.

"What's up, baby?" She yelled.

"Our apartment's on fire! I'm pretty sure it was John! Tell the others! Meet us there, okay?"

She grabbed my face in her hands and tears had begun to well in her eyes. "Go! We'll be there soon!"

We ran. The taxi was the longest two minute drive of my life. I threw a few bills, not really caring if it was enough or too much, and launched us out the door. The building was indeed in flames on our corner of the building. I noticed our apartment seemed to be the only one on fire. I thanked God for small blessings. They must have gotten there pretty quickly.

"No!" Harper yelled.

We wound our way through the throng of people and found a fireman on a radio.

"That's our apartment!" I yelled over the sirens. "Did everyone get out safely?" I asked.

"Everyone! Are you Callum and Harper Tate?"

"Yes, sir!"

"You two were the only ones we had yet to locate. Please, stay nearby!" He said, running off another direction as a section of Harper's bedroom collapsed into the street, shattering into a flaming mess, making us both cringe.

So, Harper and I were forced to watch our apartment burn to a black crisp. Harper was openly sobbing, clinging to my shirt, burying her face in my neck. I tried to soothe her by rubbing her hair but it did no good. What could I possibly do or say? We both knew who started it. He ruined everything we had worked for. All those years of shopping for frugal purchases, investing an astronomical amount of time into making our house cozy and everything wonderful, gone. In a blaze of hate. I absently remembered that we had renter's insurance and breathed a small sigh of relief knowing we'd get to at least purchase a new life if we ever survived John Bell's wrath.

Then, I remembered Harper's copy of *To Kill A Mockingbird* and almost cried for her. I wasn't going to bring it up. I hoped for a small favor in that it might be spared but I knew that would be unlikely. We were literally losing all our possessions. We were being left with less than what we had when we met, which was absolutely nothing accept for a motorcycle and a book. I'd come to terms with my bike being gone but Harper's book was the *only* link to one of the *only* happy memories she even had.

I barely remember hands being wrapped around our bodies. They stood around us, enveloping us in their warmth and kindness. Yet again, pillars for us to lean on. I don't know how long we stood like that, as they fought the scorching inferno that was John Bell, but they never faltered. They held us until a fireman came up to let us know that it was cleared to scope out the damage. We nodded and waited to hear word on just how bad the injury was.

I remember Cherry and Charlie discussing where we should stay and they'd decided Charlie's was best and he'd go stay with her, but that at least for the night, none of us should be apart. Cherry sent the girls out to pick up essentials for both Harper and I; toothbrushes, underwear, basic clothing, things like that. Charlie told Tom and SO to ready his apartment for our arrival. I couldn't speak, too engrossed in caring for a grieving Harper but I remembered feeling an overwhelming gratefulness to our generous and considerate friends.

It was almost light out when it seemed all the trucks were gone. The only ones left were us and a few investigators. All had been cleared to return to their apartments. There was no structural damage. Our apartment was the only affected. The police had arrived shortly after that and we answered as many questions as possible. The fire investigator confirmed it was arson. He returned to his truck while we spoke to the detectives and brought back a clear plastic bag with a large metal case inside. I didn't recognize any of it so I knew it had to have been something John left.

"This is a fire proof box we found in the middle of their living room. We figured it was left by the arsonist. It had a name written in marker across the top and a melted bow. It looked out of place," the investigator told the detective.

"That's definitely not ours," I said.

"Can we take this?" The detective asked.

"I need to process it. You can have all when we're done with our investigation. Is it something you'd be interested in?"

"Well, yeah, the suspect in their assault case from a few weeks ago is probably our number one in the arson as well."

"Ah, I see. Alright, well, I'll hand it over to you then. Yours takes precedence. Just let us know when you're done," the investigator said, starting to walk away.

"Wait, what do you think is in it?" Harper asked, clinging to my side.

"We're not sure, Miss. We suspect a message of sorts," he answered.

"We'll process for prints at the office, Harper," the detective said. "Once it's opened, we'll let you know what's inside."

"Will you call tonight?" I asked.

"You mean, this morning?" He asked, squinting at the rising morning sun. I nodded. "Sure, I'll be sure to do that."

The detective took my cell phone number. The investigator led Harper and I and the remainder of our group, including Cherry and Charlie and led us to our apartment. When we reached our floor, it looked normal but the smell was intense.

"What about our neighbors?" I asked.

"I think they're staying at a few friends' homes until it can be cleaned."

I nodded, feeling slightly guilty at the inconvenience our psycho was causing others.

The hallway half way to our door was splattered

239

with gray and grew to a menacing solid black once we reached the open hole where our door used to be. I gripped Harper's hand as we entered our living room, barely recognizing it. Cherry gasped once inside and held Charlie's hand as he stood and shook his head back and forth in disbelief.

The couch was a charred mess, the wingback we spent hours recovering was non-existent. I wrapped an arm around Harper's waist as we inched toward her room, absorbing our scorched surroundings. Her bedroom was a giant gaping hole, exposed to the outside. The closet that held both our clothing was gone as well as an entire wall of art Harper and I had spent months collecting. The only room slightly left intact was the kitchen and it was the only room we could probably care less about. I felt like hunting John Bell down and murdering him with my bare hands.

"My book!" Harper suddenly exclaimed.

She broke free of my grasp and tried to enter the bedroom. I clutched at her waist, preventing her from entering.   "No, Harper! The floor is unstable!" Cherry went to Harper's side, trying to console her.

"Where is it?" I asked.

"It was wrapped in plastic and placed in a plastic shoe box on the top shelf of our closet."

"It's gone then," I said, going to her.

She wrapped her arms around my waist and held me closely. "Why?" She whispered. She pulled away a little to peer into my face. "I'm so sorry. He took our home, Callum."

I forced her back into my chest. "No! He didn't take *my* home, Harper! Because *my* home is right here, in my arms."

She clung to me harder, squeezing my waist, before

reaching up and throwing her arms around my neck.

She spoke into my neck. "I'm still so very sorry."

"You have nothing to be sorry about. They're just things, Harper."

And for the first time since the incident, I realized just how much I didn't care for those things. Yeah, it was an inconvenience, I'll admit that, but I was forever grateful that everything I truly cared about in this world was standing right in front of me, wearing my ring. I knew I couldn't wait anymore to tell her how I really felt.

"Come on," I said, guiding her toward the hall. "Let's go," I told Cherry and Charlie.

We took a taxi to Charlie's and the place was empty when we got there. Cherry told us she had encouraged everyone to go home and get some rest and try to come over later that night. Since, Harper and I were beat, Charlie and Cherry left, leaving Harper and I alone. We showered, brushed our teeth, and dressed in the pajamas Cherry had the girls buy us. It all felt very normal, save for the fact that it was anything but.

I practically spilled into Charlie's bed, not even bothering to get under the covers. Harper followed suit and squirmed to my side of the bed, entangling her arms and legs within mine. We slept as one person for a couple of hours before being woken up at noon by my cell phone, whose battery was on its last leg. *Have to remember to stop by the store and pick up a charger*, I thought, yet another thing you never think of until you need it once it's gone.

"Hello?" I answered groggily, still holding Harper. She stayed fast asleep.

"Hi, this is Detective Carson. We spoke earlier this morning at the scene of the fire?"

"Yes, is this about the box?" I asked.

"Yeah, would it be too much trouble to ask for you and Harper to come down to the station."

"We need to ask you both a few questions, if that's okay?"

I couldn't help but yawn. Four hours of sleep just wasn't setting well. "Of course, we'll be right there," I answered and hung up.

I shook Harper gently. "Harper, honey, wake up."

She groaned and looked up at me sleepily. "What's wrong?" She asked, studying my face.

"Detective Carson asked us to come up to the station."

Harper

The station was teeming with people, the smells of lunch permeated the air around us. The girls, who always thought I dressed a bit too lax, were true to form when they purchased a change of clothes for me. I was so grateful to them but they picked the tightest pair of skinny jeans they could find, a pair of grey boots to wear over, and a ridiculously low cut and tight t-shirt. I thanked God that I still had my jacket from the night before to cover up. I giggled to myself slightly as I thought about how much I wanted to kill them and hug them both at the same time. Kill them because I felt ridiculous but hug them because of the amazing look I got from Callum when I came out of the bathroom at Charlie's. I needed to rethink my boy wardrobe slightly if I was going to get looks like that.

I was tired of waiting to tell him how I felt. I refused to wait until after graduation as I'd planned. I knew I couldn't make it that long. I'd decided that night, I'd spill my guts. The night of the fire I couldn't believe where our conversation had gone. My stomach flipped just thinking about it and it gave me more hope than I dared to dream. Every time he held my hand, touched my skin, hugged me, now had a very different meaning. I wondered now if it wasn't just as one sided as I'd always thought it had been.

"Mr. and Mrs. Tate?" An officer asked, breaking my train of thought.

The giddy, crazy feeling I always got when someone called me his wife would never leave me, I thought.

"Yes?" Callum answered, standing up, sending a deeper thrill coursing through my stomach.

"If you'll follow me," he said.

Now the nerves took over. I wanted to stop in the middle of the hallway, beg Callum to run away with me and start fresh in another state just so I wouldn't have to deal with the crap we were destined to deal with very soon. We rounded a corner and entered an older looking gentleman's office. This was not Detective Carson. Carson was younger, maybe mid-twenties, had light blonde hair and bright eyes. This man was much older, maybe sixty, pudgy around the middle but had a very kind face.

"Hello," he said, standing, holding out his hand for each of us. "My name is Detective Lewis. Carson needed some shut eye and I promised him I'd go over the evidence with you. I'm the second detective on the case now."

"Hi, nice to meet you," I said. "I'm Harper Tate and this is my husband, Callum." Callum winked at me when I'd called him my husband. It was the first time I'd ever done that.

"A pleasure," the detective said and we all sat. "I'm not looking to alarm you but the box the investigator found, you have suspicions it is John Bell, correct?"

"Yes, sir," I said.

243

"Okay, we found prints on the box but they weren't John's."

"What?" Callum asked. "That's impossible..."

"Wait," the detective interrupted. "They belong to a woman who 's been missing for several weeks now and is now believed to be deceased."

"What?" I asked, all the breath leaving my body at once. I was choking on the news he'd given me. If I wasn't already sitting, I would have trouble supporting myself. "Why do you believe she is deceased?" I asked, not really wanting to hear why.

"Well, unfortunately we found her fingers inside the box he left at your home."

"Oh my God!" I said, clutching Callum's jacket sleeve.

The detective shook his head. "Yes, terrible and I'm so sorry to be the one telling you this but we've had a slew of missing persons cases over the past six months, right about the time John Bell was released. Now, we suspect him in most of the cases because the timing just fits."

"Why else do you suspect him?" Callum asked, reading into his statement.

Detective Lewis sighed loudly and fell into the back of his chair, making me sit up ramrod straight in mine. "There are *characteristics* that each girl possesses that we feel may be a common link."

"And...what would these characteristics be, Detective Lewis?" I barely asked.

"This girl, the one who's fingers we've found in the box, well, her name is Harper as well."

I began to sway in my chair. Callum gripped my shoulder to keep me from falling forward.

"And the others?" I asked.

"There's no need to burden you with this," he said.

I was too far gone now. "No, please."

"Well, there is a girl missing from Harlem that we realized could be your twin. Another missing from Flushing with the exact same color hair and," he sighed again, "one went missing last week that shared the same street name and apartment number as yours."

They're probably dead and it's all my fault. I reached for the trashcan by his desk and began dry heaving. I hadn't had anything to eat in over twelve hours and my stomach had nothing to give.

"Oh my God!" I panted, trying to keep the tears from falling. "If it weren't for me they'd be alive, wouldn't they?" I asked Callum.

"No, Harper!" He said, "We don't know that they're dead." But not even he believed that. I could hear the hesitation in his voice. "Nobody is responsible for those girls going missing," he continued, "but John Bell."

"Of course not!" Detective Lewis said at the same time as Callum. "No one is to blame but him, no one," Lewis said when Callum was done. "Listen, we need you two to stay under the radar. That means no attending classes, no visiting friends he would know about."

"Would he know about Charlie's?" I asked Callum.

"I don't see how. He's not in The Ivories. There'd be no way he could find us."

"Just in case," Lewis said, I'll have a patrol car out there throughout the night until we find this guy. We've checked all his known addresses and he's not at any. No one seems to know who this guy is."

"There's one person," I said absently.

"Who?" He asked.

"There was a man there the night John killed that woman. He was trying to get John to leave. I doubt he really knew John's true nature. I have no idea how you'd find him but..."

"We'll check the records for that night and see if he doesn't come up. In the meantime, please stay out of sight."

Callum and I both nodded.

"What else was in the box?" I asked.

"Um, I don't really..."

"Please, Detective Lewis."

"Alright, video tapes of you and your husband sleeping."

"How?" Callum asked.

"He must have set up surveillance video but all evidence has since been burned we suspect."

I felt my face turn bright red from embarrassment, not that Callum and I did anything but, still, I felt an unbelievable invasion of privacy. My body felt sick at the thought that he watched us when we thought we were alone.

"Is that all?" I asked.

"No, there were letters inside addressed to you and your husband."

"Can we read them?" Callum asked.

"They're being processed. I've read them. Most of it was gibberish, basically he was letting you both know that he would never forgive Harper for not waiting for him and for marrying Callum. Also, he threatened both of your lives. I know, this is a lot and it is very serious. I want you both to know we're working very hard to put him in custody.

"Also, we have video of him in your hall with the box in hand and a metal can of accelerant, breaking in to your apartment, and then leaving right after, smoke trailing behind him. Once he's caught, he's not coming out for a very long time." Thank God our building had surveillance. "If we can link him to these missing girls, God willing, find them alive, he'll never come out."

Callum and I left the station together an hour later. I wanted a reprieve, wanted to run, wanted to hide. As we descended the steps to the street, I grabbed fistfuls of Callum's shirt. It was all proving to be too much and I hated myself for bringing my baggage to Callum's doorstep.

"Callum, I'm sorry I dragged you into all of this. I...I know you won't but I wouldn't blame you in the slightest if you wanted out."

He grabbed my shoulders severely but not hard enough to hurt just strong enough to drive his point home. "No more talk like that. You hear me? No more. You're my best friend," he said, breaking his grasp and pulling me in tightly for a hug. "I love you, Harper. More than you could possibly know." He spoke so low on the last part I barely heard him.

"Let's get to Charlie's," he said but stopped short. "Wait, I've got to pick us up a few chargers for our stupid phones first. Then, we need to call our insurance company about the fire. I'm afraid that will be your job, love, because I have no idea who we go through."

"God forbid something ever happen to me," I said, not thinking.

He stopped short once more and glared at me fiercely. "Don't say things like that, Harper." He positioned himself in front of me and held my face in his hands. "If you left me, for whatever reason, it would be the death of me." He let out a shuddering breath, and then gripped my hand, like he couldn't stand the thought of breaking the touch.

Oh my God, I had it so bad. I loved him more than I thought I could ever love another. When we first met, it had been a new love, a genuine love but not as deep as it became with time. As the years passed, Callum became my everything. My happiness was tied to him in strands of transparent steel cables, nothing could break those ties except for Callum himself and I trusted him so implicitly. Callum was as selfless a man could be and in a world where an attribute of that caliber was more rare than a pink diamond, I clutched him tightly to my heart, fully aware of just how priceless he doubtlessly was.

Unexpectedly, as we walked to the phone store, I knew that time was as precious as his selflessness. I promised myself to reveal all despite the possible consequences.

"What are you thinking about?" He asked softly, as we held hands walking the sidewalk, like our lives weren't in mortal danger or that our home hadn't burnt to a crisp.

"I'm thinking," I teased, "that tonight is going to be an amazing one."

"Is that so?" He questioned, one brow strategically raised, his head cocked back a bit, adding a tiny, sexy oomph to the way he swung our hands.

I loved flirting with Callum. He was dynamite at it but he always kept it in check, like he was afraid to lead me on. Suddenly, I wasn't so sure about my plan to reveal all but just as quickly, I steeled myself again. I had to do it. I *needed* to do it.

"Yes, most definitely," I thought but also said out loud.

His cheeks pinkened a bit and he fought a smile, making him gorgeous and humble all in one blow. His teeth were white and *perfect* and, dang, if I hadn't just heard a bell tinkle as the sun shone off them like a mirror. *Damn, that boy is going to be the death of me*. All

248

my worries evaporated when he smiled at me and it was more than welcome. I tamped down all my irreverent thoughts, focused again on walking instead of tripping on the random crack in the sidewalk I always ended up falling over because I was too busy ogling my husband like a complete and utter goofball.

Chapter Fourteen
Electric Feel

Callum

Back at Charlie's, Harper called the insurance company and arranged for an adjuster to come out. They would issue us a check on the spot the following Tuesday. That made both of us feel a heck of a lot better about getting our lives somewhat back to normal. We decided to get a new place as soon as possible but we'd put it in a different name not associated with us personally. Also, we wrote our professors and let them all know what was going on. Ninety percent of them were already aware and agreed to send our assignments to us via email until we returned so we wouldn't get too far behind the progress of the other students.

We laid down around four in the afternoon, exhausted, but not even an hour later, our crew came piling in, in droves, and we knew that would be it on sleep. They came bearing gifts and by gifts, I mean a meal fit for a king and a ton of red wine to 'take our minds off the fire' but, the truth was, they just loved their wine as these 'gifts' were a Saturday night staple if the band didn't have a gig.

Harper and I rarely drank and if we did, it was only a glass or two with dinner and we were set. I had no idea if Harper would partake that evening due to the stress. I hoped she wouldn't. I needed her sober for my confession.

"Time for dinner!" Cherry called to the group as she laid a very large bowl of pasta in the center of the table. We all gathered around the presentation but before we sat, Cherry spoke up. "I think we should start a new tradition!" She announced to the group. "And Charlie's in agreement. In fact, it was his idea. Charlie?"

Charlie stepped forward and wrapped a hand around Cherry's. "I'm not sure why we never did this before as we've got an incredible amount to be thankful for but I just want to start off our meals in a prayer, if that's okay with everyone?"
Everyone nodded in agreement.

"Lord, we are humbled by your generosity. You have given our entire family here tonight something to be truly thankful for. We thank you for this food. We thank you for our health and life. For all this, we thank you and ask that you continue to watch over each one of us, especially Callum and Harper as they are going through a particularly harsh time. In Your name, we pray."

"Amen," the group sounded and it was abruptly obvious that hearts were lighter, eyes brighter.

"Let the merriment begin!" Charlie sang.

We both got caught in group conversation until very late at night as the wine poured freely and the food was plentiful or maybe it was that I was nervous and avoiding the inevitable. *Enough*! I told myself. I stood up when Cherry left her seat to join Charlie at his end of the table, leaving the seat next to Harper vacant. I practically sprinted to the empty chair and sat beside her, eager to profess it all. I noticed a rather full glass of wine beside Harper's plate and hoped it was Cherry's.

"Hey," I said with a wink.

"Hey," she said back, boldly threading her hand with mine. "I thought you'd never come over here."

"Why? Did you have something you wanted to say to me?" I asked, a brow cocked over one eye.

"I have an unbelievable amount I'd like to say to you," she said, bringing her mouth to my ear, "but nothing I can say here."

I shuddered, making her laugh sexily in my ear. An incredible warmth spread from her mouth to my ear and down my neck.

I leaned into her ear and whispered, "Then what are we still doing here?"

She leaned back a bit, taken aback at how open we were being.

"Lead the way, Callum."

I picked up her hand and lead her to the window that opened to the balcony garden that Cherry had grown for Charlie. I scooped my arm behind her knees, reveling at her sharp intake of breath, and sat on the sill before working our bodies through. I swung my legs over and stood up, still holding Harper. Her mouth was open slightly in curiosity. I slid her body down mine to set her upright again. *If I'm doing this, I'm* doing *this. No turning back.*

I inched my face closer to hers, our mouths an inch apart, a repeat of that day in front of The Hope House. I couldn't believe I was about to confess all. I closed my eyes and breathed in deeply through my nose in preparation but her delicious scent sent me reeling forward into her mouth, devouring every square millimeter of her lips.

I breathed out years of pent up frustration at having tasted her once but denying myself every day that we were married and *she* kissed me *back*. I consumed a passion from her I'd never known could exist. She threaded her fingers through my hair and I nearly whimpered at the feel of them, my eyes rolling to the back of my closed eyes. I clutched her waist tightly, inhaling her breaths as I practically swallowed her beautiful tongue. We traded control, back and forth, back and forth, kissing in undulating waves and she tasted incredible, like honeydew and strawberries. I couldn't stop myself from licking her bottom lip to savor the flavor.

I lifted her by the back of her thighs and pushed her into the bit of wall near Charlie's window and as we collided, our breaths rushed out in a huff. She wrapped her legs around my waist and purred with satisfaction, practically giggling. I broke free from the kiss, both of us panting from the exertion. I feverishly kissed below her jaw, her neck, and along her collarbone as she ran her nails along my shoulders, a moan barely escaped from her lips earning a light chuckle from me. She amused me. *Oh*, how she amused me.

"What's so funny?" She wheezed, the back of her head resting against the wall, giving me better access to her neck, her eyes closed but her mouth smiling.

"You're so amazing," I whispered into her neck between kisses. I squeezed her hips between my thumbs and forefingers.

I kissed her mouth again, in disbelief. She smacked

intensity. It made me want to bow in acquiescence, to bend prostrate before this woman, if she let me. I would worship the ground she walked on.

"Take me home," she whispered without thinking.

"You are home, Harper," I answered, running my hands up her sides, feeling her beautiful ribs, stopping just below her breasts.

She looked at me like she'd just woken, sleepy and confused. "You're right."

"I want to yell at everybody to leave," I laughed into the crook of her neck.

"Why don't you tell them we're tired?" She said between soft, caressing kisses along my jaw line.

"I am feeling a bit sleepy myself," I joked, squeezing her thighs and contradicting my words. She gasped lightly and, again, married her lips with mine.

I knew I would never get my fill of Harper, never.

"Callum?" We heard Sam calling through the apartment.

"Damn it!" I exclaimed, letting Harper down, *really* not wanting to let Harper down.

I kept her pinned to the wall as we tried to steady our labored breathing.

"We're here!" I yelled in frustration, never taking my eyes from Harper.

I leaned about six inches from her but kept her restrained with my arms on either side of her face. All she could do was stare at me, breathless, making me want to attack her with everything I had. I kissed her softly on her cheek, making her shudder. I smiled in flirtation, a promise of things to come.

"I want you, Mrs. Tate," I whispered in her ear.

"I want you more, husband," she countered, making me shiver as well in ecstasy.

"There you are!" Sam said, poking her head through the window.

Obviously noticing the intimacy between us, Sam wedged through the window anyway and shook the dust of the brick from her hands.

"Whatcha' doing?" She asked, awkwardly walking to the bench Harper had just sat at.

I never let Harper escape my arms. "Oh, just flirting with my *wife*," I answered, never taking my eyes from my Harper. She bit her bottom lip and smiled.

I slowly released Harper and she stood straighter, breathing hard through her nose, her chest rising with each intake. I placed my hand on her chest, feeling her heartbeat, elated I was making it race at light speed.

Sam cleared her throat, reminding us she was there, breaking our trance. I grabbed Harper's hand and led her to the bench opposite the one Sam was sitting in. Before Harper could sit, though, I yanked her into my lap, making her laugh. I couldn't stop myself and gently nipped at the top of her shoulder. She yelped in response, making us both laugh.

"I see you're busy," Sam said, racing to the window and crawling in. "I'll come back later, then." Neither of us acknowledged her, too engrossed in the other.

Harper wrapped her hands around my face and kissed me softly but the kiss turned deadly, heated, desperate. I knew I was losing track of why I'd come out there in the first place and I didn't want anything to happen until I'd told her what I needed to tell her. I started to peel her unbelievably amazing body off of mine but she unexpectedly straddled my lap and in an instant, I forgot what I was so worried about talking to her about. *No, the truth, Callum*, I thought as her mouth melted into mine. Her moans spurred me on and I gripped her waist with

255

tight fingers, pressing her hips into mine as I kissed her like I'd never kissed anyone.

When I married Harper, I loved her. Tremendously. But after two years of living with her, knowing her the way I did, I was desperately *in* love with her and tasting her brought forth every memory that made me fall, like flashing cards of vibrant feelings and overwhelming images. Our wedding day, the way her hair whipped in the wind that night, framing her face, another still I referenced often in class when I should have been paying attention to the lecture. The first day of classes, I walked her to each one. I told her it was because I didn't want her to feel overwhelmed but I truly did it so I'd have an excuse to hold her hand. I remembered looking down into her face, her eyes bright with new adventure and a little piece of my heart fell into her hands. My heart tumbled in pieces at her feet as she chipped away at it with her wondrous ways, and it didn't form a whole again until half a year had passed and the end product was a living, beating organ in the palm of her hands.

The first year of our marriage, on New Year's Eve, Harper and I, with the rest of our group of friends, dressed warmly and trekked it all the way to Times Square. We all danced and drank hot cocoa and as the ball dropped, she and I gripped each other's arms and counted down, laughing louder and louder with each number. I remembered her pink cheeks, her ears covered by her wool hat. On one, she reached up and ran her cool gloved hands down my cheeks. I regret we only kissed cheeks. I had lots of regret those past two years. In retrospect, I could see that my youth was what prevented me from making moves, solidifying a relationship, so, instead, I fell deeper and deeper in love with Harper, making me more frightened of losing her.

No more. It was a risk I was willing to take because being in love with your best friend can only carry you so far.

"Ha-Harper," I gulped, my mouth begging my brain to keep it locked with hers.

"Hmm?" She asked, her eyes still closed, her mouth resting against mine.

"I need to tell you something," I said.

"Tell me," she whispered but we continued to kiss for a few minutes more.

When I finally emerged, my lips were raw and Harper's chin was red from my stubble.

I sighed, realizing I let it go too far. Now, I knew she'd think I was making this profession because I wanted sex but that wasn't the case. "This wasn't supposed to happen," I said more to myself than to her.

"I'm sorry?" She asked, practically jumping off my lap. Her hand flew to her mouth. "Oh my God, I'm so sorry Callum." Tears began to spill but abruptly stopped. "You know what?" She yelled. "Screw you! You kissed me back! I felt it!"

"Harper! No! That's not what I meant!"

"No! Don't you worry your pretty little head! You don't owe me any sort of explanation!" The sarcasm was dripping off of her but she sobered quickly, hanging her head. "I shouldn't have kissed you when you've been drinking and with the fire and all things, we're emotional." I started to interrupt her, to tell her I hadn't been drinking, but she stopped me with a finger in the air. "Don't worry, Callum. We'll go back to how things were." Her thoughts turned inward but she spoke them aloud. "We'll pretend to be married again. Yeah, we'll go back to pretending because that's how it's supposed to be. No one has to find out. I don't know what I was thinking kissing him. I'm such an idiot."

Harper walked toward the window and I sprinted toward her, grabbing her arm.

"Let go, Callum. I'm going to go lay down. I don't feel so hot."

"Wait," I said, "Let me explain."

She placed her hand over my mouth and shook her head, her eyes were wet.

"Don't say anything we'll regret. Please, Callum? I can't handle truths tonight."

What? She knew what I was going to say. There was no other way she could interpret it and yet she didn't want to hear it. I initiated the kiss, she had to know what I was planning and she wanted me to keep it to myself.

Humiliation washed over me. A hundred emotions flew through me. I was angry at her for leading me on, for kissing me when she didn't feel the same. My chest ached at the loss. The most awful pain, a heart attack at twenty.

She slid through the window and I slid down the brick wall, clutching at my heart with the palm of my hand, pressing hard in attempt to alleviate the pain. Except, it wasn't a heart attack in the traditional sense, was it? The attack would probably shorten years from my life, yes, but it wasn't from high cholesterol or a genetic disorder. No, this was an acute burn that resonated from the center of my heart and if it were words it would read 'you wanted the truth and now that you have it, you want to give it back'. With each pump, my body wanted to shut down from the agony it caused. It was a rhythmic, pulsing wound. Each beat, a question.

Harper

When I fell through the window, I immediately ran, feeling sick to my stomach and headed toward the kitchen. Thankfully, no one was in there. I turned on the water to drown out the sound and vomited into the sink. I rinsed the sink and my mouth, turned off the water and sank to the floor as one of the biggest fools this side of the Mississippi. He hadn't meant any of it and I'd made a massive ass out of myself. I wanted him to want me so badly I didn't bother to ask.

My heart felt like it had been ripped from my chest. I couldn't stay in that apartment with him by ourselves. I stood, grabbed my bag from my dining chair as I swiftly ran to the door, nobody taking notice of me. I entered the hall and quietly shut the door behind me. I noticed that SO was in the hall on his cell.

I looked at him with tears in my eyes and sunk against the wall, falling to the floor.

"Let me call you back," he said into his phone and ran over to me.

"Harper, what's wrong?" He asked, almost frantic. "Let me get Callum."

"*No!*" I practically yelled. "No, he's the reason I'm crying."

SO sank to the floor next to me, throwing his arm around my shoulder. "No worries, Harper. Men can be boneheads sometimes. He'll come around, you'll see."

"No," I said, shaking my head back and forth, "not this time." *I won't.* I wiped the tears from my eyes. SO removed a handkerchief from his pocket, deftly earning his nickname. I laughed without humor.

"What happened?" He asked kindly.

"I can't say," I said. "Just trust me?" I turned to face him.

"Of course," he said, squeezing my shoulder. I could tell he was trying to decide whether or not he should try to pry a little further but he respected me enough not to.

"I can't stay the night with him, SO. Do you think you could get Cherry for me?"

SO's eyes widened before he stood up and went into Charlie's flat.

This wasn't supposed to happen, he'd said, confirming the only real fear I'd ever felt my entire life. I felt so foolish. I stupidly felt like I could somehow make our arrangement more than what it really was. Somewhere in the back of my mind, I knew that men didn't do anything they don't want to and it works the same in reverse. When a man wants something, he'll do anything to get it. I should have known that if Callum wanted me he would have taken me...a long time ago.

I felt like an even bigger fool knowing that I was scrunched down in Charlie's hallway by myself when John Bell was out to kill me or take me or whatever plans he had for me. I visibly shivered. I wanted neither. Understatement. That's when I realized I couldn't stay at Cherry's because John would know that Cherry was part of The Ivories. I needed an alternative arrangement. The door opened just as I was deciding to ask Marty if I could stay at hers.

When I looked up, Callum, Cherry, and SO came out. "Crap," I said out loud, earning me a look of admonishment from Cherry.

"We'll just be in here," Cherry said, pulling SO with her back inside. He tried to protest but Cherry would have none of it.

I stood quickly, faced Callum, and knew immediately that his face was the most beautiful but most painful thing I could possibly look at...ever. I hadn't realized it but I was retreating backwards, slowly. Callum followed me just as slowly, watching me closely, afraid I'd flee.

"Wait," he said, holding a hand out.

I don't know why, but I took it.

"What are we going to do?" He asked, grasping my hand.

"I - I'm not sure," I told him, on the verge of losing control.

"Do we go back to pretending?" He said, shocking my heart. "That we're married?"

"Is there much of a point now that John Bell knows of our identities?"

Something washed over his face, startling me. *Relief? Hurt?* I couldn't tell.

"I suppose not," he said, "but..."

"But?"

"But we'll at least stay friends, right Harper?" He softly slid his hand up to grab my upper arm, sending an alarming pain to the center of my chest, unbeknownst to him.

I had to step back to be rid of the pain. He looked hurt but not as much as I was.

"I don't know. Can we? We both know that when one friend is in love with the other, it never bodes well," I said bluntly.

Callum's shoulders hung limply in defeat at my statement, no doubt feeling guilty for not being able to give back what I wanted so badly to get.

I couldn't stop myself and ran to him, throwing my arms around his neck, sobbing into his shoulder. "I wish it didn't have to be this way," I said. "I don't think I can live without you, Callum. Despite everything, you're still my best friend."

He squeezed his arms around my back and held me close. "I can't do it either. Maybe it's not healthy," he stops, choking on his words. "No, I *know* it's not healthy

261

but I can't do it. I can't leave you."

I cried harder. "Can we still live together, Callum? Do we," I gulped. "Do we stay married?"

"I think we remain roommates. If you can do it, I can do it."

"And our marriage?" I asked, tearing my face from his now wet t-shirt and peering up at him.

He closed his eyes and sighed loudly. "I think we should divorce," he said.

The word hangs in the air like a noose. A new wave of pain inundates me and I sob harder into his shoulder. "I'm so sorry, Callum. I wish I could change how I feel." *I wish I wasn't so in* love *with you.* But I don't say it. I can't. It's too fresh to say the word out loud.

"Shh," he says, wrapping his arms tighter around my torso. "Me too," he whispers.

Callum

This wasn't supposed to be how it happened, I thought. I felt so foolish. I stupidly felt like I could somehow make our arrangement more than what it really was and I had forgotten how to be a man. I wanted her - more than anything - I wanted her to be mine and was too much of a coward to take what I wanted from the beginning. I could have spared myself all this heartache if I'd only been honest with her from the start.

"Callum!" I heard over the street noise below. "Callum!" It's Cherry but I can't muster the voice to call back to her. It doesn't matter because she and SO find me anyway. "What are you doing out here?" She asks, climbing through the window, SO following behind her.

"Harper's out in the hall crying, Callum," SO says, eyeing me carefully, folding his arms across his chest. I can see he wants to accuse me of something but he's waiting for a preemptive explanation. I don't give anything. There's nothing to tell. What am I going to say? *SO, I fake married Harper yet, still, foolishly fell in love with her but she doesn't feel the same way.* No, I don't think so. "She's crying like I've never seen her cry. Did you - you didn't cheat on her, *did you*?"

Cherry hits SO's shoulder in my defense. "SO!"

"Ow! What?" He asks, rubbing where she hit. "I've never seen Harper so upset!"

"Callum," Cherry said, "she's out in the hall by herself. It's not exactly ideal since, well I don't want to bring it up but John Bell. She shouldn't be alone."

I shot up like a light and sped through the apartment with both Cherry and SO close on my heels. We opened the door and breathed a sigh of relief, she's alive and well. 'Crap', she says. What a strange situation we'd found ourselves in. Cherry escorts SO back into the apartment, leaving us alone.

She stands quickly, facing me, and I knew immediately that her face was the most beautiful and most painful thing I would possibly look at...ever. She slowly stepped backwards toward the elevators. I follow her, memorizing her every move. I hold out my hand and, surprisingly, she takes it.

"What are we going to do?" I asked.

"I - I'm not sure," she said, wary.

"Do we go back to pretending?" I asked. "That we're married?"

"Is there much of a point now that John Bell knows of our identities?" She said, stunning my heart to a still. Her words shoot through me like a poison tipped arrow. Mortally wounding. The effects, I'm afraid, contort my face but I try my hardest to fix it before I hurt her own feelings.

"I suppose not," I said, "but..."

"But?" She asks, her eyebrows raised.

"But we'll at least stay friends, right Harper?" I softly grab her arm, sending an alarming pain to the center of my chest, unbeknownst to her.

She steps back to put distance between us, piercing me yet again.

"I don't know. Can we?" She asks. "We both know that when one friend is in love with the other, it never bodes well."

It seemed careless, her statement, its damaging effects making my shoulders hang limply. She cut me down once again. She knows I'm in love with her, she just said it with her own words and she's reminding me she can't return the favor.

Seemingly in regret, she throws her arms around my neck, sobbing into my shoulder. "I wish it didn't have to be this way," she said. "I don't think I can live without you, Callum. Despite everything, you're still my best friend."

I squeezed my arms around her small back and held her close, pretending she was mine. "I can't do it either. Maybe it's not healthy." I stopped, choking on my words. "No, I *know* it's not healthy, but I can't do it. I can't leave you."

She cries harder. "Can we still live together, Callum? Do we," she gulped. "Do we stay married?"

"I think we remain roommates. If you can do it, *I* can do it," I said, coming to terms with what I must say next.

"And our marriage?" She asks, tearing her face from my t-shirt and peering up at me.

I close my eyes and sigh loudly. "I think we should divorce," I say thickly.

The word hangs in the air like a noose. A new wave of pain inundates me

"I'm so sorry, Callum," she said. "I wish I could change how I feel."

Me too but I wish more that I wasn't so in love with you. But I don't say it. I can't. It's too fresh to say the word out loud.

"Shh," I say, wrapping my arms tighter around her torso. "Me too," I whispered.

Chapter Fifteen
Boo

Callum

Harper and I met our insurance adjuster at our burned down apartment. Seeing it in the light was so much worse, making Harper and I all sorts of crazy depressed. We took our check to the bank and stood in line, together yet alone with our thoughts. Things were extremely awkward now that our friendship was so defined. We had no idea how to act around one another. I could only hope that these new boundaries would be what it took to help me fall out of love with Harper, though I knew that was unlikely.

I accidentally bumped into her and apologized like we were strangers. She waved it off as an accident and refused eye contact whereas before she would have stomped my foot in playful response and laughed whole-heartedly. I wanted my old Harper back. Then again, the old Harper drove me crazy with want.

After the check was deposited, Harper and I agreed

with a strange sort of politeness that we should look for a new apartment...one with *two* bedrooms since 'we make a little bit more money now, we can afford it and that will allow us privacy', she'd said, leaving a rotten taste in my mouth but I mindlessly agreed. We looked for new apartments and found a decent one in a building similar to our old one, lots of old history, lots of tile and wood and plaster. This one had a doorman though, which was nice.

We got a two bedroom with two full bathrooms, making it possible never to see one another once during a school day. I'd have to get used to it sometime, I guessed. Slowly weaning myself off of her seemed like a good idea in my head but my heart couldn't help but thump wildly in protest. The week we were off school, we did our work at night, never seeing one another except once when I needed to get a water from the fridge and Harper happened to come out as I did for the same. We clumsily danced around the other when I tried to leave and she tried to enter, both laughing stiffly. I basically sprinted toward my room and never emerged after that.

Furnishing the apartment was equally painful, although sleeping on a real mattress after enduring two years on a sofa bed was sort of nice. Beds were the first thing we bought and it was much easier since it truly didn't have to be a joint decision. When we entered the store, we went opposite directions. I couldn't decide on which one I wanted and needed so badly to get Harper's opinion but couldn't dredge up the nerve to bother her. She already knew I was in love with her, no sense in making myself look more pathetic.

For the rest of the apartment, namely the living room, we went to the Ikea in Brooklyn, deciding that fishing for 'cool pieces' was too much work since we were in the thick of school and the whole John Bell thing. Plus, we would never be able to recreate our old apartment because firstly, that took two years to accomplish, hunting little used furniture stores and the weekly trips to the flea markets and secondly, and most importantly, the old apartment was a piece of the *old* Callum and Harper. The *new* Callum and Harper were reserved, neither having an opinion anymore and therefore creating an Ikea explosion in our living room. A one stop shop. I have to admit, it was really nice looking but we basically took a catalog room, pointed to it and said, 'we want this' to a sales associate and had it delivered.

Also, since we had to replace both our wardrobes, we gave one another five hundred a piece and visited a few stores on our own. In a rare moment of unusual friendliness, after Harper came in to our Ikea vomited living space, we took one look at each other in our clothes and burst out laughing. Both of us had feet clad in red Chucks, distressed jeans, and vintage t-shirts. She went to change so it wouldn't be weird and came out in a freaking skirt, which I'd never seen her wear before of her own volition and wish she hadn't started since her rejection of me that night at Charlie's. Any headway we had made with our moment was completely gone when I saw her in that skirt and boots, effectively sending me to my room for the rest of the evening.

We put the apartment in a completely different name from ours. That was a recommendation from the police department. It was harder than I thought to list the apartment in someone else's name but somehow we managed. We also couldn't go to one of The Ivories' biggest shows because John had yet to be caught. I was prisoner in a torturous cell that week. I was Loki and she was my snake.

When it was time to return to campus, Harper became extraordinarily chatty, chattier than even before our incident and I found myself venturing to her side of the apartment, leaning against her door jamb as she explained to me how she was going to be walking to her classes now, since a new route had to be determined. I had yet to see her bedroom. This was a lot more feminine than her old room, lots of textured fabrics, velvet, Dupioni silks, crazy patterns, a lamp I noticed from our old apartment that must have survived the fire.

I entered without asking and stopped short.   "Can I come in?" I asked.

"Of course," she said, sighing. "You don't ever have to ask."

I smiled sadly and walked over to the lamp.

"It survived, did it?"

"Yeah," she said, walking over and running her hand along the fringe. "I didn't tell you?"

"I knew some stuff did but I never bothered to find out, too depressing, I guess."

"It's depressing but at the same time makes me feel a little bit better knowing he couldn't destroy everything." *Yeah, he destroyed the only thing that* really *mattered, though*, I thought. She stopped talking but continued twirling her fingers in the fringe. "I - I never really thought you would forgive me for what John did to us."

The blood rushed to my face in frustrated anger. "Think about what you just said, Harper, it's what John did to *us*. I don't know how many times I have to tell you this, but I don't blame you for his craziness. Shit happens. He fixated on you and that's not your fault. Please believe me when I say this, Harper, because I don't want to keep reassuring you about it. You need to start believing it yourself."

She nodded, giving me a half-smile.

"Are we ever going to go back to normal?" She asked after an awkward moment of silence.

I stepped back a bit and fell into her bed, sitting down and placing my hand on the edge of the foot board. "I don't know, Harper, but I sure as hell am going to try."

She stepped beside me and sat next to me, not as close as she would have before but close enough for me to know she was trying. "I promise, I'll give it my darndest."

"So, school," I said, changing the subject.

"Yup, I'm nervous about it. I'll be by myself most of the day."

"I know you're nervous but I'll still walk you to every class and there will be that hour we have for lunch. I promise it'll be okay. Just make sure you always stay in a crowded area but where I can find you."

"And work?" She asked.

"Already took care of that. You and I have the exact same shifts for the next six weeks. Laura said she can arrange the same schedule as long as needed if they don't find him within that time frame." Harper shifted uncomfortably. "You don't need to be worried about being alone there. Besides, I think that's the one place we're safest as he isn't aware we even work there.

"Plus, and I know you hate it, but I had her put us on a lot of the one a.m. shifts to organize the stacks."

"Blech!" She said, making me laugh. It wasn't long until she joined in. "Alright, that sounds okay, I guess."

Harper and I worked at Bobst, or the Elmer Holmes Bobst Library. It's the main library of NYU but we usually worked on the third floor at the Fales Library, a rare collection of books and manuscripts in English and

American literature. Harper *loved* it, seeing as her favorite thing in the entire world was reading. She had a healthy respect for all things literature.

The Bobst is a daunting place, housing close to three and a half million books and journals, a twelve story square building, home to one of the largest academic libraries in the nation. When you step onto the black, white and gray marble stereo-grammed floor, your gaze shoots straight up to the ceiling. There's glass as far as the eye can see, surrounding the lobby in a translucent square cocoon. The library fits within a square ring of sorts, all glass interior walls, allowing you to see through the lobby and into the other side, a magnificent sight especially to those first visiting.

A particularly creepy fact about the Bobst is that a six foot Plexiglas wall had to be installed on all its open air crosswalks because there were two suicides in the same year a few years back. I remembered reading about them when I was in high school. I shudder to think the stress those poor students had been under. It made me wonder what things were being put in place besides barricades to prevent further deaths.

The first week we returned to class, I walked Harper to all her classes without incident though they hadn't caught John yet. The second week was our last before Christmas break and we were swamped with finals and work, both grateful for the distraction since the detective handling our case had called to inform us that yet another woman fitting Harper's description was reported missing that Monday. I stayed particularly close to Harper that week and by Thursday, finals were over, and we only had to work that night in the stacks before we had the next *month* off.

Friday was Christmas Eve, we'd planned on

visiting my uncle in Seattle before our 'incident' but hadn't talked about it since. I never bought the tickets and she never brought it up so I never bothered either. I did write Ames and he basically gave me an open invite to visit, letting me know he was aware that I had a few weeks off and that I could stay as long as I'd like. I told him I'd think about it, knowing the answer was most likely no. I would never leave Harper alone without John caught and would never risk John Bell following us to Ames', getting my only surviving family member mixed up in my craziness.

That night, the night before Christmas Eve, Harper and I shared a silent train ride to organize the stacks for the last time until the break was over, both of us hiding from one another by immersing ourselves in our iPods. I had Pinback's *Boo* on repeat. It just felt appropriate. I wore a simple thermal and t-shirt under my utility jacket. It was especially cold that late at night so I threw on my wool cap, tucking my longish hair behind my ears and wrapped a scarf around my neck. I glanced Harper's way and couldn't help but take her in. She didn't wear anything unusually different that night yet she looked completely different to me. Her faded jeans hugged her legs well, her bright red military jacket with the large black buttons was buttoned all the way to her neck, her chunky blue knitted beret covering her ears. She decided to wear her black combats, probably because the cold here in the city could penetrate even the thickest sneaker. The concrete just held the cold better than anywhere else. As I watched her, I realized that it had been weeks since the declaration and I was still in love with her, nowhere close to getting over her.

We had agreed to continue wearing our rings to keep up appearances but it made me ill to look at mine.

My eyes followed the line of my arm until it met the ring on my finger. It was a huge lie, that ring. I suddenly felt tired, not from the late hour, but from carrying the massive burden of our lie and the heavy weight that she didn't love me as I loved her on my back. As much as I hated to admit it to myself, I didn't think I wanted to be married to Harper anymore. I knew I couldn't have her so why torture myself any longer? As soon as John was caught, I'd divorce Harper, that was already decided, but I needed to take it one step further than that. We hadn't agreed to separating our friendship as I think we both wanted to remain friends, even after the divorce but I knew that if I ever wanted to have a semblance of normality, I'd have to cut myself off from her, completely.

I looked down at my feet, a stinging, burning sensation overtook my eyes as I realized I was on the verge of losing it. I sucked it up, not wanting to alert Harper to any sudden change. I rolled my head onto the back of my neck and stared at the ceiling, relieved when the speaker announced our arrival as it sobered me quickly. Both Harper and I walked quietly to Bobst, entered the building and went to work, never removing our headphones.

This was it. The beginning of the blasted end.

Harper

Callum and I walked into Bobst surrounded by the terrible unspoken words the last few weeks' had given us. Words like 'grief', heartache', and 'rejection' rolled off my back and onto the warm floor. I desperately walked faster, throwing a secret glance over my shoulder, trying to shake their relentless pursuit. The phrase 'he doesn't love you, Harper' crept down the walls, crawled over the tile, and invaded my body. It pounded against my head, making my temples throb.

We entered the elevator and hysteria crept into my throat as the doors closed. An overwhelming sense of finality hit me like a blast of freezing air as we rode the elevator to our floor, forcing me to lean against the wall for support. I almost choked on the regret pressing down on my body from all directions and just when I thought I would collapse from the weight, the doors opened and that building pressure burst through its barrier, spilling out into the stacks, relieving a bit of the panic residing in my chest.

Callum chose a few stacks in the back and I, to keep my distance, stayed to the stacks near the tables in the archives. After a few minutes, I finished most of the shelves there and moved further from him, to the stacks on the opposite side of our floor. We rarely worked like that but I wanted to be alone and, much to my dismay, he looked like he wanted the same. I stopped working for a moment to peer across the glass, over the lobby, and into the other side to watch for him. I noticed he'd sat on his haunches, scrubbing his face, before turning back to his own work.

My stomach constricted for him. I was tired. Very. I wanted Callum more than I'd ever wanted anything in my entire life because he was better than anyone I'd ever met. He genuinely cared for me. He would have given his life for me, I knew it, and my jaw clenched knowing that he just couldn't give me his heart. It was such a strange sensation knowing that someone loved you enough to die for you but not enough to fall in love with you. I shook my head at that, wondering what was so bad about me and went back to work.

After a few minutes, I could hear him approach me from behind but I was too heartbroken to turn his direction, my arms and legs too heavy to even bother. He tapped me on the shoulder and I didn't have a choice but to acknowledge him. I pulled my buds from my ears, letting them fall to the floor. I stared at the shelf in front of me, readying to see his beautiful face.

"Hello Harper," I heard, making me freeze. Tiny, electric bugs crawled up my back at the recognition of that voice. John Bell's voice. My hands begun to shake as he continued. "It's been such a long time, sweetheart."

I slowly stood up, hoping to everything Holy that Callum wouldn't glance my way. I was a goner, I knew that, but at least I could save him as long as I didn't bring him to John's attention. I turned around, ready to comply to any of his demands as long as it saved Callum. *Look who's getting ready to die for someone now, Harper,* I thought depressingly.

I studied John. He looked the same to me, frighteningly scary, obsessive eyes, perfectly straight white teeth in his perfectly formed face. He was an enigma. A beautiful, horrible face on a handsome, threatening body. Tears formed at the corners of my eyes.

"John," my trembling lips whispered.

He wrapped his arms around me, warm and inviting, and squeezed me to his chest. His tenderness contradicting the murderous look in his eyes. The smell of the pine cologne he'd worn even in high school swum in my nose as he pressed me into him. "Shh," he said, guiding his hands gently down my hair, "I'm here." My body shook in anticipation, waiting for it to hit me. He held me tighter and tighter and *tighter* until I could barely breath. Finally, his fingers bit into my shoulders and I braced myself. He slid his cheek across my own and dipped his lips to my ears. "You've really disappointed me, Harper." He shoved me against the stacks hard, knocking the breath from my lungs, making me gasp for air. There was a bent piece of the shelf near my neck and it pierced my flesh. I could feel something warm trickle down the side and into the collar of my shirt.

He shoved me harder into the shelf and I whimpered, earning me a sick grin from John. He stared at me, holding me too tight to his chest before grabbing my chin, his fingers pressing deep into my cheeks, and forced me to look at him. He stuck his nose in my hair and inhaled deeply, his eyes rolling into the back of his head, making me want to vomit. When he opened them, his pupils were dilated, and he smiled wickedly. My lips trembled, giving me away.

"I've wanted to do that for a very long time," he said, bending slightly and bringing his face dangerously close to mine. I sunk into the shelf as far as I could go but he just moved with me. He bent further and ran his tongue up the side of my neck, making me shudder in fear. "I can taste your fear, you know?" He said. My body recoiled from him but he grabbed and brought me even closer. "And you should be afraid." Tears spilled down my cheeks.

"I loved you," he whispered against my face, almost choking on his own words, my hair feathering back slightly from his breath, "and you screwed me over so badly, Harper. I just can't believe you've done me like this." His jaw clenched tightly. "You screwed me!" He yelled, hitting the shelf loudly and I involuntarily glanced Callum's direction to make sure he didn't see us.

That was my first mistake. John smiled at me, clenching a meaty hand over my throat as he stared through the glass windows over to Callum's side. He noticed Callum working and his grip tightened around my throat, cutting off my breath. I clawed at his hand with both of mine, drawing blood. I felt the blood vessels in my eyes begin to pop and black spots dot my vision.

Suddenly, John let go and I sucked in a burning breath. My throat was on fire and I doubled over, dry heaving. I felt sick to my stomach that I was forced to lean on him for support.

And John had seen Callum.

I tried to scramble away from him, to run to the windows. My plan was to warn him but John tossed me onto my back, straddling my legs. He pinned my arms above my head and brought his face in close. He kissed me hard, sucking my bottom lip into his mouth and bit down hard, drawing blood. I cried out in pain.

"Do you think your husband might enjoy watching this?" He asked, sitting up. When I didn't answer, he slapped me hard across the face, making me wince. "Answer, you stupid, selfish bitch!" He yanked at my left hand and brought it up to him, pinching my thumb between his own and his forefinger before walking his fingers over the tips of my index and middle finger, stopping at my ring finger. "I'm gonna' cut this ring from your finger, whore." I softly began to cry. He was going to torture me before my death and he was going to thoroughly enjoy it.

John stood up and dragged me by my hair toward the window facing the lobby. "Come on, Harper."

I grappled at his hands as a monster headache began to split through my temple. John brought me up to his level, my feet dangling over the ground, before slamming my face into the glass, my head pounded harshly. Callum still had his ear buds in, thank God, and he didn't hear us. I prayed that John would give up but knew that was unlikely. He reached behind him and removed the pistol he'd been hiding in the waistband of his jeans. He lifted the gun and placed the barrel against the glass, pulling the trigger and shattering it into a million pieces, making me scream and finally catching Callum's attention.

Callum sprung up from his position, throwing his iPod down, and ran to the glass on his side of the fourth floor. I shook my head at him as he pounded against the glass, screaming my name. 'Please', I mouthed to him. He began to run our direction but I screamed for him to run away. Callum's hands pressed against the glass and he walked them across the panes towards the door that lead to the open walkways, as if that could get him any closer to us.

Callum threw open the door, slamming his fists into the Plexiglas of the walkway directly across from us. "Let her go!" He yelled, his request echoing across the marble lobby flooring and bouncing all around us. His voice soothed me, each word caressed my skin, giving me a peace I didn't think could possibly come in that moment.

John dragged me across the glass on the floor, over the metal divider that once held the thick glass window pane, and slammed me against the Plexiglas. "You!" John screamed, silencing Callum's demands. He brought the gun up and pointed it directly at Callum. Calmly, he said, "You're going to pay for taking her. Simply put, she belonged to me and you had no right. Granted, she should have told you as much, and trust me, she will pay for her dishonesty, but so will you. If you want to be mad at anyone, it should be this untrustworthy slut!" He said, his words growing in heat until he was spitting the last. He slammed my head against the Plexiglas on the word slut.

"If you kill Harper," Callum gritted through his teeth, slamming his fists into the walkway cover loudly, making me flinch at the unusual aggression, "so help me God, I will hunt you down like the dog that you are. I will string you up by your feet and flay your skin from your body!" He bellowed in a fit of rage, the veins in his neck growing thick with the exertion. "Get.Away.From.Harper! Let her go and we can finish this man to man!"

"Temper, temper, mister Tate. Remember yourself, sir. Remember that *I* have her. *I* have the gun. You have *nothing*. And nothing's what you'll leave this world with, I'll make sure of that."

Callum's chest pumped three times with heavy breaths, his loaded stare icing even me over, before he began to run, skidding along the floor, when John aimed his gun and shattered the Plexiglas wall nearest him, causing me to scream his name. He ran out of sight, visibly making John nervous.

"Walk ahead of me," John said, pushing me the direction Callum had been running.

We walked the length of the walkway before entering back into the library, circling around the front, heading towards the room we saw Callum disappear into. As we walked past the elevators, I breathed an inward sigh of relief that I could hear the thrum of the cables and John didn't. We walked straight into the book sorting room, John slamming the door behind us and locking it. The room was pitch black so John pulled me to the floor with him, dragging me behind him as he searched each dark crevice. I wasn't frightened, I knew Callum wasn't here, that is until John pulled me up with him as he stood against the wall.

He covered my body with his, pressing his front to mine as close and as hard as he could. John pushed his nose to my throat and inhaled me again, making me want to vomit. I held back the acid though as he kissed up my neck and trailed his lips along my jaw line.

"At first," he whispered, startling me, "I'll be soft and drive any idea of that asshole out of your mind. I'll make it so good, you won't remember him." I pinched my eyes closed and swallowed hard in disgust. Then he kissed me, slowly, taking his time, running his hot tongue over me and I could feel the bile rise in my throat. I almost wished I'd vomit in his mouth but I knew he'd make me pay dearly if I did. "Kiss me back," he begged, breathless, like this intimate moment was totally normal. I clenched my teeth together and dug the back of my head deeper into the wall. He slammed my body hard against the wall. "Kiss me back!" He yelled, striking me hard in the face.

"N-no," I trembled.

He pushed his face close to mine, nose to nose. I could feel his breath fan across my face. "Kiss me back or I'll take you right here on the floor, slut." I tremulously inched closer to his face and pressed my closed mouth to his, squeezing my eyes closed as if that could make me forget. "Open your mouth, Harper," he said, but I just couldn't voluntarily do it. I knew it would anger him but I couldn't make myself do it.

He yanked me to the floor hard, bruising my hip. "No!" I cried. "Please, please!"

"Shut up!" He screamed in my face, making me sink away from him, turning my head into the floor. "God, you don't get it, do you? You make me do these things to you, Harper. I never wanted it to be this way." He started unbuttoning my coat and I fought with what little nails I had left. He grabbed hold of my wrists and pinned my hands beneath a leg strait-jacket while he went back to work, undoing each button like he had all the time in the world. I was openly crying now, wondering where Callum was and hoping he got away to call the authorities. When they showed up, I knew it'd be too late. I'd either be raped, dead, or both. It looked like both. "If you had only obeyed me, Harper, all those years ago we'd probably be happily married ourselves and those girls would never have had to suffer."

"No!" I screamed, thinking of what he must have done to those innocent women.

He slapped me across the face again to shut me up and kept working. When he edged the jacket off my shoulders, he kept it there for extra restraint and began unbuttoning my plaid shirt, exposing my white tank top. He sighed loudly, grotesquely happy at his progress and the sight before him. His fingers were unusually warm as he lifted the hem of my tank. As it edged up my torso, he pressed delicate kisses to my stomach, stopping at my belly button, sinking his tongue inside. I turned my head and vomited all over the floor next to me.

He sat up abruptly. "Do I disgust you, Harper?" He asked, the hurt evident in his voice. "*Do I*!?" He roared. "Get up," he said. "Can't have you tasting like vomit." He threw me out the door and I stumbled onto the carpet. He gripped my upper left arm hard as he pulled me up and walked me toward the restrooms on the opposite side of our floor. He pushed me inside over to the nearest sink. "Wash your mouth out," he ordered.

I obeyed him, rinsing out my mouth but when I raised my gaze into the mirror above the sink, I barely recognized myself. My face was bruised and bleeding. My bottom lip was swollen as well as my right eye from each back hand I'd received. I was surprised to see that the blood vessels in my eyes hadn't actually burst, that it had been my imagination.

John stood behind me, caressing my hair, straightening out the strays from our scuffles. I shuddered in revulsion. He bent over me and pulled several paper towels from the dispenser at my left. He ran them through warm water, never taking his eyes from my reflection. He squeezed out the excess water and began cleaning up the dried blood around my mouth that I had yet to clean as well as the blood from around my busted brow and neck.

"There," he said, kissing my temple, "now let's get out of here before your asshole husband returns with the police."

I gripped the sides of the sink. "Are-are you going to kill me?" I asked point blank.

"Eventually, yes."

Chapter Sixteen
Dream is Collapsing

Callum

I'd called the police, briefly spoken with the detective handling our case, and been advised to leave the building. Sure. Now that they were on *their* way, I was on *my* way to beat the living shit out of the murderer who had my Harper on the fourth floor. I tipped over one of the reading tables on the third floor not caring if he heard me or not and unscrewed one of the heavy legs to use as a makeshift bat. I knew if he'd touched her, touched a single hair on her head, that I was going to smash that bat in his disgusting face.

I spun open the door, studying the floor I hoped they were still on. I edged up the crosswalk stairs but stopped at the top. I knew I'd have to make a sprint for the door as there was no hiding from all the glass windows but I wanted to know exactly where they were before I did that, knowing John could just shoot through the glass the second he saw me. I desperately tried to see but it was of no use. That's when I heard the most blood-curdling scream come from behind the glass door. Forgetting the risk, I raced through to the door, practically tearing it off the hinges but they weren't visible. I ducked behind a stack and quieted myself, listening.

"It's on the bottom floor," Harper said, terror laced in her voice.

"Where?" John asked softly.

I followed the sound of his voice until I came upon them stuck between two stacks. He had her pressed against the shelves, his hand studying her face like they were lovers. Harper looked beyond frightened and John looked like he loved it all the more because of that. *Sick bastard.* I bit my heels into the floor when he kissed her neck intimately, making Harper's bottom lip tremble. He acted like he had all the time in the world which made me wonder if he didn't care if he was caught. And there was only one reason he wouldn't care about being caught and that terrified me.

"Walk," John ordered her toward the elevator, walking right past me. I burrowed deeper into the shadows.

As they walked to elevator, John leaned over Harper and pressed the button. I stalked closer, trying desperately to stay as quiet as possible. The wait for the doors to open was agonizing. Finally, they opened and I made my move. Heaving the bulky table leg over my head, I swung on John and it smacked him square in the back. Unfortunately, the brute was so large, it barely made an impact. I shoved Harper in the elevator and pressed the first floor button, turning back to John as quickly as possible and swinging the table leg toward his head but missed, just as the doors began to close, I jumped in with Harper. The doors closed completely and Harper startled when John began to beat at the doors.

"Harper!" Bang. "Harper!" Bang. "I'm going to kill him for that! And you're going to watch, you stupid bitch!" John screamed, making Harper tense beside me.

We began our descent but it didn't last long. John was pressing the button and the elevator began its ascent once more. Harper wisely pulled the stop switch as well as the alarm bell. I didn't have time to tell her that was useless, that I'd already called the police, because we heard John bellowing out Harper's name. She sidled up to me and I wrapped my arms around her. Three clear shots rang out, making us both tense.

"He only has one shot left," I said absently, trying to gauge how much further we needed to go to reach the lobby and if it was close enough that John wouldn't be able to run down the crosswalk stairs before we could make our escape.

"How do you know?" She asked, tucking her arms into herself.

"Because his gun is a revolver. It can only shoot six."

"Unless he reloads."

"Yes, unless he reloads but I doubt he will."

"How do you know?" She asked eerily calmly.

"I don't," I said, looking her in the eyes.

"What do we do now?" She asked.

"We wait for -" I started but stilled at the sound of metal bending. "Oh my God, he's opening the doors. He's going to jump."

"No," Harper whispered, backing into the corner of the elevator, staring at the ceiling.

Immediately, I pressed the stop switch once more, repeatedly pressing the first floor button. Much to my relief, we were moving downward. I hoped to God we'd reach the first floor before he reached us. A loud thud sounded above us and Harper and I stilled. I bent to grab my wood 'bat' and backed my way to Harper's corner, tucking her behind me. The elevator was still moving but we were nowhere near the first floor. I knew John would be joining us soon. I turned to Harper just as John began to peel back the escape hatch above us, the sound of metal twisting and bending.

"Harper," I said, meeting her eyes.

"No," she said, crying and grabbing my face. "No, Callum. Don't do anything stupid, please?"

"Listen," I said, ignoring the feel of her warm hands on my cheeks, a feeling I never knew if I'd feel again, "I'm going to fight with everything I have but as soon as those doors open, I need you to run like hell, okay?"

"No!" She said, frantically searching my face with her hands. "Please, don't, Callum. I can't leave you!"

"Harper!" I said, grabbing her shoulders. "He only has one bullet left and I swear to God if that bullet comes anywhere near you I will never able to forgive myself."

"And you!" She screamed in my face. "Will you-" She started but John came crashing to our feet just as we rounded the second floor.

Almost there, I thought. I grabbed the table leg and rushed him, swinging at his hand as he aimed the gun for my head, knocking it away. Harper immediately reached for the revolver but john kicked her in the stomach before she could reach for it, making her double over. I swung as hard as I could for his head but he leaned back just enough for me to miss and my bat met the wall beside him instead, giving him just enough time for his fist to connect with my jaw and I staggered back against the wall.

When I righted myself, John had bent to pick up Harper, sickeningly attempting to sooth her with troubling words that she made him do that to her, so I took advantage, swooping up my makeshift bat and cracking him over the head as hard as I could. John fell to the floor in a massive lump.

"Oh my God," Harper cried, reaching out for me.

I tugged her to my chest just as the bell alerted us we'd reached the first floor and the doors opened to reveal surrounding officers, their guns drawn. We practically fell from the elevator as they swooped in to collect a very out, very heavy John Bell, the sickest bastard I've ever come across in my entire life.

"Thank you," Harper said, tears streaming from her face. "You saved my life, Callum."

"Shh," I told her, rubbing her back. I placed my hands on her face, pushed the coppery hair from her tear soaked cheeks, and rubbed my thumbs across the salty wetness. "It's over, love. It's over."

It's all *over.*

And my stomach plummeted to the floor, a strange mix of relief and colossal regret.

Chapter Seventeen
I'm On Fire

Callum

Harper and I watched as two EMT's placed John in an ambulance and drove away with a police cruiser following behind, a collective, pent up sigh came barreling from both our lips. The detective took our statements on the scene and we were given the clear to go home around five in the morning. We rode the subway in a dazed disbelief, quiet, and afraid of what this meant next for us. I opened the door to our apartment, closed it and locked it as Harper began a sticky walk all the way to her bedroom door. She didn't want to sleep alone but didn't know how to ask me.

"Come on," I said, dragging her by the hand to my bedroom.

The room was pitch black despite the fact the sun

was coming around soon. I need complete and utter darkness to fall asleep or it won't happen. I closed the door behind us and felt around for my dresser, pulling a random large t-shirt from my bottom drawer. From the feel of it, I guessed it was, ironically, my Barcelona tee. I explored my nightstand with my hands, looking for the remote for my stereo. Finding it, I hit play and my Stateless album rang softly through the room, drowning out the sounds of the city that never sleeps.

I felt Harper sink into the bed and reached for her, pulling her across the top, towards me, and sitting her up. I pulled her hat and coat off, peeled off her t-shirt, and pushed my own on top of her head. I unlaced her boots and tossed them at the end of the bed. Shaky hands reached for the top of her jeans but she'd already started undoing them. I heard her slink out of them and toss them with her boots.

The intimacy of the situation didn't escape me, nor Harper, I'm guessing, but undressing her in my bed never played out like this in my dreams. In my imagination, she wasn't practically catatonic, or bruised, or beaten, or scared out of her wits. No, that was not how it was supposed to be. I peeled back my steel gray sheets and tucked her beneath them before enfolding her in my arms and we were both asleep before our heads hit my pillows.

A loud pounding woke me from a dreamless sleep. I sat up right, still on edge, glancing at my alarm clock, nine a.m. Harper sat up, but I pushed her back down.

"Go back to sleep, Harper."

I got up to put some clothes on but realized I'd fallen asleep in mine. When I opened my door, a sliver of light fell into the room, highlighting Harper's hair and neck, making me almost wish she wasn't sleeping in my bed, a sad reminder of what I what I couldn't have. In five steps, I had the door thrown open, revealing a distraught Cherry and an amused Charlie.

"Oh thank God!" Cherry said, reaching for me and throwing her arms around my neck. I lifted a brow at Charlie as if to ask what was up but he only offered a shrug. A slap to the chest brought my eyes back to Cherry. "Why in the hell didn't you call us?" She demanded, hands on her hips, tears in her eyes.

I tugged her close and hugged her. "I'm sorry, Cherry. We were just so exhausted. We needed sleep so badly by the time it was done, we didn't think to call anyone." I looked over at Charlie. "How'd you find out?"

"The news, Callum. You can't seriously think it wouldn't have made the news."

"I really didn't." I pushed Cherry back softly to look at her. "Forgive me?"

Just then, Harper threw my bedroom door open wide in my t-shirt, nothing covering her legs and panic written all over her face. "What's wrong?" She asked. "I heard crying."

Well, if there was any doubt in Charlie's or Cherry's mind that we weren't 'together', the sight of her would have squashed them. Ironic that shortly I'd have to admit everything to the both of them. She peered down at herself and blushed. "Sorry," she offered, hiding behind the door and peeking over the edge.

Cherry didn't care though. She pushed past the door and hugged Harper fiercely, closing the door behind her, I assume, so Harper could throw on her jeans.

I stood staring at the door when I felt Charlie's hand on my shoulder as he pulled me into a slap-hug.

"Jesus, Callum. If you scare Cherry like that again, I swear I will hunt you down and kill you myself." He pulled away, throwing his stare at the wood below. "You terrified us."

"I'm truly sorry, Charlie."

"It's alright," he coolly said, throwing himself on our couch. His eyebrows pinched as he took in his surroundings. "Good God, did Ikea vomit in your living room or what?" And just like that, Charlie was his normal, chill self making me recognize the rare sight of emotion he had shown me as the precious thing it really was. I must have truly shaken him. Cherry and Harper emerged arm in arm, smiling and happy, though glassy eyed. My heart constricted in my chest.

"We've got to go, Cherry," Charlie said from behind me.

"What? You've just gotten here," I said.

"We were supposed to leave this morning but when we heard what happened, we changed our flights to come check on you," Charlie said.

"Where are you going?" Harper asked Cherry.

"Charlie is taking me to meet his family," she answered.

I turned to meet Charlie's eyes but he subtly shook his head as if to say 'later. "Well that sounds like fun." I walked over to Cherry and wrapped her in another hug. "Do you forgive me?" I asked again.

"Yes, you fool but let this be a lesson to you, Callum. Next time I hear of you on the news and you don't call me to inform me, I'll be forced to interrupt you and your lovely wife here," she teased, pulling Harper in and kissing the top of her head, making my stomach clench. "I love you both, so very much," she said, with tears in her eyes.

"Oh no," Charlie said, pulling her away. "Come on, dear.

We don't have much time." Then he grabbed Harper and squeezed the life out of her, whispering in her ear. I only caught the latter half but he essentially told her what he told me. The look on Harper's face was priceless as he pulled away, seeing Charlie 'unhinged' from his usual collective. I almost laughed out loud.

Harper said she was hopping in the shower so I took the elevator down with the both of them and walked them to the curb to hail a cab. The bright yellow car swooped in next to them and Charlie opened the door for Cherry, settling her in, and closing it.

"Listen, I've not much time," he basically whispered, heading to the other side of the cab, "but I'm in love with her, we've been secretly seeing each other these past few months, and I plan on proposing to her in London. If you so much as breathe a word of this to Harper, I'll kill you, Callum."

I laughed out loud. "Lots of threats on my life today, Charlie."

"Yes, well..." He said, a smirk at the corner of his mouth.

"Congratulations, friend," I said, warmly.

He smiled fully at that. "Thank you," he said, pulling open his own door.

I ran back inside, feeling high from Charlie's news but by the time I reached our floor, the merry had worn off from the task ahead of me. I opened the door and remembered that Harper was showering so I tore off my t-shirt, too lazy to pull off my jeans and fell onto my bed, desperately trying to convince myself that there was another way. I buried my head in the pillow Harper used and almost lost it. Her scent assailed me just as Stateless' *I'm on Fire* began to play. I rolled over onto my back and drug Harper's pillow over my face, clutching it there, breathing her in while the song thrummed through me, haunting me.

I heard Harper clear her throat and I tossed the pillow off my face, hoping she didn't realize what I was doing. The song had yet to finish and all I could think was how appropriate its soundtrack would be for the conversation I was about to have.

"So," she said, leaning against the door jamb, her arms folded across her chest, her hair dripping onto her shoulders and back.

I sat up and scooted to the edge of the bed, unsure of what to do with my awkward body. "I'm leaving," I said matter-of-factly. She seemed to have expected that.

"I see," she said, moving to sit beside me. Neither of us could make eye contact so, instead, we stared blankly at my closet. "I'm going to miss you."

"And I, you." We were so quiet.

I opened my mouth to tell her everything, to confess everything I felt for her, to really verbalize it, but lost my nerve as Harper stood, leaving the right side of my body bereft of her amazing warmth just as the song came to an all too soon close. *I gotta' get out of here.*

After a quick shower, I threw some clothes in a duffel and grabbed my school bag but as I turned the knob of my door, I let them fall slack at my feet. There was one thing I needed to do. I sat at my desk, grabbed a piece of paper and a pen and began to write.

Harper,

There's so much to say. I never planned on doing it this way but things have become so strange between us, I don't feel like myself. I feel like the honesty that used to be between us has evaporated into nothing but I know I at least owe you this letter. I owe it to myself as well, to be honest. I need to get this off my chest if I'm ever going to get over you.

I'm in love you, Harper, gut-wrenchingly in love with you. I dream about you. Every second I am awake you are in my thoughts in some manner or another. And I've always loved you. Unbeknownst to you, you've tormented me for years and though I felt I might have been strong enough when we first married to endure, now I know my heart can't take it anymore. Each time you sit next to me on the train, warm and folded into me, I have to force my hands to stay buckled at my side, to keep from seizing you. When we study on the sofa, your feet in my lap, it's everything in me not to drag your body onto mine and kiss you senseless. Every time I've placed my lips on your neck, I've imagined guiding those lips up your soft skin until they reach your mouth and owning that mouth with my own, possessing you with my tongue, Harper. And as if that wasn't bad enough, just the smell of your beautiful scent sends me reeling, careening deeper and deeper into an attraction I never thought possible.

The hardest part is that you know me, probably better than I know myself. You feel a part of me, Harper. You can read me like no one ever has. You are my best friend in this entire world and I will never have the friendship I have with you with anyone else. I know this.

Remember that day, we sat in our old living room, talking about nothing yet everything that seemed important? My heart felt so heavy that night as our conversation felt bittersweet to me. I came so close to revealing all but couldn't risk losing your friendship but now as it seems

I've lost both and since I literally have nothing to lose anymore, I have to confess all because if I can't get over you, Harper, I don't know how I'll live, how I'll function without you.

That's why I'm leaving. Tonight, actually. I hate to leave you one day before Christmas but I feel like I'm struggling to breathe around you. You are everything that is important to me and yet you don't belong to me, you never really did. And that's the most painful thing to admit to myself. I've been lying to myself all this time and now I have to pay for my carelessness.

I'll be at Ames' in Seattle if you need to reach me for anything. I need the distance to get over you. Let me find out on my own if I'm doomed regardless, Harper.

I'm sorry, more than you could possibly imagine.

Callum

I laid on my bed, the door closed to the rest of my shared home and listened to music until I was sure Harper had gone to bed for good. I felt like a coward but such was life. I needed distance and couldn't face her lovely face for a second longer than I had to. And so, with my letter wrapped in an envelope and sealed, I slid the message underneath her door and made my way to the bus depot. I was getting the hell out of Dodge and not a moment too soon.

Because Harper was like a bullet to the heart and if I'd stayed even a moment longer she would have obliterated it and no amount of medical attention would've been able to revive it.

Harper

I cried myself to sleep. I'd lost him, I knew that. I'd lost my best friend and the one person I loved more than anyone in this world, more than myself. I woke startled, thinking I'd heard something but it was nothing. I'd only slept for maybe an hour. I glanced at my clock, it read eleven fifteen in the morning. I had no intention of doing anything but sulking in my bed the entire day save for the fifteen minutes I planned on throwing on a pair of jeans to answer the door for Chinese.

"You can at least shower, you dolt," I told myself. I climbed out of the bed and shuffled my feet across the chilly wood floor and into the bathroom.

Turning on the hot water, I pulled my hair from its ponytail and glanced at my swollen red face in the mirror. My hair was dramatically creased from sleeping with damp hair the night before. I'd have to rewash to get it out. I leaned in closely to examine my red eyes and hoped the steam would so something for my raw skin. I washed my hair twice and conditioned and as I reached for my body wash, my hand slid across the expensive bath soap Callum bought me last year on a whim. I grabbed the gifted soap and opened the cap, inhaling its heavenly scent. The tears started again but I tried my best to ignore them. I had been saving it for a rainy day.

"What better day than today," I said out loud with a sigh.

I turned off the shower and stuffed the plug in the porcelain tub with my toe, letting it fill half way with hot water before I emptied the little bottle of bubble bath. I watched as the running water churned the soap into

296

frothy suds for a moment before resting my head against the lip of the bathtub. My tears felt cold as they silently ran down my cheeks and neck. I breathed in the steam, letting my thoughts swim hazily through its fog.

When the water turned cold, I forced myself out and wrapped a large, thick towel around my body, using a second to squeeze excess water from my hair. The steam fogged up the mirror and I used my hand to get a clear look at myself. My eyes looked clearer and my head felt it a little as well. *Just keep yourself busy, Harper*, I thought to myself. Not about to waste the warmth of the room, I took out my blow dryer and dried my hair completely. There wasn't anything I hated worse than a wet head in a chilly apartment. Happy with how quickly it dried, I decided to distract myself further by curling my hair, something I never did because my hair already had a bit of a wave to it.

Half an hour later and I was desperate for another distraction so I did my makeup. That only ate up a measly fifteen minutes. I was running out of diversions in the bathroom and since all the warmth had seeped out from underneath the door, I moved to my closet, threw on a pair of panties and a bra and went on a full on search for my most comfy pair of Yoga pants. They were buried deep in the back of my closet right next to my 'Frankie Says Relax' tee.

"Why not."

Dressed, hair and makeup ridiculously done, like I had a Christmas party to go to or something, I ventured out into the living room. I hadn't heard Callum rise yet and thought I'd be safe. He liked to sleep late when he didn't have school or work. I swept past his room but couldn't hear him, his room was quiet, too quiet.

Ignoring every protest my common sense was

screaming at me, I approached his door and knocked softly, at first, then harder when he didn't answer. I don't know why but I began to panic and threw open his door. He wasn't there. It was one o'clock on Christmas Eve. Where was he?

Deciding he went for a jog, I walked back to my room and slipped, my right foot shooting forward on a piece of paper beneath my Teenage Mutant Ninja Turtle slipper.

"Damn it!" I bent to pick the paper up, to toss it in the waste basket but was stunned when my name appeared across the middle of an *envelope*.

My heart racing for reasons I had no idea, I tore open the envelope and fished a letter from the pocket. It was from Callum.

"No, no, no," I begged myself, panicked. "He left me already?" I mused out loud, my voice laced with a tremor. My hands cupped my mouth and the letter dropped to the floor. I couldn't read it, couldn't bring myself to see what he had to say. My heart was already broken. I didn't need another reminder of why it hurt so badly.

Squeezing my eyes shut, I picked it up from the floor and folded it once more but when I attempted to place it on my dresser table, I froze. One single world jumped out at me from the partially folded letter in my hand.

I ripped it back open and began pouring over its contents.

"Oh my God," I said, setting myself on the edge of the bed as I finished his written confession. "He *loves* me? *Loves* me? Of all the stupid, idiotic, ridiculous misunderstandings I have ever known...this has to be the most glorious of all."

I let the letter fall to my feet as I ran to my laptop, swinging it open a bit too forcefully and crying like I've never cried before.

"Okay, okay, okay." I breathed deeply. "One way flights to Seattle."

I found one available seat leaving that evening at five fifty-five, which wasn't ideal, but I couldn't feel too disappointed that I'd have to wait a few hours to leave. It was Christmas Eve after all. I felt lucky to get anything at all. I'd arrive half an hour before midnight with an hour layover in Philly.

"It'll do, Harper."

I grabbed my credit card and charged it, not feeling the least bit guilty. I almost felt like I should call Callum, warn him, but two reasons stopped me. One, I didn't have a phone because it was confiscated at the library after 'he who must not be named' attacked me and...almost killed me. I wasn't going to think about that. Sometime in the future, a therapist would get a very nice kitchen makeover courtesy of my sessions but until then I decided denial was best for my mental health. The second reason I didn't ring Callum was because I wanted it to be a surprise. A nice, pleasant, incredible surprise. You know, a 'look up, baby. Yeah, that's Mistletoe' kind of surprise or an 'Oh my Lord, Harper I'm so glad you're here. Let me ravish you' kind of surprise.

"What the heck am I going to do with the next two hours?" I asked myself.

I grabbed my suitcase, packed everything I needed and still had an hour and a half to spare. Fixing my hair and makeup with the care I did that morning was the rarest of rarities and the irony didn't escape me that I did it on a day I'd be flying to meet my freaking *husband*. The husband who thought I didn't love him like he loved me. The very husband I could have had a real marriage with if we'd just been real with one another. I felt like a jack ass.

No worries, you'll remedy that very soon. Realizing, I didn't have anything for Callum to give him for Christmas, I got dressed in the outfit I wanted to fly in, threw on my coat and scarf and headed toward the department stores.

I couldn't believe how strange my day's events had become. Never in my wildest dreams would I have thought this would be happening to me that day. In just a few short hours, I would be wrapping my arms around Callum confessing my own feelings for him. I wanted to kick myself for letting our situation get so out of hand, for not being forthright and for letting assumptions take over. *And what if he doesn't want you anymore, Harper?* A funny, prickling sensation crept up my neck but I shook it off. *Surely, he still wants you. He left to get over you.* The sensation never really left me as I walked the rest of my journey, scraping my hand over the back of my neck, frenziedly trying to shake the uncomfortable feeling away.

The department store was packed but I expected as much. As I admired a scarf on a mannequin, I froze in terror, thinking I'd seen John Bell walk across the marble flooring in front of me. My hand flew to my chest and my adrenaline started pumping. I ran quickly his direction to make sure.

"Jesus," I exhaled when I noticed it was just a man who looked like him. *Get a hold of yourself, Harper. Therapist. Need to call a therapist when I get back home.*

The rest of the shopping trip was a blur, I bought a sexy little sweater dress and leggings for Christmas day, an attempt to be a bit more feminine because the girls were starting to insist, a pair of orange leather gloves for Cherry because they seemed her style, and a few bobbles for the rest of our crew for Christmas. We all celebrated

Christmas together on New Year's Eve for dinner, that way we could all take advantage of the after Christmas sales. We wanted to be generous but were broke. It was a nice little compromise. Half an hour had passed and I'd found nothing for Callum. I felt horrible, nothing stuck out to me.

When I'd given up, resigned to the fact that I'd have to show up with nothing, I passed by a table at the entrance I hadn't noticed coming in. On it, was real live mistletoe wrapped in a fancy box.

Merry Christmas, Callum Tate.

Chapter Eighteen
Teardrop

Harper

When I got home from shopping, I rode the elevator still trying to shake the uncomfortable feeling in my gut. *It's just nerves, Harper.* When I opened my door, a small white card fell at my feet. It must have been wedged between the jamb and door. I bent to pick it up and noticed the words, 'Call me ASAP', written in hard blue pen strokes. I flipped it over and read that it was the card of Detective Carson at the NYPD. But I had no way to call him because my cell was with them most likely and, to be honest, I wanted nothing to do with the possibility they'd want to interrogate me for another four hours, making me miss my flight. I promised myself I'd call them in Seattle and let them know they could question me after the holidays. John Bell wasn't going to take up any more of my time for at least a couple of days, not if I had anything to do with it.

I stuffed the card in the back pocket of my jeans and let the thought of John Bell seep further into the recess of my brain's 'don't even go there right now, Harper' closet. I locked down the apartment, ran over to the Super's and let him know both Callum and I would be gone for a few days, made sure all the appliances were shut off, emptied the fridge of things that would grow three or more heads while we were gone and took out the trash. I deciding emptying my bladder would probably be best since the airport was probably crowded as hell and I'd rather not need to take a leak after waiting in a line full of women who'd been flying for hours and ready to plow me down if I so much as looked at them wrong. I gathered my bag, threw on my coat, locked the front door and I was on my way.

I took the LIRR, or Long Island Rail Road, from Penn Station to the Jamaica Hub and caught the Airtrain to JFK. It took closer to an hour because of how busy the day was but I got there with two hours to spare. I thought that would be sufficient until I checked my bag and was immediately greeted with the Security Check Point. Good God, the line was horrendous. I thought seriously for a moment about just turning around, convinced there'd be no way I'd get through in time. I cursed myself for dallying in the department store for so long.

The burning returned to the back of my neck again and I became seriously agitated. *You'll get through. You'll get through.* I kept turning behind me, rubbing my neck over and over, looking to see whose eyes were scorching through me.

"You okay?" The guy behind me asked. He was young, probably my age, well built, dark hair.

"Uh, yeah," I answered with a small smile.

"Nervous flyer?"

"Something like that," I said, turning back to face security.

But he kept at it. "Where ya' flying?" He asked me as I turned back around.

"Uh, Seattle."

"Really? Quite a long flight from JFK. I'm headed back home for Christmas. St. Louis. You going back to family?"

"You could say that," I grinned.

He laughed. "Something tells me there's a lot to that story."

I laughed with him. "Definitely." I proceeded to tell him the basics of my story, leaving out the really disturbing parts, no sense in scaring a stranger.

"Wow, that's...unbelievable." He hoisted his laptop bag higher on his shoulder, his face a mixture of disbelief. He realized how serious he'd become and fixed his expression. "So, you're married, huh?"

"Yup." I smiled.

"Good ones are always taken," he jested.

"You seem 'good' enough," I teased.

He smiled. "Thanks."

"Of course. So, this family of yours, what's it like?"

He laughed at my obvious attempt at making light of my depressing life story. "It's about as wonderful as you could possibly imagine. Granted, sometimes I'd like to strangle my sister but at other times I don't know what I'd do without her." He eyed me, squinting, and nodded his head. "I have a feeling you'll build quite an amazing family yourself there. All you need is time."

"Thank you. I think you may be right."

The Security Check Point was tedious. I had to place my lap top in its own container, unlace my ridiculous boots and place them in one as well, then stuff my purse and carry on through as well. I passed through the metal detector easily enough and went straight through to gather my stuff. My shoes were back on, lap top back in its bag but I had to wait a moment while they checked my carry on a little more thoroughly. I glanced down to see that my boots were laced properly and unhooked the hem of my jeans from the back of my right boot. When I glanced up, my breath caught in my throat.

I noticed in the reflection of the mirrored window in front of me, John Bell, bending to put his own shoes on. I spun around quickly but he wasn't there. Adrenaline pumped through my veins at an alarming rate. I admonished myself for torturing my heart the way I was. *Keep it together, Harper, or they'll take you in for drug use or something.*

"God, I have to call Detective Carson. I'm losing it," I whispered to myself.

One glance at the terminal clock told me I didn't have time for that. I'd have to call when I arrived in Seattle. I arrived at my gate just as they were calling for all remaining passengers. I huffed down the aisle to the very last row, where my assigned seat was, stuffed my carry on above me and plopped in the window seat. I listened to the flight attendants ready to close the plane's door as I settled in for the not so comfortable six hour flight ahead of me.

I almost laughed at loud when I noticed that every seat was full yet the seat next to me was vacant. *What luck!*

Just when I thought they were closing the doors, the attendant whipped it back open for a moment to let the last minute straggler board the plane. *Damn, there goes my luck.* I grabbed my laptop bag and purse from the seat beside me and began shoving it under the seat in front of me.

"Thank you, miss," the passenger said to the flight attendant as I removed the iPod Callum got me for my birthday last year from my bag. I stuck the buds in my ears, closed my eyes and rested my head against the pane.

The passenger beside me settled his ginormous body next to mine and I almost groaned out loud. The plane's engine roared to life and I was suddenly in a much better mood. I was going to see Callum! As we prepared for take-off, I felt a tap on my shoulder. The flight attendant had to lean forward, the engine was so loud.

"I'm sorry, miss! All electronic items must be turned off for takeoff."

I nodded and apologized with my expression. She stood and started walking away as I glanced down at my seat belt and made sure it was buckled.

"Flight attendants, prepare for takeoff," the captain came over the intercom.

The last thing I wanted was to get in more trouble. I'd be flagged by the National Guard as an uncooperative passenger. I started to laugh at my own little joke as the plane positioned itself on the run way for takeoff but the chuckle died in my throat when I saw who the late passenger sitting beside me was.

"Jesus!" I yelled, propelling myself against the window, but no one could hear me over the rumble of the engine.

John Bell.

He was smiling. An evil, wicked, demented smile.

306

Tears came of their own accord and I began to shake, squeezing my eyes shut, then opening them to see if he was real. And he was. *Very real*. I opened my mouth to scream and struggled to remove my belt but he clamped his hand hard over my mouth.

He leaned in closely to my ear. "One peep and I'll strangle you to death. Believe me, no one will notice." He kept his hand over my mouth and waited for me to respond. Salty tears clouded my view but I nodded as best I could despite the fact he was pressing me hard against the hard plastic of the interior plane wall.

He slowly released his grip on my mouth. I tried to catch any sort of eye contact with *any* passenger around me but they were all too focused on the impending take off.

"Good girl," he said, leaning in closely to my ear again. I shuddered in response.
He leaned back and studied me, making sure I'd remain quiet. My eyes searched his face.

"I escaped," he excitedly told me. Though I hated myself for wanting to know, my eyes asked how and he continued. "I head butted the officer transferring me from the patrol car to the jail and ran. They didn't stand a chance."

That's why Detective Carson wanted me to call him so urgently. I felt like such an imbecile. I should have known something like this would happen to me. This was my luck. My shitty, awful luck.

"Sweetheart," John said, running his meaty hands down the sides of my face. It was revolting and made me gag but I steeled myself. "Now we can be together." He kissed me hard against the mouth, smashing his wet mouth against mine. He dug his tongue through my tightly lined lips and almost choked me. He pulled away, nipping me with his teeth a little. "How many times will it take for you to learn, Harper?" He admonished. "You belong to me."

He grabbed my hand and squeezed it between his fingers. I turned my head away and began to tremble. This angered him, I could tell, because his grip tightened uncomfortably before releasing me. He grabbed the back of my neck harshly and pulled me toward him.

"Do you know that I know where Callum is right now?" He asked. I shook my head. "Ames is his uncle, right?" I didn't answer. "That's right. I know everything, Harper. In fact, I have many things planned for both your asshole husband and his uncle. I'm going to show you, actually. Right after I remind you of why you're mine."

I knew now what I needed to do and thought to try the only thing I could think to save John from hurting anymore people in my life.

"You win," I said, swallowing hard as the plane began to level off.

John seemed surprised. "Excuse me?"

"You win," I repeated after the captain removed the 'fasten seatbelt' sign. "I will do whatever you want. I'll be with you forever and do it willingly just as long as you don't hurt Callum or Ames." I knew it was idiotic. It was my attempt at being reasonable with the unreasonable. It never works. Never. But it was the only bargaining chip I had.

And it seemed to intrigue John. "Willingly?" His perversely handsome face said, amused. I nodded sharply once. His hand worked up my jean clad thigh. "Prove it."

I sunk even further into my seat as the flight attendants drove their beverage cart past us toward the front of the plane.

"Wh-what do you mean?"

John's cheek grazed mine as he whispered in my ear. "What do you *think* it means, Harper?"

"Tell me what you want," I asked bluntly.

"John," he corrected.

"Tell me what you want...*John*."

His eyes rolled to the back of his head in sickening satisfaction and he smiled. In a lightning flash movement, he unbuckled my seat belt, then his, before lifting the armrest that separated us. He brought me as close as possible and I was practically on top of his lap.

He spoke into my hair. "Put your hand here," he said, guiding my shivering hand onto his thigh, making him moan softly. The bile that had risen in my throat began to threaten an appearance but I tamped it down. He offered me his neck and I seriously considered biting it hard but thought twice. If it didn't get me the reaction I wanted from the rest of the passengers, I still had a few hours to survive with John and I'm sure that would make them even worse. I hesitantly kissed the bottom of his throat with tight, trembling lips and struggled with the nausea that caused. I retreated slightly. There was a twinkle in John's eye.

He crushed his mouth to mine and I willed myself to kiss back but couldn't. When John's grip on my arms tightened, I knew my chance to 'prove' myself, or whatever the hell he called it, was fading away and fast. *Pretend, Harper,* I pleaded with myself. *Anyone. Pretend it's anyone...but Callum. Whatever you do, don't taint Callum.* I wanted him to always be that pure part of me, to remain the only good part of my past and whatever future I had left. I reluctantly moved my hand to John's hip, fingers trembling the entire journey, and reached deeper with my tongue. The kiss became feverish, heavy, and altogether revolting. I fantasized it was the guy

309

across from us to keep the knowledge it was actually John away from my thoughts but that did nothing but make me even more uncomfortable, if that was possible. I decided to act like I was kissing a stranger and that seemed to help, if help is what you'd call that.

John was forgetting where he was. Reaching beneath the hem of my shirt, pressing the warm skin of his hand to the bare skin on my back. Instinctively, I shoved him off me.

"I need to pee," I lied, trying to recover.

His pupils narrowed and grew cold. "Come then," he said, gripping my hand harshly in his.

"I can't go by myself? It's not like I can escape," I argued, like an idiot.

"Right but I can't risk you alerting anyone." He dragged me out of my seat, and shoved me in front of him.

Since we were the last seats on the plane, the walk to the lavatory was but a few feet. He shoved me inside and closed the door behind him.

"Go ahead," he said, crossing his arms at his chest, leaning against the door, as if he was about to enjoy the show. His eyes bore creepily into my skin and I wanted to rub my hands over myself to shed the feeling.

"Turn around," I said.

"No," he said, an evil grin spread flush across his face. "Just a warning, if you don't piss right now, I'll make you pay for interrupting when things were just getting good."

I maneuvered my clothing so that I wasn't exposed as I sat on the toilet. We sat there, John's eyes revealing just what a sick bastard he really was.

"I can't pee with you watching."

"Stage fright? Please, Harper, you probably did

plenty of personal things with that bastard around, including taking a piss." He shook his head, his body began to shake. "You're such a slut!" He spit out, trying not to yell. "You shouldn't have any problem peeing in front of me in light of the fact that you and I will be doing a lot worse soon." He leaned toward me closely. "You belong to me now, bitch. You've always belonged to me and I'll drive every single smear of disgraceful stain he placed on your body. My tongue will know your body better than he ever did."

His words shamed me, made me feel dirty and disgusting and violated before he'd even laid a serious finger on me.

"Do it, Harper." Tears were streaming harshly down my face. "Do it, Harper," he gritted out, his face growing red with restraint.

Suddenly, a loud knock came to our door, making me simultaneously terrified and relieved. "Excuse me! *Excuse me!* I know you're both in there! Out! Right now! We don't tolerate that behavior!" The flight attendant said, all the time rapping loudly at the door.

I stood quickly and rebuttoned my jeans. I stupidly flushed out of habit. John flung the door open and walked out confidently, pretending to zip the fly of his own jeans. The flight attendant stood there, her hands on her hips, her lips pursed in disgust. I followed John out, humiliated, my face red, tears still streaming.

"Take your seats," the woman ordered. As we passed her, she glared at me, shaking her head, a snippy retort on the tip of her tongue but when she saw me crying, her face softened slightly and she bit her insult back, probably confusing my tears with shame. Though I was ashamed, I could give a flying eff what she thought of me. I only wanted her to see the pleading in my eyes but she was too distracted by what she thought we did. I looked across the aisle of the plane as we walked to our seats, everyone stared at us, some looked revolted, others amused.

The other passengers watched us carefully for close to an hour, unknowingly but, more than likely, only temporarily, saving me from whatever torture John had planned after the lavatory incident. Ironically, I actually needed to pee but I wasn't about to tell John that.

I wanted a normal life. And I don't mean normal, like, I wanted a mom and dad where we lived in a two story in the 'burbs with a white picket fence. I'd play hookie from school some random Monday to shoot hoops with the neighbor boy and get grounded for a month.

No, I wanted normal as in there weren't any psychopaths obsessed with me. The kind of normal where I didn't have memories of my foster mom and dad *sleeping* with each other in a living room I was expected to walk through to get to school on time, or swimming in a sea of wine corks, avoiding another set of foster parents' drunken, abusive rants. Or the kind where I wasn't threatened with rape every day by the kids who loitered on the corner near my school. Or even the kind of normal where I didn't fall in love with a normal family only to realize I loved them *way* more than they ever loved me.

I wanted Callum. I just wanted Callum and I wanted be married to him, to finish college and build a family where our own kids weren't aware that there were people out there who don't even deserve to breathe the same air as they do. I wanted them oblivious. I wanted them naive and sheltered and totally in love with us as we are with them.

I know a lot of people probably think that my dreams are unrealistic, that the world is too harsh not to prepare children for how awful it really is. You know what I say? Eff that! Why should I let my kids grow up knowing that? They'll find out eventually on their own. Why make them jaded before they've even gotten a chance to live, to figure out what's really important in life. And what's wrong with innocence, anyway? Huh? I don't get it. I grew up with no innocence. None. From day one, I was contaminated with the 'real world' and you know what? It sucked. It royally sucked.

Listen, I'm not an idiot. I know that eventually the world would deal them some awful blow but I wanted my kids to know that they could have what I didn't, that even though fate may deal them an occasional shitty hand, it doesn't make the game not worth playing. It doesn't mean that they can't create their own amazing, incredible life because, by God, your happiness is what you make it and if you want to be happy, damn it, that's your right! And it's not impossible because I had it once...with Callum Tate.

I turned my head toward John and watched him watch me. I decided right then and there, that this guy wasn't going to take anything away from me that I wasn't willing to give and I wasn't in a very charitable mood that day, either. I was gonna' fight this guy with every ounce of fire I had in me.

When the plane landed, every antsy passenger, ready to see their families for the holidays, stood, gathering their bags, purses and carry-ons, poised for the few inches they'd be given every ridiculously precious five seconds as the passengers ahead unloaded.

And we were the last. John stood and yanked me up brutally beside him. If the stupid people around me were paying one iota of attention, they'd see this guy for what he truly was but, instead, they immersed their heads with visions of sugar plums or whatever else people dreamed of on Christmas.

"Come on, dear," John said sarcastically, tugging me callously through the door of the plane. The flight attendants glared at us, the heat of their stare attacking the back of my head.

Just to embarrass me, John threw me just beyond the doors and kissed me brutishly on the mouth, grabbing my butt and pinching hard. I yelled in pain but they interpreted it as the perverted action John wanted them to think it was. He pushed me up the jet way, laughing at his own lewdness. He was being careless, like he wasn't afraid of losing, which scared the hell out of me.

He forced me hard against his chest and breathed in my ear. "Don't even think about running *or* asking anyone for help because I'll just run myself...straight to Callum and kill him with my own hands *way* before the cops could *possibly* save them. Run, Harper, and be prepared to identify a few bodies."

That was exactly what I'd planned on doing the second I saw an airport security guard but when he revealed his plan, it deflated mine. I just couldn't risk Callum. I needed to reach Callum somehow, warn him, then make my move.

"I have amazing plans for us, Harper," he said, wrapping his arms around my shoulders like we were best friends, squeezing lightly. "I've got to get a room first. We'll shower and you'll dress for me like you'd dress for your asshole husband." He paused. "We're going out." He smiled down at me, revealing the devious plans that lay just beneath his seemingly innocent statement.

We took a taxi in utter silence to one of the most broken down motels I'd ever seen. I wondered if it was even open for a moment before noticing a few people milling around a room with the door open. They looked exactly like the kind of people you'd see gathering around a broken motel door. One was most obviously a prostitute, one was possibly a dealer and the others were probably his users.

John walked us through the door to the front office. The walls were grimy, yellow, and black in a few spots. The carpet was close to the same. The lighting was artificial and sucked the life out of the entire room.

"What can I do for you?" The man behind the bullet proof glass asked.
He blended in with the room quite nicely with his dingy yellow sweater full of holes. He missed a few buttons on his once white shirt.

"We'd like a room," John said.

The man eyed me carefully. "How many hours?" He asked, before adding, "You look too expensive for this part of town."

"What?" I asked.

"She's not a prostitute," John said through gritted teeth. "This is my *wife*." My eyes widened a bit and my heart started racing. I'd rather he thought I was a hooker.

"Whatever," the man said. "A night's stay is thirty-seven."

"I'll pay cash," John said.

The man didn't argue which scared the crap out of me because most overnight establishments required some sort of credit card to secure a room. The fact that he didn't want one was alarming for two reasons. One, the owners and management didn't much care what went on in their rooms which was concerning to say the least and, two, there would be no way to trace us.

The man handed us a key, an actual key, like it was the freaking fifties or something. The key was attached to a hard bit of plastic that had seen better days.

"One-seventeen," the man said and slumped back into a chair, raising a paper to his chest.

We walked towards the room in silence. I looked up to see we were passing the unsavory group I noticed when we arrived.

"Hey, baby, something I can do for you?" The prostitute said when she noticed John, her eyes following the length of his body. Something told me this 'John' would be one she'd service for free the way she drunk him in. *Have at it,* I thought, *but be prepared for a messy death after*.

"Not if you paid me a million dollars," John said, laughing.

This offended her. There's something about prostitutes that screams demure, right? Exactly.

"What the hell does that mean?" She screamed, shaking her body and readying to get in his face. Two men I assumed were users or maybe they were just drunk, I couldn't tell, came to stand behind her. I doubt if they were any sort of knight in shining armor. They looked more ready to rob us than anything. Opportunists, really.

John smiled cruelly her direction and she actually shrunk inside herself a little, the fight inside died the moment he revealed his true nature. She'd seen enough of evil to recognize when she saw it right before her. She turned and ran toward the street but the men behind didn't take her flight seriously. They stood ready for a fight.

I found myself wishing they'd engage John, that would free me just enough time to ring Callum and warn him before I could run myself but after properly taking in John's size, they decided against it. The risk seemed to outweigh their reward.

I pleaded with my eyes for help but they didn't take any notice of me whatsoever. John pushed me toward one-seventeen and opened the door. It was disgusting. If there was maid service, this room hadn't seen anything but a sheet change and possibly towels for weeks.

"Get in the shower," he said immediately, making my body tremble.

I grabbed my bag and walked toward the shower. The sink was outside of the room with the shower and toilet, so I placed my bag on the worn laminate there trying to avoid the bed and carpet. John came behind me and pushed me slightly out of the way, rummaging through my bag, pulling out the dress I planned on wearing for Christmas dinner. It was short, came just above mid-thigh, a deep red silk chiffon, with a five inch silk detailing at the hem. The sleeves were long though and billowy and the dress fit snuggly with a choker neckline. It had paisley velvet details throughout the bodice the same color of the chiffon. I was saving it for Callum. It was my Christmas gift for him. Well, the girl inside it was going to be. The girl and the black lace underwear I bought to wear underneath it, that is.

"This will do nicely," John said, infuriating me. He rummaged further and pulled out the underwear I'd been saving. He smiled at me. "And these will as well." He shoved the pile back onto the top of my bag. I showered quickly, laying a folded towel down in the tub itself to avoid disease and fungus. It seemed smart at the time despite the other dangers just outside the door. I was so tense during the shower I had hardly any time to think of an escape plan. When I got out, I wrapped two towels around my body and emerged into the room, praying to God that John was somehow miraculously gone but he wasn't. In fact, he had positioned a chair a few feet away, facing the sinks.

"Dress," he said, casually resting against the back of the chair, twisting a pen in his hands.

"Turn around," I said hopelessly.

"Not a chance," he said, smiling.

I angrily yanked my underwear from the top of my dress and slid them up my legs, desperately trying to keep the towels around my body. John only laughed more.

"I can't wait to see how you attempt the bra," he said.

This was actually a lot simpler. I placed the bra over the towel and fastened it around it, tugging the towel underneath it and rearranging as best I could without exposing myself. I looked up, proud of myself but noticed the anger in John's clenched jaw. He yanked the towels from my body, causing an involuntary shriek from me. I frantically reached for my dress but John stood fully, clasping my wrists in his hands.

"Oh my God, Harper," he breathed, extending my arms out. He took a good, long drinking, look at me. I tried to bring my arms to my chest but he just tightened his grip more. "You are breathtaking. Much more beautiful than the other girls." I assumed he meant the innocent girls he took because of me and I wanted to vomit. My body shook as he trailed his hands up my arms. I brought my hands to my chest but he yanked them away. "Keep them here," he said, bringing them to my side. He ran his rough hands over my shoulders to the back of my neck, trailing his fingers down my spine. He brought the palms of his hands over my sides, then down the flat of my stomach. "So soft," he said quietly, eyeing me with a revolting hunger.

I pushed away from him, making him laugh and brought my dress to cover the front of my body.

"Get dressed," he ordered. "We'll have time for that later."

With trembling hands, I pulled the dress over my head. I just stood there, grateful to be covered, fighting tears that begged to trail down my cheeks.

"Dry your hair. Can't have you getting sick."

Chapter Nineteen
Please Don't Go

Harper

Wearing the very outfit I wanted Callum to see me in first, John dragged me out the crap motel door and into the freezing cold.

"Where are we going?" I asked without thinking.

"I didn't tell you you could talk, Harper," he said, suddenly and inexplicably angry slamming me against the door after he shut and locked it, unexpectedly surprising me.

His eyes seethed as he stared into my face. I inhaled sharply as John cupped my right breast and squeezed hard, making me yelp in pain. His eyes softened slightly and he grabbed the back of my neck, bringing me close.

"Why do you make me do these things to you?" He asked grittily.

My mouth gaped slightly and I furrowed my

brows slightly. "I haven't made you do anything. As much as I loathe to admit it, you're the one in control. Does it make you feel like a man forcing a woman to do things she doesn't want to only because she can't defend herself?"

This was a mistake. The second it started spilling from my lips, I knew it was a mistake and he showed me why by slapping me harshly across the face. I brought my hand up to ease the sting. Tears burned behind my lids.

"I'm sorry, Harper," he said, removing my hand and rubbing his thumb across the red mark he only just placed on my cheek. I was revolted by him. He caressed the side of my face with a tenderness that made me uneasy. "You told me you would cooperate."

"I-I..." I began to stammer but he cut me off by squeezing my jaw roughly, the direct antithesis to his previous gentleness, giving me emotional whiplash. "A promise is a promise, bitch."

I nodded, convinced I wasn't going to live out the evening.

"I want to show you something first," he said, pinching my upper arm between his meaty hand and squeezing hard, practically dragging me toward a waiting taxi. "Get in," he ordered, shoving me into the backseat.

"Twelve-twenty-seven First," he told the driver, making my throat run instantly dry. Ames' address. John leaned into my ear, his hot breath against my neck. "I think you need a little reminder."

He nestled me closely to his side and I gagged from the proximity. The driver was eyeing us strangely through the rear view. John suddenly leaned forward, banging his hand against the Plexiglas separation.

"Get a good look at my wife, old man?" He bellowed, making the man jump.

The man only steered his eyes toward the road, not looking at us once for the remainder of the trip.

"Get out," John said, when we pulled up to a beautiful old building near the pier. He paid the driver and the man peeled away, desperate to get away from us. *Thanks, old man.*

Ames' home looked exactly like he had described it in his letters. A five story building of old architecture. It reminded me a lot of our own building back home. Ames' flat was on the second floor, right above a coffee shop. I stupidly wondered if the noise was tolerable during the day but was abruptly brought back to reality when John's body ran flush against my back.

I sprinted for the front door, losing a heel as I threw myself up the steps to the building's main door. The door was locked. I quickly found Ames' buzzer, which wasn't difficult as there were only ten names available, and pressed repeatedly until John caught up with me, slamming me into the door behind me. I hit the corner of my head, the sensitive part right above the hairline, making me feel dizzy.

"You stupid, bitch! Fine! You want to play this game! You got it. You've just made the biggest mistake." He slammed me again, hard, against the door.

"Hello?" Callum answered through the intercom. I sucked in a harsh breath.

I opened my mouth to warn him but John clamped his hand over my mouth. I bit down on his hand but it did no good, he didn't budge, only tightened his grip, painfully straining my jaw. I thrashed around as he waited for Callum to give up. "*Hello?*" He asked again. "Kids," he muttered before breaking off the connection.

John smiled disturbingly into my face and tightened his grip, making me gulp for air. "You've sealed your deal, princess."

He dragged me down the steps by my throat. I lost my the other heel as each foot bounced against steps on the descend. At the bottom, he dropped my body and punched me in the stomach as hard as possible, sending vomit all over the pavement.

Tears began to flow and I folded myself into a fetal position to avoid anymore blows to my stomach. The pain was excruciating. A volatile mix of nausea and unbelievable agony pricked at my insides. A thick blanket of darkness approached, begging me to follow it. John repeatedly kicked me. I fought with myself against the black but it beckoned me with every blow from John's boot. My hands protected my face from each swing of his foot at my head but my fingers suffered intolerably. I manage to scream out in pain once when he finally fractured two fingers on my right hand.

I was granted a ten second reprieve when he moved to the other side of my body but soon sharp needles of extreme torture came with each swift blast of his boot. I arched my back, writhing in agony, the pain was so intense, I couldn't find my voice and just when I thought I couldn't take any more, just when I thought death was imminent with the very next hit, he stopped.

Kneeling beside me, he cradled my body close to his and I was powerless to stop him, my body limp and I realized I could no longer feel my legs, my arms lay feebly around me.

"Why must you make me do these things to you, Harper?" He said, squeezing me tighter. I wanted to scream in pain but my throat wouldn't allow it. *"You make me do these things, Harper!"* He yelled, searching my body wildly with his eyes. "Get up. We need to go." But I couldn't move, not a single muscle would obey.

"Get up!" He bellowed as I could barely open my eyes. He shook me soundly, urging me to stand. "Get up right now, I said. It's time to leave." I just lay slack against him, praying that God would just take my soul. John's eyes followed the length of my body, realizing what shape I was in and began to cry. "It's okay," he said, soothing the sides of my face with his hands, tears staining his disgusting face. "I didn't mean for it to get so out of hand but you left me no choice. You'll recover from this though and we'll live the way we were meant to." He clutched my broken and bruised body closely to his and began to rock back and forth. "You'll see," he told me but it was more for himself than for me. "You'll see. Everything will be just fine. Let's get you back to the room and we'll just start over." Panic laced his voice. "Come on." He picked me up and I screamed from the movement, positive he had broken my back. He tried to stand me up but my legs fell loosely beneath me.

John suddenly gripped me harder, cocking his head to the side. I strained to listen to what he heard. Laughing, I heard laughing and talking about a block from us, heading our direction. John became noticeably panicky, the indecision in his face. He began to run. Every jolt of his step sent inconceivable suffering up my back. With each ragged movement I yelled in torment until he cupped his hand over my mouth and hugged me closer, squeezing my body hard, with his right arm. I screamed at the top of my lungs but it was muffled by his hand. His breath was hot and harsh across my face in his desperation. "*Quiet!*" He gritted through teeth. "They'll hear you!"

"Hey!" I heard one of the men from the approaching group yell. "Hey! Stop that! What are you doing to her!"

Hysteria painted John's face and his own sense of self-preservation kicked in because he dropped me on the ground and ran toward the pier, disappearing into the darkness.

"Help me..." I barely spoke out.

"Oh my God!" A woman screamed and the last thing I remember were a cacophony of running feet coming to my rescue just as the darkness consumed me.

Callum

"Here, Ames, let me get that for you. It's the least I can do after such an incredible dinner," I told my uncle.

"No, no. You are a guest in my home and there is no way I'm letting you do this," Ames countered, stopping my hands with his as I tried to pick up his empty plate.

"You at least need to let me help. Please, we can share the sink, get done in half the time and leave us enough time to watch some random Christmas flick."

He smiled appreciatively. "Fine and stop begging. It makes you look pathetic." I laughed.

Getting to know Ames was proving to be an almost perfect distraction from my broken heart. I say almost because it only slightly dulled the pain, which is more than I thought possible.

I liked Ames. He was funny as hell, generous, and laid back.

We stacked the dishes in the sink and I began to run the hot water just as the buzzer connected. Ames' hands were already soaked so I ran, for the second time that night, to answer it, prepared to yell at the prankster kids this time.

"Yes?" I clipped shortly.

"Uh, yeah, we're looking for a Mr. Callum Tate?"

Surprised, I answered. "Uh, this is he."

"Mr. Tate, this is the Seattle P.D., we'd like to speak with you, if that's alright?"

I couldn't imagine why the Seattle Police Department would want with me near midnight on Christmas Eve. Suddenly, I began to worry, thinking that something had changed with the John Bell situation and the N.Y.P.D was looking to reach me.

"Of course, come right up," I said, buzzing the door so they could enter.

Ames walked near to me, drying his hand on a towel. "What could this possibly be about."

"Uh, I'm not entirely sure," I told him honestly. The wait for the police was anxiety filled. I sat at the dining table, my foot tapping at an unreasonable speed.

"Are you okay, Callum?" Ames asked, sitting in the seat across from me.

Just then, the knock came at the door and I launched myself at its handle, throwing the door open and stepping back slightly. Two uniformed officers removed their hats and asked if they could enter.

"Of course," Ames said, gesturing to his sofa.

"Actually," the larger of the officers said, "it might be best if you sat down, Mr. Tate."

My heart beat rapidly and I had trouble catching my breath. I sat and Ames lowered himself next to me in support.

The officers sat in the chairs opposite us, seemingly taking their time, reluctant to reveal whatever news they were tasked to repeat. *It's just a message about John, Callum. Nothing's wrong with Harper. She's perfectly safe back home.* I foolishly tried to convince myself but deep down I knew that if the N.Y.P.D wanted only to speak with me they would have rang me. Two uniformed messengers meant bad, awful things. My stomach wrenched itself and I wanted to vomit.

"Please," I begged, "just tell me."

The larger of the two sighed, obviously the spokesperson and leaned forward as if to catch me. I didn't like where this was going at all. "Mr. Tate are you married to a Harper Tate?" He asked.

My world began to spin and it felt like the floor would drop beneath me. I gulped. "Y-Yes, sir," I answered shakily, shifting forward in preparation.

Ames looked at me with wide eyes, obviously shocked at having learned I was married but wisely kept his mouth shut.

"I'm sorry to have to tell you this, Mr. Tate," the larger officer began but I cut him off.

"Please," I begged, my voice breaking. "Not Harper...not Harper." I slid from the sofa and onto my knees hard. All three men lunged for me but I held them away with a quivering hand. "What happened?" My trembling voice asked.

"She was found not a block from here, badly wounded. She's been airlifted to Northwest."

I launched myself at the door and threw it open. I ran down the steps, not knowing exactly where I was going but knowing that if I didn't move, didn't do *something,* I would lose my mind. I heard the officers' steps as well as Ames' but paid no attention. I looked up the street toward the city and decided to run but Ames caught be before I could flee, throwing my coat over my shoulders.

"You can't run to her, Callum! Be reasonable! I'll drive us!"

Ames ran around the building to the garage for his car and I collapsed on the steps of his building.

"Son, she's alive, hold on to that," the smaller officer

assured me. I closed my eyes and nodded once in acknowledgment. His hand rested on my shoulder, letting me know he was there. "We'll escort you there."

Ames' car pulled up short at the curb and the officer helped me inside. He climbed into the passenger side of their cruiser and led the way, sirens blaring, to Northwest.

"She's alive," Ames' said quietly. "The officers told me she lives, Callum."

I turned to my young uncle, unsure of what to say but finally found the words. "Do you really think they would have come to your apartment, given us this escort, if they suspected she would live?" I asked incredulously. My jaw clenched at hearing myself say the words.

Ames said nothing, only pressed harder on the gas pedal.

"I can't live without her, Ames." I told him but turned inward. "I think I always knew it. I was a fool to think I could come here and forget her." I looked at his profile, highlighted by the neon lights of his dash. "I'm ridiculous in love with her."

"I can tell," he told me. "Is that why you never said a word about her? You two are no longer together?"

"In a sense, yes," I answered, unable to reveal more.

The drive to the hospital felt like it took hours. My legs were sore from bouncing repeatedly in anticipation. When the emergency room at Northwest came into view, I removed my seat belt and scooted up in my seat. Ames rounded the driveway in front of the entrance and I bounded from the car before he'd even come to a complete stop.

I ran through the automatic doors and practically assaulted the woman manning the desk. "My wife! Where is she?" I asked.

"Your name, sir?" She asked professionally.

"Tate. Callum Tate. My wife is Harper Tate."

When I said Harper's name, the woman's eyes briefly flashed wide before she checked her expression. Her tone softened. "Uh, yes. Um, if you'll just come with me," she said quietly.

I buried my hands under my arms, hugging myself tightly as I followed her to a single empty room. "What is this?" I asked.

"Um, I thought you'd be more comfortable in your own private waiting room."

"No," I said, refusing to step through the door. Flashes of the day my parents died came flooding my senses. These were the rooms they put family of patients not expected to live. These were the rooms they stuck you in so you wouldn't make other families uncomfortable when you lost your shit. I'd been in one of these rooms once before. "No!" I screamed, buckling under my own weight, falling to my knees once more. The woman signaled to someone for help and one of the officer's from earlier in Ames' apartment helped me up, leading me into the room I detested with every fiber of my being. They sat me down on a leather love seat and my head fell into my hands. "Just tell me," I said.

"She's in surgery," the woman said softly, earning a soft, exhausted sigh from me. Her hand went to my shoulder, "but she's in critical condition." Tears began to flow freely and my fingers tore into the back of my head. "A doctor will be here shortly to enlighten you more on her condition." She stood as Ames came into the room. I stood quickly and he hugged me tightly as I lost control of myself.

The door clicked behind the woman, leaving just Ames and I. "She can't die," I told him.

329

The two officers came into the room and waited patiently.

I pulled myself from Ames' embrace and turned toward the officers. "What happened?" I asked.

Ames and I sat down. "Well, we've been in touch with the N.Y.P.D and unfortunately their prisoner, John Bell, had escaped the night he was arrested." I sucked in a breath. Confusion, anger, and pain flashed across my chest, thinking that I'd left Harper there alone that night. "They've been desperately trying to get a hold of the both of you. We confirmed that John Bell was following Harper through surveillance video obtained from airport security. We suspect he engaged her on the plane and, essentially, kidnapped her."

"Where is he?" I asked, my jaw clenched, my hands in tight fists on my thighs.

"We don't know," he admitted.

"Jesus!" Ames said.

"We're doing everything we can!" He insisted. "He can't get very far. We've alerted all means of transportation that he is a wanted man as well as the media. He will *not* be getting far." he paused, thinking. "Is there any place you can think of that he could be hiding?"

"None," I answered. "He has no family and I believe he knows no one in the city."

"Good." The officer seemed to relax a bit. "We'll be checking all hotel and motel establishments in the area. We've got men manned at every airport and bus depot. We'll catch him." Both officers stood and shook our hands, exiting swiftly. The larger officer stood by the door and turned toward me quickly. "We'll let you know if there is any progress."

"Thank you," I told him as the door clicked behind them.

Ames and I waited for hours. Each minute that ticked by, the tightness in my chest constricted to unbearable levels. I paced the length of the room at least a thousand times, praying to God, offering myself in her place, if He would just give her back. I knew God didn't work like that. If He did, I would have had my parents back, but I wasn't bitter about it. That was life. I just wished He'd bend the rules, just once, for me. Though I didn't deserve it, I prayed He would.

A knock came to the door and Ames left my side to answer it. A tall man in his mid-fifties came inside, shutting the door behind him. He looked haggard, tired.

"Mr. Tate?" He asked me, my red rimmed eyes giving away my title.

"Yes?" He took my hand and shook it. "I'm Doctor Matthews. I just came from surgery with Harper."

"How is she?" I asked, dejected.

He breathed a large sigh, removing his glasses from his red face, and rubbing his eyes. "She's stable but still in critical condition." He replaced his glasses on his face. "She's in ICU and I expect her to wake within a few hours. She's doing remarkably well...considering."

I swallowed. "What - what happened to her?"

All three of us sat. "Her back was broken," he said, ignoring my trembling body, a product of his profession. "Her spleen ruptured and we were forced to remove it. She had several small internal bleeds but we believe they will heal without difficulty. I'm most worried about the possible damage her spinal cord suffered as well as her kidneys. She has acute renal failure and will more than likely need dialysis while her body heals to bridge the gap."

"Is she," I swallowed, " expected to live?"

"I believe she will survive but any permanent damage

can't be determined as of yet. Only time will tell."

"Can I see her?"

"Not yet." He glanced at his watch. "It's close to two in the morning now. ICU visiting hours quit after nine, you won't be allowed back into ICU again until the morning. She'll be asleep anyway. I suggest you get home, get some rest and come back here bright and early."

Doctor Matthews stood to leave. "Thank you, Doctor Matthews," I said, taking his hand.

"Of course," he said, his eyes softening. "I'd say she is nothing short of a miracle, son."

"I already knew that," I said, a small smile touching my lips. He smiled back and shut the door behind him.

"She's going to live, Ames."

"I heard," he said, gripping my shoulder next to me on the sofa and sending me a large grin.

My whole body shook as the relief poured over me. I couldn't think of the possibility that she may never walk again. One obstacle at a time. I was grateful I even got the chance to worry about any damage at all, if that makes any sense. I was so ecstatic she was alive.

"Did you want to go back to the apartment?" Ames asked.

"Not even if you threatened to drag me," I said.

"I figured as much. Let me grab a change of clothes for you and some food. I'll be back in an hour, Callum."

"Thank you, Ames," I said, slapping his back.

"You're my family, man."

I offered him a large smile.

The ER nurses let me know of a family waiting room right outside the ICU and I immediately left for the fourth floor to be as close to Harper as possible. As I boarded the elevator, a woman came bounding up to the closing doors.

"Mr. Tate?" She asked, a bit breathless from her trot.

"Yes?" I said, stopping the doors with my hand.

"Your wife's belongings, sir," she said, handing me a plastic bag.

"Thank you," I said, grabbing the sack and clutching it close to my chest.

When I reached the waiting room, I was the only one there, thank God and threw my body onto a sofa, exhaustion setting in. I had been a live wire while she was in surgery and the relief of knowing she was alive just beyond those glass doors brought on a new sensation. Residual fear. Now that I was alone, I fell to my knees and let my body wrack with the sobs I'd been holding back worrying about my wife. And I prayed. I prayed like I'd never prayed before, thanking God for keeping her on earth and asking for Him to watch over her.

I wiped my face with the inside of my jacket, took a deep breath and drug the bag holding Harper's things onto my lap. I unclasped the plastic handles and pooled everything inside onto my thighs.

My eyes began to water when I took in her shoes, dress, and undergarments. I squeezed her tattered belongings into my hands, feeling the garments that were recently upon her body. Tears began to threaten once more but I sucked them back.

I studied the clothing on top of the pile, spotting a folded piece of paper tucked into the inside of her bra. I picked it up and unfolded it.

Callum, I love you more than you could possibly know.

"Oh, God!" I bellowed, crushing the note to my chest. She hadn't thought she was going to make it.

333

I cried myself to sleep on that sofa, my face buried in her dress so I could inhale her scent.

"Mr. Tate?" I heard. Someone was shaking me awake. I shot up. "Yes?"

"I'm Doctor Sullivan. I'm sorry to wake you but I thought you should know that your wife's vitals have crashed and they're working to revive her. I..." But I wouldn't let him finish.

I pushed the man away from me and sprinted for the ICU doors but they wouldn't budge. They needed to be opened by the ICU operating desk.

"Open these doors!" I yelled to the nurse manning the desk. "Right now!" I bellowed when she shook her head. "That's my wife in there!" I screamed, punching the glass with my palms.

I heard a slight buzz and the door clicked open. I ran to a room filled with people. I knew this was hers. I forced my way through the line of waiting nurses, working my way around the physicians attempting to revive her. I stood at the head of her bed and bent toward her ear. I ignored how beaten and bruised she was.

"Harper," I whispered, my voice catching in my throat. "Sweetheart, please. Please, Harper, stay here with me. Our life has yet to begin, Harper. You belong with me here. Stay, love."

I watched them shock her heart multiple times but it refused to beat. The room moved slowly around me, people yelling, tugging at Harper, reading machines. Nurses, stoic in this very experience, yet looking on me with pity. I couldn't stand looking at them. I wanted to tug Harper from all the wires and drag her back to New York. I wanted to pretend they weren't working to bring her back to life. I wanted to pretend none of this happened and that John Bell, that bastard, didn't exist.

Two men forced me away from Harper saying something about the paddles but I didn't catch all of it. All I could do was stare at my beautiful wife and think that this was not how it was supposed to be. I stared at her thin frame, her long copper gold hair, dull, her tan skin, pale, her usual pink, full lips turned blue and thin. *Get up, Harper. Get up, baby. Give me the life we both deserve, Harper. Screw what we used to be. Screw the shit our lives used to be as children. Let's make our own way, Harper.*

"Wake up, Harper," I began softly. "Wake up, Harper!" I said a bit louder. "Wake up!" I screamed at her finally, fighting the men holding me back. "Wake up!" Tears streamed down my face. My hands dug into the shoulders of the men pinning me against the windows. "Please," I tenderly requested. I closed my eyes. "God, I'm begging you," I prayed softly. "Please, God, don't take her from me yet. I've had enough tragedy in my life. I need something to keep me from taking the tumble over the edge. I don't think I can live without her."

Seemingly out of nowhere, a nurse came from the line and placed her hand on my shoulder, silently praying along with me. The men looked from one to the other and relaxed their hold on me, praying with me as well. Soon, the entire room was filled with prayer, including the physicians working to revive her. I even noticed, family members visiting their own loved ones drifted to the large glass windows that was Harper's room and folded their hands.

They worked for what seemed like forever but a calm entered the room and they worked methodically, no more panic in their motions. They worked with an efficiency I'd never seen before but nothing was happening. Her body laid limp on her bed, her chest still without breath. I continually prayed but was losing hope, my stomach clenched in nausea. I was preparing myself for the worst and contemplated how I could possibly bury another family member. I wondered how in the world I could place the love of my life in cold, hard dirt. That's when I knew. I knew I couldn't do it, I would only throw myself in the hole with her. I clenched my teeth and fisted my hands, pressing my eyes closed. She had to stay with me. *Had to*.

Suddenly, Harper gasped and my tears turned to wracking sobs. "Thank you," I told God. "Thank you," I told the doctors and nurses quietly. The nurse who placed her hand on my shoulder, squeezed it and left the room, letting the doctor stabilize my wife.

Unnecessary staff left the room, but there was an eerily quiet blanket that descended on every person inside the ICU, realizing the miracle that was their prayers. A breathing tube was placed, and eventually she was stabilized enough that the ICU staff could leave me alone with her. I pulled a rolling stool over to her side and held her hand. She wasn't conscious but it didn't matter to me. She was alive.

I breathed deeply, my body exhausted from the fear. "God, Harper, He gave you back to me." I gripped that hand with both of mine then. I rubbed the back of her swollen hand with my thumbs, making lazy circles over her pale skin. "He gave you back."

I was astonished, to be honest. I reached my hand up, sliding it over her gown, and placing my trembling hand over her chest to feel her heart beat. 'Thump, thump, thump', it told me, steady and strong. I buried my chin into my chest and reveled in the miracle that was

Harper's beating heart. I released a pent up breath and sat up straight, leaning over her face and tracing her hair line with my fingers.

"I love you," I told her, "*so much.*"

Over the week, Harper healed at an astonishing rate, according to her physicians. She was still in a medically induced coma because of some swelling in her brain but was expected be woken soon and moved to a regular room once she was breathing on her own since her back was healing so remarkably well and the swelling was completely eradicated.

The nurses were incredibly helpful to me, not making a big deal about leaving Harper's side. Essentially, I refused to leave her but Ames convinced me that I should probably shower because, and I quote, I would 'scare the shit out of Harper' if she woke and found me days without a shower and a full beard. I still refused to leave the hospital but thanks to Ames and the kind nurses. I was able to shower in one of the hospital rooms and had a change of clean clothes. Ames even brought me my meals on break from work and visited me for hours each night.

Five days after Christmas, the physicians decided it was time to wean Harper off the barbiturates keeping her comatose. When I knew she would be waking, I made a long list and sent Ames to a local department store to get all the things I thought she would want and a few things I just wanted her to have.

"Okay," Doctor Sullivan said, to me outside Harper's room. "I've taken her off the drugs."

"And how long before she wakes?" I asked, my tired arms wrapped around my chest.

"It's up to her," he told me with a smile, "but if she was

a smart girl," he teased, "she'd wake so you'll get off my back."

I laughed. Doctor Sullivan and I had an understanding. He made jokes and I laughed so I didn't lose my mind.

"Seriously, within a few hours is usual. We'll be transferring her to the third floor within the hour. Chelsea will let you know what room. I'll see you in a bit."

"Thanks Dr. Sullivan."

"Of course."

As Doctor Sullivan walked away, my cell rang. "Hello?"

"Hey, Callum."

Cherry.

"Hey, Cherry."

"What's the progress?" She asked for the sixth time that day. I loved her all the more because she was so concerned. Cherry and Charlie were still in England but kept tabs on Harper throughout the day. It was three a.m. there but Cherry said she didn't mind setting her alarm to catch wind of any progress.

"She's been taken off the drugs that's keeping her comatose. It's up to her now when she'll wake."

"Oh, thank God," Cherry sighed into the phone. "And you'll..."

"Yes, Cherry, I will call you the second she wakes." I laughed.

"Good." She yawned. "Alright, buttercup. Catch you on the flip."

"Bye, Cherry."

Chelsea, an ICU nurse who helped make my life easier, came bounding up to me as I slid my phone in my back pocket. "Three oh-seven," she said, smiling.

"Excellent! Thanks, Chelsea!"

"No problem," she said, sliding by me to enter the room next to Harper's.

338

Chapter Twenty
Young Blood

Harper

I woke to the sound of his voice. *His* voice. "...No, not yet," he said. Pause. He was on the phone. "Because it takes time, Cherry. She'll wake when she's good and ready." He sighed. "I know, I know. You'll be the first we call. Okay. Alright, I love you, too. Send our love to Charlie. Bye, Cherry."

My eyes were heavy as well as my arms. All I wanted was to lift my sluggish lids to look at his beautiful face. I felt trapped inside my body. I inhaled deeply, catching the soothing scent that was Callum's cologne.

I could hear him slide a chair over the floor toward me, toward the bed I was in. When he took my hand in his, small, salty tears cascaded down my cheeks. His breath caught.

"Ha-*Harper*? Are you- Are you there?" I tried to

squeeze his hand but lacked the control. "Can you hear me, Harper?" He asked, coming close to my face. The warmth of his body radiated over me and the tears came faster. "Oh, love, listen, you were hurt." *John.* My heart rate accelerated. "But I'm here..." My eyes fluttered open to a dim room. Night. Callum took in a sharp breath. "Harper," he said softly, caressing my face with his hands. I watched him and tried to smile. "Oh my God, Harper." Tears began to fall softly down his own face. "You're here. You're really here." He tenderly cupped both his hands over my face. "Harper." He broke down, making my insides twist in agony. I squeezed my lids shut, flushing out fat drops of my own tears.

"I got your note," I gritted out.

"I love you," he told me, looking straight into my eyes. A small smile played across my lips. "I love you. I'm *in* love with you."

"I love you too," I told him, my voice raspy from disuse. "I've always loved you," I continued, clearing my throat. "You're the love of my life, Callum."

He laughed lightly, coughing to avoid a sob. A massive smile splayed across his gorgeous face. "I think I've waited my entire life to hear those words from you, Harper Tate."

***

It took me eight weeks to leave that hospital. By the time, I was done, I knew every single person employed there, as did Callum. It was bittersweet leaving but it was most definitely time.

The good news was that I regained control and feeling in my legs which was nothing short of a miracle according to Doctor Sullivan. I'd need extended physical therapy back home but I was healed well enough to travel which is what I wanted more than anything. I just wanted to be home, in my own bed...with my husband.

I could walk short distances only, forced to utilize a wheel chair for any kind of extensive trips. Callum would cart me around like a doll, lifting me into bed, even helping me bathe which was somewhat embarrassing the first time but the nurses would have thought it strange that my *husband* wouldn't eventually be the one who assisted me. The first few times, the nurses did it but they told us he needed to learn how to care for me once we left the hospital and insisted he try. Who were we to argue?

The first time he saw me naked was...*strange. Gorgeously strange.*

"Lean on me," he had whispered into my ear, making me shiver. I stood on my feet but he held me tightly against him. He had begun to close his eyes but I stopped him with a hand.

"I want you to see me," I told him quietly, making his eyes shoot wide. I almost laughed but checked myself.

He gulped audibly. "Uh, okay." Trembling hands came toward me and undressed me slowly, being careful not to jostle me too much, when he pulled my top off. My heart began to race inside my chest, pounding against my ribs at an unhealthy rate. If I'd been hooked into any of the machines sitting inside my room, five nurses would've come bounding through the door. I smiled shyly.

Piece by piece, my clothing laid in a pile by my feet and eventually, I stood completely bare, accept for a pair of panties, against him. We both breathed in pants. Callum would see me naked. Callum and naked...in the same sentence. He still had yet to look at me and wrapped me in a towel before he could get a good look. He laid another towel on one of the shower chairs and picked me up, tucking his hands behind my knees. I felt my breath whoosh from my lungs. This was it. Until he sat me there while he filled my bath. I felt my cheeks redden and my feelings were sort of hurt that he didn't want to see me. A heat crept up my neck and into my face, ashamed that I couldn't tempt him the way he tempted me.

I had been healing for weeks and all my bruises had disappeared, use of my broken fingers restored. I looked completely normal from the outside, the only thing that ailed me was some soreness in my back and a definite lack of strength but that wasn't visible to the naked eye. I had just given him permission to look at me naked and he didn't freaking do it. I was feeling so vulnerable and open it was almost excruciating. Tears began to make an appearance but I bit my bottom lip to prevent them from spilling over.

I watched his broad back as the running water captivated his attention. I bent slightly to the side to see what was so interesting about this seemingly so amazing water. I was offended. Callum's back rose and feel deeply with each breath. *He's nervous,* I realized. His hands made tight fists, then released, over and over and over. *Signature, Callum.* I sat back and enjoyed the fact that I made my husband nervous. It was flattering.

Once the bath was filled, there was nowhere else for Callum to go. Slowly, he turned my direction and began to undress himself making me tremble a little on my own. All my fears and insecurities dissipated in one swift motion as he shrugged off his button up shirt and pulled his t-shirt over his head.

"Um," I said, suddenly nervous myself. "Are you,

uh, going to fill the bath with soap?"

"No," he said softly, deliberately taking his time with the buttons of his jeans. Massive pause. "I won't be able to see you very well if the foam is in my way, will I?" He asked, a knowing smile tugging at the corners of his lips.

My throat closed. I could only nod my response.

He was breathtaking, literally, the lines of his stomach and chest were hard and conditioned like a toned athlete. He was lean and absolutely the most handsome man I had ever seen in my entire life. I loved the way his hair curled around his ears and the way his eyes sparkled in the subtle lighting above him. The heat that had crept up my face before turned into a delicious, warm blush and I couldn't stop my hand from flying to my chest as I inhaled deeply. A small, smug smile fought to make an appearance on his lips. Never taking his eyes from mine, he pulled his jeans off his legs and stood in his boxers. This is the most I'd ever seen of Callum's naked skin. I shivered, actually shivered like some romance novel harlot.

Callum walked to me, both our hands quaked but the instant they met, all nervousness disappeared and we held firmly onto the other. He helped me to my feet and I balanced in front of him. Slowly, I removed my towel, letting it pile onto the floor at my feet. I blushed furiously at his own sharp intake of breath.

His head shook lazily from side to side as if in disbelief but his hands fisted at his side, betraying his easy look. Another gulp. "Lord, Harper. You are *beautiful*." Callum paused while his eyes roamed my entire body, making me blush an even deeper red. "My God was it worth the wait," he barely murmured under his breath.

343

He stepped closer to me, wrapping his arms around my shoulders being careful not to squeeze too hard.

And then he kissed me. Deeply.

His tongue found mine and I almost melted in a pool at his feet. He broke away too soon and I felt slightly abandoned but he quickly remedied this by finding the underside of my jaw with his lips, moving up to the side of my neck and across my chin, meeting up once again with my mouth. I wrapped my hands around his neck, running my fingers through his disheveled hair, tugging lightly at the base of his neck, inciting a groan and even deeper kiss. The kiss slowed and he finished with three pecks on my lips.

"Come on," he said, winded, "before the water gets cold."

He knelt at my feet. I held my breath as he stared into my eyes, sliding my panties to my ankles. I stepped from my underwear and he stood as his boxers came off. He picked me up, sliding us both into the water. He nestled my back against his chest and I fit perfectly inside his arms. The water was the perfect temperature and I sighed from the proximity of our bodies. I closed my eyes as Callum wet my hair and began to massage shampoo into my scalp, eventually finding the tips of my hair with the soapy lather. He conditioned and lathered my entire body, washing me from head to toe.

When he was done, I sighed, content with being relaxed and clean against him. The bath wasn't large enough for me to shave my legs with my back against his chest but he wouldn't let me bend to do it myself anyway, opting to set me on the sink counter later and do it himself over the sink, he told me. He got out himself and wrapped a towel around his waist before hooking his arms around my body and lifting me from the water. He wrapped yet another towel around my torso and took another to my hair, languidly drying it from root to tip. We watched each other quietly as he worked the cloth through my long hair, leaning down occasionally to kiss my lips.

"You drive me crazy," he almost gasped.

I kissed him yet again before leaning into his ear. "Do something about it."

He closed his eyes and exhaled from his nose, waiting a moment before opening them and staring straight through me. "Harper, we can't right now." His jaw clenched at his words.

"I know," I said smoothly, "but soon, Callum. Soon."

"Oh, very soon, Mrs. Tate."

Gorgeously strange, indeed.

The flight home was rather difficult. I made sure not to drink anything during the flight so Callum wouldn't be forced to help me use the restroom. I could have probably walked the short distance to the lavatory but I knew Callum wouldn't let me without him. Not to mention, I had a new aversion to all airplane lavatories. God forbid, Callum and I ever venture out of country. The flights would be torturous.

Turns out, Callum is a nervous flier. That, coupled with the fact that I wasn't exactly in 'fighting' condition, and Callum was a giant bundle of nerves, didn't help his unease.

"You need a drink, Callum. Something strong," I

jested, prodding my shoulder with his, adding a tiny smile.

"Nothing short of moonshine would take the edge off of me right now," he teased. Callum turned to me, running a crooked finger down my jaw line. "I want you, Harper."

My breath sped and my heart beat pushed the boundaries of normal, threatening to rip itself from my chest. I inhaled slowly, closing my eyes. I opened them. "You can't say things like that on a crowded flight, Callum."

"Why not?" He asked, his eyes twinkling with mischief.

I took in the people around us. "Because these people seem nice enough and I wouldn't want to traumatize that little kid staring at us three rows down."

Callum peeked down the aisle in the direction of the little girl before turning back to me. "We wouldn't want to do that now, would we," he said, leaning closely to my face, his lips inches from mine.

I was forced to swallow. "Nuh uh," I said, leaning closer to close the gap. His breath tickled my face and I sighed in exasperation when he put, what felt like, way too much distance between him and myself. "What a tease," I said, wrapping my right hand around his neck then letting go for fear I'd do something drastic.

Callum and I made out in the back seat of the cab we took home from the airport like a couple of sex-crazed teenagers. I had forgotten there was a person even driving the cab but when we pulled in front of our building, my face flushed a brilliant red when the cabbie winked at me while placing our bags on the curb. *What, ya' perv? We're married.* And before you go all, eww, on

346

me, know that I hate PDA, hate it, but you know my story. Can you blame me?

Callum threw our bags in the elevator, using one of them to hold the door open. He lifted me up and carried me 'over the threshold' of our building's front door, and placed a kiss at my temple. He kicked the bag holding the door open into the lift and we rode up to our floor, kissing like our lips weren't already red and swollen.

As we passed each floor, Callum would groan at each bell alerting to us to every floor. We were close, sending my heart into a frenzy. The doors dinged, signaling we'd arrived. Callum set me down right outside the lift doors and grabbed our bags, tossing them in front of our door. I walked closely to him, his hand gripping my waist.

On the door, were ten or so messages from our landlord, letting us know about packages that needed to be picked up or letting us know about visits from the N.Y.P.D, etc. Callum grabbed them all before opening the door to our home and tossing them onto the hall table, the bags came next and then me. He wrapped me in his arms again, locking the door behind us, and made a beeline for his dark bedroom. None of our friends knew we were coming home that night for, um, obvious reasons.

Callum laid me gently on his dark bed before standing to close his bedroom door. "Are you comfortable, Mrs. Tate?"

"Very much, Mr. Tate, thank you," I told him.

He lowered himself next to me and kissed me like there was no tomorrow. "I'm so unbelievably grateful to be lying next to you, wife. You feel like a dream to me."

"Maybe it is a dream. Maybe we're not even

awake right now. Maybe you're a figment of my imagination and this entire ride has been a trip down unconscious lane. Maybe I'm still in my coma," I contemplated, irrational fear creeping up my healing spine.

Callum kissed me deeply. "Does *that* feel like a dream?" He asked.

I smiled, inches from his lips. "No, it most certainly does not." He began to kiss me again but I stopped him. "Help me up," I told him.

"You're not going anywhere," he said seductively.

"Yes, I need, uh, to shower."

"What? No, you don't." He buried his face into my neck and inhaled, kicking up the perfume that laid dormant on my skin. His cologne and my own fragrance mixed well, making me feel faint. The two mixed oh so perfectly together. "You smell amazing," he said.

"Callum, please? This is a big deal for me. I want it to be perfect."

"Harper Tate, you're here, it's already perfect."

"Please, I want a shower, babe. Just help me up."

"Can I watch?" He asked in all seriousness, making me laugh. His eyes twinkled lightly.

"If you want."

Callum helped me up and brought me to my room. "I guess this really will be the guest room now?"

He chuckled, his chest shaking with the effort. "I guess so."

I slowly turned the water on, my back still slightly sore. The hot water would help get rid of any stiffness I had and that was the real reason I was showering right then. It wasn't ideal my first time being just after I was recovering from a broken back but I couldn't complain, not really. Callum made himself comfortable on the marble counter of my sink as I began to undress. He slid to the edge of the marble, his right knee bouncing up and down.

I stopped unbuttoning my jeans and peered his direction. "Don't even think about it. You stay right there."

Callum groaned into his fist. "God, you're making this hard on me, Harper."

"Go into the bedroom then if you can't handle it."

"No, no. I can handle it. I-I'll be good. I promise," he remedied with little boy-like excuses.
I laughed.

I shimmied out of my panties, not quite being able to bend all the way over, then stepped out of them before turning towards the shower. Before I knew it, Callum was at my back, running his hands up my sides, up my neck and back down, all the while kissing my shoulder.

"Callum," I playfully admonished.

"Fine," he grated before forcing himself to sit back down.

I tied my hair up, having just washed it that morning, and stepped into the water. It felt amazing on my back and I sighed at the relief it was giving my poor muscles.

When it felt like all the kinks were worked out of my back, I poured a generous amount of white ginger infused body wash and began working it over my legs and over the rest of my body. I turned around and found that Callum was leaning against the wall, the shower curtain pulled slightly back so he could see me. His eyes looked faintly glazed over. I smiled innocently at him. He flirtatiously smiled back, the grin touching his eyes. He turned his head trying to stay cool and rid himself of his shit-eating grin.

"It won't work," I told him, making him smile even

wider. He coughed into a fist and righted his expression only to lose it again, making me laugh. "You're adorable."

"And you're sexy as hell, Harper. Please tell me you aren't going to shave."

"Not needed," I told him. "I did that this morning."

"Then what are you we still doing here?" He asked.

"I'm rinsing the soap from my body," I teased, having more fun than I thought I'd ever have teasing Callum.

"You're done," he insisted. "You're rinsed. If your back wasn't so newly healed, I'd have already tossed you over my shoulder."

"*Callum!*"

"Get out."

"So bossy. Sheesh," I teased. I stepped out of the shower and towel dried off. "Go back to your bedroom. Get comfortable. I'll be there in a minute."

He hesitantly obeyed me, walking backwards from my room. I shut the door in his face and almost laughed out loud at his stunned expression. I put on deodorant, spritzed myself with a little Wild Bluebell and paced slowly in front of my drawers. *Don't be a coward, Harper*, I told myself. *It's for him, just put it on.*

On my wedding night, Cherry had passed me a little discretely wrapped box through my overnight bag. When I unwrapped it that night, I blushed like a schoolgirl at its contents. She'd bought me a sweet, little baby doll nightie. At the time, I was so incredibly embarrassed but now it seemed like the perfect thing to wear. Huh. Maturity. Who'd have thought.

I slipped it over my body, reveling at how soft it felt against my skin. I wrapped my robe around myself, shook my hair out, applied a little mascara and lip gloss and opened Callum's door. Seductively, I leaned against the doorjamb, preparing to shed my robe *but he wasn't*

350

there. Jeez, you're bad at this, Harper. I closed my door and the room went pitch black.

Slivers of lit the frame of his bathroom door. I listened for a moment. The shower was running. Laughing, I slid my robe off and laid it across his reading chair in the corner of his room. I crawled over onto the bed, leaning my back against the pillows at his headboard, stupidly shifting my body this way and that, trying to decide which was sexier. Nothing was sexy enough, I'd decided and thought about surprising him in the shower.

I knee walked to the edge of the bed, trying not to make too much of an effort but just before I was going to spin my leg down and off the bed, Callum opened the door, steam spilling out beneath him. His hair dripped onto his broad shoulders. I sucked in a breath in total disbelief that the impressive specimen standing before me was actually my husband.

He stopped short when he saw me and his mouth dropped open, matching my own. "Oh. My. God." He said, sauntering over to me, his towel still around his waist, and stood in front of my kneeling form at the corner of the bed.

He bent his head to mine and kissed the sense out of me. If you'd asked me my name, I'd have told you wrong. He had that kind of ability and he was mine, maybe it was *because* he was mine and *because* I loved him the way I did that his spell could cast itself over me with such ferocity. He moaned into my throat, causing a pool of heat to settle in my lower belly.

He gently laid me on my back, being careful not to bend me or put any strain on my back. Callum explored me with his hands and the heat that spread into my belly spilled over every inch of my skin, making me flush from head to toe.

Callum made love to me for the first time as husband and wife right there on those dark sheets, in that dark, cool room.

And it was the most amazing experience I'd ever had in my entire life. Both our pasts escaped our conscious that night. It was just the two of us, together, desperately in love with the other.

His body fit mine like a glove.

Callum was right. He was *so* worth the wait.

Epilogue
Believe

Six Years Later...

Harper
"Callum Tate," the man announced over the loud speaker.

I watched my husband take the stage to receive his diploma and stood to cheer him with the rest of our group of friends.

Freddy and Sam sat a few seats to my right, spinning their noise makers and jumping up and down. I sat between Cherry and Charlie, a husband and wife now themselves. Charlie stood, whooping and hollering with me. I couldn't really expect poor Cherry to stand since she was seven months pregnant with their second baby. She put up a good show from her chair, though. I smiled down at her. She beamed back up at me, her eyes glassy with hormones but mostly pride. I couldn't help myself and bent to kiss her cheek, making her outright cry in happiness. Tie-Dye Tom, my closest friend next to Cherry, sat next to her crying like a little baby.

"I feel like a mama bird," he said through choking

sobs, making me laugh out loud. I could only shake my head at him when he smacked my cheek with a tear soaked kiss.

SO sat next to Tom, smooth as ever, though his moist eyes may have betrayed him a little bit, not that I'd say anything. He winked at me. *Our secret,* I told him without words. Ames sat next to Charlie, yelling at the top of his lungs Callum's name, telling him how proud he was of him.

"I can't believe it!" He yelled to me, eyes bright with happiness.

Kelly, Cross, Marty, Aaron, Nat, Jared and Josiah were all there as well, scattered in our row, shouting and dancing around like the goofs we all were. I studied the people around me, knowing they were my family made my heart nearly burst from happiness.

I was complete and very much unafraid. Unafraid because John Bell had been found dead two weeks after Callum and I returned home. He'd thrown himself off the pier, his body turned up on the shore after a two and a half month man hunt. Suicide. He took the coward's way out. Not that that surprised me. He was an incredible coward. I barely thought of him anymore. Barely.

Callum turned toward the crowd after accepting, searching the sea of faces for mine. I stood on my chair and waved at him. He stopped, smiled and held out the hand sign for 'I love you'. I sent it back to him along with a kiss. He caught it and pretended to put it in a little folded bag, stuffing it into a non-existent front pocket. "For later," he'd always say. 'I love you', I mouthed, tears streaming down my face. He nodded and threw a fist in the air, making the crowd and our family especially go wild with excitement.

I had graduated with honors, thanks to my

amazing Callum, four summers earlier and wrote several columns for a local paper. I worked from home which was nice, though I was forced to visit my editor once a week to catch up and go over whatever I was working on. It was the best job in the entire world but it could get better apparently because I had surprised Callum last night with the news that I earned a monthly featured column in a national magazine with a circulation of over two million.

Callum accepted an internship position the previous week at his first hospital of choice in the city. Yes, our lives were plugging away nicely in the direction of amazing. Nothing could make it better. Nothing. Well, *almost* nothing...

...If I could just get home to wrap his graduation gift.

It comes with a card that has nothing to do with graduation, though. It reads, "Congratulations on your new human alarm clock".

The End

The Paranormal
Plumes
Society

Fisher Amelie is a member of The Paranormal Plumes Society.

http://theplumessociety.com/

Callum & Harper Playlist
fisheramelia.com/thetunes

Please enjoy an exclusive excerpt from Shelly Crane's YA novel, Devour. It's available now for purchase through Amazon and Barnes & Noble.

There's a game you play. The one where you guess what the shapes and objects the clouds have made above you. Today there was a lady with a long witchy nose, a rabbit, a sailboat. Everyone's perception is different; we all see different things. I personally think you see what you want to see.

I was solely entranced in my gazing. The sun was bright behind me as I lay in the grass, my head on my jacket. My insanely dark black hair was long and almost too warm as it fanned around my head and caught the sunlight. The small hill on the edge of the park was the perfect spying spot. Spying on clouds, on people, on squirrels, but I was alone. Alone here and alone in life. My family used to come here together, but no more. My sister was gone, joined the Navy and would be gone for four years. She couldn't handle the fact that our parents died and decided to fulfill my dad's wish for us to be in the armed forces.

The burglary, and the burglar who took their lives, was something we all wished to forget. Even the Montana police hastened the investigation because things like that just didn't happen in our town. But there I was, stuck in my last year at high school, living with my Pastor's family as a temporary custody home until I graduated and went off to college. I was as alone as I could be.

The sun so bright behind me made the shadow that was suddenly loomed over me startling.

I looked up to see a guy standing by my head looking down at me. He had a little smile, almost wistful, on his lips as he cocked his head to the side. I sat up and twisted to see him better. His eyes were a freakishly bright violet. I'd never seen a guy with purple eyes - well, I'd never seen anyone with purple eyes. It was a rare thing, I guess, but now looking at them like that, they almost seemed natural.

He was wearing a deep green button up shirt with the sleeves rolled up and jeans with a small tear in the knee. Aviator sunglasses hung from his collar. His hair was as black as mine and close cropped. His hands were in his pockets and he continued to stare at me until I spoke.

"Hi."

"Hello, there," he finally said, his voice deep and lilting with a small accent that I couldn't place.

"Can I...help you with something?" I asked since he continued to gaze at me unabashedly.

"Nope. Just enjoying the view," he said and then smiled slightly as he turned to look up at the clouds and then back down to me. "There always seems to be a rabbit and an old lady doesn't there."

"How did you know I was..."

"I guessed. Why else would you be laying here, alone, looking at the clouds?"

I laughed nervously and twisted the ring on my finger; my nervous tick.

"Are you new here? I haven't seen you around. Big Timber is a small town so, you kinda know everyone whether you want to or not."

He laughed and it was delicious and rich making my stomach flip. I frowned. I had a boyfriend. What was wrong with me?

"Yeah, I'm new. Just moved stateside from Zimbabwe. My parents were teachers at one of the schools there. I'm Elijah Thames, but everyone calls me Eli," he said and knelt down in front of me, sticking out his hand in greeting.

"Clara Hopkins."

I took his hand, almost expecting something to happen when our skin met. Though his hand was warm and rugged, it was just a normal handshake.

"Nice to meet you, Clara Hopkins."

"You too, Eli. You came at the perfect time I guess. Second semester starts tomorrow so we all get new classes. It won't just be you getting a new schedule."

"That's nice, I guess. I'm pretty used to being the new kid though."

"Are your parents missionaries or something?"

"Of sorts," he said vaguely and stood. "So, what's there to do in this town on a Sunday afternoon?"

"You're looking at it," I said through a giggle. "This is about it, I'm afraid. There is an old theater in town but it only plays one movie at a time and there's a club here, but I've never been to it. We usually just hang out at the burger place."

"Who's we?"

"What?"

"You said 'we hang out'. Who's we?"

"Oh. My friends and I. My boyfriend," I said and was shocked at how reluctant I was to tell him that.

"Ah, I see. I should have known it wouldn't be that easy, huh?"

"What wouldn't?" I asked though I felt the blush creeping up, knowing exactly what he meant.

He just smiled.

"Well, can I walk you home at least? It'll be getting dark soon."

"Um...sure, I guess." I took the hand he offered and then picked my brown corduroy jacket up, slipping it back on. "So, do you always walk up to strange girls in the park and start conversations?"

"Nah," he said slyly and bumped my shoulder. "They didn't have parks in Zimbabwe."

I burst out laughing and was intrigued by how comfortable we seemed to be together already.

"Where do you live?" I asked him as we hopped onto the sidewalk.

"We bought a place on Buxton."

"The bed and breakfast?"

"Yeah. My parents are all about trying something new."

"Wow. Well, it's a nice house. I've always loved that place."

"It's nice and big. Too big but I guess once you get a house full of guests it won't be big enough. I made my room the basement though, so that should help with the privacy."

"The basement? Won't that be cold and muggy and...creepy?"

"You watch a lot of scary movies, do you?" he said in amusement.

"Maybe I do," I spouted playfully. "I'm sure it's nice enough anyway. But you know, it could be the attic," I said and shivered in mock horror.

"Oh, attic's are *way* creepy."

We laughed and it resounded in the quiet darkening street.

He seemed to know right where he was going so I just walked beside him and let him lead us. Buxton was only a few blocks away from the city park and I lived beside the church near there.

We walked and talked for about a block before trouble turned the corner.

My boyfriend, Tate, was coming down the street in his big 4x4 truck. He was on the wrestling team, the town's pride. He was really good to me, very attentive, and while I enjoyed spending time with him, I wasn't in love with him. And he was a very jealous guy. All he ever talked about was us going to college together next year, but I didn't want to go to college. I wanted to go on a mission trip or maybe apply to a Music or Art school. If my parents were alive, they'd be so disappointed. My dad dreamed of his alma mater and the Army and my mom wanted me to marry right away and find a man to take care of me. Both of those dreams were nil.

But Tate was a sweet guy. Even though he was popular, he was pretty nice to everyone...except guys who tried to talk to me. He once almost pummeled my science lab partner when he stopped me in the hall to get my notes.

Apparently, his mom cheated on his dad all the time and his dad had no inclination to do anything about it. The whole town knew about it but they held a position of status and prime real estate in the town so no one cared, essentially. But Tate had always cared.

"Oh boy," I mumbled.

"What? What's wrong?"

"Nothing's wrong, just my boyfriend. Just don't listen to anything he says for the next five minutes, ok? I'm sorry ahead of time."

"Ok," he said, dragging it out in apprehension.

Tate stopped the truck and I saw it overcome him. His fingers turned white on the steering wheel, his lips grim in a tight line. He opened the door and closed it gently, too gently to be considered normal. It was a façade.

"Hey, Tate. Were you coming to see me?"

"You weren't at home. I was headed to the park to give you a ride...but I see you don't need one what with prince charming walking you home and all," he sneered, glaring daggers at Eli.

"Tate, this is Eli. He's new here and lives near me. We were walking home together, talking about school tomorrow."

"Uhuh."

"Tate," I chided and went to give him a kiss on the cheek. I felt his skin, hot and angry on my lips before I pulled back. He flicked his eyes to me once before looking back to Eli. "Tate, this is ridiculous," I whispered to him. "Why don't you trust me?"

"It's other guys I don't trust!" he yelled, making me jump. "You have no idea what guys are thinking about."

I took a deep confused breath. He'd never been that vehement before. I glanced over at Eli to apologize but he looked strange. Almost like he was...in ecstasy. His mouth was slightly open and his eyes hooded as he watched me. His breathing was heavy. I squinted at him and he seemed to snap out of it.

"Come on, man," he said to Tate. "Really, it was nothing. She was just telling me about classes changing and all since I just moved here. She told me she had a boyfriend within the first two minutes of talking to her."

Tate looked at me, his eyes softening a little. I looked at him pleadingly. He took a hesitant step towards me and when he saw I made no move to step away he caved and pulled me to him.

"I'm sorry, Clara, you know how I get. I can't... It's dumb, I know. I'm really sorry." He pulled back to look at me. "I didn't mean to be like that."

"I know you didn't," I said softly and him being the blonde, beefy guy he was who stood right at my height level, put his forehead to mine.

"How do you even put up with me?" he whispered.

"I don't know," I said jokingly, "you're pretty cute. I guess it makes up for it."

"Pretty cute?" he joked and suddenly dropped to one knee and in his best English white knight accent began to beg. "Oh, please, my darling. My love. Forgive me and my assness!"

This was the Tate I knew and cared about. He was fun, playful and not afraid to make a fool of himself.

I laughed and bowed a little.

"You're forgiven. Now. Tate, this is Eli Thames. Eli, this is Tate Richman. He's captain of our wrestling team and his dad's the mayor," I said proudly.

"Hi," Eli said cautiously and stuck his hand out.

Tate stood and took the hand offered.

"Hey, man. Sorry. I'm can be a bit of an ass when it comes to this girl. I'm sure you can understand," he said with a wry smile.

"Understood." Eli looked back to me and smiled a little sadly. "Well, I guess I'll see you guys tomorrow."

"You can have lunch with us tomorrow," I threw out. "I'm not sure if I'll see you before then, but we eat at the long table right in the middle of the cafeteria."

"Ok. Thanks."

"See ya, man," Tate said and waited for Eli to turn, then pulled me to him, snuggling into my neck. "Oh my gosh, Clara, you smell like something I very much want to eat."

I giggled and pushed him back a little.

"You think you're getting off that easy, buster?"

"What do I owe you this time?" he asked amused

and touched his tongue to his lip to think. "Diaper duty? Because if that's it, it was nice knowing you."

"Hey!" I yelled playfully and smacked his chest. "No. Mrs. Ruth has the kids tonight, but you do have to take me home and...watch the last Vampire Diaries I DVRed."

"Ah, Clara," he groaned. "Anything but that."

"Come on, it's not that bad."

"It's torture," he said pointedly and then smiled. "But for you I'd do just about anything."

"I know," I agreed and I did. Tate had reasons to be the way he was and the way he normally treated me would put the Salvatore brothers to shame. But for some reason, I just couldn't move past the feeling that he was just some guy I liked, had feelings for, but knew it wasn't going anywhere. "Come on."

He helped me into the truck and drove the short distance to the Parish. Once we stopped in front of the house, I started to get out but he stopped me.

"Wait. Before we enter the no-touch zone..."

He pulled me to him across the seat and kissed me. Tate was usually a gentleman and knew how far I was willing to let him go. Sometimes he casually tried to push the envelope; he was a guy after all. This was apparently going to be one of those times.

His hand gripped my leg, as if to tug me into his lap. I let him. He seemed fueled by that and as his hands on my hips pulled me closer to him. I heard him groan a little. It rumbled through me and made my heart beat a little faster. I knew it was only torture to do this. I'd never let him do anything more than this. We were both virgins, though I was happier about it than he was. But sometimes, I just needed to feel the glue to the envelope strain a little.

I let him kiss me for a good while, just like that. I ran my fingers through his hair. It'd been a year since we started dating. We'd both always gone to the same school together, always lived in this town. We hung out with the same friends but he'd never seemed interested in me before and I never thought about him that way. I'd been on a few dates with other guys but never really dated anyone exclusively. Then one day, he met me at my locker, alone. It was odd because usually there was a group waiting there for me. As I made my way to him, he smiled bashfully.

"Hey."

"Hey," I had said cheerfully ignorant.

"How was Spanish? I have that next semester."

"Brutal."

"I was afraid of that. So, um...there's this movie playing at the Cineplex, Adam Sandler is in it. Looks pretty good. I was wondering if you wanted to go tonight?"

"Sure. Who else is going?"
"Just you. And me."

"Oh," I had said and even I heard the odd note to my voice. He mistook that as reluctance.

"It's ok if you don't want to go, I just figured it might be fun. It's ok," he had said and started to walk away.

"No, wait. I didn't say I didn't want to go."

"Do you want to?" he'd asked and came to stand

closer than he'd ever stood before.

I remembered my pulse had suddenly jumped and I noticed how green his eyes really were for the first time.

"Yeah. I do."

His smile was genuine and a little surprised.

"Great. I'll pick you up at five thirty. We can get something to eat first if you want."

"Yeah. Sure."

He'd walked backwards, grinning, away from me. That night he'd picked me up and we had fun, lots of fun. When he dropped me off I couldn't help but ask why he was all of a sudden interested.

"I can't say it was all of a sudden," he'd answered. "I just wasn't sure if you'd want to and I didn't want things to be weird so I just watched you. But you never looked at me different...so I took a shot." Then he touched my cheek, his thumb sweeping across my cheek bone. "I'm glad I did."

"Me too."

Then he had kissed me and I felt something in me burn, like slow lava. We'd stood there on my parents porch and kissed slowly and gently for a good while before my dad turned the light off and on, making us laugh.

Two months later, when my parents died, he was there for me like no one else. He was the first person to meet me at the hospital waiting room. He held me - just held me - for hours in those uncomfortable chairs as I bawled my eyes out. My sister had been gone on a skiing trip with friends and wasn't there yet. I had been to a movie with my friend who moved to another town, Addison, and found my parents when she dropped me off. Tate stayed with me all night. Took me home, held me as I finally fell asleep on the couch. I don't know what I would have done without him.

And now as he ravished my mouth with skill and restraint I was still thankful for him but, I didn't love him. He had never said the words to me and I wasn't sure what I'd say if he did. I couldn't lie.

"Mmm, Clara, you are driving me every kind of crazy," he spoke huskily against my lips.

"Then maybe we should stop."

"No. No, don't stop," he said and took my lips again.

"Tate," I whispered. "You're not making this easy."

"Then give in to me," he suggested and I could hear the smile in his voice.

"Tate," I chided.

"Ok, ok." He blew a long breath. "It should be illegal for you to look the way you do and me not be able to have you."

"That's so cheesy," I said through a smile.

"I know," he laughed. "Alright, fine. Vampire Diaries in the preacher's house it is."

"Thank you," I said and pressed one last kiss to his lips before climbing out of the truck.

We spent the night like we spent a lot of nights; watching television on my bed, with the door open and a clear view of us from the door. I was allowed to lay by him but there was no kissing in the house. The preacher, Pastor Paul, was very lenient with me but there were certain rules of conduct, especially with Tate, that he was strict about. Despite us being young and all, we were both kind of home bodies. I'd rather sit and watch a movie at home with him than go out with a whole bunch of people. Our friends and I usually had to work pretty hard to get Tate to go out somewhere. He much preferred to be alone with me.

~ ~ ~

I was back, laying in the grass in the park. It all looked so real. The sun was bright and gorgeous behind me as it cast sparkles on the lake. A perfect day. I saw a shadow over me. At first I thought it was Tate but this person was taller and leaner and I felt something coming from him. Like I could feel his interest in me like a tangible thing. He knelt down beside me and I sat up. His face was covered in shadow from the halo of sun around his head. He reached out and touched my face. I gasped at the pleasure his touch elicited from my skin, goose bumps spread widely and I tingled all over. A response I'd never felt before, not even with Tate.

He moved in to kiss me and I was helpless to stop him. His lips almost touched mine. I felt the heat from his breath and a tremor ran through me. I suddenly felt afraid for no apparent reason at all and he moaned, seeming to enjoy my reaction. He pulled me to him and I whimpered as my terror spiked and he continued to hold me to him, like I was something he couldn't live without.

I jolted me eyes open with a start. What was that? I wasn't even asleep yet. Too many vampire shows for me...

The next morning I woke feeling a little strange. The first face I saw was Eli's and I immediately felt guilty. Tate was good to me, though he had his flaws like everyone else. He was very desirable; a hot commodity at our school, and I was lucky he wanted to date me. At least that's what everyone told me. It couldn't be that he was lucky to be with me.

So I threw on my school uniform. Most people hated them, but I loved them for some reason that escaped me. It was a typical uniform; red and black plaid skirt, white collar shirt and a vest that matched the skirt. No knee highs though, thank goodness. We were instructed to wear black ballet flats. After I fixed my hair and threw in some earrings, I made my way downstairs.

After helping Mrs. Ruth with all the babies breakfast - she had five kids under the age of five, the latest being twins who were only four months old - I rushed off to school, a little later than I'd wanted. I came through the gray concrete halls of our prison looking high school looking for Eli. I had wanted to get there before homeroom bell to make sure he found his class easily, but the bell was about to ring. Dang, I was going to be late. The church and the parish were across the street from the school. They shared a parking lot in fact, so I never got a ride with Tate; I didn't need one.

I ran to my new home room just as the last bell rang. I slid into the first empty seat I saw by the door. I noticed Tate across the room, looking at me with amused eyes. He made kiss lips at me as we both turned to face forward.

After the bell rang, we made our way to the hall. I waited for Tate and he studiously threw his arm around my shoulder and kissed my temple.

We walked to my locker and there was Eli. At first I thought he was waiting for me there and wondered what Tate would do, but I saw him reaching into the locker next to mine. He was now my neighbor.

"Hey, Eli," I said.

He looked surprised to see someone knowing his name and almost dropped his books, catching them very cutely in a jumble before they hit the floor and stuffing them in his locker.

"Oh. Hey, guys," he said in that low rumbling voice of his.

"Who do you have for homeroom?"

"Mr. Winepeeno?" he tried and Tate and I both laughed.

"It's Winepegofski. I know, it's an impossible name. I think he's from Russia or Poland or something."

Someone called my name and I looked up to see Ashley. I waved and turned back to Eli.

"A Polish guy teaches U.S. History?" Eli asked with a smirk.

"Welcome to America, Mr. Zimbabwe."

He laughed and leaned on his shoulder against his locker. I looked up to Tate to see him no longer smiling. He was looking between us with a slight frown gracing his brow.

"Tate, who do you have next?" I asked, trying to include him.

"Bishop. Shop," he spouted shortly.

"Ugh, well, we definitely won't share that class. I have Menendez."

"Me too," chimed Eli.

"Huh," Tate said, clearly annoyed. "I'm out. Gonna be late and Bishop will ride me all year."

"Tate," I called and grabbed his arm. "I'll see you at lunch, ok?"

"Ok," he said tightly.

"Hey," I pulled him to look at me and saw a couple freshman giggling at us from across the hall. I ignored them. "I'll miss you," I said to appease him. "It's too bad we don't have anymore classes together."

"Yeah, I'm sure you'll really miss me with Zimbabwe over there," he said low where Eli couldn't hear us.

"I will. He doesn't watch vamp shows with me and follow silly rules at the house I live at. He doesn't know exactly where to find me when he comes to see me and I'm not home. He's just a guy, Tate."

He laughed a small breathy laugh.

"Ok," he conceded. "You better miss me," he joked and poked a finger at my chest gently.

"I already do," I said and accepted his kiss. He usually didn't kiss me on the lips in school, but right then he was letting me have it. I felt his hand on my lower back, pressing me closer. In the distance I heard a whistle from someone and I pulled back to breath. "Wow."

He chuckled.

"I can definitely deal with wow."

"Bye."

"Bye, babe."

I watched him walk away as he bumped fist with someone and they started to jog across the campus.

Then I turned to see Eli still standing there, with a wry look on his handsome face. The fluorescent lights made his hair even blacker. He looked almost ethereal like that. Today he'd worn his hair spiked to the side and I noticed he had his right eyebrow pierced with a small silver rod. I hadn't seen that last night. He was wearing the same jeans as before but with a Queen 1986 Tour shirt. It was his first day, so he didn't have his uniform yet. It always made the new kids stick out like sore thumbs.

"Hey, sorry. I told you he's...I don't know. And I'm sorry about last night too."

"No worries. It's not your fault. So," he grabbed a black messenger bag from his locker and threw it over his shoulder, "can I walk with you to our next class or will I get my spleen removed for it?"

"Ha ha. Yes, walk with me. It's way over on the other side of the gym, so we better get going."

We walked and I saw he was getting quite a lot of attention. I even got the stink eye from a couple of girls and I couldn't help but laugh. He was definitely cute with a bad boy thing going that made me cringe with the cliché of it. He wasn't hot in the traditional sense, I guess. He was a little rugged and jagged, but he was extremely nice and not cocky so that added to his appeal.

"Hi, Clara!" Sarah called as she passed.

"Hey."

"Who's this?" she said and walked backwards beside us to eye him appreciatively.

"This is Eli. He's new."

"Oooh. New meat. I'm Sarah. I'm single by choice, a Pisces, and I'm on the spirit squad with Clara. I'm also free this Saturday."

Eli chuckled and it had the same effect on Sarah as it had on me yesterday. She looked about to jump him right there in the hall, so I saved her some embarrassment.

"Sarah, we're late. You can ogle him at lunch, ok?"

"Ok. Bye, babe! Bye, Eli," she sang his name and flounced away.

"She eats lunch with you?"

"Afraid so. You may as well get used to it now. We hardly ever get new kids at our school and the girls I hang out with are...forward when it comes to guys. You can back out now and I wouldn't blame you."

"No. No, I like a challenge." I looked at him sideways to see him smiling in his profile. "So the spirit squad? I didn't peg you as a cheerleader."

"You pegged right. I'm not," I laughed. "Spirit squad decorates for games and sells tickets and ribbons and stuff. We try to pep people up for events."

"I see. Sounds interesting. And cheerleaders can't do this?"

"Not when they're too busy *getting* busy in the bathroom before the games."

He laughed and I looked at him with a smile. He was so different somehow.

While gazing at him I forgot to watch where I was going and plowed right into a freshman, but he may as well have been Andre' the Giant. He was huge and the fact that I was a girl apparently had no effect on him.

"Watch it," he growled.

"Sorry."

"Why don't you just take your," he slapped my butt hard, "pretty little pampered spirit squad butt back to where you belong and get out of my way."

"Whoa, pal," Eli said and pulled me behind him. I was surprised by it but grateful. "Don't talk to her like that and don't *ever* touch her again."

By this point there was an eager crowd with the word fight dancing in their eyes.

"Who are you, Pippy?" Everyone laughed and snickered. "If I were you I'd watch it. You're not making a very good first impression at this school. First, you're hanging out with spoiled ice queen over here, and now you're messing with me. I'd just go around me and pretend you never got in my way if I were you."

"Sure. I'll do that after you apologize," Eli said calmly.

"I don't apologize to brats who get everything they want. She should apologize for bumping me."

"I did," I mumbled at the same time that Eli said, "She

did."

"Whatever-"

"Get to class!" Mr. Brank called from his classroom and everyone scattered. "Now."

"Later, Pippy," the big freshman jerk called. "Later, spoiled brat."

We started to walk and heard the bell. We were still a couple hallways away from class and I saw no point in rushing now.

"Thank you," I said after some time. "I have no idea who he was but he apparently knows me."

"I don't think he does if he thinks you're a pampered spoiled brat."

"You don't know me," I said but thought it sounded defensive so I added jokingly, "I could be a horrible drama queen who stomps freshman under my leather stiletto boots."

"I highly doubt that," he rebutted and looked at my feet, then dragged his gaze back up to my eyes. "Besides, I don't see any stilettos."

I realized we'd stopped in the hall and were now just standing there, looking at each other.

"Thanks. Really. You didn't have to do that. Now you've already made an enemy and it's the first day."

"Yeah, but I made a friend too."

Gosh, his eyes were so breathtaking. It made me feel like I had Jell-O knees looking at him. His face changed and he cocked his head a little before opening his mouth slightly. He looked surprised this time though. He had that same look before, last night, when Tate and I had been fighting; like he was in ecstasy.

"What is it?" I asked.

He shook his head and smiled sheepishly at me.

"Sorry. You're just...um. We better get to class."

"Yeah," I said nodding.

We walked into Menendez's class well after the bell, everyone turning to look and see the new guy. I saw a couple people I sat with at lunch in this class too and dreaded the conversation I knew would take place later as we took the only two seats left; the two sitting right next to each other in the back.

End of Preview

You may find ways to purchase Devour as well as more of Shelly's other books and information at her website

www.shellycrane.blogspot.com

Made in the USA
Lexington, KY
16 May 2015